It's 1982, the fourth and nastiest year of the Civil War. With war prices for some things going through the roof, there are some cargos too tempting and tucked down in places too risky, and a ship captain has to weigh both if he wants to make a profit and stay afloat. Last I saw my parents, they were going to do the sugar run to Jamaica. Up in the cold North sugar cane simply doesn't grow. You have to go where it's warm and for us in the U.S., that means the Caribbean, which is unfortunately down next to the Confederate States of America and we have to sail right past Florida with its people doing their best to be unpleasant. I won't kid you. It's a dangerous run. Normally, they would have been back in port a week ago, but they're overdue. Nothing to worry about yet - much.

Mark Bondurant

Red Jacket

The Autobiography of Calista Antoine

Mark Bondurant

RED JACKET
The Autobiography of Calista Antoine

Copyright © 2014, 2021 Mark Bondurant, All Rights Reserved
http://www.markbondurant.com

Cover and Illustrations by Mark Bondurant
Edited by Sara "Birdee" George and Gaven Claypool

Published by Bongo Books
http://www.bongo.net

Publisher's Cataloging-in-Publication (Provided by Bongo Books)

Bondurant, Mark.
Red Jacket / by Mark Bondurant. –
2st ed. p. ; 16x23cm.

Trade Edition
ISBN: 1-940995-03-5
ISBN-13: 978-1-940995-03-8

1. Teenage girls. 2. Schooners. 3. Merchant ships.
4. Congo (Democratic Republic). 5. Steampunk
fiction. 6. Science Fiction. 7. Alternative histories
(Fiction), American. I. Title.

Dedication

I dedicate this, my second book, to my mother and especially my father, whose writing career was cut short before he could finish a book of his own.

CONTENTS

Chapter 1 – The End of School   2

Chapter 2 – The Wounded   11

Chapter 3 – A New Wardrobe   18

Chapter 4 – Farewell to Boston   28

Chapter 5 – France!   37

Chapter 6 – Meeting the Enemy   50

Chapter 7 – Always Ready to Trade   65

Chapter 8 – The End of Childhood   76

Chapter 9 – The Prince   88

Chapter 10 - Dracula   100

Chapter 11 – Pastel Vasco   111

Chapter 12 – The Congo   122

Chapter 13 - Interred   135

Chapter 14 – My Birthday   150

Chapter 15 – Logs in the River   166

Chapter 16 – Msuata Trading Post   189

Chapter 17 – The Hunt!   200

Chapter 18 – An Unfortunate Incident   211

Chapter 19 – Dengue Fever   229

Chapter 20- My Introduction   240

Chapter 21 – The Final Dance   250

Chapter 22 – The Retreat   269

Cali's Songs   276

Bibliography   278

A Bad Crossing   283

Author's Foreward

My publisher first informed me of the certainty of a book contract for the autobiography of the Duchess of Tervuren on Christmas Eve of 1902; the telegram delivered to my snow covered step in the late afternoon carried by a breathless boy, barely topping my waistcoat. Needless to say it was the best present an author could hope for. This was the infamous German spy "The Rabbit", the violin that had seduced Paris, the Sea Witch, the recluse Duchess. No writer had yet managed to interview her let alone write her story. Needless to say--I tipped him like an American and wished him a merry Christmas to boot. This would be the work of my lifetime, I thought. There was no luckier writer in Europe.

But, as any author can tell you, no matter how much you plan, no book ever turns out like you think it will. As I grew to know her, I found her to be nothing like the stories, the good or bad. Instead, at age 26, I found a frightened girl who loved to dance, neither spy nor pirate. A woman who fought to protect those she loved, her eye never wandering from the sea and escape, never toward fame that seemed to chase her footsteps.

Our first meeting was in Amsterdam, over lunch at De Silveren Spiegel, Canal Straat efficiently blocked by soldiers in plain clothes who needlessly looked through my satchel and coat. She was waiting, which was strange since I was early, sitting alone at a table in a dim corner, hidden behind the golden slanting sunlight that spilled in through high set windows. We had the whole restaurant to ourselves, this in busy central Amsterdam. The owner had still seen fit to light the candles at all the tables.

I first noticed her Irish heritage, evident in her hair. She seemed small, somewhat thin, eyes pale green, almost blue, her skin unmarked despite all she had apparently experienced. Her dress was simple and unremarkable. Just a short coat with straight sleeves, a plain skirt. Beneath she wore white blouse and a simple gold locket. Her hat on the seat next to her was smallish, adorned with only a blue ribbon. All very unfashionable. I could have mistaken her for the wife of a servant or a school teacher, except on closer inspection, the quality of the cut of her clothing and, of course, the intensity of those who guarded her.

"M. Bondurant," she said, as I approached.

"Yes, ma'am," I replied. "Duchess?"

"Yes," she sighed, as if to brush it aside. The accent definitely American. "Please sit. I'm so hungry. I missed breakfast. I'm afraid I'm often too late or too early." She had seen my assessment of her clothes and for a moment I saw a fleeting, mischievous smile.

"Then lunch it is," I replied.

"I've read several of your books." Bluntly to the point. "They are admirable works, and you seem to produce them regularly." Definitely American, although her French was quite good.

"Thank you. I'm glad you appreciate them," I said.

"I need to learn a little more about you though . . ."

But then she stopped and laughed, looking at my eyes, and then down at her dress. "I supposed they are a bit odd. Paul works very hard on them and I have very difficult requirements. He's the only one who takes me seriously when I say I don't want to wear a corset."

"Pardon ma'am, Paul?"

"Paul Poiret. You don't know him? He's a friend from Paris. A precocious youth and now a terrible huckster." She shook her head.

"Huckster?" I asked.

"It's an American word. I'm sorry, I don't know the French. A salesman, only with overtones of the circus."

"Ah, I think I understand. A *Bonimenteur*. And he makes clothing." I was getting names already. Realizing that I should be taking notes, I reached for my satchel. Someone stirred behind me in the shadows.

"He designs them to order, at least he does for me," she continued. "He mostly goes for oriental fashions these days. The current fare, I'm afraid, is definitely not to my taste. The fronts of women's dresses look like a tug prows and the corsets bend your back. It's nonsense. I don't see why I should to wear them. At least not unless required to."

"No, of course not," I replied.

The waiter came with the menus and we discussed the food. She ordered tea with her lunch.

"If you don't mind my asking, are the Duke and your son here with you?"

"Albert is back at the hotel. The Duke is flying in this afternoon. He'll almost certainly want to interview you tomorrow. Hopefully he'll land in time to make it to the Concertgebouw." She leaned forward looked at me with barely disguised glee. "They're playing Bach!"

"Ah yes, I haven't seen it myself yet. I wondered why we were meeting here in Amsterdam," I said. I could see callouses on her fingers from her violin as she poured her tea. I wondered if I'd get to hear her play.

"It's not the concert. My family should be making port tomorrow or perhaps the day after." She frowned, then she looked back at me. "The Concertgebouw is just an extra. It's sad they'll miss it." She thought for a second. "We might arrange for you to meet them."

"That would be helpful," I replied.

Her face seemed to cloud for just a second, perhaps a difficult memory. It was strange. But she recovered quickly, back to the moment.

We discussed her family and friends. I made a list, their locations. She had very few, which might simplify my research, or hinder it if they were unavailable.

"Do you think it will take long?" she asked.

"Take long?"

"The book." She seemed worried.

"I don't know. I have no way to tell yet."

"Of course."

"Is there a need to hurry?" I asked.

"No. Of course not." But I thought from her tone that there might be. Our food arrived, which broke the thread of our conversation. It arrived very quickly I might add. It was almost rude. I suppose when you have the kitchen to yourself, things happen. Then again, perhaps they wanted us out. It was quite good. Their food and wine cellar are excellent.

We talked about Albert, a subject she warmed to quickly. I could see it woke a need to get back to the hotel. At two, I learned, he was already speaking well and reaching for his mother's violin.

We then turned to her family's shipping business, and I felt we were progressing well, when she suddenly pushed back her chair and stood. Grabbing her hat, she declared, "Let's go for a walk. It's too close in here."

She looked down at me staring back and asked, "Do you mind? I need air."

"No, not at all." Honestly, I was down to toying with my fish.

"They'll pick me up soon and I want to have a chance to walk a little."

She waited while I put away my pen and paper. We walked out with no indication payment, heading east toward a low bridge.

"I've been asked to avoid the harbor, though I do so dearly want to go there," she said. "If it were just me, I would go anyway. But it's not fair to cause inconvenience and to put others in danger. So I pick random directions."

"So they're still trying?"

"No, at least it seems that way," she sighed. "Not lately at least. But that only makes it worse."

Two of her men appeared on the curb, between us and the road. I hadn't noticed they were so near. Then a strange carriage overtook us, clopping up behind us. *"Bent u op zoek naar een cabine?"* the driver asked.

"No, thank you," she replied, cheerily.

The driver nodded and drove on. Somehow, the guards walking near us managed to stay between us and the cab as it rolled away.

"They're good men," she said, nodding to them. "Many were with me in the Congo." She paused for a moment. "They'll relax once they get to know you."

We had barely traveled the two blocks to the bridge when three petrol cars rolled up. The driver of the middle one popped his head out. "Ready to ride milady?" he asked, cheerily.

"No, but I suppose we should," she said. Then she looked at me. "Can we give you a ride M. Bondurant?"

The soldier who appeared at the door and lent her a hand up the step gave me a sidelong glance.

"No," I replied. "I think I'll walk."

"It's a dear day for it," she said, smiling wistfully at the sky.

"It is."

"The Duke's secretary will make arrangements."

"I'm looking forward to it," I replied, and waved as they rumbled away.

I found an appointment card waiting for me at breakfast the next morning.

The Duke and I met alone in their apartments, the Duchess having taken young Albert to the Tropenmuseum despite it being Sunday, and the museum closed. I could see toys on the floor through the doors to their living room. I was again searched before being led into the study.

"M. Bondurant." The Duke rose to shake my hand. We were to sit in the leather chairs rather than at the desk. "I must apologize for the security."

He was of medium height, dark curling hair, 34. His suit cut along German lines, the rounded collar, length in the jacket, the lower waist. He did not, however, go so far as to oil his hair.

"I understand entirely," I said.

"Perhaps," he said, half to himself. A servant appeared with a tray. "May I offer you some coffee? I became quite attached to it in the Navy."

"Yes, please." We had biscuits too.

"We're always a little tense when we visit her family." He picked up his cup and took a sip. He drank it black. "It's one of those times. When they know when and where we will be."

"Are they really that vindictive?" I asked.

"They will have their pound of flesh," he snapped bitterly. "It's one of the reasons why I requested this book be written."

"You hope to air your side of the story," I said carefully.

"Yes."

"I'll only write the truth as I see it," I replied.

"That's all we're asking for. Your reputation is one of the reasons we chose you. There is so much that needs to be told." He had made a temple of his fingers pressed to his lips, staring at something in the distance only he could see. "And I think that it will do her good to talk about it as well."

"Surely she talks to you," I blurted and sat up. "I'm sorry. That was too forward." I had spilled coffee in my saucer.

"No. You need to know. There are things she will not talk about, even to me."

"Then how will I write? What can I write about?" I asked.

"You do research, and you have my permission to pry." He smirked. "I've noticed that you can be quite good it. That's another reason why I chose you."

A servant entered and I handed him the cup. "May I have another?" I asked him. One without coffee in the saucer.

"You will, naturally, help me with introductions?" I asked the Duke. Without them, I would get nowhere with the upper class.

"Yes. Absolutely. Whatever you need. Forward your requests through my secretary. He will instruct you in the proper protocols. We will work out your expenses through your publisher as well."

I sighed. My publisher was notoriously tight fisted.

"Is that acceptable?" he asked.

"Yes, of course. I'll need to interview you as well."

It was his turn to sigh. "Yes. But I'll need warning. My schedule is very tight."

"Naturally," I said.

I sipped my fresh coffee. It was very good and very strong. I think he noticed my smile.

"Do you like it?" he asked.

"How do you make this?" I asked. "It's amazing."

"I'm not sure. They use a steam press. I don't go to the kitchen often. They seem to feel they have to make an event of it." He shook his head, amused. Then he looked back at me. "It disrupts their day, and thus mine. I'm rather fond of it myself."

How far could I reach with my interviews, I wondered? "Would there be any problems connected with interviewing Leopold himself?"

He frowned. "A touchy subject, but we can try. I'm no longer able to predict how he will react. Not like I used to. Marriage has changed him, and the subject of the Duchess is not to be publicly discussed. The Queen Mother has seen to that."

I think I must have looked disappointed, because he chuckled. "He does like the spotlight though. Perhaps we can make something of his hunting exploits. There's a great deal to tell there. Be sure about interviewing him though. He can be quite vindictive."

"I understand," I said. "I can see that all of this will require a great deal of tact.'

"I'm glad you understand. I would rather walk through an artillery barrage than attempt to do what you have agreed to do. If you really do tell the truth, you will make more enemies than you know. Please, if you change your mind about the position, tell us soon."

"I won't. My mind is quite made up. I'm beginning to feel my age." I chuckled. "I think this will be my last work and I can think of no better way to go out. Let Leopold do what he will."

Red Jacket

Mark Bondurant

The Autobiography of
Calista Antoine

By Calista Antoine

As told to Mark Bondurant during
the winter of 1903

Chapter 1

The End of School

My father is a ship captain and my mother is his cook, and our family owns the Red Jacket, a three-masted ballyhoo schooner, and in the summer, when I'm free from school, I get to sail away in her.

Unfortunately, right now, I'm still tied down in school with three days to go and no sign of my parents. Normally, they would have been back in port a week ago, but they're overdue. Nothing to worry about yet – much.

These days, with war prices for some things going through the roof, there are some cargoes too tempting, tucked down in places too risky, and a ship captain has to weigh both if he wants to make a profit and stay afloat. Last I saw my parents, they were going to do the sugar run to Jamaica. Up in the cold North sugar cane simply doesn't grow. You have to go where it's warm and for us in the U.S., that means the Caribbean, which is unfortunately down next to the Confederate States of America. This is 1892, the fourth and nastiest year of the war so far and we have to sail right past Florida with its people doing their best to be unpleasant. So, we in the cold North can either buy it from Britain at outrageous prices or go get it ourselves, come back, and sell it to ourselves at outrageous prices, which is, by the way, why my parents can afford boarding school.

I won't kid you. It's a dangerous run. But, if nothing else, our Red Jacket is fast and Crow sits up in Crow's nest and watches when they sail past the Florida coast. Crow, Crow's nest, get it? Well, maybe not. Crow isn't his real name anyway, but that's what people call him and he doesn't seem to mind. His real name is *Iilittate Akdisshé*, which is Blood Dancer, but that's a little scary for most people. He's a Crow Indian, which isn't what they're really called either. They're the Bird People. So Crow sits in Crow's nest. Get it? Pa had it built when the war started just so we could keep a lookout and stay ahead of things. It's a tricky climb to get up there and Pa doesn't let me go up when we're at sea, but in port I can, and you can see a lot.

So I'm staring out the window, daydreaming in class. It's summer. You can't blame me!

"Calista?" That's Mrs. Johnson.

Honestly, she still calls me that to this day. Everyone calls me Cali. Even my parents.

"Calista, are you with us?" Of course, half the class snickered.

"Yes, ma'am."

"It's just a few days more. Come up to the board and solve the problem."

Naturally, it's division. I hate division because it takes forever. It's unpleasant, but that's what school is isn't it? So my term is almost over, the school is going to close, my parents are overdue, and I don't know where I'm going to stay if they come back after school closes. Maybe I'll sleep in the school basement!

I will not bore you with the details of the day. Let's just say that it went by. Classes ended, we were let out in the garden for two hours before dinner, where we got to throw a ball around. Daisy is my best friend, but don't call her that. She hates Daisy. Call her Dae.

We were tossing the ball back and forth. It's best if you do. If you just sit, they come out to find out what's wrong.

"No news about your parents yet?"

"No, Daisy, not yet," I replied, trying to sit on my temper. People had been asking about that a lot lately and things like that make me crabby. It's like they think I might keep it a secret or that everybody else in the entire town won't know before I do. Dae knows this, but she can't help asking, which is why I just called her Daisy instead of Dae.

"Have you heard from yours yet?" I asked. Dae's parents are rich. They grow tobacco. They get to ship their goods to England by steamship and don't have to go sailing by Florida.

"No, but they never write. I'm sure someone will show up." They always come in a steam carriage. "It's bath night."

"Oh be still my palpitating heart," I sighed.

At the Carrigan School for Young Women in Boston, we bathe three times a week: Sunday, Wednesday, and Friday nights. It's Wednesday. With 62 girls to bathe, discipline and organization are paramount. There are four tubs, but there are limits to modern plumbing. When first tub is full, in goes a girl and they start filling the second. When the second is filled, the first girl comes out and two girls go in and they start filling the third, then three, but on the fourth – ah ha! The first tub is dumped and refilled. Therefore, the fourth girl gets just a little bit longer to bathe while the first tub is emptied and refilled and the second girl gets the dirtiest water. This was how we filled our minds.

"Are you done with Daisy Miller?" I asked. It was probably not going to be to my taste, but reading material was always in short supply. It had come to my attention, naturally through honest and casual conversation, that someone had a copy of *Dracula*. I wish someone would tell me where it was as well!

"No, it's very slow going. Did you hear about Anne?"

"No."

"Her mother died having a baby. A carriage came for her this morning."

For this I stopped tossing the ball.

"How awful," I said. And I meant it. I liked Anne. "Will she be back next year?"

"I didn't get to talk to her. They called her out of Bible, and then I heard she had left."

Anne, unlike yours truly, was seventeen. I'm just sixteen. If she's out of school at seventeen, then that's probably the end of school for her. Next stop, marriage. Goodbye, Anne. I liked you.

"That's sad. Still, she has good prospects." Which means that she's of good family and would almost certainly have a line of waiting suitors to choose from, if her father lets her. I think Anne will make a good wife as long as she has a good husband to match.

Me? What about me? My prospects are good as long as Red is afloat and my Pa is sailing her. I'll probably end up marrying a sea captain or a shipper. Oh please, oh Lord, don't let me marry a military officer. They earn no money and more often as not sail off to a horrible death; which brings us back to my current situation. Where are my Ma and Pa?

Our Red Jacket is fast. She can pull speed from the breeze of a hummingbird's wings, but there has to be a breeze. On a good day, nothing can touch her. On a bad day a steamship can trot right up to her and do whatever it wants. The trick with Florida is to cross on a good day. Did my parents have a bad day?

That evening I was pleased to find that I was no longer a number two, which I'd been all year, but was now a number one. So shineth the light on the virtuous. It shineth for two more baths before I'm out.

In the evenings we practice our music, read, stitch, or write letters. All girls were required to learn a musical instrument. I chose the violin. I chose it because if fit in my sea chest, which is where it stays most of the summer. There's very little free time on a schooner. But while I'm in school, I have to make a show of it, and since I have no one to write to and no books to read, I practice. I practice in the dining hall along with seven or eight other girls who are in the same situation. We make quite a racket, which is why we're there and not where people are reading books and writing letters. There I am, sawing through a nasty piece of Bach for tomorrow's lesson. Can you see me roll by eyes?

You can make amazing sounds with a violin, from earsplitting squeaks that make your teeth hurt to low rasps like the lid sliding off a coffin. Oh, and you can play notes too. If you're clever, you can twist them this way and that until they flap like flags in the wind, much to the frustration of my music teacher Mrs. Hartnoll. She wants precision, but there's no real precision in the world. Just the rolling of the deck and the hum of the wind through the rigging on moonlit nights.

Oh, dear Lord, please take me back out to sea. Even if they arrive tomorrow, it'll be weeks before we make it back out. There will be cargo to unload and sell, cargo to buy and load, and repairs and provisioning.

All of which we did. I mean, they came in the next day.

What? Did you think they wouldn't?

I was, naturally, the last person to hear. They all must have said, "Someone will tell her I'm sure." I heard it from Mrs. Grayson who asked if I was packed. Clueless Cali stood there with her mouth open like some kind of gaping cod fish. They could have packed me in salt and loaded me on a barge to Albany.

Inasmuch as the act of packing itself is concerned, I'm lucky as I rarely have much to pack. My parents didn't send word but came themselves. They called me out of Math! Can you see my smile? I hugged Dae as I left and promised to write, which is nonsense. Wherever I end up going, unless I sent it airmail by zeppelin, the letter would take longer to get back than me. We might even be carrying it in our hold.

I ran down the halls to the dorm, at least when no one was looking, and threw my things in my chest. Believe me, I don't do this at sea, but there is a time for everything and everything has its place. Ecclesiastes 3:1. Bible test question, but I'm out for the summer! I wonder if they could hear my laughter in Math?

Mrs. Pettett was waiting in the front hall to straighten my clothes, the school reputation after all, and to tisk over my posture, and to pinch a little color into my cheeks for their first sight of me. Like I need that! Out the door I went.

Ma and Pa had lost weight and they looked shorter. It must have been a hard trip, but they made it. I jumped into their arms, which knocked them back a step or two – really, they had gotten shorter. And there was Mackie, our first mate, up in the driver's seat smiling. He had gotten shorter too. We are all in tears. They kept saying my name over and over.

"Pa, Ma, take me home," I said.

"She's there, berth 31a," Pa said.

"Berth 31a? Yuck! That's downwind from the cannery, Pa."

"Yes, but near Gleeson and Sons," Pa said.

"Don't tell me you broke something?"

"It was a rough trip, Hon," Ma said. "We took a little damage."

"Got shot really," Mackie said.

"I have to see. Go, go!" Now I was worried.

They let me drag them into the carriage, Pa grabbing my things as I pulled him backwards. Mackie flicked the whip and shooshed the horse forward, and we *clop-clopped* off toward the harbor. "Clop-clopped" you ask? No steam carriages for us. We are not rich.

"We've talked it over and decided we should tell you," Pa said. "You'll see anyway when we get there. It was some sort of shore patrol boat. The wind was down and they overtook us. Didn't even have any masts we could see, just smoke. They sent some shells our way and one clipped the quarterdeck and took out our mizzenmast, but didn't go off. I guess Red's wood isn't hard enough to set off shells. It was kind of lucky really. The mast dragging in the water pulled us starboard and threw off their aim."

"And then when we cut it away and turned leeward into a dead run, it threw them off again," Ma said. "Never been so scared in my life." Ma is Irish, just so you know. Red hair and all. You stay away from her. If she doesn't lick you herself, you'll find me and half the crew in some dark alley some night!

"Then they quit. I guess we weren't worth the gun powder," Pa added.

"Tell her about Ian," Mackie said, over his shoulder.

Pa whoofed, like he had had the air knocked out of him.

"What about Ian, Pa?" I'm worried now because Ian is like my older brother. He was the cabin boy when I was little and my only playmate when we were at sea.

"Oh," Pa looked uncomfortable. "He took some splinters from

the mast when it broke."

"Your Ma put 21 stitches in him," Mackie said.

Ma looked uncomfortable too.

"He's going to be all right isn't he?" I was sitting up in my seat.

"He'll live," Mackie said.

"He'll be fine," Ma said, looking sternly at Mackie.

"I suppose this means we aren't going to Jamaica this year doesn't it?" I asked.

"I'd rather not," Mackie said.

But Ma and Pa looked worried.

Red is painted black. There isn't a spot of red on her. Her hull is black, her stern castle and cabins are white trimmed in black. Nothing complicated. We're here to work. She was named by her former owners, who were British. Looking at her in her berth I couldn't help my tears. The shell had come in at a low angle. The wheel was still there, she could steer, but it had flown through the center of the deck, cut the mast, and knocked a hole through the main deck below on its way out. I am grateful, as I'm sure we are all, that they didn't have rough seas on the way home. They had done their best to shore up the hull and deck to make her watertight, but she must have leaked, and it must have been hell to keep her pumped out.

"You sure she doesn't need the dry dock, Pa?" I asked.

"No, Gleeson says the hull is sound. The shell went right through the porthole. It's just deck work and stepping the mast."

"This is going to cost, isn't it?"

Pa looked at the other ships docked. The repairs were going to cost.

"We still have the cargo, right?"

"Oh yes, cargo is fine," Pa said.

"We've got buyers, right?"

"Oh yes."

"Then we're going to be all right, right?"

Pa sighed, turned and looked me in the eye. "It'll hurt, but we'll be fine."

"That's my cabin, isn't it?!" I said, upset all over again. "It went through my cabin!"

My cabin is really just a nook, like a large cupboard, but it has a door and a porthole and it's where I keep all my things, but now it was sitting there open to the spray. I ran across the gangway, up on deck, then up on the stern castle, and down on my knees in tears. Her beautiful lines were torn. She looked naked without her mast. The aft cabin roof was smashed in. The companion way leading below was open to the spray and the main deck below had been wet. The hole through the deck showed each bulkhead the shell smashed through. I couldn't see my cabin because they had stretched sailcloth over it to keep the water from getting in, but by the way things looked, there couldn't be much of it left.

"Where's Ian?" I asked.

Pa came up the stairway behind me, "He's at the doctor's getting looked over. He'll be back tomorrow."

I could smell the cannery. It was like the icing on the cake.

"They're going to restitch him properly," Ma said.

I reached deep inside. Poise and deportment. A proper lady is calm in the face of adversity. Miss Brunche's etiquette class. A breath, then two, and finally, "Where am I going to sleep?"

"With us, in our cabin until yours is fixed," Pa said.

I nodded. "Do you have an estimate yet?"

"Not a formal one. They say the deck and woodwork can be ready in a week, the mast another two days beyond. No estimates yet from the riggers or the sailmaker."

"Shame you couldn't save the sails," I said.

"There wasn't time."

"Ho ho, it's the little missy," cried Crow, coming up the stairs. Then he stopped, "Whoa, not so little."

"Crow!" Pa said.

"Yes, sir," Crow replied.

"Hi, Crow!" I said. "Were you up in the nest when she took the shell?"

"Yup. 'Bout flung me off. She tipped when it hit. If I hadn't been holding on when she righted, I would have been flung back at them like I was a cannon shell myself."

"You landing on their ship would have been funny."

"Maybe. Depends on who had the upper hand."

"Anybody else, anything else I should know about?" I asked.

"No, that's the worst of it," Pa said.

I sure hoped he was telling the truth, because below decks was a mess and my cabin was really gone.

So we all went down to Ma and Pa's cabin where they had strung up a hammock for me. I hauled in my chest and stacked it in the corner, then I sat down on their bed. Knockers, our ship cat, came right over and started brushing up against me like I'd never been away. I picked her up and scratched her neck, and she purred. There I was, home.

That night for dinner, fried ham! My Ma soaks it in molasses all day and then she fries it. It's my favorite and they all know it, so this was my special welcome home dinner and holes in the ship be damned. I went up on deck after dinner with my violin and played slow and hard for the ship and her pain, and in the next ship up came a harmonica, and then a flute, and then a jig. We were dancing with boots thumping on the decks. Someone was pounding on the side of a barrel. We did *Squid Jiggin Ground*, and then *Jack Hinks*, a squeezebox dancing in there somewhere and people howling and singing at the moon, and around we went until I fell over laughing looking up at the sky.

Oh those stars, those stars in the sky out on deck.

Chapter 2

The Wounded

The next morning, I was sitting up in Crow's nest, staring at the blue sky, which was rapidly turning gray as the fog rolled in, trying to think of alternatives to the sugar run. Pa and I had been brainstorming all day, trying to come up with something we could do for money that didn't involve getting shot at. So far, he'd found insolvable problems with every one of my ideas.

"Pa?" I called. But of course he couldn't hear me. I started to climb down. "Pa?"

Now really, this must stop.

What do you do when you realize that you sound like a bleating sheep? You shut up and climb down to look for him, of course. What kind of upbringing did you think I had?

He was over on the dock.

"Pardon, Pa?"

He turned and, silly Cali, head in the clouds, I realized that he had been talking to someone. The man was undistinguished and I thought him a tradesman. Pa said "pardon" and looked at me.

"Could we mount guns and turn privateer?" I asked.

Pa turned red and quickly looked at the man he was talking to and absentmindedly bowed as he apologized! "I'm so sorry! She's young and understands little," he stammered, which alarmed and confused me. Then I saw the man's guild ring. He was a warehouser, dressed down for the docks!

The warehouser looks at me like I'm a piece of livestock and says, "She's marriageable, I think it's probably time to find her a husband."

Which got me *angry*. But! I am not just a lady of refined character but a good daughter as well. Remember Miss Brunche. So I took a deep breath and then addressed the warehouser, "I'm sorry if I caused you offense, sir. Father has encouraged me to think about the company and I am trying to the best of my ability, but after all, I am a woman."

This seemed to mollify him, and only confirmed to anybody listening with half a brain that he was a complete idiot.

Pa gave me a wry look. My father has far more than half a brain! I wiggled my eyebrows at him when the warehouser was looking away, which left Pa in a state of distress.

"I apologize again for interrupting," I said, with a pathetic curtsey. "I will leave you to men's work." And I went back to the ship. Now, you might think this is funny, but to me this has always been a real problem. Most men of business will not talk to me, even now. I will say no more on the subject. Well, maybe not a whole lot more.

When he was done with the warehouser, Pa came below decks and found me staring at my future cabin; right above the rope locker. Honesty, I don't mind. Privacy onboard a ship is better than gold and my cabin is all mine.

When I saw him, he was chuckling, so I beat him to the punch.

"What an idiot," I said.

"Yes, but a rich idiot. It seems to start with the second generation," Pa said.

"Is going privateer such a bad idea?"

"No, which was why you scared him. But Red's hull isn't braced for cannon. They'd shake her apart."

"We wouldn't actually have to fire them, at least not much."

"True, and some merchants mount cannon because of that. We'd have to have hire a gun crew and they would take up space and cost us money. Maintenance on a gun isn't cheap either."

Pa had thought of this already. What do you say to that? Hazzah? Tally ho?

"Could we ferry troops south and wounded north?" I asked.

"Too small," he replied.

"Could we trade directly with the South? They must smoke. There must be something we make they need."

And at that he gave me a big smile and a kiss on my forehead. I do love my Pa even though at times he seems crazy. "They would shoot us," he said.

I sighed. "We should stick to consignments, do packet runs," I muttered.

"Red's sails make it difficult to keep a fixed schedule and we couldn't remain independent."

"I know. And that leaves Africa."

"Africa needs everything, but what does it have besides slaves? Not much. We have problems with wind and currents. In order to get to Africa we'd have to sail to Europe, which means raiders, and we'd still have to come back by Florida. A long trip means higher overhead. Look at the charts in our cabin and think about the costs."

I love my Pa for that. He won't carry slaves and he doesn't dismiss me. I decided then and there that I was going to the library to learn about Africa.

Pa hired a wagon to go get Ian. A horse wagon of course. Steam trucks cost money and since time was not an issue, they offered us no advantage. Only Ma and me were going since the crew was unloading cargo. Let's be frank here. I was only sixteen and not as strong as a man, at least not yet. Under normal circumstances I'd be down in the hold pitching in, but this job needed doing too and didn't need one of the men. So we rode, clop-clopped, bump-bumped, down the street to the doctor's. I had never been to this doctor, but Ma knew the way. At school they gave us a checkup at the start of term, and other than that, there was never a need for me to see one, but I wasn't looking forward to this. I've heard stories.

His clinic was on a side street, crisscrossed with laundry and wet with poor drainage. We splashed and rolled through fetid puddles. The smell was appalling. I swear, how do you all live in cities? We stopped in front and Ma and I climbed down and went in. The front room was nice. He had a secretary behind a small desk and padded seats to sit on. His secretary only had one arm, which had become a fairly common affliction thanks to the war. There are few men walking the streets since the war that aren't either old, in uniform, or had come home wounded.

We are all worried for Ian. The draft men would love to get their hands on him.

"Can I help you?" the secretary asked.

"We're here for Ian McAllister," Ma said.

The doctor, who apparently heard us, came out from the back in his grubby smock and gave us a frown. "You're all there is? How are you going to carry him?"

"We have to carry him? We didn't know," Ma said.

He looked inquiringly at his secretary like he could help. The secretary averted his eyes. "Yes, of course. You brought payment?" the doctor said.

"Yes." Ma stood up and pulled some bills out of her purse and laid them on the desk. The secretary took the money, wrote her out a receipt, and then began making notes in a ledger.

"Well then," the doctor said. "I guess we'll have to see what we can manage," and waved for us to follow.

Inside, it was dim – and smelled too – which was hard to place at first, but I decided after a bit that it was rotten meat. We passed through his work room with its bloodstained table and sink. He was not a tidy man. Pa would not have tolerated this onboard. He led us back through a short hallway past a couple of rooms. Inside we could see patients in beds. The rooms had windows, but despite the heat, they were closed.

"You know to keep the wound wrapped."

"You've told us," Ma said.

"Good. Oxygen, that means air, promotes infection. Keep it wrapped, keep the air out."

Ian was lying in his bed, with one arm over his eyes, looking kind of pale. He was soaked in sweat, still wearing the same pants he had been wounded in. Ma had cut them up the leg in order to work on his wound. With his stitches and bandages, I suppose they were about the only thing he could wear. But for all the money we paid, they could have washed them. They were stained brown with flaking dried blood. Under his pants, he had bandages all the way up his thigh and hip.

He smiled when he saw me. "Hi, Cali. Sorry I missed you coming home."

"You sure are. We danced like lunatics without you," I said, smiling back.

"Young lady, I'll need your help with the stretcher," the doctor said.

"Yes, sir."

I followed him across the hall to a room with only one bed. An older woman was lying in it.

"Doctor, has my sister come yet?" she asked.

"No. Not yet. Just lie still."

"I need a bedpan, Doctor," the woman said.

The doctor blew air out of his cheeks in exasperation. "The day nurse is out and my assistant has been drafted. You'll have to wait. I'll be back as soon as I can."

The stretcher was leaning up against the wall. "Take it in to your friend's room, young lady. I'll be right there."

I looked at the stretcher, leaning up against the wall, a big clumsy thing and a bit heavy. I don't think he had originally intended for me to carry it by myself, but since it was folded, I found I could lean it over my shoulder and drag it. Going through the doors, I had to dip down, dragging the end of it on the floor, which wasn't easy on the knees and threatened to tip me. But get it there I did.

Ma grabbed the top when I came in and helped lower it. She knew how to open it so we could spread the bars apart and lock them. Ian looked frustrated that he couldn't help. Ian's roommate lay there unconscious. He wasn't sweating, which was bad.

"Ian, we're going to have to move you to the wall side of the bed," Ma said.

"Yes, ma'am," he said.

"We'll try to be careful, but we're going to need your help too."

The doctor dashed past the door carrying a low edged bowl.

Ma leaned out the door and called, "When you get a chance, we could use some help too."

"In a minute," he called back.

Ma looked at me and said, "I think we're going to have to do this ourselves. Here, pull the bed out from the wall."

We scraped the bed forward across the floor, trying to lift it as best we could, but it still left scratches. Ma pulled the sheet loose from the mattress. "Cali, we're going to pull him to the back edge with the sheet. Grab it here," and she took one side of the sheet and I took the other. We slid Ian over by pulling him on the sheet, with poor Ian trying to lay still. He couldn't help wincing, though I could see him try to hide it. We laid the stretcher on the other side of the bed next to him.

"Here's where we need your help, Ian," Ma said.

"It's so hot in here," I exclaimed.

"The doc said the outside air has bacteria or something," Ian said. "I think he's full of," then he stopped, glancing at me. "Hooey."

"You're going to have to haul your hooey onto this stretcher," Ma said.

"Yes, ma'am."

So we wrestled him onto the stretcher. Actually, I will not lie. He mostly did it himself and quite bravely, keeping his body straight the whole time. It clearly hurt.

Then Ma went after that secretary. I'm not sure what all she said, but it did involve some heated words which to my shame I know the meaning of, but were not part of my school education. Then with Ma on one end and the secretary and yours truly on the other, we hauled Ian out to the wagon and stowed him in back. Then we clopped back to the ship. That doctor never did show up! I know where there are people in Jamaica that can lay curses!

Mackie, our first mate, had the cabin opposite of mine. Well, opposite my future cabin. But he moved out so Ian could have a flat place to sleep instead of a hammock. The first thing Ian did was to open the porthole to let the breeze in. I agreed with Ian. That doctor was crazy. "Bacteria" in the air! There is nothing better for a wound than clean fresh air and sunshine. Then Ma went back to the dock and paid the driver to deliver the stretcher back.

That evening, after dinner, Pa came to me on the stern castle while I was staring down the channel out to sea.

"Cali, we got two notes today, one from the *Kittiwake* and the other from the *Lucky Son*. Seems they both have boys that want to try courting you."

I had absolutely nothing to say. You hear talk about people being speechless, but you really don't understand until it happens to you. I Cali, the woman of wit, was stunned witless. They were all laughing about it later. Pa said my eyes bulged out big as plates. He could see my distress and with a repressed smile said, "You don't have to answer now. The notes are on your sea chest if you want them."

The next day, two more came in. Now I really, really, needed to get back out to sea!

Chapter 3

A New Wardrobe

The next morning Ma declared over breakfast that it was time we did something about my clothes. I have to admit, she was right. How could I be a woman of poise and grace clomping around in boots, deck clothes, and a nor'easter? So we set out for Eagleston's. A block in from the wharf we caught the steam trolley, which I have always enjoyed. Ma paid the white conductor his nickels. The conductor rang his bell, pulled the big lever, and off we went rolling down the dirt street, the occasional cool mist of household steam vents drifting down around us.

We went late in the morning, so the work rush was over and we could sit away from the boiler. It's the best seat in the winter, but the worst in the summer. The negro coal man hummed tunes as he worked, keeping time with his feet and shovel. I listened, filing them away for further study. I do that a lot. There's new music everywhere, if people would only listen.

Downtown was as busy as ever with people darting back and forth across the street, steam trucks dodging this way and that, wagons parked out in the middle unloading. The conductor spent more and more time ringing his bell. I wished he wouldn't. No one listens except those who don't need to, but he has to do something besides collecting money.

Having nothing else to wear, I wore my school uniform. It's kind of like a navy uniform, dark blue, the skirt ending about ten inches above the ground. It wasn't much to look at, but it was comfortable and I could move in it, and blue kind of brings out the red and gold in my hair. Everything else went up with my cabin.

Eagleston's is two stories tall and takes up a whole corner. They sell everything and I mean everything. Well, maybe not buckets. You'd have to go to a hardware store for that. Food either. But when it comes to the day-to-day necessities of life, Eagleston's is it.

New toothbrush, new hairbrush, new nail scissors, new bloomers, new night dresses, new day dress, new stockings, new shoes, and my first ever hat. No more bonnets for me. A boater with a ribbon! The salesman continued to insist that I should be fitted for a corset and I was ready to do him bodily harm when Ma diplomatically intervened by telling him that we would work on that later. We did, however purchase three light bodices because, frankly, my school ones had gotten rather small for me. There are limits to how far lacing can extend. Really, we are not barbarians. Some things should not be left out to wave in the breeze.

Since our purchases would be delivered to the dock office, Ma said with a wicked smile, "Let's buy lunch!" Being served by someone else is a rare treat for Ma, and I would gladly forgo my lunch anytime so she could do it twice. Down the street from Eagleston's is Ma's secret sin. Ma loves Chinese food, but Pa will have none of it.

And so we entered Wong's den of iniquity.

Since the railroad opened to San Francisco, things Chinese had been flooding east. Chinese restaurants had been popping up everywhere and Wong's was typical. He had that Chinese squarish woodwork with geometric patterns, painted black and red, and pretty black lacquerware with shell inlays hanging on his walls.

The Chinese like to fry things and they do it so well. The food can be spicy too, which is nice! And Wong's gives you a lot. We staggered out with happy smiles.

I wanted to go to the library to look up Africa, so Ma gave me money for the trolley and took off back to the docks. You know I'm such a good daughter. Of course I spent the money on the trolley. Not on candy. What kind of daughter do you think I am? A smart one! The candy was yummy.

I skipped along eating my candy, secretly laughing at the clothes women had to wear. Corsets, crinolines, high heels, bustles, dresses cinched tight from their jawbones down, and hats bigger than sails piled high with every kind of strange geegaw and doodad. Women's clothes--to be blatantly and unapologetically frank--are stupid; and I wasn't sure what I was going to do when I got older, which was going to be soon. I was small for my age and thin, which gave me a little time. But girls, at sixteen, are starting to get married and I was thankful my Pa wasn't pressuring me.

Subject: Humidity and latitude. One of the great things about Jamaica is that clothing rules are relaxed. Loose and blousy is fine. You can even roll up your sleeves and show a bare arm. Skirts are simple and the legs underneath are often naked to the breeze, at least they can be when they're black.

When I was little, I ran naked on the beach, and woo hoo to all of you! Black kids, white kids, running together, who cares? But since I grew and sprouted breasts the world changed until everybody ran around in a state of tilting madness. Ooooo, like brown legs are different than white ones. Sadly, apparently they are. Even a bare foot is scandalous for me in the U.S., even in Jamaica, and if I didn't cage myself in a corset, pantaloons, and a crinoline, our family could be ostracized and I might even be arrested!

The Boston Library is on Boylston Street and looks like a large featureless brick that was slapped down forcefully by a giant. Being solid and stone has its advantages in the humid Boston summer. Inside it's cool and smells of wood and books. I love the smell of books!

At the Corrigan School for Young Women, we were taken to the library two times a year for precisely an hour each time. It's important for a well-bred woman to know where library is, but not how to use it. But I laugh. Ah ha! Give me an hour and I'll take anything apart. I love the library and I know where the good books are. Even *Dracula*, which was, unfortunately, at the time checked out. I even checked neighboring shelves just in case it had been misshelved.

I looked up Africa and what did I find? Well-thumbed books with pictures of naked African ladies. Men. Can you see me bleakly shaking my head? It took a while to find anything serious but as I've said before, give me an hour. What I found was rubber, copper, rubies, gold, diamonds, sugar, and rum. Unfortunately, the men who wrote these books were not the exactly the best sources of information. Reading about the authors in the fronts and backs of their books revealed that many of them may not have even been to Africa at all!

But, I still found nuggets of gold. Apparently, for the last 11 years crazy King Leopold II of Belgium had been trying to cultivate a rubber industry in the Congo because of some treaty or other. He had been trading it north with Europe for five or six years, but there wasn't any reason I could find as to why they couldn't trade west with us as well. So Africa seemed like it might be a good bet. Tobacco to France, manufactured goods to Spain, wine and grain to Africa, rubber, and maybe even copper and jewels here for the war effort. A four-way trade, so much better than our one way trade with Jamaica.

I looked up rubber trees. They started producing in five to six years and reached mature production levels at ten to twelve, so the first plantations had to be in full production. The Congo's principle Atlantic port was Boma, at the head of the Congo river.

It took two days to drag Pa to the library. I wore my new boater by the way, and looked quite fetching. He looked at the books, frowning. After that he looked at me and frowned some more. And then he sighed, sat back in his seat and said, "I love you." Was I beaming? "Rubber, I didn't know about that. I need to ask around about this." I didn't know it then, but that was one of the most important moments in my life. Then it got better when he said, "Of course that would mean you'd miss half the next school year."

Most of the Americans who've traded with Africa live in the South, but Pa heard about a trader in port who had been to Africa. He was berthed way over on East Island. So Pa decided we ought to row over in the yawl.

Harbors are cesspools. I mean really. Every drain in the city ends up there. They're disgusting, but the tides were on their way out, and the worst was out to sea, so this trip promised to be somewhat pleasant.

There are some beautiful boats in this world, not that our Red isn't beautiful. She truly is and we love her dearly, but she is first and foremost a working boat and that means she has a lot of function in her lines. There are yachts sailing the seas that are just for show and nothing else. They are exquisitely pure of line and liquid of form, with woodwork and brass exposed and polished, sails that are always white. And there are armies of workmen who labor over them to keep that shine. There are many rich in Boston and quite a few of these little jewels in harbor. We got to ogle them as we ambled past. On the way, as well, we got an eyeful of the Navy docks. Huge mountains of gray painted iron with great swiveling guns. How do they stay afloat? Some didn't even have masts. What would they do if they broke down? Row? They were terrifying, with guns that gaped like sewer pipes.

One big problem with the tide being out is that you have that long slimy climb up the ladder to the dock. The East Island docks aren't as crowded with ships as the main harbor, mostly because the island doesn't connect directly to the city. Instead, it has three bridges to the shore. It was easy to find an unobstructed ladder up to the docks.

Once we were on top, a glint of sun caught my eye for the merest moment. We were in sight of the Boston Aerodrome and I could see one of the big trans-Atlantic zeppelins as it left for Europe, its huge gray shape visible in between the gaps between the warehouses.. How much cargo can they can ship, I wondered? They're for the rich only and I was sure then that I would never get to see the inside of one.

But we were there to see the *Quilombo*. She was a big boxy two-masted snow with the biggest bowsprit and the widest spacing between her yards I'd ever seen. Her sails must have been enormous when they were unfurled, and they must have been hell to pull in during a storm too. At the time, her hull needed paint and when we walked up the gangway, her deck was not clean. She was amazingly empty of features too, nothing but a small deckhouse, her cargo hatches, and the wheel and binnacle on the stern. I figured this was so they could carry extra cargo on deck. It looked ugly, but I bet she could carry twice the load Red could. But Red is as much a home as a means to an end.

Looking about we saw a man up in the mainmast crosstree tarring sidestays. Otherwise there wasn't another soul around. That was until another man climbed up through the deckhouse door, turned, and saw us.

"Hello!" he called.

The man up in the mast called down, "Sorry, Captain. Missed'em. My mind was driftin."

Pa called back, "Hello."

The man, when he came over, sized us up with a squint. "What can I do you for?" he asked.

"Captain Bartholomew?"

"Yes, and you?"

"Captain Carmichael, of the Red Jacket."

"Ah yes, the one with the daughter."

Eeeeek! I didn't scream out loud. Really. Deportment first, after all. But my cheeks were certainly burning.

"This must be her," he smiled. "As lovely as I've heard."

Has everyone in the harbor heard of me?

"That's not why we came," my Pa said, bless him.

I definitely didn't get any notes from Captain Bartholomew or I wouldn't have come. Besides, he had to be at least 40. Yuck!

"We've heard tell that you have experience in Africa," Pa said.

"Who told you that?" Captain Bartholomew replied.

"O'Toole, Caddock," Pa said.

"Well, I suppose they would know. Come, let's go to my cabin." He turned and walked toward the deckhouse, with us following. "My father used to carry slaves out of Dakar," he said over his shoulder. "But that was 12 years ago."

"Why'd you stop?" Pa asked. We climbed down the steps into the darkness below decks

He was silent for a moment as he put his hand on his cabin-door latch. "Rather not talk about it," he said finally.

"Of course," Pa replied. Bartholomew's cabin was dark, split with beams of morning sunlight working their way in between the shutters.

He was fumbling with the chimney of a lantern. "To be honest, the ship's been haunted since," he stopped and looked at us, his face half in shadow. "Nothing bad, mind you, but you can hear them at night." Then he turned back to the lamp and continued on. "It's a stain we'll have to work off."

He struck a match and lit a lantern and his cabin leapt into view. He had books – and a globe! I went right to it and when he saw me, he brought over the lamp.

"Bought that in Bristol. It was too lovely to pass up. Excellent detail. Definitely intended for use."

I turned it to Africa. There was the Congo and there was Boma.

"Have you ever been here?" I asked, pointing.

"Congo?" That moment of light I saw in his eyes when he had brought over the lamp, vanished. "No. Never that far."

"How far down did you go?" Pa asked.

"Freetown, Sherbro, Cape Coast, but it was all 12 years ago or more, when my father was still captain."

I found them all on the globe. He had been all the way down to Guinea.

"If you don't mind my asking, where is your father?" Pa asked.

"Malaria."

Pa nodded and there was quiet for a moment. "Would you be willing to go over some charts with me?"

He nodded yes, but you could tell he didn't want to. He reached into a cupboard and pulled out a bottle half full of something brown. "Share a drink?"

My pa doesn't drink much, but I had the feeling that he might this time, as a gesture of support. And sure enough he did. I do know my pa! As he went down the coast on the maps, you could see the Captain reliving it. Sometimes he would shudder and then take a drink. He told us about reefs, uncertain areas in the map, traditional pirate lairs, weather, all the while Pa scribbled notes on the chart or in his notebook. What Captain Bartholomew couldn't tell us about was the political situation as it was now, who was angry at whom, or the current state of development along the coastline. He only had rumors.

"I've heard that the rubber trade is controlled by a British company, the Anglo-Belgian India Rubber Company. You can carry for them, but they demand a percentage. I don't know how to contact them. You might try the British Trade Office. And I don't know if there are restrictions on ports of delivery, either. Ivory, back then, was free for the taking. If the British are shipping for the Belgians these days, then they might know about that too," he said.

"Let me think." He took another drink. "You might want to look into exotic hides. Zebra and leopard are popular. They make interesting carvings and such too, but there's no market. They're too strange. You'll see."

"I've heard they have gemstone."

"Don't. There's blood attached to every one of them. Don't even let anyone think you might be carrying them. You aren't big enough to handle them."

"I also heard about copper."

"That's way south. You said you were going to Boma. You won't find copper until Cape Town." He stared into space for a bit, pulling on his beard.

"There has to be air travel down there by now, if not regular, then at least charter." He ran his finger down the coast. "All these ports belong to one European power or another and they all compete with each other. They'll seize a ship just because they think it might tick off their neighbor. They also get snippy about exclusive carrying contracts." Then he looked at me. "Are you taking her?"

"Yes," Pa answered.

"You shouldn't," he said.

"Why?"

"If you do, don't let her on shore."

"Why?"

"Maybe things have changed now," he said, his face troubled. "But they were very cruel to the blacks."

A book chose that time to fall off a shelf with a loud whack. For no reason. Really. We all sat there, staring at it.

"She'll like Europe though," Pa said, changing the subject. He smiled, "Yah, she'll like Europe."

Pa was a little unsteady as we walked down the gangway, and I was worried about that ladder. But he took it slow and I steadied the boat as best I could, such that he hardly made a mess of it getting in. He actually managed to row us back! I love my Pa.

That afternoon, on the dock, there was a young man with a squeezebox. When I came up on deck he began to sing:

Cali, oh Cali
siren of the sea.
Oh Cali, oh Cali
won't you step out with me.

Cali, oh Cali
step out with me.
Oh Cali, oh Cali
won't you come out and see.

Cali, oh Cali
come out and see.
Oh Cali, oh Cali
let's see what may be . . .

It went on for three more verses and when he stopped, he went down on one knee with arms spread. I was rooted to the deck, unable to run, eyes wide. What should I do? I breathed once, then twice, and it did nothing at all to help. I was no longer a lady of calm deportment.

Enter Mackie, my savior. He took one look at me, sighed, and walked down the gangway shooing him away. "Out of here! You'd think they never swept the docks around here." The young man took off and Mackie came back aboard chuckling. Then he looked at me and said, "You've got to admit, it was a good show."

"Mackie! What am I going to do?"

"That's not for me to say. You should talk to your Ma or Pa."

Ma was in the galley making bread, so I washed my hands,

picked up her knife, cut off a loaf's worth of dough, and started the second kneading. "Ma," I said, at a loss for words. Me! At a loss for words!

"It's the boys, isn't it?"

"I don't know what to do," I sounded pathetic even to myself.

"I don't know if I can help you. There were a few in my time. They came over for tea with my family, but your father wouldn't have none of that. He would come around the back door to buy bread for his ship, at least that's what he said. He was first mate on a clipper at the time. Gave all the bread away it turned out. We'd pass the time talking on the step. I could tell he was a good man."

"Didn't your ma and pa object?" I plopped the rolled loaf into one of the greased pans and started another.

"No. It turned out he was talking to them too. Invited me pa out for beer. Took them out for dinner. It was the surprise of my life when he showed up at the front door. He's always been a good salesman. It turned out he'd been talking business with me pa. Your grandpa's still a shareholder in Red you know. We bought out most of the others." She took a breath and then started putting the bread pans in the oven. "So you see," she continued. "I didn't have a whole lot of suitors. It was pretty clear that your pa was really the only one for me."

"There was someone singing," I said. Knockers was curling around my legs, so I reached down and gave her a fingernail-sized piece of dough.

"Well, I'm not surprised. You don't have to go out with any of them if you don't want to. You're still very young. I didn't marry until I was eighteen."

So Ma was of little help. Pa was no better.

"Cali, this is for you to decide," he said. "You have to decide when you feel ready,"

So there I was, completely footloose, flapping in the wind.

Chapter 4

Farewell to Boston

The next morning, the tug came to take us over to Glessons dock for our new mast. Red isn't a large ship and we were only moving in harbor, so we didn't get the big side-wheeler. Instead, we got the Nellie Thomson. Nellie is only 40 feet long and her boiler and engine are right out in the open on top of her weather deck. When she came alongside I called down, "Captain Thomson, permission to come aboard!" I had to yell. The motor on Nellie makes a lot of racket.

"Come on over, Cali!" yelled Captain Thomson. Nellie was Captain Thomson's daughter. She's a fair bit older than me, but we still played when I was young, and now she's married and gone, and I thought Captain Thomson was a bit lonely without her on deck. The Nellie Thomson had two other crew--Ed the new engineer and Nathan the boilerman. Nellie used to be the engineer. She was quite good at it too. I wonder what she's doing these days? Probably making grandchildren like a good wife.

But enough wool gathering! I hopped down with a whoop. Nellie's deck is always stained from engine grease and oil, unlike ours which is beautiful salt-bleached white. Engines will do that. They're worse than cats when it comes to piddling in the corner.

But like the calluses on your hands, that's part of her work. At that moment, she was venting steam to keep her pressure down, which blew back in our faces like warm drizzle. Warm until the wind turns and it's gone and you are left damp and cold. But that's just part of the fun.

"Hi, Ed!" I yelled. He was trying to pull the lever on the secondary clutch. That drives the pumps. I could see what he was aiming for. There was definitely wash in the shaft alley.

"Hi, Cali!" He yelled back.

"Need a hand?" I called.

"Sure. Pull the main clutch for a second. The gear teeth are square on."

"Aye aye!" I yelled, and hopped over the shaft well to the other clutch lever.

"Hi, Cali," Nathan yelled. He was mopping his forehead with a dirty red rag.

"Hi, Nathan," I yelled back and pulled the lever. You do a lot of yelling on Nellie. The main drive shaft began to turn over raising some water and prop wash from the screw in the stern. I immediately pushed the lever back before we made headway. Captain Thomson was in the stern heaving Nellie's tow rope up to Tinker and Wally.

Tinker and Wally? I didn't introduce you? I'm so sorry. They're part of Red's crew. Tinker isn't his real name. He's really Angel McGregor. He used to have a shop where people brought in things to be fixed. That was before he decided he liked it better out to sea. Wally is Waleed Jansen. He used to farm until he lost everything in a flood, including his wife and kids. Bad things like that can happen to farmers. That leaves Ed, who's no relation to Nellie's Ed. Our Ed is William Augustus, a former cod fisherman. He likes Ed better than Willy.

Tinker carried the line forward and Wally kept track of the play. Ed pulled his clutch lever just before the shaft stopped spinning and, with only a little bit of grind, managed to engage it. He let out a little whoop as he stood up on the sloping deck in the smoke stained sunshine, mopping his brow. That's life on a tug.

With the tow line secure to Red's bow, we proceeded to pull her away from the dock. Mackie was at the wheel, but he couldn't do much until she had some headway. Nellie needed to be a little hotter at this point, so Nathan kicked open the firebox door. You don't want to get down there with your hands. It's orange-yellow in there, and it feels nice when you're back a ways from it, but up close it will take your hair off. He heaved in a shovelful of coal and kicked the door closed twice, once to close it and once to set the latch. The stack on Nellie was tall, tall enough to be level with Red's deck, and the black smoke drifted across Wally's path. Wally's poor farmer's lungs aren't used to that and he started in a-coughing and had to back away from the smoke still hauling rope.

Once we were moving and Red had some water going past her rudder, Mackie could use it to help turn her into the main channel. Red and Nellie danced together as we moved past docks and boats toward Gleesons, Nellie pulling and Red helping to steer. At Glessons dock, Nellie reversed pulling back on the tow line, breaking Red and pulling her starboard at the same time.

"Cast off," yelled Captain Thomson to Tinker in Red's bow. Ed reversed Nellie's screw with no orders necessary from Captain Thomson, they had done this so often, leaving Captain Thomson free to pull in the line.

On the front of Nellie is a big bumper of woven jute and she used that big padded bow to push Red amidships, giving her a nudge to help the crew on the dock who were pulling Red into her berth under Glessons big crane. Red looked tiny underneath it, but that crane is a big help when stepping and assembling a mast.

So where was Pa when we were getting our new mast? He was going through the warehouses looking for bargains. When it comes to cargo, Pa is a master bargainer. Some kinds of cargo are straightforward, like tobacco and beef for instance. No bargains there. Their prices are set by the brokers with no room for haggling. But there are other things you can find that are not so straightforward, such as raccoon pelts, cheese, can openers, and even buffalo hide gloves, a pair of which I snagged from a big bag. We bid for these things against other ships who were also looking for cargo. Pa is constantly on the prowl for bargains to keep our holds full.

We were working at a disadvantage this time since we were going to a new port and didn't know their markets, so it was hard to estimate what prices things would fetch. We could only guess as to what would sell and for how much. If we don't like the prices

being offered at our first destination--on this trip it's Le Havre--
then we could try carrying it to our second, Lisbon, but every mile
we carry it costs us money and it might not sell at the second port
either. Sometimes it's better to dump items at a loss, just to clear
out hold space for things that will pay.

The last thing we do when we leave any port is to go to the
mail exchange to see if there's any mail waiting to go to our next
port. This isn't as lucrative as it used to be. A lot of people send
their mail by zeppelin now, even though it costs more. And then
there are the telegraph lines across the Atlantic, but those are for
really important messages only. People these days are more willing
to pay for the quicker delivery, but there's still a lot of regular mail
for us. We get paid by speed of delivery. The quicker we get it
there the more we get paid. So we wait until the last minute, and
it's best if you have alternate cargo lined up just in case there isn't
any mail. Really, the most important thing is that Red leaves port
with holds completely full.

The day came when our holds were packed, our sails were
back from the lofts, and our new mast and rigging were up. There
was food stuffed in all the corners, so much so that we had to crawl
over things to get anywhere, my cabin smelled like paint and I was
sleeping in a little nest amongst my new clothes. See? There I am,
sitting in the middle of it, smiling. We were ready to go!

Ships getting pulled out to sea get the side wheeler, The
Nantasket. She's as big as we are and I don't get to play on her like
I do on Nellie. This isn't a casual tow from one dock to the next,
even though Captain Winkler's son and I used to throw rocks at
each other. Sadly Jimbo, Captain Winkler's son, was drafted into
the Union Navy. He wasn't a whole lot older than me. The
Nantasket can reverse one of its paddle wheels and turn on the
spot, which is very handy for a harbor tug. It was those big paddle
wheels that hauled us out past Governor's Island and into President
Roads, the outer harbor, where they left us with a couple of blows
on their horn for goodbye.

The President Roads is a deepwater anchorage surrounded by
barrier islands, and several ships were moored out there waiting for
inspection. The wind was fair for standing out, it was overcast, the

tide was falling, and we had to go because others were waiting behind us.

We needed to make steerage quickly because we were drifting. Everyone's on deck ready on the mainsail, except poor Ian. The great thing about a schooner is that you do it all from the deck. The bad thing is that it's all hoisting and it can take all of us to get one sail winched up in bad weather. We coat the masts with linseed oil and tallow to make it easier, a chore that I have done more times than I can count and for as long as I can remember.

We were finally making way and the deck was moving under my feet. It wasn't the open ocean yet, but I could feel it. And it felt like the first breath I'd taken in nine months.

I hate pumping. Red leaks less than most ships her age, less than two inches a day, but we still have to pump, and we all take turns at it. Some more than others for sure, but even Ma does it sometimes. Naturally, it's worse during and after storms, especially if water is breaking over the deck. Wooden ships are built to bend otherwise they'd come apart the moment something gives them a push, like a squall or even a hurricane. It's better to bend than to break. And storms can do a lot of bending, which means that there's always something leaking. Today it was Tinker and me. Bending--we don't leak! Bending up and down. On the deck pump. I was so glad for my new gloves because yours truly had lost all her calluses.

We were a week out of Boston and every day so far we'd had to tighten the play out of our new rigging. We did it that morning. New rope stretches as it settles. I got to see them making that rope. The rope alley in Boston is 300 yards long and they run jute yarn down its length to twist them together. I helped string our new rigging too. We ended up doing it ourselves because it was cheaper to stay docked an extra day to do the work. The bids were all too high. It's the war. Everyone has to pay more for labor. Settling in new rigging was new to me, but Pa said it will take at least two, more likely three weeks before it achieves some level of contentment. That's close to our whole crossing. The new sails make our others look dingy, but time will change that too.

So we were pumping, the water was shooshing, the sun

shining, when Ed called down from Crow's nest. Wait, Ed? Don't be silly. Crow can't be up there all the time. Ed calls, "Smoke on the port fore quarter!" and we all stopped and looked. Honestly, it wasn't because I hate pumping. This was important. Really.

I couldn't see it, but that's why we built the crow's nest. The great thing about being a sailboat in times of war is that we can see those steamships long before they see us, well at least that's what I thought. It's that big column of black smoke sticking up into the sky that gives them away. This was probably some steamship hauling cargo like us. But it could be a warship too. Some of them have guns that can lob a shell miles and miles away. So we avoid them all if we can. It's best if they never see us. But we won't change course unless we're sure it's closing on us. The open ocean gives us a lot more leeway than the coast. Sadly, not all warships are steam. Many are still sail. Then it's a matter of who spots whom first. At night we lock the deadlights down over the portholes. We don't even have a lantern over the binnacle. No light must show. We use a shutter lamp to read the compass instead. That's the way it is during war.

Oh, but we were pumping! That is easy to forget. Tinker and I had only just started so there was a long way to go until the bilge was merely damp, and a long time before we found out anything about that smoke.

We were following the trade winds and the North Atlantic Current. Both will take you straight to Europe. Everyone does this and Red can skip over the water easily at six knots average, or about 165 miles a day, on a good day. Our best was 207! But really that's just bragging. Balance that with our worst on this trip so far of 63. When the weather is really bad, we can even go backwards! This all may seem like a lot, but the Atlantic is very wide and if things go well, it may take us three or even four weeks before we sight first land.

This unpredictability makes it difficult for us to convoy. The Navy doesn't like to shepherd sailboats precisely because they get blown all over. They concentrate their limited resources mainly on the steamships. Little rabbits like Red must rely instead on stealth and speed. Thinking back, I suspect that it was probably our new bright white sails that gave us away.

But we were pumping, I really don't want to think about that, when Ed calls down from above, "More smoke on the port fore quarter." That's when Pa decided he wanted to look himself. More smoke means there are multiple ships, either a convoy or a fleet. So up he went. I'm not allowed up there, of course, for reasons already stated. And that was too bad because I got all the spray when the first shell hit the water. Apparently it was a fleet, although we never found out whose.

It was a long lob and pretty inaccurate, coming down about 200 feet ahead of the bow. We were running with the wind, moving pretty fast, and sailed right through it, which brought the spray down like a small monsoon on deck and incidentally on me. Mackie was at the wheel, but Pa is the Captain and he yelled down from the mast, "Jibe!"

After a sting of curses, Mackie yells, "All hands on deck! Man the booms, prepare to jibe!" We were going to cross the wind, which is difficult and sometimes dangerous. A schooner never sails absolutely directly with the wind. Our sails don't work well that way. We're always at an angle to it. When we jibe, we turn across the direction of the wind, so it's blowing on us from the other side. The booms have to be swung across the deck in order for our sails to work again. Jibing is not a common maneuver--it's for racing boats--but I think racing was what Pa had in mind. So, it was to the sails for us all. We had to swing the booms and I was on the sheet line, the rope that controls the swing. Even with the blocking, the pull in moderate airs like this can be tremendous and if the booms swing too fast, they can break loose from the mast. It takes at least three of us to swing a boom on a light day and that day was not light.

With Ian out, Ma, Wally, and Crow still below, and Pa and Ed up in the shrouds, there was only Tinker and me on the foresail, which I had never done, at least not by myself, not in a jibe. But it's an emergency. I ran to the preventer and released it, then ran back and braced my feet against the bulwark, the mainsheet looped around my back. She was slack, but when that boom swings, that would change quick.

"Prepare to jibe!" Mackie called.

"I'm ready, Mackie," I think.

"Jibe Ho!" he calls and rolls the wheel.

The stern comes about and the sails began to flutter. I let go the lock hitches and let out slack as Tinker hauls the boom across the deck. The trick is to not let her swing freely but to let her have just enough momentum to make it across. It's vital that we try to slow her before the wind catches the sail again. The yard was across, into the wind, and the flutter snapped out of the sail as the wind caught. The rope pulled me toward the bulwark as I tried to slow the swing. Even with the loops on the cleat, the blocking, and Tinker pulling on the boom itself, we were losing. I was being pulled closer and closer to the cleat. I couldn't let go or I'd lose it and I couldn't pull hard enough to get the slack I needed to throw a locking hitch over it. I was stuck, literally, my boots planted, standing up on the side of the bulwark, pulling as hard as I could-- and it hurt. The rope was digging into my back. Another shell came in and splashed where we would have been if we had decided to come about and tack. It sent more water raining down, which was good because now no one could see my tears.

Suddenly, Pa was on the yard itself, next to Tinker. He must have jumped down from the mast. Together we eased it over.

"Let go!" he yelled.

Tinker had it tied off and I threw some locking hitches over the cleat. I let go and rolled to get out of the way. Running the preventer line across deck, I secured it on the other side. I was angry now. They were only firing one gun at us! 154 feet bow to stern, 345 tons of cargo and we hardly rated the powder. We were probably only a training exercise! Then I heard Ed. "Smoke aft starboard quarter!" he called as he was climbing down.

"Great!" I yelled at the wind, as I ran to the next sail. "There are more!"

We'd just gotten the yards shifted, and we were making good headway again, with the jibs still to do when Mackie yelled, "Prepare to jibe!" Crow, Wally, and Ma were on deck now too. Ma's skirts and hair were flying in the wind. Ed was down from the nest, and every position was manned. This time the turn went smoother. The wind was great, we had to be doing at least ten knots, the bow slicing and heaving over blue water. Pa's plan was to keep jibing, zigzagging at random, always running with the wind, in the hopes that we could maneuver faster than they could aim and maybe clear the range of their guns. It was a forlorn hope, because they can shoot a long way. Another shell whistled in sending up spray abaft our stern. So far though, it was working. We were in the middle of the next jibe when another shell flew in, landing so close I could feel the ship shift to the side. If we'd been square rigged, it might have clipped the yards. It couldn't have done the hull any good.

And that could have been it. Really. We were as good as dead. But then they stopped. I could see the smoke looming on the horizon in both directions. We were still running dead with the wind, when we heard a new sound, a low irregular thumping like someone gently blowing in your ear. Which was followed by the sound of whining shells, arcing high over our heads. Nothing little like they had been using on us, either. They were the big guns. These monsters on either side of us had spotted each other and were showing their claws. Naturally we didn't to wait around to see who won. This little rabbit was only interested in trade.

When we were gone and they were merely a memory on the horizon, we took stock. Red was wet but unscathed, the hull sound. Woo hoo! Mackie and Pa patted me on the back, which hurt a bit, and then gave me a smile, which felt nice. Sadly though, the pumping still needed to be done, which put that smile away pretty quickly. Red's purpose is business after all, and we got back to it.

That evening, I discovered I had a welt across my back and side from the rope. It stayed kind of tender for several days. But you get a lot of cuts and bruises working on a boat.

Chapter 5

France!

So we were free, running with the wind toward France, and the ocean rolling by. So what did we do when we weren't on deck getting knocked about by Confederate warships? That's easy. We slept. No really, we ate, we goofed around. Ma and I made apple pie. You have to use up the fruit and vegetables quick and there's nothing better for mealy apples than pie. We brought books, but sadly no Dracula. We didn't keep them when we were done either. Like most ships, we give them to the church store. It's the unofficial harbor library. There's no room to accumulate things on a ship. When people asked, I played my violin, and also for myself as well, just to keep the calluses on my fingers of course. We all had our little nooks and crannies where we kept our toys.

Ed had been carving the framing in the galley for years. Rabbits, vines, flowers, mermaids, whales, birds, all from his own head. He's really very good. He kept his tools in the side pocket of the locker under the bench that abuts the galley. Mackie had been weaving jute, so we had new placemats. Poor Pa only had work. Merchants have a lot of bookkeeping to do. But by and far, we simply didn't have time. There's stitching, splicing, fixing, salvaging, painting, tarring, and washing, all waiting for that free moment foolish enough to stick its head up. This is the world in which I was born and raised. I didn't live in a steam palace, I lived on a schooner!

For instance, war or not, that night was bath night. Yes, we bathed. Ma would not have it any other way. And because we had women on board, we didn't do it on deck. No, we removed the table from the mess, which is next to the galley, which makes it handy to heat the water. It's saltwater of course and you never quite feel clean. Salt on your skin feels slimy when you sweat, but at least you don't smell. Well, not for a bit at least. And, of course, really, that's not entirely true. We do get to bathe in fresh water when it rains and the cistern was full. The ship had plumbing, but it was all cold, so we heated the water on the stove.

When we were docked at any reasonably modern port, we'd have water hookup too. Red's plumbing was kind of primitive. We had running water in the galley and in the fore and stern heads. At sea we switched the galley to cistern water. Cistern water isn't really drinkable, but it works for cooking and cleaning dishes. We also had a salt water tank that provided water to the heads, but we had to pump to keep that full. The drains went right out the sides of the boat. There were backflow valves naturally, but sometimes they'd stick and we wouldn't notice. When we hit a bad piece of ocean, the water would jet up out of the sinks and toilets every time we'd go over a wave.

So what's left to tell of the crossing? Two days out, we got tired of Ian's bandages, so they came off and stayed off. After that, a lot of the redness went away and he seemed to heal better. That doctor was crazy. I'm so sorry Ma gave him good money.

Ten days out, after a squall, we discovered fresh water leakage around the stern. It might seem odd to you, but fresh water is the bane of ships, not salt water. Salt water is a ship's best friend. It preserves the wood and keeps everything tight. When a ship dries out, the wood shrinks and we leak. Fresh water promotes rot and weeds, especially around the ends of wood. If it isn't dealt with quickly then things may come apart--which is not something you want to happen 1500 miles from the nearest shore. The fix for it is caulk and tar. Tar is horrible. We heat it in buckets used only for that purpose because it never comes off, and that's off anything, gloves, clothes, hair, skin. Poor Tinker thoughtlessly scratched his cheek with his tarry glove and ended up with a black spot on his face. We paint tar on the lines to keep the moisture from rotting them too.

Eighteen days out we sighted the Isles of Sicily. The night of the 19th day, we passed the lighthouse on Lizard Point, our first sighting of the English coast. It was Cornwall, not that I got to see it. You have to swing wide of the coast to avoid Eddystone Shoals so there's no looking at England until we were past Start Point. At Start Point you're officially in the English Channel. France, here we come!

Pa speaks French. I do not. At least, not very much. It's not that I hadn't tried. We had French in school, but the effort had been wasted on me and I was scared to death someone was going to try to speak to me. If I had been able to speak none at all, then I might have been able to shake my head and look clueless, but I was in mortal fear that I might actually be forced to try to say something and I knew I was going to sound like a complete idiot.

On the way in to Le Havre we passed a lot of Confederate shipping as well as ours, including warships. One of them might even be the one that shot at us. We saw ships from both side's that had battle damage, with turrets knocked askew and sections of their superstructure reduced to twisted wreckage. We even saw one that was listing, trailing smoke. She couldn't have been making more than three or four knots.

Inside the English Channel, though, all were safe. All the great countries of Europe laid down the law two years ago in the Brussels Treaty of 1890. There will be no combat within 300 miles of the coast of Europe. Everyone was tired of our constant brawling.

It was a dreary afternoon when we were finally towed in to dock. Being towed in isn't a bad idea in La Havre, even if you don't get a break on your insurance. When we were there, there was only one entrance to the harbor and the channel was jammed with small boats. It would have been very easy to hit something. When we docked, Pa pulled on his slicker and left for the harbor office to get our paperwork straight and we were left to sit, listening to the rain come down on the deckhouse roof. End of our first big day in France. Sigh.

So Ma and I baked a cake. We make them without milk. It was great! Don't you wish you had some!

Sunshine! Everything was steaming and the air was warm and humid. Le Havre's docks have railroad tracks built right into them, which is a great idea. No waiting for wagons. It's something we could really use in Boston. The harbor water wasn't as rancid as Boston's as well. I think it's because Boston is a bit of a cul-de-sac and Le Havre gets a more constant flow.

Pa and I were dressed for town. We were going looking for buyers and bargains. Did I say "we"? See my big smile? The crew drew lots and Ed was stuck on ship with Ma. Ma didn't want to look for buyers so she volunteered. Pa would take her out that night, which suited her fine.

We were standing on the dock when I noticed the Confederate flag that was flying from the ship docked just afore us. It was a brigantine, slightly larger than us. She was well kept too, so Pa decided that we ought to go visiting. We might have a thing or two to trade. We could see two crew on deck. Neither of them had horns or a tail as I had been told more than once that all Rebels do.

Pa walked right up the plank and announced himself. "Captain Carmichael, of the Red Jacket, here to see the Captain of the *Saint John's*."

They looked up and smiled! "How do you do!" one said. "You from the schooner?" he nodded toward Red.

"Yes, we are," Pa said.

"Well, I'll go get the Captain. He's about to step out himself."

The other deck hand came over and held out his hand to shake,

"She's a sweet lookin' ship. Saw her coming in last night."

"Family owned."

He nodded thoughtfully for a second. "Wouldn't mind that myself. Maybe someday." Then he looked at me, "This your daughter?"

"Yes."

"Well, there's somethin' to look forward to."

"Thank you," I said.

"Make yourself at home. Captain'll be up in a minute. Probably lookin' for his best hat."

So, we looked around the deck for a bit. She was certainly trim. When the Captain finally did come up out the deck cabin, the crewman made a clicking sound with his cheek. When I glanced at him, he pointed at his head and rolled his eyes over at the Captain. Sure enough, the Captain's hat looked new.

"Captain Carmichael, Captain Oakley Cavanaugh."

"Call me Thomas," and they shook hands. "This is Calista."

"Cali," I corrected.

"Charming." He bowed!

And then off they went. I ceased to exist. We retreated to the Captain's cabin where they sat at his desk going over manifests and I was left to wander. He had some interesting knickknacks and books. My eyes wandered down the titles. I stopped. There it was.

"Excuse me," I said.

They looked up.

"May I?" pointing at the book.

"Yes, of course," Captain Cavanaugh said.

I pulled it down and sat on his bed, which was very properly made by the way.

"Jonathan Harker's Journal," it started. I had found a copy of Dracula!

I was in the middle of chapter four when they finished. The Count had forced Harker to write three letters, postdated to the following weeks! He had that long to live!

"May I borrow this?" I asked weakly.

"No, I'm sorry. I haven't read it myself yet and half the crew is waiting in line for it next. If there was another copy to be had,

41

I'd buy it for you."

I gave a little whimper and put it back on the shelf.

At the gangway they shook hands and promised to talk again soon and we were off.

"Did we find anything to trade?" I asked.

"Yes, we did! We picked up close to a ton of mauveine purple pigment packed in one-pound boxes, which might sell in Spain, and two hundred gallons of pyrethrum extract insecticide, which ought to sell well down south in Africa," he replied with a big smile. Pa loves cargo.

In back of the docks were the warehouses, which were, as always, fun to look through, although I could barely understand a single word anyone said. They all spoke so fast and what I understood sounded strange. The variety of goods waiting to be bought and sold was, as it often is in an industrial city like Le Havre, remarkable. At the end of the day we heard about an estate sale, which Pa wanted to go look at. Luxuries can sell well to colonials we were told. So we decided to see it tomorrow.

Then it was back to the ship for poor Cali. So far I had seen a Rebel ship and the usual warehouses. So much for French adventure! Ma on the other hand would get to go out on the town. Oh well.

But the real problem was, and I was absolutely bleeding to know--what will happen to Jonathan Harker?!?

The next day, the sky looked a little browner as the coal smoke began to accumulate after the rain. The sun rose orange, which looked pretty behind the boats in the harbor in the gray blue morning light.

This was the day that I, Cali of the Sea, got to go see a count's palace! To set the stage, I wore my boater. And for a count, especially for a dead one, I pined my hair back and show my ears, which were sadly unadorned. And my best dress, which I had never worn in public, was waiting. It was dark sea-green gingham. And because I was still a girl I got a full eight inches clearance above the ground. I could run!

I had never worn any of this gear, so the shoes were a little uncomfortable, the dress still crisp. When I walked out on deck, everyone drew a breath and whistled, which was kind of nice in a strange way. For lack of a better response, I performed a wobbly curtsey.

Pa was wearing his captain's suit, which he almost never drags out. He had somewhere, over the course of yesterday, acquired some of the local money, and we used it to ride across town on a cable trolley, which was really much nicer and cleaner than the steam trolleys we had in Boston.

French houses are older than Boston houses. In many, you can see the framing between the plaster. The streets are narrower and sometimes the houses hang out over them. It makes for more chaotic traffic. Blocking the sky, especially in the side streets, were crisscrossed laundry lines. People taking advantage of the clean air after the rain. The feeling of closeness was aggravated by airships, which were constantly passing over our heads, and the steam carriages and trucks that were always trying to squeeze by.

The air was muggy to begin with, but it was aggravated by the houses as they vented their excess steam in white jets up into the sky, momentarily popping up here and there on the tops of the buildings. Le Havre has plenty of water and coal, so inside steam power was common in houses and especially businesses, as was gas light on the streets. I saw smokestacks everywhere, and columns of black coal smoke rose above us into the sky, shifting with the breeze like seaweed in the tide.

But we were going by things too quickly and it was hard to figure out the signs on the stores, which were of course in French, in lettering that was not always clear, so I was forced to look in the windows to see what they did within. The glimpses I got were tantalizing, but never satisfying. Pastry, dresses, hats, stationery, on and on.

I could catch only little bits of the conversations around me, they were talking too fast and rarely with clearly formed words. Heaven help me if I had to ask directions. All my French study was wasted. I hate Mrs. Claveloux! But Pa seemed to know the way, although how he navigated through streets like these was beyond me. They were even crazier than Boston. The Atlantic Ocean is so much simpler. We got pulled along in the cable car until the end of the line, and then we got off and got on another.

At last Pa said, "Ah!" and grabbed my hand as we stepped off the trolley – into the path of a milk wagon. I didn't understand the driver's words or the gestures, but I understood the intent. I am, however, a woman of poise and grace, who appropriately ignored them. Wherever we were, there were no palaces to be seen. There was, however, a stone building with large windows. You could tell it was important because it had stone steps, which always makes the difference.

We made the sidewalk, shoes unsoiled. And now, we have come to the *Musée d'Art Moderne*!

"I'm not sure if you'll like this," cautioned Pa. Inside, really, it seemed at first to be more a museum of the abnormal and unfinished. Inside were paintings, some of them huge, some very small, none of them seemed really complete. They were perhaps closer to being sketches in paint than paintings.

So the art was kind of strange. Instead, I will tell you about the people. I have yet to describe them to you, have I? The French men were normal enough. Very close cut suits, mostly. The usual variety of hats. It's the women that really bear description. They were even crazier in France than they were in Boston. Somehow they managed to get their corsets tighter. I swear that some of the women looked like they might break in two! The bustles and crinolines bigger, often with giant drapery and bows on the rump or hips and huge puffed-out shoulders, and sleeves that go down looping over their thumbs and fingers covering the backs of their hands! It was like everything wrong made worse. The biggest pieces of insanity were the hats, and I mean the biggest. They were like huge platters, two going on three feet across, always wider than their shoulders, piled high with – things! Flowers, bows, ribbons, feathers, birds, and even ships! Their heels, when you saw them, were higher and their shoes tighter and colored. Their hair was done in complicated rolls and swirls. They must spend half their day fixing it up, or perhaps they never wash it. From the amount of paint and crust on their faces and hair, I suspected the latter. We'd have to use the boom and winch to get them on deck. Then again, maybe they floated all by themselves, no ship needed. They certainly had room enough for cargo under those crinolines.

That brought a snort and chuckle, which I tried to hide. Pa frowned at me, so I cocked an eyebrow at a group of women. He, bless him, rolled his eyes up and gave a little nod.

We went by one picture after another. I mean they weren't all bad. The color was certainly nice. That was until we come to a picture of the harbor. It was the view from our ship. With the help of the memory of the scene, it seemed to suddenly snap into focus. There was a sudden unexpected depth. I saw the yellow sky, the orange coal-stained sun, the blue twilight, the boats rocking on the water. It was all there. Not a moment in time like a photograph or a normal painting, but the time itself with all the movement! I went back one painting and I could see it there too. Back another and it was there as well! Sometimes I had to step back from the picture, sometimes forward, but it was almost always there. That moment of movement that set the place, like each moment of life was a dash of paint and life one big painting. The colors were so bright and yet they were perfect and in balance! I had to sit for a moment to catch my breath.

Outside, Pa suggested lunch, and why not? The French eat outside a lot, at least they do when it's not raining, and we could see at least three places to eat within sight. Pa picked the second. We sat at a round iron legged table. A waiter with a towel over his arm came up and tossed a white table cloth over the wood tabletop.

"En quoi puis-je vous servir?" He was asking us how he can serve us.

"Puix-je voir le menu?" I asked, which made Pa smile. That though, was all I was prepared to say. It took me a full minute to think that up. I had never heard of anything on the menu but the waiter mentioned eggs, which sounded nice.

We had omelets! Omelets are like scrambled eggs folded over with mushrooms and maybe spinach inside. I'm not sure. Over the top they had a white gravy or maybe a sauce sprinkled with something green. They gave us breads with a strange taste. They were shaped like big fingers and seemed to go down well with the white wine. In the end they brought us a salad with things in it. It was the strangest meal I'd ever had, and it occurred to me that I might be drunk. It was difficult to know, because I had never been drunk before.

"Pa, I think I'm drunk."

"Don't worry, half the city is too," he said, which sent me laughing. I must have been drunk.

They brought us coffee and chocolate! I had two coffees and I felt much more awake. I mean, I still had that odd drunk feeling, but it's not so bad when you aren't falling asleep. However, it was time to move on. Forward! We boarded the trolley.

Pa knew the way, which was good, because I was completely lost. I mean I knew where the harbor was. I could see the water when the streets were pointing the right way. I wasn't completely helpless. The problem was that the streets never seemed to go straight. But the houses were getting bigger, and they had gates and driveways. We had to be heading in the right direction.

We went inland and uphill and then the trolley ended. I suppose rich people don't need trolleys. I wondered if these people had yachts. It would be nice to tour the harbor, I thought, while we walked in the cool ocean breeze.

We arrived at the Count's house. It was the biggest of course, although I wouldn't be shocked if we had found bigger ones further up the hill. His house, though empty, hadn't been shut down yet. I could still see smoke coming from the smokestack in back. The gates of his big iron fence were open and guarded only by common workmen. They nodded to us as we passed through.

His carriages and vehicles had been arranged in the driveway. Everything was clean and polished. Even the insides of the coal boxes had been scrubbed and their doors left open so you could see. I suppose they were for sale. There must have been horses as well, perhaps in back, in the direction of the driveways.

His house was bigger than the museum, painted yellow with carved white marble and trim, and gas lights lining the driveways and garden. The garden was all geometric hedges, meticulously cut with square edges. It must have taken an army of workmen just to support one count. On the far side I could see scaffolding. They were using small pressure hoses to clean the house exterior, the workmen's boiler wagon chuffing smoke.

Naturally, it had stone steps with columns. How do the ladies, in all that gear, make it up the steps? Maybe they have servants to carry them? That wasn't my problem though. I danced right up. The front doors were propped open and we went straight in. Inside was a short hallway, perhaps it's a foyer? Anyway, it had rooms for keeping coats. I suppose the Count liked to throw parties. In this house, they could all be big ones and he might not even know they were there. That day, the coat rooms were empty. Then the foyer opened up to the main entrance hall, and that's where we stopped. Your dear Cali was gaping like a cod fish again!

The hall was round, more than a hundred feet across, with a high domed ceiling painted with angels. Above that was a second dome of colored glass, from the center of which was suspended a chandelier that must represent the sun--for around it, on arms radiating from the center, were the planets. I can only suppose that they must move. I could see the Earth and there, on another smaller arm, revolving around it was the Moon.

Climbing around the sides of the hall were two carpeted white marble staircases like welcoming arms that lead upstairs. Between was a golden clockwork gate that lead further into the house. Inside it was the breath of steam, but nowhere did it escape. It was playing a tune, like a hundred little bells, and little figures were dancing all over it, soldiers marching, maids milking cows, farmers riding hay wagons, trains riding over tracks, airships flying overhead, ships steaming over blue stone inlaid seas, and over it all passed the sun. The little church tower bell struck twice, two o'clock. It was a clock, I thought.

To our right and left were carpeted vestibules with high windows, ornate seats, small tables, and indentations in the carpets where other furniture had already been removed. The floor of the hall was a mosaic of colored stone showing the 32 points of the compass, the house exactly aligned with north. Considering that it was built on a hillside, the land itself must have been forced to conform to its symmetry.

"*En quoi puis-je vous aider?*" said a suited man sitting to our right at a dingy little folding table. He was asking if we needed help.

"*Parlez-vous anglais?*" I said without thinking, which got a little chuckle out of Pa for some reason. "*Mon français n'est pas très bon.*" Pa was letting me do the talking!

"Of course," he replied. "I am Monsieur Lefebvre, *avoué auxiliaire.*"

He was an assistant solicitor.

"Captain Carmichael and this is my daughter Calista," Pa said, giving a slight bow.

"A pleasure," he replied with his own smile. "I assume you are here to bid?"

47

"We are," Pa said.

"Then you will need this," and he handed Pa a flat piece of wood with several sheets of paper and a pencil. "Just write down the object number, description, and bid." Then he looked at me, "It will be best if you could write it down in French."

"*Nous allons écrire*," I said.

He thought I spoke French!

"*Très bon*," Pa said, as we walked around.

Believe me, that was just luck. He used words that I knew.

It took a while for us to find anything we might carry. He had a lot of things that were of no use to us like paintings, delicate furniture, steam appliances, and clockworks. Profit for us is a function of volume and weight vs. expected sales value and time to sell. A chair takes up a lot of volume and it can be fragile, which adds to the difficulty of shipping. Its value was unpredictable unless it has known artistic merit or a known buyer. Unlike a furniture store, we can't sit on an item.

The kitchen had all sorts of steam appliances that were connected to rows of valves in the wall. I turned one of the valves and a hot wet jet of steam come out with a loud hiss. I let out an "Eeeek!" and turned it off. No one seemed to notice though, or maybe they didn't care. He had a real observatory built into his house! The telescope was huge and the roof could open up and move. And there was a big blue concrete pond in back, just for swimming. The bathrooms, I would live in one. I used one too!

We bid on practical items like cookware, silverware, and dishes, which were practically new. The groundskeeper's tools were not for sale, which was not surprising. And yes, there was a stable, but the tacking went with the horses. Then we found the library, I immediately went to the S's, Stoker. And there it was, an English edition! The French edition couldn't be out yet. I pulled it down. The spine cracked when I opened it. The Count hadn't had time to read it.

The world was gone.

Pa came and told me that we should move on. I let out a small wail. There's a legend that when a ship is lost, bells are heard out at sea! How can I stop?

"Are we bidding on the books, Pa?" I asked.

"Yes we are. They should ship nicely as long as we can keep

them dry."

I hoped we won.

So that was it for the Count. We went back to the docks and changed clothes. Then Pa went out to dinner with Ma again. It looked to be another quiet evening. At least that's what I thought.

Chapter 6

Meeting the Enemy

Tinker came running though the ship, calling, "All hands on deck!" Banging on my door.

I was in my shoes and on deck in less than a minute. What? Do you think we sleep nude? This is a ship! I pulled on my pants under my night dress and jumped down into my boots.

We heard commotion on the dock, but there were too many lights to see properly. Really, sometimes all lights do is make shadows and spoil your night vision. The noise was coming from the Saint John's. It was a fight, a righteous big one, both on board and on the dock. Mackie ran back below decks and I followed. grabbing two crowbars off the stand in the tool locker. Then the rest of the crew was down there doing the same. I passed one of the crowbars up to Ian in his room.

Then Pa stopped me before I could get back on deck. "Cali, to the galley," he said. "Take the crowbar."

Orders.

When I got there, Ma was already there. She had an axe.

So we waited. Nothing. Then more nothing.

The suspense was killing me.

"You know, Ma, we could defend ourselves just as well from the gangway as here."

Ma hesitated, then sighed. Finally she nodded, "Let's go." She's Irish. She would have been up there already if it wasn't for me.

The deck was clear, but there was still commotion from the docks, and still no sign of the crew. Then three dark shapes loped up to the gangway. They bellowed as they charged forward, coming across single file, but Ma held her ground.

"Hold it right there!" She yelled and held up her ax.

Ma can cut a formidable figure, especially when that red hair of hers flies about. The first tried to stop, but the second collided with him and they went down. I stepped forward and brought my crowbar down on the second one's head. He dropped like an empty dress, and then the third scrambled backward, stood, and ran. The first was trying to get out from under his friend, so I hit him on the shin and he howled.

"You sit still, lad," Ma said. She seemed amused.

They reeked of liquor.

Two more figures loomed in the dark, but I could tell Ed and Crow anywhere, "Hi Crow, hi Ed," I said.

"You should have been an Indian," Crow said. "We thought we saw some heading this way," he said, looking down at our friends.

Then we heard police whistles in the distance.

"Go get the rest of the crew back," Ma said. "Hurry!"

"Yes, ma'am," they replied in unison, and ran back into the dark.

After a few minutes, the crew came limping and stumbling back. Someone was being carried. It was Tinker. Ed and Crow had him by the shoulders. Ma grabbed the man with the hurt shin by the collar and dragged him on deck. He no longer seemed to be interested in fighting. Pa brought over a lamp. He was a kid like me! He couldn't have been more than a year older. The other was 30 or 40, bleeding all over our beautiful white deck. They were both in Union sailor uniforms.

"You know, lad," Pa said. "This is a Union ship and you just attacked two women."

The kid let out a squeal and cringed back. Pa shook his head in disgust.

When the gendarmes arrived, they found us on our own ship, causing no trouble other than defending our own--with two prisoners to boot. They carried them away and we were left to bind our wounds. I pulled out my clothes from my cabin and we laid Tinker on my bed. With so many of our own always being hurt, I swear we might as well switched to being a hospital ship.

Then we went over to visit the Saint John's. They were a mess. You can't see me because it was dark, but I was shaking my head as I inventoried the wreckage. Every one of them was wounded. They had some bad ones too, and Ma did a lot of stitching. One would certainly not make it. She was pulling out pieces of skull.

The next morning we could see all the blood on the dock. The Saint John's crew had managed a watch, but it was more a matter of lying on deck as opposed to down below. They could barely walk. Ma and I made big pots of stew and coffee and lugged them over. Those that could move were just sitting down with their bowls when the police arrived on deck. None of their crew that was conscious could speak French.

"*Veuillez attendre*," I called back, asking him to wait. Ma ran to get Pa.

Captain Cavanaugh came out of his cabin using a plank of wood for a crutch. "Who is it, Jenkins?"

"It's the police," he said.

"*Gendarmes*," I said to the Captain. Then I called, "*Veuillez descendre*," to ask them down because the Captain obviously wasn't going up.

"Girl," the Captain said. "You're damn handy."

The Captain sat down and I brought him a bowl of stew.

"Damn handy."

"*Je vous en prie, nous sommes tous blessés*," I said to the gendarme in charge, telling him everyone was hurt and cannot come.

"*Bonjour*," the gendarme said, as he came down the

52

companionway.

"*Bonjour. Ceci est Capitaine Cavanaugh.*" I nodded to the Captain, introducing him.

"*Je suis sergent Durant.*"

"He's Sergeant Durant," I said. Then my Pa limped down the steps.

"*Bonjour,*" Pa said. And we had to start all over with the introductions.

They all chatted. I served coffee and stew. Real steam ambulances with sirens come to take everyone to a real hospital, to be paid for by the Union, even Ian! Woo hoo! I was very relieved because Tinker still hadn't woken up that morning. His wounds didn't seem that bad at first, but we couldn't wake him.

So what happened? Why were we attacked? Apparently a bar full of Union sailors got a bit too drunk and decided to start swabbing the deck with every Confederate sailor they could find, which they did. Gathering force as they moved from bar to bar, they then had the bright idea that they could save time by scuttling the Confederate ships in port instead of hunting them at sea, port neutrality be damned. But the Confederate warships were too scary for them so they decided to go after unarmed merchantmen instead. After all, they were going to have to sink them eventually anyway, right?

What idiots!

More ships than just our two were attacked that night. One was actually sunk with many lives lost. So we got two weeks extra port time, costs, and a share of the fine, which must have been huge, all paid for by the Union. Did I hear you say, Yippie! Two extra weeks in France! Ah, but not so fast. They didn't have enough able bodied men left on the Saint John's to stand watch, so we stood watch for them until they could get back on their feet. I didn't manage to get off the dock for a week. Captain Cavanaugh, the good man that he was, gave us the cargo we were going to trade with him for our help. I guess he was feeling kind of flush with his share of the fine money.

Most came back from the hospital the next morning, Ian came back the evening after that, with his stitches out. He was able to walk, which was a big help for us all. Tinker didn't come back for three days. He had memory loss, double vision, and headaches.

The hospital sent us pills for the headaches, but there was little else that the doctors could do. He would heal at his own pace.

Things were rolling out of and into our holds. Farm tools, machetes, and we got those books! I was opening crates one at a time, going through them book by book, and then closing them back up. There were still eight crates that I couldn't get to without rearranging the hold. It had to be in one of those. In the meantime, we now had plenty to read.

And sadly--it was time to go. Farewell, France. I've tried pastries, veal, red wine, and crepes. We went to a huge ornate church, a cathedral that was crawling with ghosts, and went for a carriage ride in the country where I saw a windmill. They roll their hay up in large rolls that Pa calls *pooks*, so they can carry it in wagons. Everywhere I looked I couldn't help but think of the paintings.

But we must make money, so we were off to Lisbon, Portugal, where the wine and grain are cheap, two things Africa lacks.

The shipping lanes down the coast were practically as busy as La Havre harbor. Pa said that the U.S. coast used to be like that before the war. The sky was full of airships as well. They were following the shoreline. We rounded the Cotentin Peninsula where the boat traffic had to clump together. Everyone has to keep station at the point, which creates a bottleneck and there's a real risk of collision. All shipping between Europe and the Mediterranean passes there. We sailed past Guernsey, Ushant and the Brittany coast, past Brest, then out of the English Channel and out to sea. No more land until Portugal.

When we reached it, the Portuguese coast was gray and rocky, with few trees. After France, it looked barren. We passed a lot of lighthouses, but that's because there's a lot to look out for. The charts are full of rocks and reefs. But it was just a coast and the weather was fine, and we were in a hurry to make up time. We swung past Peniche, which was a peninsula masquerading as a fortress, or maybe it's the other way around. It was both. It's nothing but gray rock vertical cliffs and crashing surf and then in the middle, a fortified city connected to the mainland by a sandy isthmus.

I am sorry. I'm really rushing through this part, but there really wasn't anything going on. That was until, finally, Lisbon!

Lisbon does not face the sea. It's inland, on the edge of a huge lagoon. The first thing you see when you approach is a fort. It's massive, gray, ugly, and it definitely means business. "Be clear about your intentions before entering," it says. And we were. We were there to make money. Lisbon itself is reached through a bay that narrows to a wide river that takes you to a large lagoon, three miles across.

The city is spread around the north shore. The pilot took us in to the tug, which brought us to our berth, which looked like every other berth, except that it was warmer. In fact, the weather was really nice. Warm like Jamaica, but not as humid. And the breeze was really great. I could get used to this.

"I'm sorry, *senhor*, but we cannot accept your money at this time."

"They're perfectly good dollars. I can pay in francs if you want," Pa said.

"This is for your own protection. We are having a problem with our banks. We don't know the exchange rates. We'll give you credit until tomorrow. Put your name, ship, and berth on the list over on the next counter. Please. Next!"

A big man with a black bushy beard pushed forward next to Pa, who reluctantly stepped aside.

"We need provisions, water," the man said.

"Try in town. They may accept your money."

"I don't speak Portuguese!"

"I am sorry."

The port office was in chaos, angry captains all talking at once to each other, to worried-looking clerks behind counters, and to the empty air in frustration.

Something had gone very wrong in Lisbon. Pa tapped me on the shoulder, "Come on, he's right. We should try in town."

We stopped by the ship to tell them where we were going and then started walking up the hill. Lisbon is built on a gentle slope, rising as it goes inland, which means that everything is up hill from the harbor. Most streets are very narrow and the buildings loom over them, just like Le Havre. Lisbon had steam trolleys, but they only took *reals* and we had none. Most stores had hand drawn signs that said, "*Réis não aceito*," over and over again.

"The real is their money," Pa said. "*Réis* is probably plural. Their currency apparently is having problems."

"That sounds bad."

"This will complicate things." But then he smiled. "But then again, we might be able to pick up some bargains."

In front of the bank up ahead were soldiers in blue coats standing guard. Pa stopped.

"That seals it. There's been a run on the banks. We're going to need a strategy, and to start with, I think we're going to need a translator."

"Maybe that man at the port office?" I asked.

"No. If we ask him, then we'll get into a bidding war with the other captains. Perhaps what we need is a tour guide."

A few blocks away, up the hill, we could see the spires of a big church.

"Let's start there," Pa said.

It turned out to be a good choice. It was the Lisbon Cathedral. Up close it almost looked like a castle, but there was no mistaking the stained glass. Several groups of men were lounging around out front, hoping to pick up tourists, and probably any other work they could get.

"Anyone speak English?" Pa called.

Five men jumped up, "Me! Me! No réis!"

"Francs or dollars and food," Pa replied. That got three more to stand up. They began to crowd us. "No, stand back. One at a time, and it doesn't matter which order. I won't pick until I've heard you all."

Telling them we would need a translator for the next week got them even more excited. We sat on a bench and talked to each one. They were all very rough, but Pa finally decided on one at two francs a day plus food. His name was Claudio Marcelo, in his mid-thirties, black hair and light brown skin. He wore shoes with no socks. A lot of them did. Very odd. Pa and Claudio shook on the deal.

"Great. Let's start with the cathedral. Since we're here, can you give us a tour?"

And give us a tour he did. It turns out the cathedral looked like a castle because it was. The Portuguese were afraid of the Moors, people from Africa who invaded 400 years ago. It had relics, bits of saint's bodies and things. It had beautiful stained glass, and even had people's bodies buried in the floor, like it was an indoor graveyard with shadows crawling everywhere!

One thing about cathedrals I liked was that they are made of stone and are cool. I love the Portuguese sun but it's hot, so on the way down the hill we stopped and bought shaved ice, again with our francs.

"Are we going to have enough French money, Pa?" I asked.

"That's a good question. Maybe if we stop offering francs they'll take dollars," Pa said.

"No," Claudio said. "No one knows how much a dollar is worth. Francs, pesetas, we know."

"Why are the banks failing?" I asked.

That riled him. "It is the government's fault!" I thought he was going to spit. "Giving up to the British like some kind of whipped cur!" Then he glanced around with a worried look. "I am sorry for my outburst."

I glanced at Pa and he looked a little puzzled.

Claudio saw my Pa's look as well and frowned. "We have agreed to give our Central African colonies to Britain for no other reason than they asked us to, or at least for no reasons that can be stated in public. We have spent 30 years struggling to build railroads and cities there and then we give them away, just because Britain wants to build a railroad from Cairo to Cape Town. Whatever the government's reason for doing it, it is pointless now since they are out of power. The government has collapsed. They have fallen, and the country has gone crazy."

"Claudio, we are going to need to change our dollars to something we can spend," Pa said.

"I know," Claudio said. "I've been thinking." We walked for a bit, eating our shaved ice, when Claudio says, "Do you mind dealing with disreputable types?"

"I prefer being the one they have to come to rather than one of the one who has to go to them," Pa said, which almost made me spit out my ice.

Claudio burst out laughing, "That was the right spirit!"

"We came here for wine and grain, and it's just sitting there in the warehouses. I'm thinking we could do a barter trade, goods for goods, but we're going to need incidentals, and to pay fees, and barter won't work there. And I would like to take a trolley once in a awhile, rather than walking up this hill every day."

That sent Claudio laughing again. "The government requires them to take réis. We can get those from anybody if you have more francs to trade."

So we stepped into a hat shop and traded a franc for a pile of réis.

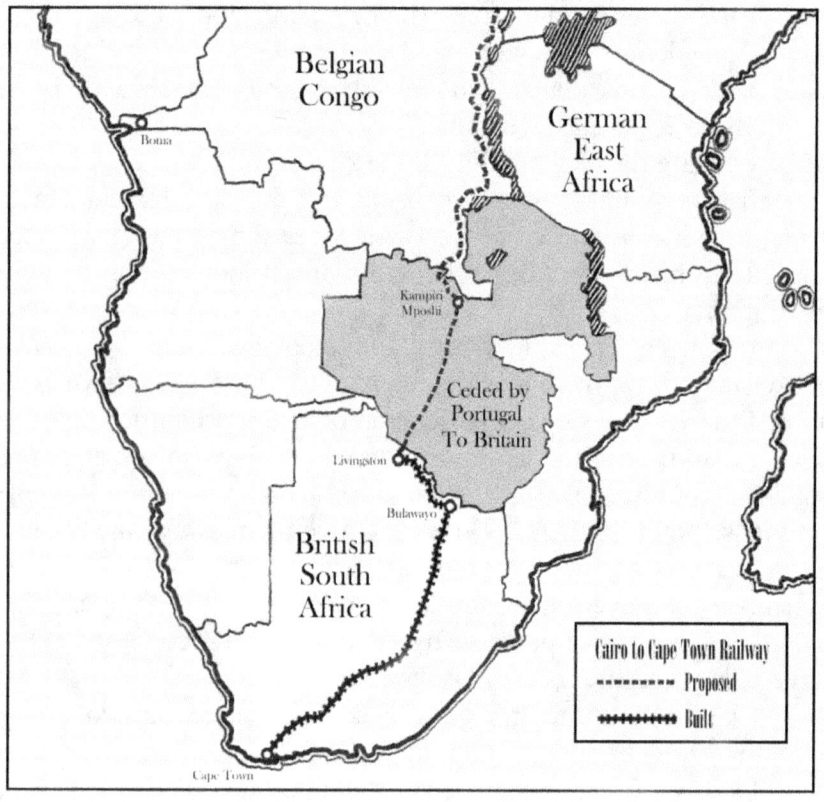

Trading went well and cargo moved in and out of our holds. If Pa went to deal with criminals to change his money, he didn't take me. Really. I wasn't disappointed. Honest!

In moving around cargo, four more book crates were exposed. I feverishly pawed through them while I could, but with no luck.

On the fifth day all hell broke loose. The first thing I heard that morning was the crackle of gunfire up in the city. Claudio was not waiting for us on the docks as usual and things were burning here and there in the distance. Columns of black smoke blew back through the city streets in the morning breeze.

What do you do when you're a schooner docked in a city going up in flames? You sit and watch. We need a tow to get out of the harbor. No, let's be honest, we could row her out, or perhaps winch her out with an anchor. Drop the longboat, pile everybody in, and drag her clear of the docks and out into the channel, but things weren't that bad yet, and we could get a fine, or worse, bump into something. That was assuming, of course, they could figure out what currency to fine us in. That's why we were just sitting and watching.

Eventually, toward noon, Claudio came running up. We were setting up to have lunch on deck. It was my idea, just to be different. I mean we had a beautiful day, and we were stuck sitting around. Let's have some fun, I thought.

He comes bounding across the gangway and yells at Mackie, "Pull the walkway from the dock!" which confused Mackie until, jumping around like a mad man, Claudio began pointing at the gangway.

Mackie gave Crow a look of deep annoyance and then said, "Do it." Then he spoke to me, "Cali, go get your Pa."

So down I went. Pa was doing what he always does when he's on board, paperwork at his desk.

"Pa, Mackie wants you on deck. Something's happening."

Pa took a moment to take off his glasses, put them in their case, and then latch the case and his pens in a drawer. You get in that kind of habit on ship, putting things away so they don't roll away and end up getting stepped on or lost on the floor.

Up on deck we could see people running down the streets, onto the docks. Some of them were hurt, bleeding. From up the street came shooting. They were trying to go anywhere to get away, breaking into the warehouses across from us. Jumping against the doors to get them open, windows are breaking.

Pa yelled, "Cut the ropes!"

Ian grabbed an ax and started chopping one of the dock lines. Great, I thought. You know who was going to get to spend an evening splicing those. Soldiers in blue coats followed the crowds into the square with guns. They were shooting. Blood was flying.

That wasn't right!

"Meara, take Cali below," Pa said. That was his way of getting rid of us both.

I wanted to stay, but it was orders. As I climbed down the steps, I could feel us drifting so I yelled back up, "Hey, Pa. Set an anchor!"

"I am," he called back.

"Set two. The tide shifts in an hour," I said. You don't want to swing around.

I could hear lots of shooting and screaming outside and I hoped everyone was taking cover and being careful. Somewhere far away in the city, there was an explosion. Something thwacked into the deck cabin above me, then two more, knocking splinters of wood down from above. Ian and Ed came running down the steps.

"It's a mess up there!" Ian said.

The rest were coming down the other way and joined us.

"There was a coup d'état," Claudio said. "Then the soldiers started shooting protesters. This is a nice boat. Maybe it should be at sea."

"The wind's off the sea and there's no room to tack inside the breakwater," Mackie said.

"We're going to have to wait until it quiets down," Pa said.

So we waited and waited. The bullets stopped, the screaming stopped too. Ian poked his head up for a second and then ducked down. "It looks quiet," he said.

Mackie poked his head up, ducked down, but then ventured back up. "Cali, stay down here," he said. It was a challenge. He should know better.

They slowly went up, one after another. No shooting. When I topped the stern companionway I saw the boat docked astern of us was burning, her smoke blowing across our deck. I saw bodies floating in the water! We were 40 feet from the dock. Across the dock's wood planking bloody forms lay all askew, like rags after a bad operation. I just stood there at the top of the stairs, stunned.

"Time to row us out," Mackie said.

"Yes," Pa said. He seemed distracted. Then I saw the tears in his eyes. After that we worked with our eyes down. Nobody wanted to look at the docks.

Getting the longboat out is far more difficult than the yawl.

Suspended by davits, the yawl drops down straight into the water. The longboat is clamped down to the roof of the forward deck house. There's no trick to it. We all lift it together with the boom, carry it across the deck, flip it, and drop it in the water. Well, not exactly, there's more sense to it than that, but you get the basic drift.

"Pull the bow up!" yelled Mackie. "She'll swamp!"

"Aaaack," yelled Ed, as his hand got stuck between the transom and the bulwark.

I was supposed to push the stern out, but I was blocked by the main boom halyards. "I need to push it forward!" I yelled.

"No!" Ed yelled back.

And on and on. Trust me. I am Cali of the sea. The longboat gets into the water. It may not seem like it, but we know what we're doing. Really. Just wait until we have to pull it back in!

So the longboat was down, floating nicely beside us, and we were getting ready to climb down, when we hear a call from behind us.

"*Atenção!*"

That's not something you expect!

"*Atenção! Você retirará à doca!*"

There on the dock were at least fifty soldiers with their rifles pointing at us.

We all looked at Claudio.

"They want us to return to the dock." He looked resigned.

Forty feet can be a long way for a ship. Pa looked a bit defeated too and I was worried. Getting back to the dock wouldn't be easy. I hoped for patience.

"Ed, Crow, into the yawl. Get over there," Pa said.

Really, these soldiers were not bright. They could have picked any other boat. I guess we were the only one with crew showing. But, we were in no position to go anywhere. I suppose we looked like we knew what we were doing, which was of course true.

We tossed a light line with a throwing weight across and then pulled over the new dock lines, which yours truly had to help haul up from the rope locker under her cabin. With all the soldiers, we had hands aplenty to haul us back to the dock. That, at least, was something a Portuguese soldier could understand. We, being good merchants, retrieved our severed dock lines. Rope costs money!

And yes, I did eventually have to splice one. Crow did the other.

"*Arranco! Arranco!*" they yelled, and damned if they didn't all pile on when we got there. They started jumping across before we could get the gangway over, the commander yelling, "*Fique a bordo, pressa!*" We were being commandeered!

Being commandeered is actually pretty common in war zones and you just have to put up with it. They have guns and the support of the local, and even the international courts. The best you can do is to try to minimize the damage and trouble, and hope they feel the same way.

Now here's the sad part. I think they thought we could just take off.

When we started piling into the longboat, the commander started yelling, "*Wjat que você faz?*"

"He wants to know what you are doing," Claudio said.

"Tell him we have to row the boat past the breakwater before we can take sail."

"*Nós temos que remar o barco passado o quebra-mar antes que nós podemos tomar vela,*" Claudio said.

"*O que? Faça o barco ir,*" the commander replied.

"He wants you to go."

"We can only go the direction the wind takes us!" Pa said.

"*Eu só posso ir a direcção que o vento toma-nos.*"

The commander looked up at the sails, as if it were the first time he had done so, and let out a cry, "Aaaaagh," and waved his hands in the air.

So, our men were in the longboat, beginning to row, towing Red. Ma and I grabbed poles to try to fend off obstacles.

"Rowing." What an easy word. Why didn't we ask those soldiers to row? I could teach you to row in a useful way. It would take me maybe twenty minutes, and to really get the hang of it, an hour. You'd want give up in ten. Real rowing isn't as easy as you think.

Luckily for us the tide had shifted and was coming in. It may not make sense to you, but in this case that helped. We needed to get out of the dock lagoon. When the tide is going out, it runs into the lagoon, which makes it hard to get out. It's like a pocket and you're getting blown down into the bottom of it. When the tide comes in, it draws us toward the river and the main lagoon, out of the pocket. So like I said, we rowed. And don't think that the tide was as big a help as it might seem. She was drifting, which meant she couldn't steer because there was no water running by her keel or rudder. We were steering with the longboat, pulling her along. It was really a matter of choosing the least amount of calamity, frantically pulling to drag her past one obstacle after another. Eventually she drifted out past the breakwater and the river took her. That's when they got to see us move!

We were all back aboard, the men climbing up over the sides like pirates, the longboat forgotten to follow behind us on its tow rope. Mainsail, jib, foresail, jib. We were making way against the wind, heading for the harbor mouth, figuring they want to go somewhere far away. We moved like a machine. The soldiers were staring in wonder.

"Where are we going?" Pa yelled.

"*Onde nós vamos?*" Claudio translated.

"*Barreiro!*" yelled the commander and he pointed at the far shore.

It was a small fishing village on the far side of the lagoon, three miles away. They had a tiny fishing harbor. We were in open water, so we changed direction and made it easily. We Dropped our sails and drifted in to dock. Mackie rolled the wheel hard a port to bring our stern around, and Ed and Tinker tossed out our bumpers just before we hit the dock. It was a hard docking because we were in a hurry, and the rickety timbers of the dock shifted and creaked as we slid against them, but there were no tugs here. Just us. Ed and Tinker jumped across at the closest moment and Wally and Pa tossed them the ropes. They looped them over the pilings and we rebounded off the pier, then hauled ourselves back up against the dock.

The troops jumped off the boat to the dock or ran down the gangway, to be harangued into rough lines on shore. At the end their commander gave us a little bow, and said, "*Obrigado.*"

"He's thanking you," Claudio said.

"Great," Pa said.

And off they trotted at a steady jog, guns held high.

They were gone. What did we do now? What is there to do in a fishing village like Barreiro?

The answer is, "Nothing". So we left Portugal.

Chapter 7

Always Ready to Trade

What do you do with bullet holes? You patch them! You mix milk glue and sawdust to make patch dough and then cut a wood plug for the hole. You use the wood dough to fill in the gap between the plug and the edge of the hole. When it dries, usually the next day, you plane it, sand it flat, and then apply more dough, if needed, to fill in any dips or irregularities. When it's smooth, you paint it. Isn't life on a ship just the heart of romance!

Knockers was on deck with me and wanting something. She crawled between my face and the wood I was sanding, and then around my arms as I was trying to work.

"Knockers!" I said with fake severity. Knockers really doesn't care about my opinions in the least. I picked her up and scratched her neck and was rewarded for my correct behavior with a purr. She wanted my hair, which was loose for a change, and climbed my neck to bury her face in it. I turned so the sun was on her back. She was sandwiched between the warm me and the warm sun. Kitty heaven.

We were sailing south down the coast toward Cadiz, Spain. If we couldn't deal with the Portuguese, then we'd deal with the Spanish. I wasn't worried. Every delay meant we would be just that much later into Boston. Who knows? I might just miss the entire term!

Honestly. Did you think I was that selfish? It also meant that we'd be that much further away from hurricane season on the way back. You didn't actually think I meant that about school, did you? But you know how much I love playing ball in the garden.

Where was Claudio you ask? He stayed in Barreiro, happy to get his full week's pay and be far away from the city for a few days. Last I saw of him, he still wasn't wearing socks.

Pa was worried by the problems the Portuguese were having. If the British had managed to take Portugal's African territories, then what had they been up to in the Congo, the heart of Africa? They'd certainly be after that too. There's all sorts of mischief they could do and mischief is not good for trade. What if they did something horrible, like burning down all of Leopold's new rubber plantations?

"Knockers," I said. "Holding you is great, but this has to get finished before we get rain." I put her all the way down on the deck in the hope that she'd either get the message or would be too lazy to jump back up onto the deckhouse.

We were making good time down the coast. Compared to the coast around Le Havre, we'd seen few ships since we passed St. Vincent Point. Most shipping heads straight for Gibraltar and the Mediterranean. The sky had been clear of airships, which was why the one following us stood out. She was one of the big zeppelins, aluminum and polished wood gleaming in her undercarriage. It had some sort of design on her upper fin and a black, yellow, and red flag on the bottom.

Knockers was back up on the deck cabin. "No," was clearly not in the cards today. I picked her up again. What a pushover I am.

"Call the Captain on deck," Crow yelled. He was deck watch.

I looked up. The zeppelin was clearly lower and closer. I could hear the motors. It was painted blue-gray and looked almost like a ghost against the sky. A very big ghost. She had six big engines crackling with little pinpricks of fire. Underneath her gondola I could see a wavering, like the heat off a sunny roof, as they dropped below the mountain tops. The shimmer was glowing blue. Then the blue flame stopped, like someone shut it off.

Pa came up on deck with his hailing horn. "Ahoy!" Pa called.

She'd finally come down low enough that I could make out the design of the emblem. It was a gold shield with something that looked like a skull and crossbones. They weren't crossed bones though, I think they were L's.

"*Guten tag!*" someone called out a big window.

Mackie took the horn from Pa and called, "*Wir sprechen nicht Deutsch!*" Mackie is German-American, not German!

"Spreekt u Nederlands?"

Pa asked Mackie, "What was that? Dutch?" Mackie just shook his head.

By this point the zeppelin had come abreast of us and had cut back its engines, which helped conversation.

"*Sprecken Sie Englisch?*" Mackie called back.

Up in the zeppelin we could see some debate and then their horn was passed to another. "*Ja*, I mean yes," the new voice called.

"What can we do for you?" Pa called.

"We are out of spirits. We wish to trade. Do you have rum?"

"Only a little, but we have French and Portuguese wine."

"French will do." Then more debate in the cabin. "We wish your rum and a case of wine."

Pa looked at Ma, the official keeper of the rum, and shrugged his shoulders. Ma nodded back and headed below deck. "Wally! Pull us out a case," he said. "Ed, we'll need something to wrap the rum in."

By the time everyone was on deck, the zeppelin had dropped a throw line. I caught it; tucked in with the weight was a British ten pound note. About five times what the liquor was worth. I passed it to Pa, who whistled. The rope followed the throw line. We tied the case on, added the bottle and a half of rum wrapped in a towel, then I hanked the throw rope and stuffed it in as well so it wouldn't tangle with our rigging. They winched up the slack until it was just clear of the deck, where upon we pushed it clear of the bulwark.

"Thank you," they called.

"Thank you, *danke*," we called back. And off they roared back into the sky. We are always ready to trade. Little did I know then that that was start of something big that would change everything forever.

Well--back to sanding, and, of course, Knockers was in between my feet again.

Cadiz is on the end of a long narrow peninsula, like a knob on the end of a cane. It's an ancient fortress city, one of the oldest in Europe. No one is sure who built it, but practically everyone has claimed it at one time or another. As such, it's a hodgepodge of architectures, overlooked by over 140 towers. Up until 100 years ago, simply everyone had to have one. Merchant princes used to have their offices in the tower tops so they could keep watch for their ships. They may still to this day.

Then, it was the home of the Spanish Atlantic Fleet whose ships we passed as we were piloted into harbor. They were a mixed assortment of sail, steam-sail, and iron monsters. No airships floated above the city. There's no room for them on the peninsula. The Cadiz aerodrome was across the bay in Santa Maria. Air visitors had to take the train in, which ran down the isthmus to the city. We could see the trains leaving their trails of smoke, back and forth across the low spit of land as we entered the harbor.

We were there to finish what we hoped to accomplish in Lisbon, to pick up wine and grain. When we docked, it felt like we had never left. Docks look like docks. These were a little warmer than Lisbon because the harbor faced inland instead of the sea breeze and open ocean.

We arrived on market day and Ma, Crow, Tinker, Ian, and I

were going out to buy supplies, especially fresh food. We eat fresh when we're in port, because most things don't last long after we're out to sea. We didn't get to resupply in Lisbon like we normally do, so we'd been eating a lot of stew. Fresh fruit would be especially wonderful.

Ahead of us was a gold-domed building with two towers, shimmering in the sun, which I was told by Wally was a cathedral. If it was, then I'd have to see it, but today we were aiming for the *Plaza de Espania*, the local market square.

The men's job was to haul stuff back for Ma and Crow to translate even though he complains they don't really speak Spanish here. I was wearing my nice dress, by the way. I will not go shopping looking like a dock tuff! Cadiz's streets are narrow between walls of tall buildings, as I was beginning to think that all European streets were. Many of the ones we passed through were too narrow even for wagons.

I brought my violin because I was going to need spare strings and a new rosin. I doubted I'd find these things in Africa if I needed them. So I was looking for a music shop.

The streets were crowded with people, dark-haired and tanned. We threaded our way between with empty bags, dodging women with baskets and bags leaving the plaza, as we hoped we'd soon be as well.

The plaza itself was a wide, open, paved square, surrounded by the vertical faces of windowed buildings and nothing more, not even a fountain. Vendors had loosely organized themselves into aisles, with tables, pushcarts, and blankets spread with wares and stacks of crates. Some did nothing more than setting their goods out on the ground, displayed for all to see. In between were thousands of people. And it wasn't just food. People were buying and selling all sorts of stuff: books, pottery, and clothing, most of it looking home or at least locally made. Someone was cooking food somewhere too. I could smell it and it smelled good.

Oh! And shaved ice! An old man was sitting on his stool with his block of ice and cans of syrup. I want to grab Ma's dress and bleat, "I want shaved iiice, Maaa!" but as I said, I am not a sheep.

"Oh, look! They have shaved ice," I said. Much better, don't you think?

But she didn't take the hint. Or maybe she did. We walked by with only a slight whimper from me.

We went up and down the rows, with Ma picking things here and there. When Ian's bags were more than full, off he went to the ship. Then when Tinker's bags were full, off he went to the ship too. Then Crow. Then somehow we are back at the shaved ice man and Ma was smiling. "Those boys will have their fun tonight on shore. It's our turn now."

Eating our shaved ice, we pawed through less practical things. I saw a pretty hair comb made of shell and Ma bought it for me! I gave her a big hug and pulled my hair back off one ear with it.

Extending off the plaza were wider roads with grander and more permanent stands lining them. Many had colored awnings held up with poles. Crates of vegetables, beautiful cloth, nuts, inlayed wood, brass bells, spices, glazed pottery, beads, and melons! Ma was looking through spices.

"Ma, can we have melon tonight?" We get melon so rarely.

"On the way back. Otherwise we'll have to carry it everywhere."

In an alcove behind us, under a tree, we saw musicians playing for money. I watched them as Ma shopped. They were a mixed lot, old and young. A boy was singing with his high voice. One man was missing the lower part of his leg, but they all look like they had gotten their meals and there was no mixture in their skills. They were quite good.

At a break I approached the guitar player. He was tall and thin, perhaps in his mid-twenties, with light sun-bleached streaked brown hair, which was what probably caught my eye. That and maybe it was his blue eyes as well. They were nice. He had calluses on his fingers and muscles in his arms. He played a lot.

"*¿Qué puedo hacer por usted?*" he said.

"Strings," I opened my case and pointed to the strings. Then I put the case down and open my arms and turn around. "Where." Then I rubbed my fingers together and said with what I hoped was a look of avarice, "Buy?"

He smiled, which really was nice too. "Marita's is best," he said. He had an accent.

"You speak English?" I said.

"It helps when you're from England. But when you play the streets, it's good to speak a little of all languages."

"Where is Marita's?"

He eyed my violin. "Stay and play, then I'll show you," he said with a mischievous smile.

My reaction was simple. These were strangers and I don't like to perform, and he could see it.

"That's the deal. Stay and play and then I'll show you," he said. Glancing around, he added, "Don't worry. We're all friends here."

"Go on love," Ma said. She had come up behind me.

"Ma!"

"Go on."

So with a deep sigh, and a muttered, "Okay." I put my case down on the low wall behind them, pulling out my bow and rosining it. The guitar player began talking to his friends.

"When you're ready, we'll start and you can pick it up when you can," he said.

Her tuning was off. We were on shore and the air was warmer and dryer, but she settled down and when I raised her to my chin, they started to play.

I didn't know the song, but the chord progression was simple and I picked it up after the first chorus. I tried to stick to the music.

"You can do better than that. Go on," he said. Ma was smiling, nodding in approval.

So I opened up a little.

"Yes," he said and closed his eyes and charged ahead, me dancing along behind.

Then the boy picked up the tune and sang, and for a little while the world was gone. We got applause at the end and I found coins in my case. People were waiting for us to play again.

"Another," he said.

I nodded. This was fun.

And they were off again, with me following. This one was a little more complicated, but I picked it up again after the chorus. Then I asked if they knew any jigs. After some discussion in Spanish, they started again, and this one I knew and we had fun. It was *Pat Murphy's Meadow*, at least that's what we call it, although it didn't come out like any way we played it at home. When we were finished, I realized that the audience had grown and that they were clapping along. The musicians didn't ask; they started again and we were dancing. I don't know how long we played, but I realized that I was hungry. I looked for Ma and there she was next to the tree smiling.

"You really are quite good," the man said. "You could make money. Actually, to be honest, you could make us all money. By the way, my name is Robert, but they call me *Cuerdas*. "Strings" in English. Please don't call me Bob."

Then he turned toward the group and asked, "*¿Comida?*" and got a general "*Sí*". They scooped up the money, including the money in my case, which had grown, and divided it up. It was all pesetas. I had no idea how much I had, but it was a heavy stack.

I put away my violin and Ma and I started to leave.

"*Dile que regrese*," one of the musicians said.

Robert frowned and called, "You don't know where Marita's is."

We stopped and Ma replied, "Do you know a good place to eat?"

"Of course!" He bowed, "At your service." Then he reached toward his things, "Give me a second." He had several picks, bars, and strings, which he wrapped up in an old faded blue handkerchief and stuffed in the pocket of his baggy trousers. "Ready!" he said with a breezy smile.

Most of the musicians were packing their things and I could see in the crowd that others waiting to take our places. Some nodded when they saw I'd spotted them.

The three of us headed down the street, threading our way between the crowds with our bags and instruments. All the way Robert told us about the city.

"We get a mixture of European and African goods, which makes for a nice market day. There's a lot of Arab trade as well. It's a lot more interesting than England, I can tell you."

Up ahead was a cafe with tables on the street, just like in France. Robert stopped and picked a large table outside. Inside, in the dimness it was just an open empty room with more tables, with no wall between it and the street, like a cave. The walls were lined with posters, one over the other, covering every square inch.

"We may be joined by friends. You piqued many people's interest." And then to Ma, "And today, thanks to your daughter, I'm rich. This will be my treat, to help welcome you to Spain."

I saw several music cases leaning against the walls, and more under chairs.

"It seems there are a lot of musicians here," Ma said.

"Andre's has been a meeting place for musicians for . . ," and then he stopped and thought. "Centuries at least. It could go back beyond the Romans even." He looked like he liked that idea.

I pulled the coins from the pocket of my dress and looked at them. "Is this a lot of money?"

"It won't buy you a palace, but it will certainly buy you a nice lunch," then he looked at the sky, "and dinner too." Then he smiled. "It'll easily get you a set of strings. Two if you want them."

The waiter appeared, "*¿Le puedo ayudar?*"

"*¿Sí, qué tiene hoy?*"

They chatted for a bit and then Robert stopped and asked us, "Is fish all right?"

"Oh, we get fish all the time," I said. "Something from the land would be nicer. Chicken or beef maybe?"

"You came by boat?" He looked interested.

Ma smiled, "Yes we did." Ma seemed to like him too.

"*El pollo, por favor,*" he said to the waiter.

The waiter bowed and took his leave.

"He's a musician too. If you drop by the tree on Wednesdays or Fridays, you'll hear him." Then he leaned back in his chair, "I'm dying to hear about you, but we should make it a fair trade, so I will start. I'm the son of a farmer. Sons of farmers don't get many choices in life, especially when you have older brothers. You can divide the land only so many ways. So I took up music rather than join the army or leaving to work in a factory. It was a good choice. Since then I've been to London, Brussels, Paris, , Barcelona, Madrid, and now Cadiz. I enjoy languages and travelling. And now you?"

I looked at Ma, but she said with a little smile, "Go on dear."

"We live on a ship, the Red Jacket. We trade from port to port. During the year I go to school in Boston."

"American. That was easy to figure out by your accent. I would love to visit the U.S. But go on, tell me about Boston."

"The streets are wider and make sense. We don't bury people in our cathedral." That got a snort out of him. "We're having a war. It's awful. You shouldn't come until it's over. They might grab you for the army. Ian almost never leaves the boat at home."

"Ian?"

"He's one of our deck hands. He has to worry because he's draft age. But they don't know about him. He's been working on Red since he was a kid. He joined in New Orleans, didn't he Ma?"

Ma chuckled. "Technically he's a Confederate and an orphan to boot. It's either prison or the army if they catch him. But they won't."

"He's a part owner now," I added.

"Earned it ten times over too," Ma said.

"You own the ship?" He looked surprised.

"Yes we do," I replied.

"Pretty, talented, and rich," he said, looking like he wanted to laugh.

"Hardly," I replied.

"It's all relative. You can't hide the beauty and talent, but keep that last part to yourself or you'll get no peace. Do you know any languages beside English?"

"*Un petit peu de français.*"

"Keep that to yourself too. If they can't speak to you, then they can't chase you."

We were still chatting, when a woman came over to the table. She was definitely older, maybe seventeen or eighteen, taller than me by at least four inches, with long straight, dark hair and green eyes.

"*Hola, Cuerdas. ¿Quiénes son tus amigas?*" she said.

"This is Cali and Maera. Cali plays the violin."

"Hello. You must be from out of town. I'm sure I would have known you before if it were otherwise." She had an English accent too.

"We came in yesterday," Ma said.

She smiled, "I'm Aleta, and I see you've already been found by the most dangerous rake in town."

Robert looked a bit hurt. "Aleta."

"We all love him because he's helpful and supportive," she said. And then she smiled, "But before you know it . . ." and she trailed away.

"Aleta!" Robert said.

"Oh, we all know you aren't a bird to be caged . . ." and then she looked at me, with faked shock, "Now!" Then she sat down. "A young thing like this needs protection."

"She's with her mother," he replied.

"Oh, you're eating the chicken. Is it good tonight?" Aleta said, ignoring him.

"Yes, it is!" I said. "Do you play anything?"

"I play the flute, but I can do percussion and sing too."

"Do you play at the tree?" I asked.

"Oh, the tree! The tree is for old men and rakes looking for young things." She gave Robert a significant look. "You should come by *El Ladrillo*. That's where the music really happens."

"Robert is taking us to Marita's," I said. "I need strings."

The waiter came back to our table.

"That's not far," she said. "*Hola Mateo. ¿Me puedes dar el pollo?*" Aleta asked.

"*¿El vino?*" Mateo said.

"*No, pero tomaremos café,*" Aleta replied.

"*Bueno,*" and Mateo headed back to the kitchen.

"I've ordered us coffee."

What was El Ladrillo?

Chapter 8

The End of Childhood

The four of us walked to Marita's.

"I think you should go see the cathedral," Aleta said. "There are old forts all around us, but they're nothing to look at. A lot of stone. Really, there's nothing in particular that's special about Cadiz. It's the city itself and the things it's built on top of that make it great."

"What do you mean?" I asked.

"It's thousands of years old," she said.

"Maybe three or maybe even four thousand," Robert added.

"No one knows. It isn't only a building here and there like most cities. Although there are those," she said. We were walking in the shade of tall houses and narrow cool stone streets. "It's the city itself. It has more ghosts than people."

"Ah! Marita's," added Robert.

Marita's was a doorway and a window with old sun damaged instruments and yellow sheets of music. Except for the lack of dust and cobwebs, it looked like nothing had been moved in there for at least 50 years. The bell over the door jingled as we entered. Inside, it was cool, dark, and smelled of books and wood.

"*Zac! ¿Está aquí?*" Robert called.

"Zac?" I asked.

Aleta rolled her eyes, "Marita died a hundred and twenty years ago."

"A hundred and twenty five," Robert said.

"True," she replied, and then she looked at me. "We still celebrate her birthday. October 4th, 1679, by the Julian calendar. The Julian calendar. Zac insists. It's part of the tradition."

The walls were covered in instruments, each hanging from pairs of pegs. From the back, behind glass cases, shelves, and bins of sheet music came, "*Deme un minuto!*" Then in walked a thin balding man wearing glasses, an old shirt, and ill-fitting pants. "*Aleta, Cuerdas, hola. ¿Quiénes son estas?*"

"This is Cali and Meara," Aleta said.

"Englisch, mine is nicht gut," Zac said.

"You're thinking German," Robert said.

"Yes, sí. What want them?"

"Cali needs strings," Robert replied.

"And rosin," I added.

He looked, then squinted at me, then at my case.

"Let me look." Zac gestured toward my case to bring it closer.

So I set my case on the counter top and opened it. He pushed his glasses up on his forehead and leaned close. He seemed to smell it as much as see it. "This is a," then he was lost for words. "*Económico?*"

"Inexpensive?" Aleta said.

"Inhexpensive one. Very heavily played. A child's one."

Aleta raised her eyebrows at me.

"I told you. She's good," Robert said.

"Time for a new one. You must be better than this."

That hurt a little. I had had that violin my whole life. "I like my violin."

"Play it for us?" Zac said.

I looked at Ma. She seemed thoughtful. "Go ahead," she said.

So I took her out. The shop was cool, the temperature throwing off her tuning.

"What should I play?" I asked.

"Something you like and know," Zac said.

So I played, *She's Like a Swallow,* one of my favorite songs. Normally, for me, it's a gentile drift, but I was nervous.

"Again," Zac said. "Be serious."

This has always been hard for me, playing in front of people, so I turned my back on them and walked a little ways away. I took a breath. Around me, I could hear music in the ancient walls and air. I could feel it. It was tugging on me like a breeze in my sails. How old was this shop? I relaxed and floated along with it.

"That was," Zac said. *"Lo que pensaba?"*

"What I was thinking." Aleta said, smiling.

"Ah, yes," he mumbled to himself. The he turned and picked up a forked pole. Walking down the wall, he reached the violins and picked one off the wall. "This will play a little flat until your hand gets used to the size. Keep your bow for this." His English was improving.

It was bigger. A lot bigger. I brushed the bow down the strings. It drawled back at me like something dark. I'd never played anything but my violin and this was strange. "It's dark," I said.

"You've outgrown yours. This is bigger. Fill it with music."

It was empty.

"Play your song. It will take, I think, perhaps three tries to know."

I played, but it was slow and flat, rolling out like black molasses. But then I noticed the wood. An odd sweet smell drifted upward and pulled at me. It reminded me, perhaps, of something I dreamed once. On the second try, I followed that. I breathed it in as I struggled to pull the notes up. The spacing on the fingering was further apart. I had to reach. It was like each note had weight. I realized as I played that there might be brightness, but it was elusive. And my fingers on the strings felt strange as I chased it. All the worn familiar spots, the signposts in the wood were gone.

Finally, I had to stop and stretch my hand and arm.

"Shake your hand," he suggested.

I did and then picked up where I left off. It was a house with twice as many rooms. I found so many new overtones and sounds, its tone so deep.

"Good. Now mean it."

I tried. Honestly, I did, but I could see so many new ways to go that I staggered around the music, missing the fingerings. Everything was so different. But there was Aleta, leaning against the counter with her arms crossed and a light in her eyes. Robert looked worried.

"Now play again on your old one," Zac said.

I put the new one on the counter and picked up mine. I held it in my hands and looked down at it. It was so small, like a toy. I started to cry. I looked down at the shiny spots in the wood that I could no longer fit in.

Ma went off like a keg of black powder. "What did you do!?"

"It was time," he said, like we were stupid not to know.

I've never seen Ma so angry, but I could only sink to the floor with my violin in my arms, sobbing.

We bought the new violin, a case, extra strings, and rosin. That first night it sat at the far end of my cabin, my old one on top. I couldn't touch them.

We sold cargo to make space and filled it with wine, grain, and olive oil, which--according to Pa--were crazy cheap.

Robert showed up at the gangway the next afternoon.

"Have you tried the new one yet?" he asked.

"No, I can't."

"Please try." He looked sad, like he wanted to say more, but then, after a moment, he just turned without a word and headed back up the dock.

That night, by the light of my lamp, I opened the new case. There was that sweet smell, overwhelming the kerosene and the smells of the harbor coming in the open porthole. What wood was that? It had a lovely polished grain, but had clearly seen use. The fingerboard was black, almost like it was made of stone. The gloss my old one had long ago come off, down to the raw wood in some places, and my neck had lost some of its black paint too. I ran my finger down a string. It didn't sound right. I took her out and tried tuning it higher, but it never felt right, always something other. The pegs were stiff so I tried soaping them, but nothing helped. How long had she been sitting on that wall?

My new bow was bigger than my old one too. I had to bend my thumb to balance it, like I was a kid again. I ran it slowly across the G. There was the coffin lid.

Everyone was asleep so I slipped out the door and up on deck.

"Hi Cali."

"Hi Tinker," I replied.

"Can't sleep?"

"No."

It was too quiet to play on deck.

"I'm just going to go on the dock."

"You aren't dressed for it." I was barefoot in my night dress.

"Nobody here."

He sighed. "Go on. I'll keep an eye open."

The night was warm and I didn't mind my bare feet. That was until I got on the dock itself. It was, as always, a mess. But there was nothing sharp, at least not particularly. Back against the warehouses, on boards that would be covered by crates tomorrow, I drew the bow across the A, trying again and again with more vibrato, then less. Then intervals, always hunting for the fingerings, and it was harder to control pressure with the new full size bow. The draw was longer. I had to keep my elbow up.

I finally grew tired and went back.

"Hi Cali." It was Ed. When had the watch changed?

"Hi Ed."

I used the drop bucket to wash my feet, even though it was nasty harbor water. It was better that than nasty dock dirt. Then crawled into bed.

Morning came and the sun was way up. No one had woken me. I had morning watch and no one had woken me! Pulling on clothes in my cabin is never easy. I have perhaps two and a half feet of head room. A palace on a ship. I rolled out the door and onto deck. And there was Crow, standing my watch.

"Why didn't you wake me!"

"Figured you needed the sleep," he said. "So take the

afternoon."

What do you say to people who look out for you? You heave a deep sigh and say, "Thanks." Ma must have heard me because she was already putting out my food. Eggs. Yes!

"Hi Ma."

"Mornin'."

I had three hours free. What do you do in a new port? Sightsee!

"Want to go see the cathedral?" I asked.

"I can't. I've got bread rising. You're old enough. Why don't you go on your own?"

"I'd be lonely." Actually, the thought kind of scared me. Except in my cabin, I had, at that time, never been alone in my life. But I gave it thought.

"Maybe you could try your new violin in there," Ma said. "I think it might sound nice."

"They would burn me at the stake."

That got a snort from Ma. She hates papists.

But then again, if something as silly as going somewhere alone was scary, maybe it was time I did. So I gulped my food.

"I'm going," I said as I put my plate in the sink.

"Take your money," Ma called.

The holds were open and everything was piled in something else's way, so I went up over the main deck to my cabin. Change clothes? Yes. My dress, hair comb, and shoes. Oh, and my boater. I grabbed my case and told Crow I was going to the cathedral as I bounded over the gangway.

"Have fun," he said. "Don't worry about the time," he yelled after me.

It may be a city of towers in the middle of the sea, but the cathedral towers over it all with its great gold dome shining in the warm summer sun. It sits perched on the seashore looking out across the Atlantic. As the merchants sat in their towers watching for their ships and cargo, the church sat in theirs and watched out for the sailors.

For me, the cathedral was just across the isthmus. A nice walk on a summer morning. But there were so many other things to see too, such as a coffee house for instance. Ma didn't make it today. We had milk instead, which was a treat. But coffee would be nice too, and I had money!

They served it at a bar, something else new. So I sat on a stool.

"*¿Que le puedo traer?*"

"*Café por favor.*" I'm not completely ignorant.

He poured me a cup and brought it over. "*Diez céntimos.*"

I sorted through my coins. I had several of those. The coffee house was mostly full of men, sitting on stools like me, or at tables. Some were eating large buns. They were pouring olive oil on them. I must try that, I thought, but I just had breakfast. The coffee was stronger than Ma's. Nice!

"Cali," a woman's voice. It was Aleta, with two men!

"Hello." I beamed.

"*Buenos días,*" said one.

She sat down next to me, ignoring the men. "How are you doing?"

"I'm fine I guess. *¿No Inglés?*" I said to the men.

They made looks of regret and shook their heads.

"*Parlez-vous français?*" Which brought only more head shaking. I sighed.

"You speak French? I wish I did," she said. Then she asked, "Can you play yet?" She seemed concerned, but the waiter came back then and they all ordered coffee and one of the men ordered a bun too.

"Not really. The size is different. No. Everything is different," I said. "Who are they?" I nodded toward her friends. The men were talking among themselves.

"Oh, I'm sorry! This is Ruben and Saulo." They looked up and nodded my way. Then she turned back to me, "I want to hear you." Ignoring men didn't seem to be a problem for her.

"I can't. It's all wrong."

"Nonsense! You sounded great in the shop," she had the light in her eyes again. "Yes, you were missing notes, but not by much. You were still better than most around here."

I stared at her.

"Come on. Open it up. Play me a scale."

"Here?"

"Why not? These people know nothing and the owner will be pleased. It will draw business."

I pulled my case up on the counter and opened it. That sweet wood smell overcame everything, even the bread. Everything except the coffee. It mixed strangely with that. With a touch of fear, I played a scale with missteps, but I covered them with elaborate vibrato. Then Aleta's flute case was on the counter.

"It sounds nice. Better than yesterday," she said. "Let's try scales," and she put her flute to her lips and started. When she finished, she started over with me following, picking up speed to follow along with her. I noticed that my coffee cup was full again.

"Do you know this?" and she started playing "*Round the Mulberry Bush*".

"Of course!" and I matched her note for note. The second time she was only following chords so I left the melody too. By the third time, the original thread of the song was gone. Our notes rolled and spun around and around each other. We went around twice more and then she stopped. Aleta took a deep breath, looking pleased.

"What's your favorite song?"

"She's Like a Swallow."

"Oooo, nice. You played that at the shop. Have you tried it again?"

"No."

"Well then, it's about time you did. Come on."

And so we did, and it went well, as did the two other songs after that. I was too afraid to play around much, but it was nice just to play.

"Come to The Brick tonight," she said.

"The Brick?" I asked.

"*El Ladrillo*," she said.

"I don't know where it is."

"I'll send an escort," she said.

"I'll have to ask my Pa," I replied.

"Then I'll go with you to ask."

So I never made it to the cathedral. We packed up. I finished my third cup of coffee, Aleta said goodbye to the men, and she walked with me back to Red.

When we got there, she stopped and let out a little, "Oh," and then, "She's beautiful." Red really is. Even with her hatches open and cargo piled all around. Which I'm not helping to move! And I've missed my watch again!

I ran to the gangway. "I'm so sorry!" I called, Aleta following.

"Not to worry, Missy," Crow said. He was crossing over the gangway to the dock and I had to step out of his way. "Who's your friend?" he asked.

"This is Aleta," I said. "Aleta, this is Crow."

"Crow?" she asked.

"Yes, Crow. He's an American Indian," and Aleta's hand stopped in mid shake, her eyes wide.

"A pleasure," she said. Crow just smiled. Did I tell you he has a gold tooth?

"Sorry I'm late Crow. I have to talk to Pa and then I'll get changed."

"No problem," he said, still smiling.

Then I skipped over the gangway, but stopped and looked back. Aleta was still on dock, looking a little apprehensive. I had to stop to think for a second. Could it be that the gangway is a foot and a half wide, two planks nailed together? I never thought about it before. I suppose it is a little bouncy, has no railings, and because we're cargo light it's ten feet down into black water. I mean, at least the deck wasn't pitching!

I walked back halfway and held out my hand. "Don't look down, just walk over to me."

She was definitely trying to build up courage. Then I stepped back on deck just in time, as she marched straight down, eyes forward, onto the deck and past me. Then she let out a little laugh. I guess it's victory.

"Welcome aboard," I said with a smile.

I could hear Pa in the hold figuring load balance.

"Come on, this way," I said. We took the aft companionway down through the quarters area.

"This is where we live, except for the mess forward. It has to be up there so the smoke doesn't blow across the deck." It was kind of dark below decks, with only the light coming down from the deck cabin.

"It's so dark," she said.

"If someone were down here, then we'd light some lanterns. Opening some hatches helps too. Let in a little air and light from the portholes. Here, see? This is my cabin."

I slid the door back and light from my porthole spilled in.

"This is where you sleep?"

"Yes." I hopped up and opened the porthole. The fresh air was nice.

"It's so small. Where do you keep your things?"

"Here." I was a little confused. It should be obvious. "See, here's where I stow my chest and my violin. This is nice. It's practically a chief mate's cabin. I have my own porthole and a door." I pushed my violin back towards my sea chest, leaving it on top of the covers.

"Who's below?"

"Nobody. Just rope." I slid down to the floor and showed her the rope locker.

We were crouching to avoid the ceiling as we walked aft through the upper hold, and what do you think I saw? Two of the book boxes I wanted, just sitting there. But I'm a lady of strong will and etiquette. I walked by.

"Pa?" He was sitting on the forklift, bent over the load slate, marking distribution in chalk.

"What is it, Cali?" he said, still looking at the slate.

"This is Aleta, a friend from shore."

"Oh?" For this he looked up.

"Hello," Aleta said. A good start.

"She plays the flute," I added.

"Captain Carmichael. It's a pleasure," and he held out his hand and they shook.

"Ma met her. She went with us to the music store."

"Cali is very talented," Aleta said.

"Yes she is, and very precious to us." I love my Pa.

"I was wondering if I could go to listen to music tonight. A club for musicians."

"She won't be alone," added Aleta.

"A nightclub? Cali, you're too young for that."

"A nightclub?" I asked.

"It's complicated," Pa said.

"She won't drink. Well, maybe coffee," Aleta said

"I want to see them play. You could send someone with me," I added.

He was frowning. Not good.

"Let me talk to Meara." Then he looked at Aleta. "I suppose

you're here looking for an answer." He sighed and then he put the chalk and board down and together we walked forward toward the galley.

It was kind of a scramble for us. Normally, we try to keep at least one aisle open so we don't have to cross on deck, but we were moving cargo. Ma was washing dishes.

"Oh Ma." I immediately walk forward to help.

"Not in your good dress," she said. She was right. I had to get changed.

"Cali, why don't you change, while your Ma and I talk?" Pa said. I was dismissed.

"Aye aye."

Aleta and I took the deck route back.

"Your Pa sounds nice," Aleta said. "I've known fathers who'd take a switch to their daughters just for asking."

"Really?"

"Yes. My own, for instance."

"How awful!"

"True. But then that's why he's in Lancaster and I'm here."

I am lucky and I know it.

We went to my cabin. I excused myself and hopped up and closed the door. My shoes were stacked in a pile against the bulkhead at the foot of my bed, next to my sea chest. I pulled the ones I was wearing off and my dress as well, folding them carefully, and put on my deck clothes. After it was closed, my violin, now violins, went on top of my chest. Pants and an old stained shirt over my bodice. Bare feet make better footing, if it isn't too cold, unless you're moving cargo. Then it's boots, so I pulled mine on over socks.

When I had hopped back down on deck, Aleta asked, "How can you change in there? It's so small."

"I guess I've been doing it all my life. I used to have a ladder to climb up. They left that out when they rebuilt it. Don't need it anymore."

"Rebuilt it?"

"Yes, a Confederate shell came right through here. Took out my whole cabin. Gleesons thinks it went right through the porthole."

"At least you weren't in there."

"No, I was at school. I go to boarding school in Boston."

"I never went to school. School's optional for girls in England."

"I can't say that I care for it. But I guess I'm glad I get to go. The way things are going, it looks like I'll be missing this term."

"You are a long way from home."

"Not as far as we will be. We're going to The Congo Free Republic."

"There?" She looked worried.

"What's wrong?"

"I've heard bad things about it."

"You should talk to my Pa."

"They're only rumors," she said. "Maybe though. Maybe there are some people he should talk to." She seemed thoughtful.

"Cali," I heard Pa calling from up on deck.

So up we went.

"We've talked it over and we think you're a little too young to go. Play at that tree place instead."

"Captain Carmichael," Aleta said.

"Yes?"

"I have a deal for you."

Pa did not look happy.

"Let her go to the club, you accompany her, and in return I'll introduce you to two men with Congo experience."

Deals are something my Pa can understand. He came about.

"At the club?"

"Yes. Stay at least until midnight."

"That's late for her."

"She'll be drinking coffee. No one gets there until after nine."

Pa nodded and said, "Done."

Then I asked, "So what's a nightclub?"

Chapter 9

The Prince

Pa was wearing his captain suit, and me my good dress. These were about the only nice clothes we had. I wasn't wearing my boater by the way. This was an evening function and we must maintain propriety. I have my standards. I was, however, wearing my new shell comb. It was warm, which was good because I don't have a nice coat. It'd be embarrassing to show up in oiled japara.

Can you guess who walks up to us at the dock? Robert of course! He was smiling at me until he saw Pa, which definitely put a momentary chill in him.

"Pa, this is Robert," I said, making introductions.

"Beautiful ship, sir." Robert, you are the smart one.

"We are proud of her," Pa said. Pa is always happy to talk about the ship.

Robert gave her a look, then continued, "She'll carry, what, maybe 400 tons at 8 knots on a fair day?"

"You've a good eye," Pa actually looked at him.

"We should go," I said. Silver tongue will have Pa talked into marriage if I let him.

"Where's your violin?" asked Robert.

"Do I need it?"

"Yes, get it."

"Go on," Pa said. I should have been suspicious. Why did I need my violin? But clueless Cali just follows orders.

I bet Robert paid someone to load him up on material to talk about because Pa and Robert were jabbering away as I ran below decks. They were still jabbering as we walked to the club. Cali was only cargo.

El Ladrillo, which means "The Brick" in English, lives up to its name. It's a door in a bare brick alley, with a single lantern. End of decoration. In the alley, around the door, stood smokers, the only thing that marked the alley as being inhabited. As we approached, the door opened letting out music and a man and woman carrying guitar cases. They walked out laughing. The man struck a match and lit a cigarette. I could see the glowing tip as they walked away down the alley, his arm around her waist.

Maybe I am too young for this, I thought. But then again, I'm not a lady who cringes at the slightest social difficulty nor am I one who succumbs to mere social fear – maybe.

The door was open so we walked in. Inside was a short landing, and a big man sitting on a barstool. *"Hola Cuerdas. ¿Estas son tus amigos?"*

"Sì. ¿Estás ocupado?" Robert replied.

"Sì. Que tenga buena noche," the door man said.

Robert gave us a little smile and said, "Come on," and then headed down the stairs. "Aleta has been trying to hold a table for us."

I heard a guitar and smelled food.

"Odd," Pa said. "No smoke."

"Not allowed inside. It spoils it for the singers. And it gets hot enough in here. Smoke would make it intolerable," Robert replied

"That must be hard for some," Pa said.

"They don't have to stay," Robert replied.

We turned right at the bottom of the steps and faced a large, warm, dark room, lit by the light from a raised platform in the center. A stage. The ceiling was high, with catwalks around it and bright lanterns hanging down, with more lights around the platform itself. The only other light came from the lamps at the bar. Sitting out on the platform were a few chairs, one of which was being used by the guitarist we heard as we came in. He tapped the guitar with his ring as he played to create percussion.

"Quite a trick," I thought.

Looking away from the stage, waiting for the afterimages to fade, I could see tables. The room was full of people, a hundred at least, instrument cases stacked everywhere.

"There she is," Robert said. "It's good we got here early."

We had to weave our way around through people standing and sitting. Aleta was sitting at our table with several men, but as we got close she waved them away out of their seats. "*Vaya, vaya,*" she said.

The guitarist finished his song with a flourish and applause.

"You arranged this well," Pa said.

"Thank you," she said, with a little smile.

The next act took the stage, a young man playing a tiny stringed instrument shaped like a teardrop and singing. It had a delicate sound, but it only had four strings. "What is he playing?" I asked.

"Mandolin," Robert replied.

"It's more like a mandora," Aleta corrected. "It only has four strings."

"It's pretty," I added, to which Aleta only nodded as she watched.

A waiter appeared and Pa ordered me coffee.

"They're musicians from the audience," Pa said.

"Yes, this is a club for musicians and their guests," Aleta replied. "We take turns."

"The idea is to share ideas, but really for most it's just a chance to show off," Robert added.

"But it's a good audience for beginners," Aleta said. "There are never rude noises and the applause is genuine."

"You don't mean. . ?" I said.

She held up a wooden square with the number 23 on it. "Don't worry. I'll go up with you," she smiled.

"Really, Miss . . ," Pa said, coming to my defense.

"Just Aleta," replied Aleta.

"Really Aleta, this wasn't part of the deal. If she doesn't want to go, then she doesn't have to."

"She needs to," she replied. "And she'll regret it the rest of her life if she doesn't."

Pa replied with cold finality. "She'll perform if and when she's ready."

"She'll be married," Aleta fired back.

"That's an unfair argument."

Aleta stared back at him.

"It's her choice," Pa replied.

It was impossible to talk after that. Three men had taken the stage with horns, a trombone, a trumpet, and a small circular horn I had never seen before. They were funny, but loud. They seemed to take pride in embarrassing each other.

Five men in black uniforms and shining boots entered the club. One was an older man with a long mustache, waxed to a curl. Two of the men parted the crowd for him. Two tables away, four men got up from their table, and the newcomers took their place.

"Rich," Robert said, looking them over.

"They were in my club two nights ago," Aleta said, over the horns. "They get loud when they're drunk. Some kind of toffs."

"Toffs?" I asked.

"Nobles," Robert answered, like that explained everything.

"Like, kings and queens?"

Robert smiled, "Worse. Their kids!"

Everyone was watching them, though most tried not to show it. For their part, they ignored us. The one with the mustache had a cigar and looked like he really wanted to light it.

An older woman was on stage singing something that made the audience laugh. She switched between singing, chanting, and talking. She had the audience clapping at one point, and then said something in Spanish, dismissing or perhaps chiding us. The audience, including Aleta and Robert, broke out in laughter. I wish I knew Spanish. She was followed by a woman who only sang, slapping her hip lightly sometimes to add a beat. She was beautiful with long straight black, shining hair and a soprano voice that rang like a bell. She got a lot of applause.

Then Aleta picked up her case. "Come on," she said with a smile. "It's now or never."

My hand was shaking as I picked up my case.

"You don't have to do this," Pa said.

"I should," I replied.

We climbed the steps on one side of the stage. The room was full of people, but on the stage I couldn't see them. The light was too bright. Aleta moved two of the chairs so they faced each other.

"Have a seat," she motioned to one of the chairs.

I was trying to look around.

"Don't look, they're just noise." Someone out in the audience, Robert I thought, was repeating what we said in Spanish.

"I don't know what to do," I said.

"Let's do what we did yesterday."

"The Mulberry Bush? That's for kids."

"Maybe, we're just kids. You remember the rules? I'll start, go around once, then you start at the second round. Just follow the melody the first time. The second time you can play within the chords. After that, you can do what you want. We'll go around six times." She was smiling.

I took out my violin and rosined the bow. It needed tuning again. It was the heat from the lights, but finally we were ready.

Aleta put her flute to her lips and began to play. It was simple, of course. One of my first songs. I picked it up in the second round; the room was forgotten. My second round was easy too, we wove back and forth. In the third we began to orbit, higher, lower, changing tempo slower faster, like we were dancing around and around each other. By the fourth, our lines of notes were describing drifting shapes, the original form of the song forgotten. After the sixth, I had lost count and played into the seventh, my notes trailed out into the darkness. I put my violin down quickly.

"I'm so sorry," I stammered. But Aleta couldn't hear me because of the applause. I shied back from it, but there was that light in her eyes again.

"You have to learn to accept it," she said. "For some it's hard."

The audience quieted quickly. They were listening to what we said.

"Do you remember the second song we played?"

"She's Like a Swallow?"

"Your favorite." Then she called out, "*¿De los cantantes sabe cualquiera las palabras?*" and Robert repeated, "Do any of the singers know the words?"

"*Lo puedo hacer,*" said a voice in the dark. She was the woman who sang before, the one with the beautiful soprano voice. She stepped up onto the stage, back up into the light. Aleta was practically beaming. "We women should stick together," the woman said to us. Her accent was thick, almost lisping. "English or Spanish," she asked.

"English, as it was written," Aleta replied. Then she turned to me. "Same rules. I'll go through it once, then you join. Stay with the melody, but I may leave you. Marta, you start wherever you feel it's right." And then Aleta began to play and I followed. At first I felt confusion and panic, but before we started the next round, I thought I had it. There was so much music in that room, it drifted like smoke, telling me where to go. The audience was gone, it was so quiet. Then Marta began to sing, her words ringing out against the walls. It went like this:

She's like a swallow that flies so high,
She's like the river that never runs dry,
She's like the sunshine on the lee shore.
She loves her love and love was no more.

It's out in the meadow this fair maid did go,
Picking the lovely primrose.
The more she plucked the more she pulled,
Until she's got her apron full.

She climbed on yonder hill above,
To give a rose unto her love.
She gave him one, she gave him three,
She gave her heart for company.

And as they sat on yonder hill,
His heart grew hard, so harder still.
He has two hearts instead of one,

She said, young man what have you done.

How foolish, foolish you must be,
To think I loved no one but thee.
This world's not made for one alone,
I take delight in every home.

She took her roses and made a bed,
A stony pillow for her head.
She lay her down, no more did say,
But let her roses fade away.

She's like the swallow that flies so high,
She's like the river that never runs dry,
She's like the sunshine on the lee shore,
She loves her love but she'll love no more.

As I followed Marta, my violin settled around her voice. The sound was so rich and deep. I could never have done this with my old one. Aleta's notes departed as Marta sang and created a counter melody behind us. By the second verse, the song had formed and we knew our parts. This was not the song as I played it. Together we were so much more, each adding something. At the end we fell into a stumbling quiet, like we had all just woken up and noticed that we forgot to set the ropes on the dock. Then came a crash of applause like a wave in a storm. It seemed like so much noise. Aleta pulled me up to stand, which I did, a little confused. And we bowed.

Our turn was over. As we went down the stairs, a man passed us and muttered a sarcastic sounding "*gracias.*"

Back at the table, Marta joined us.

"I didn't know if they'd let us play two," Aleta said. She was bubbling with energy.

Pa just looked at me, which was a little confusing.

"And who are you?" Marta said to me.

"Cali," I said.

"Cali sounds like a Hindu goddess," she replied. "This one here," she smiled at Pa, "must either be your current flame or your father."

The waiter brought us more drinks, but didn't ask for money.

"We're from Boston," I said. What's a flame? I thought.

"Yes, I can hear it in your accent. Nice voice too. You should develop that."

I wasn't understanding most of this so I asked Robert, "That was you translating wasn't it?"

"Yes. Anything for a free beer," and he lifted it toward me, which was confusing too until Aleta and Marta both lifted theirs and they all clinked them together. I lifted my coffee cup and joined, almost not spilling, followed lastly by Pa.

"Hmmm . . . a sea captain. You will not be with us long I take it," Marta said.

"I'm hoping to sail day after tomorrow," Pa said.

"Let's hope you are delayed so we can have your Cali for a little longer. It was good meeting you, Cali. Don't let anyone get in the way of your playing," she said, as she left.

Then one of the men, the "toffs" who came in earlier, came over to our table and bowed. He was medium height, a little taller than Pa, with dark, slightly curled, thick hair. His eyes were pale hazel, almost gray. He was wearing a black uniform. It was my first time I set eyes on my Lucien, and to be honest I was too scared to look closely.

"Judging from your conversation, you speak English?" he said. We all nodded. "His Highness would like to meet both of you," he said to Aleta and me. His accent was, perhaps, French?

"His Highness?" Pa said.

"His Highness Prince Leopold Ferdinand Elie Victor Albert Marie, Duke of Brabant," he replied with a slight smile. Aleta grabbed my hand. I think she was afraid.

"Of Belgium?" Pa asked.

The man had been staring at me, but he finally noticed Pa. "Yes," he answered.

I didn't want to see him. Aleta's reaction alarmed me. But then again, he might be able to help Pa. Belgium owned the Congo. I looked at Aleta.

"We should go," she said. "He might pester us if we don't."

"You don't have to go," Pa said.

Aleta smiled at Pa. "You might be one of the rare ones after all." But then she added, "Really, he will get his way if he wants

95

to."

"She's American," Pa said.

"And this is Europe, and this man could buy Boston," Aleta replied.

"Then I'll go too," Pa said.

"Just the two ladies," the man said.

"I'll go," I said.

"Let's. If you decide to perform, then you need to see what they're like anyway. Robert, watch the instruments please."

"Anything for free beer," he said.

We stood and the man said, "If you ladies will follow me." His voice was clear and sweet.

The crowd seemed to part for him as we followed behind, making our way two tables over. The stage and the poor musician on it were forgotten. All eyes were on us. Two seats had been vacated to give us a place to sit. Although they were all dressed in black, I suspected Leopold was the one in the center with the moustache. His uniform had more trim. We took our seats. The man who led us over, translated for us. Our host seemed to prefer German.

"His Highness apologizes that he doesn't speak either Spanish or English," our guide said, translating.

"We're sorry that we don't speak German," Aleta said. Aleta was being coy. I later learned that she spoke it quite well.

"Your music is very beautiful," the prince said.

"We enjoy your appreciation of it. Thank you," she replied.

"Neither of you are Spanish."

"I'm from England," Aleta said. "She is from the United States."

His eyebrows went up at this. "Perhaps I could hear her speak for herself?"

"I'm from Boston," I answered.

"Charming. Are you a wandering minstrel?"

"No. My family owns a ship. We're just visiting."

"Really. What ship?"

For some reason, I didn't want him to know about Red. I didn't want him connected to my home. "She's just a sailing ship. Not a very big one."

"In harbor here. American. I hope you didn't bring that war

with you."

"We hope so too," and at that I couldn't help but smile a little.

"Charming. It's annoying that we can't smoke here. I will not smoke in an alley. We may have to leave soon because of it. Would you two like to accompany us?"

"We have appointments," Aleta said.

I shook my head, scared half out of my wits. Some lady of social grace I am.

"Charming." There was something in his eyes, but I couldn't place it.

It went on for five or six minutes, but we finally managed to make our excuses. Back at our table, I buried my face in my hands. "I was so scared." Pa looked like he had been holding his breath the whole time.

"He seemed to like you," Aleta said. "That might not be good. Let's hope he takes no for an answer." And then she frowned. "I don't know if I should be relieved or insulted."

We talked and listened to music. Aleta wanted to see my new violin, so I asked to see her flute. It was heavier than I thought, and it seemed very complicated. Unlike the ones at school, hers had holes in the lids. This would seem to defeat the purpose of the lids entirely. But there was too much sound and confusion to ask her about them. Maybe later, I thought.

Then Aleta looked up at the door. "Time for me to meet my end of the bargain," she said, and then waved. Across the room were two older men, one had a violin! Perhaps I'd get to hear him play. They saw us and walked our way.

"Captain Carmichael, this was Captain Rousseau and his first mate Andre Braud," Aleta said. "Le, ah . . . gentlemen, *ceci est Capitain Carmichael.*"

"*Vous parlez du français?*" Pa said.

"*Nous sommes belges,*" Captain Rousseau said.

"Oh, that makes it easy," Aleta said brightly. "Come on Cali. Let's leave them to their manly talk. We women can retire to the parlor." She picked up my case and handed it to me.

"Coming Robert?"

"No, I want to listen," he said.

"You don't know French," I said.

"I know more than you think," he replied.

"Good, we won't lose the seat," Aleta replied cheerfully.

When we were out of earshot of the table, which was about 6 feet in the confusion of the club, I said, "You should be nicer to Pa. He's really a very good man. I could stay and listen too and he wouldn't mind."

"He does seem like he's one of the good ones," she said wistfully. "Too bad he's married," she added, which surprised me.

She led me up the stairs to the top of the landing. "Cali, I would like to introduce you to Rafael, the bouncer. Rafael, *esto esta Cali*."

"*Hola Cali,*" he said with a smile.

"Rafael taught me a lot about how to defend myself, especially from unwanted male advances. Not all men are gentleman, and especially after tonight I think you may need some help with this. This is something every woman on stage needs. I'm hoping we can spend some time tomorrow working on it. What do you think?"

"What's a bouncer?"

Aleta gives a little smiling laugh. "He makes sure people behave. He's good at fighting."

"Like a policeman."

"Exactly."

I couldn't sit around being scared for the rest of my life. "I think that sounds like fun," and I shook Rafael's hand.

It was only Pa and me walking back to the docks. Robert wanted to talk to Aleta about something.

"What an evening," he said, and he didn't sound happy.

"Did I play all right?"

He turned and gave me a look and then hugged me, which was a big surprise. Pa isn't one for displays of affection. "You were wonderful." So we walked some more. "I guess you're growing up," he said. "We'll all be sad when we lose you."

"You won't lose me."

"A real prince tonight. Who else is going to show up at our door."

"Pa, his intentions were less than honorable."

Pa snorted. "You have a lot to learn about men."

"Aleta thinks so too," I said.

"It's too bad we're leaving. I think she might be just what you need at this point."

"Pa, she wants me to learn how to protect myself tomorrow," I said.

"How is she going to do that?" Pa asked.

"Rafael, the bouncer at the club. Can I?"

"Considering where we're going, that might be a good idea."

Chapter 10

Dracula

The next day, at 11:00 a.m., Aleta and Rafael showed up at the dock. Pa and I were there waiting for them with the crew sitting around out on deck.

"Captain Carmichael," Aleta said with a smile. "May I introduce you to Rafael Cortez. Rafael, *esto es Capitán Carmichael*."

"*Honorado para encontrarle*," Rafael said.

"A pleasure," Pa said. "I've been thinking about this."

"You aren't going to say no, are you?" interrupted Aleta.

"No, quite the contrary." He paused, trying to think of the words. "You can't teach her much in one day, so I want the crew involved. If you go through it with the crew here to see, then they can help her continue after we leave. All of these men can fight, even Cali, if she has a crowbar." I'm proud to say that got a chuckle from the crew. "But this is something that will take time."

Aleta was translating for Rafael and he was nodding his head yes. He looked relieved.

"Good," Aleta translated. "Then my time won't be wasted. I've been trying to tell Aleta that a little training can sometimes make things worse. Poor resistance can invite a worse beating."

"Wait, he said something else," Pa said.

Aleta grinned. "He said I'm stubborn."

We went through the parts of your body you use for hitting, like not using your fists but your palms, and places to hit, like the instep and knees. How to break away when people are trying to hold you, and that you should always run when you can without wasting time looking back.

Ma made lunch. Aleta and Rafael had never eaten onboard a ship before. They were both appropriately impressed by Ed's wood carving.

Halfway through lunch, the man in the black uniform from the club, the one with the prince, showed up at our gangway and Tinker called down from on deck. "Captain to the deck!"

Pa sighed and tossed down his napkin and headed up the steps. The rest of us ate and talked, wondering what could be up, when Pa came back with an envelope.

"It's from that prince," he said.

I opened it and inside was a handwritten card. His highness himself couldn't have written it since he didn't know English. "You are invited to spend the afternoon and evening aboard the Marie Henriette, his highness' private zeppelin. Please give your acceptance to the courier."

"He wants me to go on his zeppelin."

"It's your decision," Pa said, looking worried.

That's easy. "No," I said.

Pa smiled a bit and headed back up on deck. Then came back

down, standing on the companionway. I guess he was tired of walking back and forth. "He wants to talk to you, Cali."

I was not happy. Sighing, I headed up. Up close in the daylight, I could see him better. His black uniform was crisp and carefully tended. It matched well with his dark, almost black, hair and hazel eyes. Unlike his boss, he seemed to have a nice smile. It's odd, but I felt like it was something he didn't share with just anybody.

"I wish to apologize for my lord. He is not used to being refused. I'm afraid that he may become a nuisance, so it would be best if you could avoid his path. He's watching now, through his telescope."

"I'm sorry, but I don't know your name."

"Oh," he looked aghast. "I'm so sorry. One loses one sense of self when in service." He looked down for a second thinking. "I am Lucien Antoine."

"Calista Carmichael."

"It is a true pleasure," and he clicked his heels and bowed! "Excuse me while I wave in the direction of my lord's zeppelin as if I'm trying to persuade you. Now that I can see you in the daylight, I'm very glad you are not going. He crushes flowers trying to catch their scent."

"He's that brutal?"

"No, just thoughtless of others. Really, he has no conception. He generally gets what he wants. Untold numbers have died in his colonies trying to satisfy his demands. You are a strange occurrence, a . . ," and he thought for a moment. "A paradox, I think."

"His . . . colonies?"

"Yes, his personal properties include Santo Tomás in the Caribbean, Isola Comacia in Southern America, a concession in China, and of course the largest, his personal estate, the Congo."

No silent scream for your Cali this time. My blood ran cold. "So you think he might cause trouble for us if he can?"

"Very likely. I would suggest that you try to stay out of his way. He has a very short memory. In a few weeks, he'll have forgotten all about you."

As Pa and the crew were watching from a discrete distance, they heard none of this. I shoved the invitation back into Lucien's hand and shook my head no for the telescope. "Thank you for being frank and trying to help."

"Excuse me while I frown and show imperial displeasure," he said, but there was mischief in his eyes! "It works on some. I suppose it's because you're American. I suggest you shake your head no again," which I did. "I'll take my leave and say that although I would like it to be otherwise, I hope in my heart that we never meet in the future and that his highness never again hears your music."

I didn't tell Pa about the prince owning the Congo. He might do something foolish, like skipping it altogether. Our cargo wouldn't sell well in the Caribbean. We'd been working up toward the trade with Africa. The insecticide would be a big seller anywhere in the tropics, but the rest was next to worthless in the Gulf. And we couldn't go home with little to show for our trip but maintenance and dock fees.

This was our last night, and a work night for Aleta. So we decided--with some less than subtle suggestions from me--that Ma, Pa, and I might go to the restaurant where she works for dinner. It was upstairs, above a small bar, a large room with a stage, several smaller private rooms, and for us, a balcony with four tables that overlooked the harbor. We got there a little after seven, early for Spaniards, early enough to see the sunset while we ate. Then we moved to the main room.

Aleta paired with a guitarist and to be honest, they were only fair. The guitarist had to be holding her back. She joined us at our table after and I whispered to her, "What was wrong with that guitarist?"

"He's a lazy pig," she whispered back. "Did you bring your violin?"

"No, but we can play at the coffee house in the morning," I said. "We're leaving with the evening tide."

"That would be nice, 9:00 a.m.?"

"Then I could try one of those loaves with olive oil."

"Ew, that's for old men," she said.

"It looks like it might be nice," I replied.

"Try it with garlic and tomato pesto, and maybe egg!"

And on we went.

The next morning we met and played music and drank free coffee for two hours, and then she came and sat with us on the ship.

"I wonder where Robert is," I said.

"He hates goodbyes. Just ask any of the women here," Aleta said.

Pa walked up. "Hello, Aleta."

"Hello, Captain," she replied.

"What are your plans? Are you going to stay in Cadiz?"

"Probably not. It's really a matter of saving enough to move on," she replied.

"You couldn't sign on to a ship?" Pa asked.

"You know ships don't take women," Aleta said. "When I was younger than Cali, and much smaller, I was deck crew for Lufthansa, but I'm too big now. They like their crewmembers small to save weight. That's how I got out of England."

"You flew in zeppelins?" I exclaimed.

"Yup, it was amazingly dangerous work, but so much fun too," she replied.

"Dangerous? It seems like you just ride around all over the world and say *yes sir, no sir*," I said.

"The passengers just ride around. Crew do things like bag stitching at 5000 feet, cleaning the acid tanks, or regrounding envelope segments with a million volts going by because of static charge buildup. Oh, and then you get to say *yes sir, no sir*."

"You speak German?" asked Pa.

"*Sprechst du Französisch?*" she replied.

"Want a job?" he said.

"Doing what?" she asked.

"Travelling to Boston?"

"You're offering me a berth?" she exclaimed.

"I'm offering you a chance to work 24 hours a day for the next four months. If you take it, you'll probably spend the first two or three days sick in bed."

"You're kidding."

"Nope."

"I'll be back in thirty minutes!" And she was off like a sky rocket.

Pa yelled after her, "Two and a half cubic feet of personal storage." He was shaking his head and smiling, "I don't think she heard."

Then, just as he turned back, I leapt on him with my new fighting skills and gave him a big hug.

We were rushing to buy wood because we needed to build a new cabin for Mackie. He deserved it. He was getting old and needed room to stretch, and he didn't need to climb to get to his bunk. A little personal space, like a desk would be nice too. But we needed to get the preliminary work done before we sailed. The starboard rope locker had been emptied and, for the moment, the rope was stacked in the hold along with the foul weather gear, which had been the locker above.

We were the middle of doing the best part, the part where we knock stuff apart. Out came the locker walls. We were going to build new lockers for all of this gear back amidships. Of course, that meant losing a bit of cargo space, but we'd gain a proper cabin for Mackie, and a guest cabin that Aleta could sleep in. It's fast carpentry, but on ships resourceful fast carpentry is what keeps us afloat.

Mackie was going to have a real door. We bought it prebuilt, pocket and all, with louvers for air. Pa was having fun with this. Mackie will have a shallow cupboard with edged shelves, a small bookshelf and desk. We built locker space under his bed, but only some of that was his. We had to put the spare blocks somewhere. We can't stop for forgotten pieces out at sea so we had to have it all figured out that day.

"But Cali," I hear you say. "You were going to sail that day." We were, but now we are going to be sailing the next day.

So it's yo ho ho and bang with the sledge and whack with the hammer and chisel. I was working the wood splinters off the bulkhead with the chisel, and Aleta was breaking the framing up for disposal with the small sledge. Tinker was cutting the new framing, walking up and down from the deck to try fit. And Ed was hammering things together. We were hoping to paint the cabin that evening. The paint would not be dry by the time we sailed in the morning, but when it did, they would both get new mattresses on top of everything else. For the next few days, poor Aleta would have to sleep in a hammock, but she was so excited about going to out to sea that I didn't think she cared.

Knockers had already taken a shine to Aleta. Really, I think it's the long hair. She likes Crow too. Knockers just likes hair. How can you complain about that? Especially when you have it!

Our next port was the Canary Islands, *Palmas de Gran Canaria*. Pa wasn't sure what to expect there. Long ago, they were a center for sugar, but times had changed and sugar production had moved to the Caribbean. We'd been advised not to expect much. But some cheap sugar would put the icing on our cake! Yes, that was Cali humor. Consultation with Aleta's friends had put Pa in the mind that we had over-purchased grain and wine. Unloading some and replacing it with sugar, and especially rum, might be helpful. Mostly though, we were stopping because we needed fresh provisions and water. I personally love fresh eggs. And besides, of course, we had never been there, or at least in some cases, not for a very long time.

To introduce Aleta to the glamour and fun of sea travel, we spent the morning before we left tarring the upper rigging and greasing the masts. This is best done in port, without a pitching deck. The job has generally fallen on me, being as I'm the smallest and lightest. To get to the upper mast you have to be hauled up in a bosun's chair, where small and light makes big sense. Having Aleta up there with me was a nice change from Ian. It's fun to have a friend to work with. Somehow that can make everything easier.

As soon as we hit open water and began to heave through the waves, poor Aleta began to heave too. I pulled my things out of my cabin and we laid her there. At least there was no paint smell to aggravate things, and, sadly, no way to tell how long this would go on for. Usually, it's only a few days, but some people never recover, and there have been very rare cases where people have actually died of sea sickness! You have to wait and see.

The regular shipping lanes swung us wide of the North African coast. That part of the coast held nothing but trouble for us, like pirates and slavers. It was mostly controlled by the French, but they hardly policed it, and those that traded there were not the kind of people we wanted to deal with. So we were making way south out in the wide open sea and sun. This was sailing at its best. Blue water and fair wind. Most of the ships out there were heading south to catch the tradewinds and currents across to the Caribbean. They would, like us, stop in the Canary Islands for that last chance at fresh water and food before they took the big leap to the Caribbean.

Aleta was staggering around the deck the next day, trying to work. We pushed her back into bed, but she was out again at dinner. She didn't give up. I felt very proud of her. She helped Ma with the dishes, but then had to stagger back to bed pale as a sheet. I called out words of encouragement outside her door, "You are doing well" and "This will pass." Then the next day she emerged newly born, like a butterfly. Still weak and pale, but triumphant. She ate only toast, but she managed to keep it down. Later she ate an apple and then half her lunch. After dinner, she announced that she would like to work, so I offered to share deck watch with her that evening.

We had one of those best evenings. The moon was waxing past half and the sky was clear, the deck lit in silver so bright that the bow and binnacle lights seemed pale yellow. This wasn't a war zone so we could keep them lit. The spray from the bow sparkled in the moonlight. Tinker was at the wheel with his eye on the compass and the wind, so our job was pretty simple. Keep a second eye out for ships, and run and raise the crew if Tinker thought we ought to. To make the time useful, I started teaching Aleta knots and ropes. We passed a steamer and then some airships passed us. We stood on the bow and felt the pounding of the water as Red sliced through it. Every drop of the bow sent a spray to our sides. Aleta tried to ride the deck without holding on, but she was still too weak, and so we retired amidships where things were calmer and practiced our bowlines.

Las Palmas is built on the isthmus of a little peninsula that juts out from the base of a huge volcano. On the seaward end of the peninsula are three hills, ancient cindercones, the main aerodrome for the island. The Las Palmas Aerodrome is almost as big as the city itself because it's an important stopping point for airships heading west. I counted at least two dozen great zeppelins moored and at least a hundred smaller airships at the aerodrome on the hills when we arrived. Our trading friend's zepplin with the pirate L's on her tail was moored there too. They were probably in the Canaries to load up on more spirits.

We couldn't see the harbor until we rounded the point, but when we did, we saw three big Confederate warships anchored there in the harbor and not a single Union ship in sight. We were back in the war zone. Technically though, the Canaries were still Spain and by law we were safe.

We were followed into harbor by dolphins. This was something new for Aleta and she was just a little bit in awe. Their gray backs shone as they leapt in front of our bow, laughing at us for being so slow.

Except for the volcano, as I've said, harbors are harbors. The volcano itself was so big that the closer we got, the less we could see of it. You couldn't see it at all from the harbor. Just its foothills.

When we docked, Pa popped ashore, as usual, and headed for the harbormaster to do our paperwork, leaving us with the job of rearranging cargo to get the grain and wine exposed. This can be a tricky business. When the ship is heavily loaded like Red was, load balance is very important. Uneven distribution can twist the hull. Red doesn't leak because we're careful and took good care of her. Because of balance requirements, we do a lot of moving of things back and forth in ways that might not make much sense to someone watching.

As we were moving pallets and crates, lo and behold, what did I see? An as yet-unplumbed box of books! Your Cali knows where the crowbars are and that lid was off.

"What are you doing?" Aleta asked.

"Dracula," I replied.

"Dracula?" She was clearly not up to date on current reading.

"Dracula. He drinks the blood of his victims with his fang-like teeth!"

She lets out an unconvinced, "Oh."

"Help me?"

"Sure."

So we pulled books out in stacks, skimming their spines, until finally! Yes! It was there near the top of the next stack!

"It looks creepy. You're going to read that?" Aleta said.

"Yes." I replied, with conviction.

"Can I read it next?"

"Sure!"

So it was books back in the crate, hammering it closed. I had to put *Dracula*, yes, yes, yes, away, no, no, no, until I had free time.

When Pa got back, he announced that we had a buyer for the books. I had found it just in time! Unfortunately, the crates had become spread out all over the hold. The problem was that the book crates were so uniform in size and weight, that they'd become convenient counter weights. We had them tucked into all sorts of odd spots, which meant more rearranging. We didn't achieve any sort of satisfactory order until after lunch.

"I'm going to be so sore," Aleta said. She was lying on top of stack of sacked grain. The men were all up on deck and we had the upper hold to ourselves.

"Me too," I moaned. "Moving cargo is hard. The worst is mucking out the bilge. You're lucky we did that before we left."

"That sounds horrible."

"It is," I said, with conviction.

"How can you play your violin after doing this all day? I'm going to be a cripple for the next week."

"I was born on this ship. Off the coast of the Belgium, coming in to Antwerp."

"Really?" She laughed. "That's nice."

"You were born in Lancaster?" I asked.

"Yes. My family worked in the cotton mills. I started there when I was eight."

"I thought cotton needed warm weather. England is cold, especially in the north."

"Grey days most all year long. We only processed it. It all came in from America. Cotton and slaves."

"Slaves?"

"Yes." This time it came out kind of dead. "We could see the docks from the factory. They'd force the ones who could walk out on the docks, then carried out the ones who couldn't. Just piled them there, chains and all. If the wind was right, you could smell them. The bodies, those who couldn't walk and the dead. They all went in carts someplace. That was until the river silted up and the big ships couldn't make it in anymore."

"That's awful," I said.

"The world is full of awful. You have to try not to get stuck in it."

"If you didn't go to school and you worked in a factory," I asked. "How did you learn to play the flute?"

"The vicar."

"He taught you to play?"

"Among other things," she sighed. "Then I ran away when I was fourteen."

"Why?" I asked.

"It was better than getting pregnant."

There isn't much you can say to something like that.

Chapter 11

Pastel Vasco

That afternoon we had some time off, so we decided to go out to dinner. The local money was still the Spanish peseta, which I had, but why pay money for what you can get for free! We were going to play for our supper.

Poor Aleta practically hobbled along the dock, stopping to stretch when no one was looking.

Docks. Oh, I do a lot of sneering at them, but you may never have seen them so they deserve some description. They're mostly wood, although sometimes stone, and their purpose is to get people and cargo out to water deep enough that boats can float in it. Some docks don't quite manage that. With those you have to be careful of the tide. Boats left dry in the tide can be damaged. If you're empty, it's not a problem, but as I've said before, cargo can twist a ship and it's doubly bad when there's no water to support it.

Sometimes, the docks have cobblestone paths that workers can use to slide the heavy stuff. Stone doesn't bind as much as wood. Sometimes too, they may have a crane to help lift. Those are for the big ships and cost more to berth at. Ships stay at the dock as little as possible because it's expensive. It's cheaper to moor out in the harbor and take a boat in. We have a yawl for that. But Pa doesn't like to wait around, so we generally start loading and unloading as soon as we hit port. Today, for instance, we sent out a big load of grain.

We often hire dockhands, stevedores or steves, to help with loading and that day they came by with wagons, both hired by the clearinghouse to take our grain to a warehouse. We don't usually allow strangers to do this, but steves are professionals, often out of work sailors with experience.

Ships, when they're loading and unloading, will sometimes have cargo piled on the dock while they sort their holds. You have to take things out to get to the stuff you want. So docks can be crowded with both men and cargo, and they can be empty and quiet as well.

The warehouses are behind the docks. This is where goods are stored while they await sorting, purchase, and pickup. Those wagons may have been taking our grain to a warehouse, or they may have been taking it directly to the buyer. Grain is a bulk commodity and our little contribution of 40 tons probably went into a larger pool of grain being worked by a broker who is himself working for a clearinghouse.

Docks are also home for a lot of interesting people. Ship fitters, riggers, lofts, shipwrights, but to name a few who provide services. Of course there are women who provide yet other services, but they tend to stay closer to the navy. There's always a section for fisherman, which can be fun, but you have to be up three or four hours before dawn. That's when the fish market is lit. You might think you've seen it all, but you should go and see the kinds of things they haul out of the deeps. Then there are sailors looking for berths. Someone asks us almost every day and we have to turn them away. In the corners, in the shadows, there can be thieves and beggars. It's best not show your money near beggars. They might be fronting for thieves. Stay out of the dark spots in general.

Just back of the warehouses the bars start. These are not bars you want to go to unless you're particularly looking for trouble. They're there because some types of people want just that. They'll exist no matter how anyone feels about them and people seem to think that the docks are where they belong. Not all sailors are crazed bullies. Some of us have families. But that's docks and that's why we rushed through them to get into the town proper.

Downtown Las Palmas has cement sidewalks and gas light. It's altogether quite civilized. We were heading into town when we heard a guitar let loose a rattling staccato like a stick on a picket fence.

"Flamenco," Aleta said with a smile. Then she looked at my questioning gaze, "It's a Spanish style of music and dance. It's, it's . . ," but she shook her head frowning. "Let's go look."

It was coming from a restaurant, but it had walls with no roof. At least most of it didn't. The kitchen was built into the wall. The tables were set around the floor and vines edged the insides of the walls, growing right on them. No one was dancing. Instead we saw a lone guitar player who sat on a stool in an open space in the center. He was thin, wearing a loose cotton suit with an open collar, smoking a cigarette. Judging by the butts on the floor he'd been sitting there for a while.

He was working his guitar, alternating between picking and strumming, splitting out the melody and the accompaniment. He nodded to us but didn't miss a beat. It was early and only three tables were occupied. They all looked foreign. If this was like the mainland, no self-respecting Spaniard would be here for another six hours. We were thinking of playing in the street for our dinner money then coming back later with escort to eat. But a waiter showed up and Aleta looked at the hand written card he offered.

"Oh, *pastel vasco!*" She was practically jumping. "*Dos pastel vascos y café por favor*," and we made for a table. "You are going to like this. I've only had it once. It is so good."

I noticed that the music had become louder and a shadow loomed over our table.

"*Buenas tardes señoritas.*" Then he was nodding toward our cases, "*¿Tocan eso?*"

"*Si señor,*" Aleta said. "He's asking if we're musicians."

"*¿Saben melodías agradables en español?*"

"He's asking if we know any nice Spanish tunes. It's all they'll allow here."

"*Sí, pero estoy cansada de ellos,*" Aleta told him. And then to me, "I told him no, nothing nice."

"*El oueño está lejos. ¿Quizás podríamos divertirnos un poco? Estoy muy cansado de esto.*"

"He wants to play anything but this. He's going out of his mind."

We looked at each other and Aleta nodded at me, so we opened up our cases. A waiter brought three cups of coffee. Mind you, he's still been playing all this time, even when he pulled out a chair with his foot to sit.

I tuned and rosined. The sound of my violin was oddly disjointed from his guitar. It would take some thought to get them to mix.

"*Cinco más barras y termino.*"

"He's finishing the song," Aleta explained.

"*¿Puede hacer un fandango?*" he asked. "*Asino me meto en problemas.*"

"He wants to do a fandango. They start slow and then pick up speed. A I IV V chord progression in the key of C, usually something like C minor, F major, G major, E major, followed by a D minor. There's a dance that goes with it involving castanets." She saw my confusion. "They're things you click in your hands. We can follow the chord progression, at least."

More negotiation, and then it was agreed that he would start and then we would pick it up when we could. Then he started, and I heard that chord progression, but he danced around it, sometimes rattling out notes and then stopping altogether. This was going to be hard, but after a bit, I could hear a sensible progression to his breaks.

His music dodged around so much that I decided to come in slow, half time with tortuous vibrato. He only smiled, his cigarette dangling from his lips, waiting for Aleta. She would have nothing to do with it and came in playing tag with the melody. And then he stopped and turned, chasing her a half a beat behind. I turned and followed down a twisting path of dodging flute and guitar. We pounded out music and then stepped back. At least they did. I missed it, leaving a string of wandering notes only to have them drop back in again to hammer on the melody. The ground under our feet felt like it was alive, the walls rang. Then we stopped, with me almost tipping over out of my seat into that chasm of silence.

People looked in the door of the restaurant. The kitchen staff had come out. Everyone was applauding. The guitar player leaned back in his seat with his squinting smile and took a long pull on his cigarette. He wasn't done yet. He wasn't going to let us go. He started again. We played for over an hour and a half. So much for our dinner money. There wasn't time and it isn't wise for two lone women to cross the docks after dark, so we went back.

Oh, but let me tell you about pastel vascoe. It's a small pie, but the crust is sweet, like a cookie, with some kind of custard inside. We had it with sweet thick black coffee, oh! I was so awake with coffee that I was thinking that I'd switch watches with Ian and stay up until midnight.

I was up 'til midnight, then up until two. That coffee was something. How did Aleta sleep? I finally crawled into bed, exhausted, and there was Dracula, sitting unread. This is unfair, I thought.

I woke up in the morning, sun shining in my porthole, my mouth dry, Dracula open on my chest. I tried. I really did.

It's ten! At least I didn't miss my watch, but Aleta was up already, standing her watch on deck, practicing her knots even. How can she do that? Ma made me eggs, which made me think that maybe the sunshine was perhaps just a tiny bit appropriate.

Pa had found our sugar! But this meant we had to move our expected sales out of the way in order to load it. We were going to take a chance and put it all up on the dock. I tell you this, just so you know how we spent our day. We didn't sit around. I didn't get to read Dracula. There was laundry, and then I helped Ma make bread and pie. It's funny. Forty tons of wheat off, and then we buy it back as flour.

We were lying on our backs on the pallet blocks of the remaining eighty tons of wheat, looking up at the underside of the main deck, taking a break. The afternoon sun was lighting everything shades of gold as it shone in the open cargo hatches.

"Cali," Aleta said.

"What?" I sighed.

"I found out where there's real flamenco. Want to go tonight?"

"I have watch."

"Trade with Ian," she answered. "He owes you for letting him out last night."

"When did you find this out?" I asked.

"That guitar player. He wanted under my skirts, I swear I've never seen a man so persistent."

"Funny, I didn't notice." I smiled.

"You should learn Spanish."

"I should. Spain is fun."

So trade watches I did. We took baths, of course. We were in a hurry so they were cold. If this were Jamaica, I'd have jumped in the sea, but Palmas de Gran Canaria is a nasty dirty harbor, albeit one with fresh water hookup.

Did you know that Aleta has real jewelry? She has a pendent of green stone on a thin gold chain and real earrings. She had someone make holes in the lobes of her ears. Ow! Normally she keeps thin gold rings in them to keep them from healing. Again, ow!

And--she insists it doesn't hurt--which is just crazy.

I showed my money to her and she shook her head. It wasn't going to be enough for a flamenco club, so I did something I'd never done before. I asked Pa for money.

He was, as always, at his desk.

"Pa," I said, carefully.

"Cali, you're blushing like a peach. There isn't trouble?" He frowned

"Aleta and I would like to go see flamenco tonight, and I don't have enough money."

"How much do you have?"

I showed him. Pa looked at my stack with a frown.

"Where did you get this?" he asked.

"From playing at the music tree."

"From only that one time?" Pa looked a little surprised. Then his eyes turned thoughtful.

"Yes, but I've had to spend some and Aleta said it isn't enough."

He sat back in his chair thinking. "Cali, I've made a mistake. We've been buying everything for you, but you need to learn to handle money on your own. I'll give you some money for tonight, but you're going to have to take one of the crew with you. I need to talk to Meara. We need to set an allowance you can budget."

"An allowance?"

"Yes," he said, but then sat back in his chair. "But it has to be for something." Pa talks to himself when he's thinking. "Something you can have complete control over."

"Pa?"

"The money for tonight." He unlocked a drawer and counted out some coins. "This should be plenty." He handed them to me and then pulled down the petty cash ledger. "Technically, you're crew and are entitled to wages and as a co-owner you have your dividends, so really this money is yours. We just have to figure out how much you have so we can deduct it."

"I'm a co-owner?"

"You didn't know? You've had four shares since you were born. You have money in the bank in your name in Boston. It's there in case something happens to your mother and me. So you don't end up in some orphanage while the courts figure out our estate. You could stay in school."

"Oh." The thought of Ma and Pa dying was not a pleasant one. "I'd be really angry with you if you died, Pa. Thank you for the money." I was raised to be polite and a lady of etiquette and grace. I'm a co-owner! It was a strange thought.

"Be careful tonight," Pa said.

Crow agreed to go with us. No better protection in existence.

The streets that night were busier. People, families, couples, were out walking the gas lamp lit sidewalks. Carriages passed by us, most of them horse-drawn. We could hear music coming out of restaurants and clubs all around us. I wanted to go in every one, but Aleta seemed to know where she was going.

"It's supposed to be here," she said, but we could see only doorways and shop windows on a quiet street with two bars.

I was determined not to ask any of the stupid questions people feel obliged to ask. Are you sure about the directions? Are you sure this was the right street? Can you trust a Spanish guitar player who wants under your skirts? No. I, Cali, am above this.

Just then a door opened and a laughing couple came out. From inside, we could hear music.

Aleta said nothing and strode right up to the door, but it had closed and was locked. We knocked, and a man opened it.

"*Si?*," he asked.

Aleta started to walk in, but she was blocked.

"*Solo por invitación*," he said.

"*Alberto nos envió*," Aleta replied. "It's invitation only."

"*Alberto no es bienvenido aqui.*"

"*¿Rechazaría un indio norteamericano?*" Aleta replied. "I told him about Crow."

Crow managed to look very feral and threatening. "*Lo puedo maldecir*," Crow said. The man's eyebrows go up.

"*¿Realmente?*"

"We're from America," I said.

"*Es su guarda espalada,*" Aleta added.

I think it was the gold tooth that did it. He waved us in. It was another basement club.

"Alberto isn't particularly liked, apparently" Aleta said. "Thank you, Crow."

"*De nada*," Crow said.

"You speak Spanish!" I said.

"Not like these people," he replied. "I can't make out half of what they say."

At the bottom of the steps, it was much the same as The Brick. A stage in the center, more tables, less open space. But they had colored glass panels that they put over the lime lights, to tint them so the dancers on stage were fantastically colored. A woman was dancing accompanied by a guitar. Her dress--her dress was indescribable. It flowed around her like water. Bright red, shining in the colored light. Her black high-heeled shoes tapped the floor as they moved, sliding effortlessly across the stage. She had things in her hands which clacked as she moved them around her body in intricate patterns. They creating percussion for the music, moving around it like a frame for a picture!

I was stopped in my tracks. Your poor Cali was a little speechless. This wasn't singing, where the voice is just another instrument. I could match that note for note. No, the entire being of this woman was an instrument! The music rolled out and around her as she moved across the stage.

"Come on," Aleta said. She was pulling me along while I stared. Then she was somehow back, having found a table for us. The dancer's hands traced patterns through the air, like smoke. An old woman, I hadn't noticed, began to sing. Her voice was harsh but strong. I could see the dancer as her, in her youth. She sounded so sad. Then the music stopped and there was only the sound of her feet, the things in her hands, and the audience clapping along. The music built to a crescendo. Then it stopped! She stood there frozen, while the audience erupted in applause.

In the next dance, I watched her feet. They did not connect with the floor in any way that I could see, and yet they were never still. She slid like she was walking in some other world, somehow taping and pounding the floor. They brought us food, which I didn't remember ordering.

"What is this?" I said, looking at my plate.

"I ordered for you," Aleta said. "You wouldn't answer. It's some kind of pork. Try it."

Crow looked amused.

"Her whole body is a musical instrument," I said.

"Sometimes Cali, it's kind of hard to understand you." Aleta frowned. I think she was impatient with me, which as weird. "She's dancing," she said, like I didn't know.

I could only shake my head. I took a bite of these long white things. They were some kind of vegetable. They were good.

The guitar was playing music again. Someone had dragged a chair up on stage and the old woman was playing it like a drum. She made it sound like rattling rain drops. The woman in the beautiful dress was clapping and then there was a man singing. He was wearing black and when he danced, he drew me forward, and forward.

"*Mierda*," Aleta said. I woke.

"What?" Crow said.

I looked around. There, not two tables away, was that same prince. He and his entourage were still dressed in black. I reached for Crow's hand.

"So that's him," Crow said.

His highness, smiling, nodded in our direction. Lucien was there.

I had a hard time eating and enjoying the dancing after that, but I tried. My food was cold. He shouldn't be a problem and my fears were baseless of course – didn't I wish.

At the next break a man from the club came up to me. "*Tenemos una petición para usted jugar*," he said

"He wants you to play," Aleta said.

"I don't have my violin," I replied.

Aleta told him in Spanish, and then he left. It was clear where this came froM. We could hear consternation at Leopold's table, and then the man came back. "*Tenemos una petición para usted jugar*."

"They found you a violin," Aleta said. "Don't do it."

"No," I said to the waiter.

Aleta talked to the man, but he was insistent. I wouldn't budge.

Crow was staring daggers at the prince's table.

Finally I looked the man in front of our table in the eye through my tears and said, "Please."

He was embarrassed and I think I might have seen a little pity too. He nodded and left.

Finally, Lucien came over to our table.

"His Highness wishes to hear you play," he said.

"I can't," I said.

"He has told me to say that he will pay you five thousand pesetas."

I felt myself pull inward. I looked at my plate. I could feel tears, but I managed to make no sound.

There was an angry murmur through the crowd. Crow was about ready to start breaking necks. He was standing, his fists clenched.

Lucien looked at Crow and around at the people and said, "I'm sorry." I could see pain in his eyes too. He retreated back to the prince's table, where we heard hard discussion. Then Leopold was practically dragged out of the restaurant by his men.

Aleta had her arms around me. Crow was standing next to me with his hand on my shoulder saying, "Don't worry."

A buzz of conversation filled the room.

A man came over to our table, I think he was some sort of manager.

"We are so sorry. We didn't know he was a problem. He paid us so much to ask you. And he is the heir to the throne of Belgium after all."

I nodded and tried to calm down. He left. Then the woman in the beautiful dress came over.

"We are sorry," she said. It was an odd accent, almost a lisp, and she spoke slowly.

"I'm sorry," I said. "I should have been calmer. He's been . . ." and then I couldn't talk.

"I know, there are always men," she said. "Some of us are curious though and wouldn't mind hearing you play."

"I can't. Not now."

She put her hand on mine. "Of course," she said, and then left too.

Aleta stood up and said, "Let's go."

I nodded, we picked up our things, and left. The bouncer at the door looked at us sadly and said, "*Buenas noches.*"

"Why can't we get rid of him," I said, as we walked.

"It is odd," Aleta said.

"I bet he's going the same place we are," Crow said.

"Oh God," I moaned. "I'm never leaving the ship. He can have Africa."

So it was an early night for me.

Chapter 12

The Congo

On three hills, looming over the Gran Canarias Harbor, is its aerodrome and it occurred to me that I'd never really been to one. When I mentioned it to Aleta, all she said was, "They are all the same." Does that sound like me and docks?

"But I've never seen one," I replied.

Really, that almost sounded like a whine!

Aleta stopped, and stared up at the hilltops, crowded with airships, like clusters of grapes. She sighed and said, "I suppose everyone should see one – once," and so we set out that afternoon. It was a mile across the city and then the climb up the hills.

We took a steam trolley. Unlike American steam trolleys, Spanish ones have Spanish coalmen, and they don't sing interesting songs to pass the time while they work. No, ours just grunted. How can someone shovel coal while smoking a cigarette? It must be horrible!

The car rattled across the time-smoothed cobbles. We passed squares and shops which were neither as novel nor as interesting as Le Havre nor draped in time as Cadiz, so I won't bore you by describing them. Las Palmas is all work, and yet, there looming over it all, is that great volcano. It became more visible as we moved away and up. Its base was lush and green, dark lava sand beaches, and black rock stretched to either side. Steam trucks chugged by and we rolled past wagons clopping up the hill carrying cargo and people to and from the aerodrome.

The aerodrome's airships loomed over us like a shelf of clouds, blue with altitude and distance. They were all sizes, but I couldn't tell really how big they were because, some higher, some lower, there was nothing to compare them to.

We brought our instruments. After we finished with the aerodrome, we were going to try to play for our supper again. But I was bored and the trolley going up was somewhat empty, so I pulled out my violin and after tinkering with the tuning, played one of the songs I heard on the trolleys back home. Aleta sat back listening.

"That sounds fun," she said. "I've never heard it before. Where did it come from?"

"A coalman," I smiled.

"*Ser Schön*," she smiled back and then she pulled out her flute. "Can you do it again?" she said. We played with it for a bit to pass the time.

"It had words, but I don't remember them." I said, with a frown.

"That's too bad," Aleta said, amused. "You should write them down next time."

"I suppose I should, but the tune was nice and I remembered it. Mrs. Hartnoll hates them."

"Mrs. Hartnoll?" Aleta asked.

"My violin teacher. She likes precision. I play the same music over and over again." I launched into Haydn, sawing at my violin like I do sometimes in class.

Aleta looked at me askance. "She must be a very grouchy woman."

"I suppose she is," I said. When I thought about it, I realized I'd been pretty awful to her.

"Have you tried playing it nicely?" Aleta asked.

"Of course. But it's so self-important and simple as candy. Bach is better." I played part of one of his violin concertos, playing it like I actually cared, fast and jumpy.

Aleta sat back, looking shocked for some reason.

I squinted at her. "It's all technique. The song is so simple. He's just jumping around it, only he does it all for you. Really it's very confining. That's why Mrs. Hartnoll likes it. It's a show-off piece. I mean it may sound nice now, but play it for five years and see how much you like it. I have a folder full of pieces I'm supposed to work on."

"You've been playing that for five years?"

"Oh yes, I think it's been that long. Yes, at least five years on that one. I have an hour of class, two hours of practice most nights, and then sometimes recitals, except Sunday," I said thinking. "I think since I was five. Really, it's either practice or stare at the walls."

"Oh," she said, flatly.

"You have to love private school," I said. "Literally. You have to. Or they make you sing songs until you do!"

That got her smiling again, which made having to play Bach like I cared okay.

We could see the markings on some of the airships and the smoke from their camps. There was *Lufthansa, Aria Europea,* and *Trans America.* Definitely some had coats of arms, although some national flags can look like that as well. Aleta explained that the big companies had permanent buildings with kitchens and quarters, but that the smaller ones had to pitch tents. Clumps of buildings and tents spotted the hilltops, the grass grazed down by the sheep who wandered freely in between.

"Believe me, you get tired of bunking onboard. Even camping on the ground is a pleasure," she said. "Although, after you spend enough time in the air, the ground feels like its rocking more than the airship does," which made sense to me. My bed rocks for weeks when I'm back on shore, but it only makes me homesick.

We pulled into the trolley station at the top, its glass paned roof arching over the platforms, the low sun lighting everything in gold. The platforms were full of people, all shapes and sizes, speaking a dozen different languages. They had come in during the day and wanted to trolley into town for dinner and fun. We were hardly out of our seats before people were pushing past us to take our places. Outside, steam taxis were waiting for fares, but we had no clear destination and little money, so they were useless to us. Above and around were airships, lit by the low afternoon sun, like huge half-moons. The sea breeze keeping them all aligned, the air thick with taut anchor lines.

"This is just about the biggest aerodrome I've ever seen," Aleta said, as she stared upwards. "I've flown all over Europe, but even Berlin, London, and Paris aren't like this."

There had to be at least two hundred airships above us, with even more winched down on the ground. The road we were walking down was dirt, but it was well graded and flat. Of course Lufthansa, being a major carrier, got a spot near the trolley building. We peered in one of their big windows, then entered through the swinging doors in front. Inside their huge waiting room it was light and airy.

"*Guten Tag. Darf ich Ihnen helfen?*" a small trim woman in a crisp uniform said. She was standing behind a counter by the door.

"*Können wir Englisch sprechen?*" Aleta said.

"*Na ja*, I can speak English."

"I used to work here, up until a year and a half ago, and I wondering about some of my friends," Aleta said.

"The crews are all working or are in town."

"Maybe you might know of some?"

"I can try," she said with a smile. "Many pass through here."

"Elsie Grammer?" The Lufthansa lady shook her head no. "Helga Schmitt? Dietrich Grohmann? Lisa Bruce, the Mouse?"

She shook her head until she heard "the Mouse" and then her

eyes went wide. "Oh!" she exclaimed. "She's in hospital in Berlin. It was a fire. She walked right into it."

Aleta's eyes grew wide, "No!" she exclaimed.

"I am told that we had a combusting leak in a ground generator. She got caught between it and a wall."

"Couldn't she see it?" I asked.

"Hydrogen flames are invisible, at least on a small scale like that," Aleta said. "Is she going to be all right?"

"She's been in their burn center for the last six months," the woman said, with a look of concern.

"Oh, Lord," Aleta said, and she backed up until she tripped into a seat. Yes, Lufthansa has padded seats, not benches.

"We read updates about her in the company newsletter."

Aleta's eyes were leaking, "Can I send her a note?" which ended in the beginnings of a sob.

"Of course," and she fetched ink, pen, and paper from a drawer. We pulled over a table, and yes, Lufthansa had tables. Coffee, tea, cookies, and spirits too, the last I wasn't allowed to have. But this was hardly the occasion to be wondering about these things!

Aleta began to write while I ate cookies. She crossed some things out, but mostly it was straight from the heart to paper. I was not sorry that I couldn't read it. It was in German. I really didn't want to know. The worst for me was that I didn't know if I should hug her or not. What should I do? She was hurting. I finally went for it. She was warm and soft, and she sobbed on my shoulder. "She saved my life once," she said. "We were stitching shell cloth. It was a bird flock and I lost my grip and fell," she sobbed. "Lisa stood on the cleat holding my rope for 20 minutes until we were noticed and help arrived."

You couldn't argue with that. We've all saved each other's lives on Red. Well, maybe I haven't saved Crow's yet. But I'd cry if anyone died and so I started to cry too. Yes, it was Cali, miss deportment, thinking about Ed not getting to finish his carvings because he drowned. That was too much for me, I was sobbing next to her. Even the Lufthansa lady looked a little teary.

So, that was Lufthansa.

We calmed down eventually and went back outside. The afternoon breeze blew past us. In the distance, I could see an airship being cranked down for loading. They used big iron steam winches set in the ground. The airships were amazing, but the day was wearing on and we had to work if we wanted our dinner. So! It was back to the trolley hub.

The trolley station was still clogged with people, most dressed for dinner. But what were they thinking? Spaniards don't eat dinner before nine! They clearly knew nothing. They were all going to end up at Alberto's! We bullied our way past the tourists. There was no playing this time on the crowded car. We were clinging to our instrument cases as we bounced down the hill crammed into our seats, people holding on to the sides around us, down the hill past the usual shops and traffic toward the city center. The coalman was still smoking his cigarette, and for some reason he nodded at me.

At the end of the line we left with the crowd, out past the station doors and into the street. Cabs and carriages were waiting, whisking away most. The unlucky rest, like us, fanned out on foot into the streets. Along the sidewalks, the first few walkers were out, alone or with their children, doing their evening business after the heat of the day.

We stopped and listened. Nothing. Not a note drifted in the wind. So we walked toward the center of town. Then we came across a club, but that was just Alberto again and we passed it by. Honestly, he's not that bad, but we had already been there.

The shops grew nicer as we walked and I wanted to look, but Aleta was determined to find it. Somehow I could feel where the center was and pulled her to the right. This street was not as nice, but where I wanted to go was just beyond it. She stopped, and then smiled. We were going the right way. At the next corner we saw people moving to and fro. This was clearly where the locals did their daily shopping. The shops were filled with the practical rather than the interesting. There were vendors on the street. The next street was filled with more people, which led to a square filled with tables and blankets covered in goods. From down a side street, off the square, we heard the roll of music.

Every city has a tree. Maybe it's twenty, a hundred, or even a thousand years old. Maybe it's the hundredth generation of its kind. Like stone walls there's really no telling. Under it they sit, playing their music, talking to each other through their instruments or their voices. Passing the wisdom of millennia on to each other and sometimes, with the grace of their skill, their audience. I could see a dozen or so sitting around it and seven playing.

But we were new and so had to wait, standing at the edge of the crowd. The musicians were clearly curious for we were foreign, and perhaps even exotic. We could be rank amateurs who would spoil the evening's take, or a new breeze of ideas. Complete unknowns. I wondered if there was a Robert here. Strangely, some in the audience seemed to recognize us. "*¡Permitan que toquen!*" they called. The day just got stranger, I thought, but believe me, that wasn't the end.

The calls grew, and so they made room for us. "*¿Debes conocerlos?*" one said to me as I was rosining my bow. Don't ask me. I don't know Spanish.

"*Yo no puedo pensar por qué no,*" Aleta said. I could only sigh. Really I was clueless. Maybe they could teach me Spanish back at school if I asked.

They started into some folk song. The chord progression was easy and I rolled my eyes at Aleta as we danced around it. Aleta was jumping on their notes. She gave me a wicked smile between breaths. I thought that she was still a little broken up about her friend and in a mean mood.

One of the players, a little exasperated, said, "*¿Entonces qué quiere jugar?*"

"He's giving us a choice of songs. How about that slave song? That should shake them up," she said.

I smiled. I hadn't given it much thought, but there were so many possibilities in that simple tune. I started off with a long deep drawl, then took the beat forward at a vigorous clip. Aleta leapt up and danced along like a child skipping. She was a rabbit and I was a bear, my violin drawling then dancing around, batting at her. The other musicians listened transfixed as we wove back and forth, and then one tried to pick it up. He stumbled and bounced then caught the dirt under his feet and there he was beside us. His guitar was sweet, adding sideways motion. Then a bass and the color was deeper like cool water or sleep.

We were bouncing around until there came a dissonant note. Someone new. It's a wolf or a fox and it wanted to pounce, to make us stop. He dove through us like a hawk and then we went around and around, again and again drifting with the difference until we are standing there, standing in the square and people were applauding and I saw money in my violin case.

We went on like this until eventually Aleta made everyone stop and forced me to play Bach. Bach! In the town square. Can you believe it? The entire square was silent. But it brought in the money. So that's how we got our dinner money. Not that we had to pay for dinner. Some of the local well-to-dos paid for it for us. They raised their glasses to us from their table across the room.

I showed Pa my pile of coins. They were wrapped up in some paper fliers. I had no place to keep it. His eyebrows went up and he looked at me thoughtfully. Really, my parents have been doing that a lot lately! I wish they'd let me in on the joke. "I'll convert it to paper. You'll have no problem then." He handed me some bills, 210 pesetas, and a very much smaller pile of coins. My first personal encounter with paper money. Ma had always carried it for me. My first thought was that it was beautiful. The print was so fine and the feel of the paper was strange, not quite like paper. I wasn't sure what I'd do with it. Maybe it was enough to get some earrings like Aleta.

But we lived on a ship and there are always chores to be done and watches to stand. I showed Aleta how to splice and fret rope while we sat on deck with everyone on shore having fun. Then we practiced trying to push each other over, which was part of self-defense. Balance or something. I finished Dracula. I was really looking forward to Aleta's opinions. Oh, and it was really such a pity about Lucy in the end and, of course, the Count's escape (wicked smile). We played one more time at the tree before we left, and there was no hesitation from the other musicians about letting us in. Then, back to sea we went in beautiful weather and silver spray as our bow cut through the blue swells.

And there we were. As ready for Africa as we would ever be.

We stayed away from the coast, far out to sea, as we headed south toward Boma. The coast was full of reefs, pirates, warships, and all sorts of trouble. But luckily, thanks to Pa's notes and charts we saw nothing but dolphins, birds, and schools of fish.

On the second day out we hit a squall. Really, it was only a squall, but it was Aleta's first storm and she was impressed. Below decks she steered wide of the masts as they worked in their steps, shifting back and forth with each roll. Their grinding can be fearsome loud, but the rigging was all well and set and this was normal. We took turns pumping, but Red's a tight ship and it was really unnecessary. We were just getting ahead of the next day's work.

Aleta and I clomped around amidships in our big japara coats watching the waves break across the bow. We were in the middle of hurricane season and somewhere, out in the middle of the deeps, there was a whopper building steam, heading for Cuba. This was only one of its babies.

Finally the day came when we were eating breakfast and Tinker said to me, "Did you see the coast?"

"We can see the coast?"

"As clear as church bells on Sunday."

Aleta and I looked at each other, then we grabbed our plates and headed up on deck. The morning sun was bright and the air already a little humid. Pa was there with his telescope looking at the shore. To me it looked like a dark flat strip on the horizon. No hills or mountains.

"Looks swampy," I said.

"It is," he replied with a shrug. "It seems to be all jungle. Boma is, I think, about 20 miles south."

"Boma," I repeated.

I don't know why that word took the luster out of the morning.

We were heading for a big river, the Congo River. The Congo is all about the Congo River. It leads everywhere, like the Mississippi in America, the Nile in Egypt, and the Volga in Russia. Boma itself is 10 miles inland. Getting into a river port like Boma is all about the breeze. We needed enough sea breeze to beat the river current and make headway.

That day was perfect. We had great sailing weather, the wind coming in strong offshore. We would have no trouble.

The water at the mouth was deep, a deep blue turning green and the breeze warm and fresh. The shore was just swampy grassland.

"We'll need to break out the mosquito netting," Pa said. The shore looked interesting to me, although a boat could get lost in all those reeds, but he was looking at it with a critical eye. "We may need to keep some of that insecticide for ourselves too," he said quietly.

The shore closed in around us, the river immense, miles wide, at its mouth. The grass and reeds come up in bits at the edges, then thickened with breaks for little rivers and streams in between. But that was all far away, the channel was so wide. The river current was slow at the mouth, and balancing the current against the wind was easy. Still, it would take us most of the day to get through those ten miles to Boma.

We passed a skow, dirty and a little disreputable, going downstream, flying British colors. They did not wave, but they were low in the water with cargo which was encouraging. They were breaking with sail, which was important to remember. We could leave the same way.

Back from the water, between the tall grass, we could sometimes see villages built on stilts. It must be awful living in a swamp, but there had to be profit in it or they wouldn't be there. Then I saw something big slide into the water. I hadn't noticed it until it moved. By the time I looked, it was gone. Then, it happened again. They must be crocodiles, I thought.

Then, with a splash, we were surrounded by dolphins leaping from the water. They were shorter than those in the ocean and had long, long snouts like a swordfish. They were colored brown too, not blue. But they acted just like dolphins everywhere and they raced around and around us until they became bored. Then it was off as they went to look for a new toy. Birds flew over us that looked like giant herons. They worked their way into the air on their great wings with lazy slowness.

I realized that I'd been gawking and looking around the deck and realized everyone else was too, which wasn't good. Mackie was at the wheel. I hopped back up on the sterncastle and then up onto the stern deckhouse roof, sitting down cross-legged facing him.

"How deep's the river?" I asked.

He gave me a half smile and said, "It'd be nice to know, wouldn't it?" He thought for a moment and then called, "Ed, take a sounding!," and then he muttered to himself, "We're in a river, should have been doin' that all along. We don't know the channel," and then louder, "Tinker, get our speed."

We were going to find our water speed, which gives us the current. For this we use the log. Tinker hauled out the log box from down below. Inside is a big spool of string attached to a little triangle of wood--a quarter off the bottom of an old keg--called a chip, and a little hourglass. Aleta seemed interested so I said, "let's go watch," and we hopped up onto the stern and followed Tinker.

"It's really simple," Tinker said carefully. I had the feeling he had eyes for Aleta. "We toss the chip in the water and turn the sand glass. When the glass is empty, we reel the string back counting the knots."

"The chip stays still while we move," I added.

Aleta nodded, but she looked confused. There's no better way to learn than by doing so we gave her the chip and the glass. "Drop the chip in the water, then flip the glass," I said. She did, then Tinker played out string. We watched the sand grains fall, making a little pit in the center, falling down to the bottom in little waves. We were staring at it when we heard a "kerplunk" in the water and Tinker's line began to run out by itself! He grabbed it and tried to hold it back. Back from the bow I could hear Ed call six fathoms. He'd been dropping the sounding line. Tinker dropped the spool and gripped the string instead.

"What is it?" Aleta asked.

"Looks like you've hooked something," Ian said, who'd come up behind us and was looking over our shoulders.

"The chip's gone," I added.

"I know that!" Tinker snapped. He was flustered. He was letting out line for fear it would break. The pull was fierce! Luckily, we had a big spool of it. Then he was playing the line, being careful; because this wasn't fishing line. Suddenly, it went slack. We all stood there for a confused second and then Tinker shook himself and began to reel it back in.

"That's not how it's supposed to work," I told Aleta.

"That's pretty obvious," she said with a smile.

The end of the line looked like it had been sliced with a knife.

"Lovely," Ian said, staring at the end. "What kind of teeth do that?"

"I think we should stay out of the water," Aleta said, restraining a smile. I love her humor.

"Might be a good idea," I added, and then, "We're going to need a new chip." Ed called seven fathoms from the bow. That's one deep river, I thought.

Up ahead was a fork around an island. Okay, I admit it, I'm a little out of my depth in rivers. Another Cali joke. But really, seamanship 101, one side of a fork is always shallow, the other deep. But the Congo was so big that that might not matter. And the charts were no help because rivers shift all the time. Boma was somewhere on the other side, or maybe down one side or the other. So we were holding position, trying to decide, but the wind kept shifting. The land breaks up the breeze this far inland and it can't be trusted, so we couldn't safely keep station.

"Wider is shallower," Mackie said.

"I think we should tack back and forth and try to measure the current," I suggested.

"Best to call your pa," Mackie said to me.

What we needed was a ship coming down channel to use as a guide. That skow for instance. There had been many choices as we'd come upriver, but this was the first time the main channel wasn't obvious and we were so close to Boma. Both looked inviting.

Then as I was calling below for Pa when I heard a call from behind me, "*Ahoi!*" Well actually, we heard ahoy with a German accent. So intent were we on the channels in front of us that a motor launch had snuck up behind us. It was the port pilot!

"Hello," we called back.

"*Wir kommen Gehilfe!*" the voice said.

"German, in Belgian Congo?" we all thought, except of course for Aleta.

"They want to come aside," she called from the bow. "They're harbor pilots."

Mackie busts out laughing with relief. "Drop the ladder!" he called.

The pilot boat was a small, open-decked steamer, it's engine pushed rocker pistons up and down as it labored to keep up. It carried only the pilot and two crew, none in uniform. As they crossed abaft of us, their grey wood smoke crossed our deck. I noticed that they were stoking the boiler with wood!

They dropped off the pilot and pulled away. Aleta had to translate, not that you really need to with pilots. We all know what to do. It turned out the smaller channel on the left is the one, just in case you're crazy enough to want to sail to Boma.

The docks reminded me of Jamaica. They were small, wooden, with none of the normal amenities, like dry docks or cranes. A straight line of rough wood dock backed by dusty dirt and ramshackle warehouses, sided by cleared mud beaches with boats on them, or at least old hulls and hulks. Most looked like they'd been sitting there awhile. This was definitely not Jamaica.

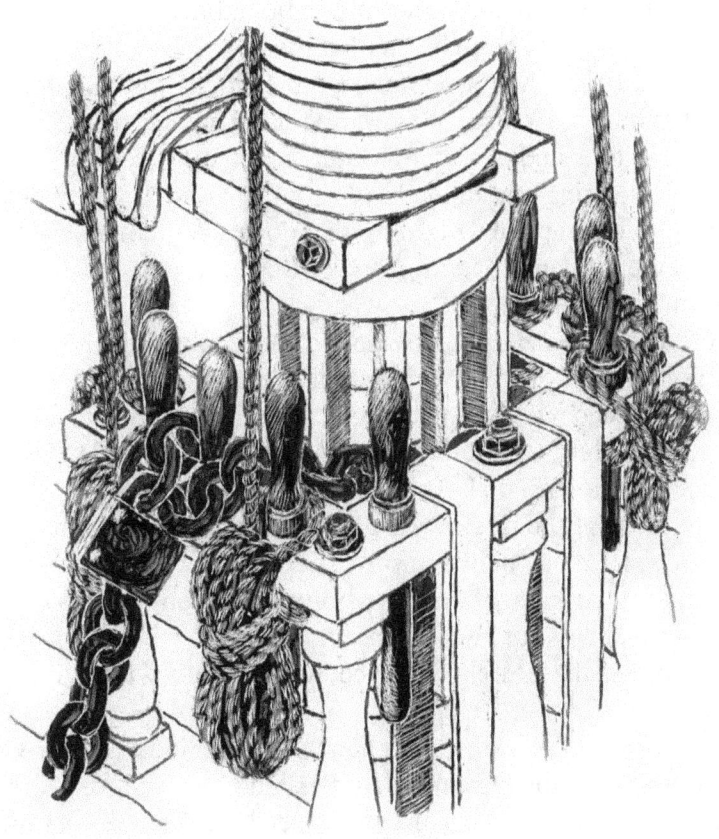

Chapter 13

Interred

No tugs. We docked ourselves. This would be impossible if the wind weren't with us. Maybe it always blows that way. I only have the experience of my one trip, and I'm not going back. We counted four ships in port, two British, one Dutch, and one wreck. The Dutchman had been docked for too long. She was a mess. Her yards weren't even crossed. Someone had been working on a sail. It was spread across the deck, with no sign of anyone on watch.

The wreck, a ketch, was on the bottom, still moored to the dock. Her deck was half under water, masts tipped toward the river, sails gone. Both the Brits were hives of activity.

Pa eyed the river's depth near the docks with doubt in his eyes. It would be close. When we finally managed to dock, we only had a foot and a half of water under our keel. Not a lot of leeway for loading and unloading.

The pilot hopped off onto the dock the moment we were within three feet and made for one of the buildings, without asking for payment.

We could see cargo moving on the docks. Black men were moving it on and off the British ships, supervised by black soldiers with rifles, who were in turn supervised by two white men with pistols. The white men, of course, got to sit in the shade. The black men were all thin as sticks, both soldiers and workers.

The Brits at the dock were a lugger and a yawl. Both are good coastal carriers, but neither up to deep water routes, which made me wonder where they could possibly have been bound. The Gold Coast, maybe? That would be a difficult run. And still no movement on the Dutchman! She was a snow with a high hull, light in the water too. No cargo.

The whole harbor was practically deserted. No movement anywhere except for the cargo handlers and their guards. No traffic at all, with only dust and dirt that stretching between us and the warehouses. The far shore of the river, a half mile away at this point, was flat swamp giving way to low jungle. Both up and down river in the distance were low hills that look oddly barren. That was it, except for the wind, the gulls, and the occasional dust devil. Pa made for the harbormaster's office while we pulled open the hold. There had been no inspection yet, so we figured it would come later. He took Aleta with him because she spoke German, which was what they seem to speak here, at least the pilot did. I wasn't jealous. This time I mean it. Boma gave me the creeps.

Mackie leaned on the rail next to me on the stern castle and we stared at the blacks working. "This isn't the worst I've seen," he said. That was hard to believe. "This looks like a company town. They may not give us fair prices. Might try to load us down with fees too. We'll have to wait and see."

Pa came back furious and said the harbormaster was passed

out drunk, but his assistant would be down shortly to look at our holds. So we waited.

"The office was awful," Aleta told me, when we were alone. "They'd been drinking rum, everything was dirty, papers and stuff stacked about."

"What did they say? Did they explain?"

"I don't know. They spoke French to us. Your father did all the talking."

We waited two hours. When he finally showed up, the assistant was red-eyed, unshaven, unwashed, and stank of drink. The first words out of his mouth were, *"Puis-je avoir de l'eau fraîche s'il vous plaît?"* He wanted water, which he gulped down. All he spoke was French and Dutch so Pa settled on French, which I will translate for you.

"We are short of water," he said after he had drained the tankard.

"But surely there's so much of it about," Pa said.

"All infested with parasites and we have no wood to boil it." He wiped his mouth on his filthy sleeve.

"But there are trees," Pa said.

"And no one to cut them. The natives run away or die."

"Die?" Pa frowned.

"There's no way to explain. Either starvation or the heat."

"So you're short of food?"

"We are short of everything, even bullets to shoot them when they run."

"But you do have rubber?"

"Oh, yes." He smiled. "We have rubber. But what have you brought us?" and then they were lost in manifests and trade.

That night, Pa doubled the watches. We stood in pairs, a night watch for each of us. Between that and the heat, I didn't get much sleep. Ma made coffee in the morning and set the pot in the bilge to cool before serving it. It was too hot out for hot coffee. We had hard bread, canned peaches, and fried dry sausage, since we didn't have fresh food from shore.

Time passes slowly when you're uncomfortable. It crawled past for us with no action from shore. Since we seemed to have the time to spare, Pa, Aleta, and I went to visit the Dutchman. None of us spoke Dutch, but Pa thought it likely that they would speak

English, French, or German, or as Mackie put it, "Some mess of all three." Apparently, as Mrs. Claveloux might have put it, they had some odd dialects.

The dock was dusty, blowing away in gray streams under our feet as we walked. Everything was so quiet, it was quite unnerving. When we got to her we could see that she'd been chained to the dock. They had been impounded, which made Pa's mood all that much grimmer. The gangplank was down. As I crossed, I looked down at her hull. It was thick with weeds. She needed cleaning and sea salt. How long had she been sitting there? No one was on watch, the deck covered with gear. It looked like someone had been trying to patch a sail, but from the dust and dried dirt, caked on by rain, it had been sitting untouched for a long time.

Pa called, "Ahoy!" but there was no answer. The companionway hatch was ajar, slowly creaking back and forth in the breeze. Below was a mess as well, the crew gone. The captain's cabin had been emptied. She'd been abandoned.

So we spent the day back on our ship. No cargo moved. We did chores. Since food and water were short in Boma (non-existent really) we inspected and inventoried our supplies. Mackie said we could make it back to the Canaries, but I would be a sad, much thinner Cali when we arrived. If we were going to stay docked in Boma for any length of time, then we were going to need supplies, at least fuel to boil water. That or rain.

So, we didn't have time to waste, but that was all the dock master seemed to want to do. The next day was no different. I heard Mackie and Pa, in Pa's office. "Did he take the bribe?" Mackie said.

"Of course, but it seems to have done no good," Pa said quietly.

"I say, leave while we can, or we'll end up like the Dutchman." Mackie's voice was a hoarse whisper.

"The Brits are moving cargo."

"You know why."

"Maybe they can help. We have a British charter after all."

Mackie just grunted.

Honestly, I didn't mean to listen, but there's little privacy on a ship. That morning, Pa paid a visit to the nearest Brit and came back looking grim. "When's the tide shift?" Pa called to Mackie as he came up the plank.

"It's ebb now. Six hours down river. We pull out right now or tonight."

Pa sighed. "Tonight, then."

It was a bad choice, because the soldiers came at dinnertime.

They were all black, except for the two white officers. They wore a motley array of uniforms and tatters, carrying mismatched guns. Two even had muskets. But there were twenty of them and we didn't have but a revolver and a rifle between us, which were locked in Ma and Pa's cabin. There was nothing we could have done, so we put up our hands. Poor Wally was in the head when they rousted him out. They chained Red to the dock with thick chains, looping them around our masts, and then ate our meal while we were hauled off to a dingy warehouse, me with no shoes.

We sat on crates while the soldiers milled about jabbering in who knows what language, their supervising officers gone. When we asked them for water, using signs and motions with our hands, we were pushed roughly back to the boxes. So we sat, Ma resting her head on Pa's shoulder and stared at the flickering shadows from our one lamp.

As the night wore on, some of the soldiers curled up on the floor and slept. I thought this was very brave of them, or perhaps desperate, as we could see rats scurrying behind crates and in the corners. It was completely dark except for our little island of light and the moon coming in the windows. Mackie and Tinker found two crates that were the same size and pushed them together. Motioning to Aleta and me, Mackie said, "Get some sleep." We tried, but it wasn't easy. I may have slept, but we had a very long, very hot night.

At one point I thought I heard Ma crying quietly to herself. I could see her curled up in Pa's arms sitting on the floor with their backs to their crate. The worst of the whole experience was having to use the dark corner as a toilet while a soldier watched, rats scurrying around and all and me with bare feet, but they left us no choice. Every time we stood up to ask for something or try to talk to them, they pushed us back down, pointing their guns.

In the morning we were all so tired and hungry, but most of

all, so thirsty, our captors as well as us, although they were able to leave in shifts. The warehouse was hot and getting hotter with biting bugs everywhere. I was uselessly trying to cough out dust, my throat was so dry. I had an awful headache, my eyes were sticky, and my lips were dry wanting to crack.

We saw the sun rise though the glassless windows, the sky turning gray, then blue, then green, and then orange. The time crawled by like that. I saw the sun's first rays touch the top mast on Red as she sat at the dock, my head resting on Aleta's arm. Red looked trim, clean, and beautiful. At least they put two guards at her gangway. I wondered if we would ever sail her again. Me and my stupid ideas. Africa!

As the sun rose, the heat rose with it, drifting from uncomfortable to unbearable, until it became something unreal. It can't be described. Everyone sat and worked on breathing. Even the rats seemed to have left. Then along about midday we heard commotion outside. I was too thirsty and miserable to look. I could only lay there, enduring.

"You were told to detain them, not *something* them!" someone yelled. He was speaking French I realized. Whoever was giving commands said, "Take him away. Put him under arrest." More commotion. And then the door opened and in strode Lucien in his spotless black uniform. Behind him came a half dozen proper soldiers in clean black and white uniforms.

Lucien's eyes darted quickly around and then locked on me. I swear that at least half a dozen expressions crossed his face in that instant. He finally settled on stern. He reached his hand back toward one of his soldiers and snapped his fingers. "Water," he said. The soldier unclipped his polished canteen and passed it forward. As he reached back to take it Lucien said, "Find water for them all. Quickly."

We were back on Red. We could barely stay on our feet. At first we drank our water sparingly, but then greedily. Lucien had given me the first drink. Someone was preparing us a meal in the galley. It wasn't me, and Ma was sick in bed. I will again swear for the last time, I promise, that we should just give up and open Red up as a hospital ship. Between sickness and injury, it had to be a calling. The meal was good, brought to us by Lucien's soldiers. It was some kind of stew – and oranges! The oranges hurt my mouth, but they tasted so good. I love oranges. And then, for some reason, the assistant harbormaster was sober, bathed, and ready to move cargo.

Those of us who could stand were sitting in the galley. Crow gave me the eye as we ate. "He was that nob from the club wasn't he?" he asked.

"Yes," I said, eyes on my plate.

"This is about that Belgian prince, isn't it?" added Pa.

"Yes."

The meal was very quiet after that.

That night we had a meeting, in whispers. There were guards on deck who could overhear so Pa posted Ian on deck watch above us. He would tap on the galley stovepipe with his ring if he could hear us.

"So what do you think of the chains?" Pa asked Tinker.

"They're anchor chains. Probably off those ships. There's three and we only have two saws."

"We've got three files," added Mackie. "What do you think Ed, maybe an hour?"

"Yeah, if we could work together, uninterrupted," Ed said. His eyes said more.

Pa knew. "We couldn't hold them off that long if they wanted back on," he said. "They can sweep the decks from the warehouse tops, and there isn't a thing we could do about it." Then he stopped to rub his eyes. "The funny thing is," he continued. "They didn't take our guns." There was a general look of surprise. "Or the safe either. But even with the guards' guns added, it wouldn't be enough."

"Someone would get killed for sure," Mackie said.

"That nob that pulled us out of the warehouse. He seems to be in a different faction," Tinker said.

"Lucien?" I offered.

"Is that his name?" Pa asked.

"Lucien Antoine."

"He's the one who speaks for that prince," Crow said. "Maybe we can use him."

"I think he's on our side," I said.

141

Pa gave me another odd glance, then added. "We need to find out more about who we're dealing with. And I think I have some ideas about how to go about it."

It's a sad fact, but the nabbing of merchantmen is a fairly common practice in the world as a whole and we have insurance that covers it. I should say, it would probably cover it, after a year or so of investigation and a court hearing or two, probably somewhere far away like London or Brussels. But in the end Red would be gone forever along with everything we hold dear. The British are especially notorious for it, but most countries treat their merchantmen like wheat, something to be reaped as a whole with losses here and there to be expected. No one would miss Red but us. We were completely alone and on our own.

The next morning a line of dock workers arrived. All horribly thin, just like we'd seen working on the British ships, guards and all, followed by the assistant harbormaster. He walked right up the gangway asking no permission, requesting to see the captain of the ship. Pa came up from below to meet him on deck. We were not going to offer hospitality.

"I have been ordered to offer every assistance," he said to Pa.

I knew Pa was hurting, but he stood tall. "Then you're going to remove the chains?" he asked.

The assistant harbormaster shook his head and replied, "Every assistance but that, at least for the moment."

"And may I ask . . ."

"Hold it right there!" yelled Mackie, walking quickly to the gangway. A long line of workers had started to follow the assistant harbormaster onboard, only to be stopped as Mackie blocked their way.

"They are here to unload your cargo, as we agreed," the assistant said to Mackie.

"We work our own holds," Mackie said, angrily.

The guards behind the workers were looking agitated and began yelling and pushing the workers forward.

"Tell them to stop," Pa said, to the assistant.

The assistant called out to them in their language and they quieted. "Captain Carmichael, I am a bit confused."

"We load and unload our own ship," Pa replied.

"Why would you do that when we have blacks?"

Pa was, for a moment, at a loss for words. "Just trust us on this, we'll unload. You can take it from the docks." We do not support slave or indentured labor. Especially labor so badly mistreated.

"This makes no sense," the assistant harbormaster replied.

"Why are we chained to the dock?" Pa asked, ignoring his response.

The assistant yelled something at the workers and their guards and they began to back away. "It is a standing order. We are to impound all non-association ships."

"We have a charter from the British Trade Ministry."

"This port is administered by the *Association Internationale du Congo*, not the British Government."

"Aren't these British ships?"

"They are, but they work under the Association. You will have to take that up with the Association administrator, Sir Nigel Prendergast."

"He sounds British," Pa replied.

"He is," the man replied.

"Could the harbormaster help?" Pa asked.

"I'm the new harbormaster." He did not seem to relish the promotion.

"What happened to the old one?"

"He's been arrested. He made some unfortunate choices."

"And who does Sir Nigel Prendergast work for, if not the British?"

"He works for His Highness, Prince Leopold," he replied with impatience.

"I see," Pa said. Frankly, I didn't. But I did understand the important part. We were impounded by the order of His Highness.

Weak as we were, we moved our cargo to the dock ourselves. We had to take it slow because we'd had some bad days. In my case the bottoms of my feet were burned, but my boots and my thickest socks made it tolerable. The dock workers took the cargo from the pallets and carried it away on their backs, like a line of malnourished ants. They had no wagons.

When our trade goods arrived, our African cargo, it was so

new and different! The rubber came in rough spun bags filled with fist sized black balls. It stacked easily, like grain, but lighter and it didn't sag in the stack, which made it easier to load. We piled the ivory, some of it still bloody, in stacks, like wood. They also had some sort of tree bark that was used for medicine, which we tucked into empty corners.

Oh, but I have to tell you about the pelts! Captain Cavanaugh was so right. They were amazing in their color and variety. Stripes, spots, yellows, oranges, and even black and white! All of it had short hair, except for one which had a big shaggy head. The harbormaster called it a lion, and there were absolutely huge immensely thick gray skins, which were delivered in big stiff rolls.

Our provisions were less interesting. They were delivered unasked for. The Congo has no coal, so we took on wood instead. They just stacked it on the dock for us. It was fresh cut and still wet, which meant it wouldn't burn well. We left it on deck to sit in the sun and worked it in with our own coal. For food they gave us dried bush meat, odd sorts of beans, and thick roots, thicker than carrots, that were supposed to boil well. We had eggs too. Not chicken eggs, but smaller. Still not bad. Oh, and also some unidentifiable leafy vegetables. Everything had to be boiled and was rather bland. Our 80 tons of grain vanished into the city. Perhaps, we hoped, we could buy some of it back as flour.

All this good fortune didn't come for free, and the price arrived the next day in the form of Lucien bearing two invitations, one for Aleta and one for me, to a ball--a ball in this jungle--in ten days! Ten more days at dock in Boma. In case you were thinking that we could just turn this down, I should remind you, Red was still chained to the dock.

It's not that we didn't try.

"We have nothing to wear," Aleta said, as if that settled it.

"Or any way to work with our hair," I added.

A small half smile leaked out of Lucien's face, but was quickly hidden under that veneer of formality. "Of course. We understand," he said. "Tomorrow after breakfast you will visit the dressmaker. We have it all accounted for. Fear not."

"Even shoes?" I asked.

"Even shoes," he replied.

"Lucien, when are they going to unlock Red?" I asked.

"I told you to stay away," he said. "You're going to have to play his game, at least for the time being."

"I thought I could stay onboard. That we would be lost in the harbor traffic. And I couldn't toss the entire year's profit in the sea. It wasn't mine to lose."

Aleta turned on me. "You knew he was here?" Aleta snapped.

"Yes!" I snapped back.

"You should have said something!"

"And then what? Turn around? It was always all about Boma. Everything depended on it."

She frowned. "We could've thought of something."

"What? Our cargo is worthless anywhere but here!" I yelled, and then clomped off on my padded hurting feet and plunked down with my back to them on a crate half full of tar bricks.

Lucien frowned, and then looked thoughtful.

"What?" Aleta asked.

"Just a stray thought." There was another ghost of a smile. "Until tomorrow then?"

You won't understand what I'm going to tell you, at least not yet. But I'm going to try anyway. If there is a human hell on Earth, then Boma is in the next berth down. It sounds trite doesn't it? There are many trite sayings about the Congo. Perhaps you will, in time, come to understand them all.

The docks, the warehouses, seemed like hell on Earth to me then. I knew nothing. The harbor itself was ringed by a wood palisade, patrolled inside and out by what I later learned were colonial soldiers or militia, as opposed to those with Lucien who were imperial soldiers. Colonials were black, led by whites. Imperials were all white and properly equipped. At the time, it was probably best that I could see little beyond the harbor walls or I would have panicked then and there. It was a blessing that it came to me slowly, in little bits.

Pa had been pacing and running his hands through his hair all morning, which he does when he's worried. When the time came to go see the dressmaker, he gave us both big hugs before we walked down the gangway. Aleta and I walked across the dirt toward the gate, raising little puffs of dust with each step. The sea

145

breeze was down and the air muggy. I wore my day dress by the way, not my good dress, spots and stains and all. This was hardly the occasion for celebration or formality. And I wasn't in a good mood.

Above the wood palisade, as we approached the gate, I could see black ribbons of smoke from a thousand open fires drifting up into a general brown haze. I felt like I was walking to my death. The worst was that that day, of all days, was my birthday! Did I tell you? No? Well, now you know. And so far, it hadn't started out well.

Outside the gate, which was opened by militia, Lucien had a carriage waiting. A horse carriage, not steam by the way, and it needed a lot of work. It had peeling paint, worn and broken upholstery, dry wood, and dark rusting iron, but it all seemed to be working. The drivers were black. They wore no livery, but instead worn but serviceable work clothes. The horses at least appeared well kept and healthy.

The brown dust street outside the gate was empty of people, with only Lucien and four mounted imperials waiting for us. He was dressed like his guardsmen, in a black uniform, a bit dusty and careworn. I looked around the street. The dirt must turn to brown mud soup when it rains, I thought.

Lucien clicked his heels and bowed. Aleta immediately went into a curtsy, which threw me for a moment, and then I followed quite awkwardly, which brought a friendly snort and a smile from Lucien.

"Good morning, dear ladies," he said, his voice sounding loud in the empty air. "We have a busy schedule today. I'm afraid this is the best we can do for transportation. This climate is very hard on equipment and what we have is always in use."

The houses on the street were low and ramshackle, made of rough split wood, piled together and held in place with leaning stones and woven cords. They had no glass in their windows. Obviously, the harbor district was where the poor lived, but the bits I could see beyond looked no better. I could see thin black figures down the streets, but none near us. It was dead still as we clopped and clattered down the dirt road. Then a door creaked open and an old black women looked out. She was missing a hand, which was sad. She saw us and fell back, pulling the door shut quickly.

Lucien and I were sitting in the back facing forward. Aleta was sitting opposite us facing back. Lucien was silent as we rode. He seemed to not notice the old woman. He was watching us instead, which was puzzling. Then I saw Aleta's look of astonishment as she looked behind us over our shoulders. I turned to look back too. Black stick figures were dashing out into the street, fighting over the dung left by the horses in the street. Some of them were missing hands too. It was such a strange sight that I was stunned to confusion.

"What happened to their hands?" Aleta asked. She leveled her eyes at Lucien.

Lucien had been collecting his thoughts. He'd been expecting this. I could see a great deal of conflict in his expression. "There was a rebellion which was put down cruelly. You'll see a lot of them here in town. Former rebels."

"Cutting off their hands. That's somewhat extreme," Aleta said.

"Yes, and wasteful. Now they can't work. They just starve." Lucien was looking at anything except the city and us. Then he turned back, glanced at each of us in turn and said, "I suggest that you not bring up the subject with him, or anyone else we meet. Discuss it with your shipmates if you want. They'll be seeing it soon enough."

"His highness, you mean," Aleta said.

"Yes. The king himself ordered it, but his highness did nothing to stop it. He is very indifferent to the feelings of others. We must be careful if we are to get you both and your ship back to the ocean." Then he glanced our way again and saw two women struck wide-eyed with fear.

He feigned surprise drifting to amusement. "Don't worry, at least not that much. Today, we'll have fun. New clothes and some pampering. We have to get you ready for your introduction. Introduction to court is a huge event for most women. It's a shame we don't have the resources to do it properly here."

Introduction to court? I looked at Lucien, trying to read him. Did he really want us back in the sea?

Aleta wasn't falling for it. "Lucien, you can't mean that," she said, flatly. "There's no court here and we aren't noble."

"Nobility isn't necessary, at least not in this case," he said, with a touch of bitterness. "And court is wherever he is. To His Highness, the Congo is more his home than Brussels."

To be frank, "introduction to court" sounded like an execution to me, but I said nothing. Aleta too, seemed to be ready to let the subject drop. We had no choice. And the sight of the city itself was enough to stop any conversation.

We clopped on, the land slowly rising as we tipped and rolled about the uneven rutted dirt alleys. Boma was less a city than a vast poorhouse with shack after shack lining fetid dirt paths crossed with stinking ditches, all of it the same shade of dusty brown. We passed wells with lines of people who scattered as we approached.

There was always the lingering smell of human waste and burning wood, with lines of smoke rising in thin trails above the expanse of roofs to drift with the thin sea breeze. The town and the jungle merged at its edges as if the consumption of trees had yet to catch up with the growth of the city. Then again, I thought, perhaps the cutting of wood was regulated, at least in the richer districts.

About a quarter mile away, through the trees ahead, I could see the tops of airships, and amongst the trees, the proper smokestacks of better homes.

Lucien, for the most part, just sat and stared off into space, deep in thought.

As we neared the trees, things did improve. Mud brick walls, windows with shutters, tin chimneys, and then curbs with gutters. Trees arched over us that lent shade. Even a horse carriage or two with white people dressed in white. Then we stopped at a shop with a real glass window and a real door. In the window were bolts of cloth with various colorful patterns. The color was dazzling after all the dirty brown.

Lucien was up and stepped down to the street before we realized that we had stopped. I felt numb.

"Dear ladies," he said, and again held out his hand, with an honest smile, to help us step down.

We each said thank you as we stepped down to the curb. The shady sidewalk was stone-edged clean packed clay. A bell jingled as we entered the cloth shop. Inside, it had two more large-paned windows letting in light that fell over long work tables snug against the walls under them. In the back were shuttered doors that opened on a small courtyard filled with green shade. Sitting on benches were black women, stitching and sewing. One of them got up and came forward with a pleasant smile. She was slight with graying hair pulled back in a neat frizzy ponytail.

Chapter 14

My Birthday

"What have you brought Omama today, Lucien? Are these the ones?" Her accent was deep and slow. Strangely, it sounded Jamaican, and she spoke English. Not African at all.

"Yes, they are, and you're to take good care of them. They have a ball to attend."

She walked around us tisking. "Do you dears have your own foundation garments?"

I was a bit stumped by this. Foundation garments? But Aleta came to the rescue. "No, I'm afraid not. We've been aboard ship for some time. It's a pleasure to meet you by the way."

"Yes, a pleasure," I added. I was still confused and tried to curtsy and made a complete wreck of it.

"You must be the American," she said, eyeing me. "Nice color. You both have good complexions, but too much sun to be fashionable. It's helped the color of your hair though," she said to me again, running it through her fingers. "Makeup may be of some help here. We will see." Then she turned on Lucien. "Lucien, we have no stay wire or proper boning available. I asked for it, but it hasn't arrived. What am I going to do for corsets?"

"I think they're very nice without them," he replied. My opinion of Lucien went up.

"It won't do," she replied, with a half-smile.

"Then you'll do what we all do and that's make do. If you need it, adapt something. Maybe we can pry something off that old ship. Barrel rings maybe? They seem appropriate," he said with a smile. I think he was laughing to himself.

"I'll need a smith who can work steel. Anton?" she said. She wasn't to be distracted.

"Anton won't work cheap, not for us," Lucien replied.

"Then we need to enlist someone he owes," Omama said, pressing forward.

"That's a short list," Lucien thought. "But I may have some ideas."

"You always do," she said. "How high will the heels be?"

"They have no experience with them. Short, I think."

"An inch and a half, two inches?"

"An inch and a half. They may need to move quickly." Then Lucien paused a moment in thought. "I need to attend to some business." Omama nodded back.

He turned to us, "I'm sorry to drop you off and run. I'll try to be back in an hour." Then he gave us both a careful look, "You're in good hands, don't worry."

Aleta said, "Thank you" as he left.

I just eyed him, not knowing what to think of him. I was very conflicted. My family was in grave danger and he was offering help. But was it real?

Then I looked back at Omama as the door tinkled behind us.

"Yes, well," she said. "Let's see what we can do with you."

She and her two assistants, who also sounded Jamaican, measured us in dozens of ways, held cloth up to our faces, and made us walk back and forth, Omama frowning in thought all the while.

"Please excuse me, but you don't sound African," I asked, as Omama took a break from measuring to go get something from a cupboard.

"I'm not," she replied, as she reached inside. "I was taken as a slave when I was five." She looked grim as she walked back to us with a black leather box, the size of a book.

"Are you Jamaican?" I asked.

That got a little twitch of a smile. "Close. Saint Martin."

"Dutch or French?"

"Dutch."

"So you're a slave?" Aleta asked.

"Not anymore," she replied, and she put the box down on a table and opened it. Inside were some bottles, a tin, and a pair of pliers, each in its own blue velvet-lined hole.

"Oh!" Aleta exclaimed.

"What?" I said, looking at Aleta.

"You're going to be wearing earrings," Omama said.

My head snapped back. "You're going to poke holes in my ears?"

"It won't hurt a bit," Omama replied.

"They won't have time to heal," Aleta said.

"She'll be over the most of it," she replied with a smile. "And she won't notice it a bit once she gets her corset on!"

It did hurt! And I didn't notice them once I had that damned corset on.

By the time Lucien came back, I had two little gold rings in my ears, and instructions on how to keep them clean. Then, before we left, we were given two worn but serviceable umbrellas, men's umbrellas by the way.

"You are to stay out of the sun from now on," Omama instructed. "I will not have you burnt."

"Yes ma'am," we replied in unison.

"You will go light on your meals. These dresses will be tight."

"Yes ma'am."

"Are they ready?" Lucien asked.

"For now," Omama replied.

"Then let's move on."

In the carriage, with our umbrellas raised and unfurled, Lucien addressed us. "This is normally where I would take you both out to lunch, but I'm afraid that the best meal to be had at the moment is back aboard your ship."

"Food is that short?" I asked.

"Food is that short," he replied with a sigh. "What quality food we have mostly comes in by airship. That wheat you brought caused some excitement."

"Why don't you have regular shipping?" I asked.

"That is a complicated question. I'm not putting you off. We need to discuss it, but I want your father there when we do. We'll have to work together if we're to get through this. Maybe tonight, over a bottle of that French wine you brought."

When we arrived back at the gate, Lucien hopped out again to help us down. "I'll be back at 2:30 to pick you up. We have an appointment with a shoemaker."

When I showed everyone my new ears, Pa frowned, but Ma eyed them with interest.

"I suppose we'll have to shop for earrings when we get back," she said with a smile. I think maybe Ma wanted some too.

That night, Lucien came to dinner. He brought bread and wine carried by two imperials.

"Permission to come aboard?" he called from the dock when he arrived. At least he was polite. Of course we'd seen him coming and Pa was already on his way up from their cabin.

"Hi, Lucien," Aleta called from the stern castle. She'd just dashed up the stern deckhouse steps. She'd been fixing her hair before she came up!

Crow was standing watch, giving him a stern look of warning.

"He's okay, Crow," I said.

Crow nodded.

"Okay?" Lucien asked, as he topped the gangway. "That's an American word?"

"Choctaw," Crow replied, still eying Lucien.

"They're a tribe of Indians," I said. "Is it really Choctaw,

Crow?"

"Yup," he replied.

"Amazing," Lucien said, genuinely amused.

"My good Duke, welcome aboard," Pa said, as he arrived on deck. Surprisingly, he was using his best sales face.

Aleta and I both said in unison, "Duke?"

"My apologies," Lucien replied. "But we haven't had a moment for proper introductions. I hope it doesn't matter." He looked a little worried.

I learned later that Pa had been plying the new harbormaster with rum while we were gone and now had a fairly long list of the principal players in the Congo, and a fair idea as to who was on what side of what. My Pa is brilliant. By the way, it was my birthday. Just in case you didn't remember.

Lucien, having stopped at the top of the gangway, clicked his heels (really, he does that a lot) and bowed. "Allow me to introduce myself. Lucien Philippe Marie Antoine, Duke of Tervuren. To be clear, it's largely a ceremonial title, with only the district and city of Hasselt, some land, and a few estates in Flanders. It's necessary for me to function in court."

"A pleasure. Come, let me show you the ship," Pa said. "She's not very big, but she's our home." As they were walking away I could hear Pa say, "So you're the prince's brother?"

"Younger half-brother," Lucien replied. "Unrecognized. Your ship is very beautiful, and well kept. Did I tell you I was in the navy?"

"No you didn't. And thank you. We take great care with her."

And they passed below decks.

"Yikes, a duke," Aleta said, after they had gone down the companionway.

"He seems so nice. It's hard to believe they're related," I said.

"Much better looking too," she replied.

"I hadn't noticed," I said, and gave her a weak smile.

She laughed, then added, "It must come from the mother."

Since half our cargo was out on the dock, we fired up the forklift and moved what was left aft to make room to extend the galley. With our table twice as long, there was room for us all. That night we left the watch to the imperials and did something that I have only done three or four times in my life. We all sat down to dinner at the same time. It was my birthday dinner, and it was fun!

We ate stew, partly from local ingredients. It was good, but tasted a bit different. Lucien's bread went well with it. I had wine, which was probably why everything seemed so silly. We were laughing and falling over at even the dumbest jokes. Lucien seemed so relaxed and ate his stew with seeming relish. He wasn't at all like what you'd think a noble would be. Really, I think we all needed to relax, even Lucien. The situation had been, for us at least, so grave for so long.

Aleta and I ended up playing our instruments after dinner; and we danced. Then Ma brought out my birthday cake and coffee. We made it, as we often do, with no milk. Lucien seemed genuinely hurt that he hadn't been told about my birthday, but rolled his eyes appropriately with each mouthful of cake, which made Aleta and I break out in laughter all the more. We had one of those best evenings.

But I can hear you asking, "What did you get, Cali? What did you get for your birthday?" We live on a ship and there isn't room for things in general, so we don't give gifts, at least not usually. We pretty much have whatever we need so I didn't get presents. We all got to share a good time. A good time, that was, until Lucien finally said, "Sir, we must talk. Your daughters too, if they can."

"Aleta is crew. Calista is our daughter."

"Your only . . ." and then he sighed. "Your crew can stay or go as you feel best, but we must discuss the situation and our strategy. And may I have more of that wonderful coffee? It really is in short supply here and I have a great deal still to do tonight."

"Of course," Pa said, and then after some thought, "I think we should go to my cabin. Aleta, Cali, will you join us? You coming Meara?"

"No," Ma said. "I'll stay and supervise cleanup." Which got a few mock moans from the crew.

In their cabin, I dragged Ma's and Pa's sea chests out for Aleta and me to sit on. Pa sat on their bed while Lucien and his mug of coffee sat at Pa's desk. "As you may have guessed . . . oh, very good work with the harbormaster, by the way." Lucien looked over at Pa with a bit of a smile. He knew.

But then he turned grim. "There's far more at stake than your daughter's reputation," he said bitterly. "There is a far larger game being played here, and I'm afraid you're in it. The problem is . . ." and then he trailed off in thought. "The problem is that you're American. Not just American, you brought us a very useful load of goods. The British have a clandestine trade monopoly here. They're very aggressive about it. You've surely seen that ship just down the dock, and the one sitting on the bottom. The difference between that ship and yours is that you're not European, thus neutral from our point of view. The British would like to leave you to rot, but as far as His Highness is concerned, you're something new and interesting," he said, glancing at me, which I don't think Pa liked.

"Could you get the key to the chains?" Pa asked.

"Perhaps," Lucien replied. "But I'm not ready to give up everything, my position and holdings, and sail away with you, which is what I'd be forced to do if I let you go. I would be a criminal on the run. And, as I've stated, there are bigger issues. The future of my country is at stake. Although I have great sympathy for all of you," he continued. "I have much greater sympathy for the millions who have died here and the millions more who will die very bad deaths if something isn't done."

"Millions?" Pa asked.

"The Congo these days is little more than a death camp. We're being strangled by conflicting colonial interests and treaties, most significantly by our clandestine ally, Britain."

"They want that railroad," I said.

Lucien's eyebrows went up. He was staring at me. Pa just sat back and smiled. "That, and the rubber," Lucien continued. "They may get it too, in the end, but it will change nothing. They're no better at colony management here in Africa than we are. And I'm not about to cede the entire continent to them. This is a Belgian colony."

"Are the British arming the natives?" Pa asked.

"Not as far as we know--yet."

"Why don't your people have bullets?" I interrupted. Sadly, I'm good at that.

"There are always shipping problems. Again," he said, looking at me. "It's because of the British, but we have more than they think."

"Then why aren't you using them?" I asked.

"We don't trust everyone who might get them," he replied, looking at me levelly. Then he turned on Pa. "Is she always like this?"

Pa chuckled. "Yes."

"You must be careful." He looked at me and then at Pa. "This was not a game where honesty and directness is a virtue. It only makes it easier for your enemies. Guard what you say at all times."

"But we're alone here," I said.

"I'm sure you trust your crew, but there are the guards on deck and who knows who else. This is a very difficult game we are going to play. If we do it right, we may save an empire as well as your ship."

"And why should we trust you?" I asked.

"Because you have no alternative," Lucien replied. "And, in this, our interests lay on the same path. The British want this colony, and they'll get it unless we can change His Highness' mind about a few key policies. The one that's important to you is open trade. At least trade with you Americans. To accomplish this, you two," and he was looking at Aleta and me, "are going to have to learn to be courtiers. Quickly too. We have less time than I originally thought. He's talking about a hunting trip in two, maybe three days."

"What's a courtier?" I asked.

"They're like lobbyists," Pa answered.

"What's a lobbyist?" I asked again.

"They're people who try to influence the decisions of government." Pa said.

"Oh."

Then Aleta jumped in, "I've never shot a gun before."

"Me either," I added.

"We can work on that," Pa said.

"Good, I have enough on my plate as it is," Lucien said. "Shooting is optional for women at these events, but I think it may change his impression of you favorably if you could. I warn you, this won't be like hunting in the English countryside. It will be somewhat dangerous. The guards will be primarily watching out for His Highness, not you. And many of the animals here are very large and very dangerous. They can charge when wounded. Being able to shoot is best."

"Will you be there?" Aleta asked.

"Of course," he said. "He needs me to translate English."

"I speak a bit of French," I said.

"I speak German," Aleta said.

Lucien's eyes widened for a second, "We already know about the German. Say nothing in French. He mustn't know. It will be harder for me to protect you if he can talk to you directly."

"What languages does he speak?" asked Pa.

"Just German and French, although he rarely uses French and doesn't like people to know he can speak it."

Just then we heard a steam whistle.

"Odd," Pa said.

"It's a riverboat," Lucien said dismissively. "It's dark, and they want to dock."

"Can we go see?" I asked.

He seemed surprised for a moment. "Okay," he said, and then he stopped and chuckled. It had a nice sound. "Choctaw, is it?"

We all stood and adjourned to the sterncastle, Lucien handing his coffee mug to Ma with a little thank you in passing. At the rail we looked up river. Lucien standing next to me.

Men were moving around on the dock with torches, spacing themselves along the edge of the wharf. The steamboat was holding station off shore, lit by lanterns and silver moonlight. She was a flat-bottomed stern wheeler, hull low to the water, about eighty feet long with an open deck piled high with cut wood, crates, and sacks. She had no deck house, but instead, a small section covered by a tin roof in the stern. Her engines, amidships, were open to the air. I smelled the wood smoke from her boilers as it blew in over the river. The moon, waning third quarter rising, cast long black shadows across the silver flecked water. The tide would be coming in, I thought.

Wood sparks rose with her smoke out her stack and blew across the dock as she neared. She was edging in sideways. Her captain was cautious and took his time, a good trait in a riverboat captain. The further in they came, out of the main channel, the more they edged back on their steam, just matching the current as she drifted slowly sideways toward the dock, venting excess steam in bursts of fine silver mist. Then she cut power altogether, letting momentum take her the last few feet. At five feet, they tossed their lines and pushed their bumpers over the side. She edged in just kissing the dock. It was a perfect docking.

"Beautiful," I said to myself.

"Hmmm?" Lucien said, looking down at me. "Was it? I'll have to find out his name. A good riverboat captain may be useful."

"Pa, can we go visit?" I asked.

"It's late, Cali," he replied.

"Don't worry. You'll be seeing quite a lot of him soon," Lucien added.

Does Lucien ever sleep? I didn't get to sleep until 2:00 a.m., but there he was, looking spotless and awake at the bottom of our gangplank at 9:00 a.m.! It was a blurry Aleta and Cali rolling along in the carriage to Omama's.

"How can you be so awake?" Aleta moaned.

"A lifetime of practice, and a long stretch in the Navy."

"Belgium has a navy?" I asked, genuinely curious.

He looked at me with those hazel eyes. I felt he was looking for something. I wanted to look back, but I was suddenly afraid. "It's small, but well equipped," he continued. "There have been efforts to expand it, but they've all met with failure. So we are forced to focus on quality instead."

"What's stopping you?" I asked.

"The British," he replied.

I frowned. They seem to be everywhere, I thought.

Omama had requested that we bring our boots along, which we did, although I felt a little embarrassed to show them. They were just work boots, and they had seen work. It's strange, but I'd never worried about them before. And we were wearing our nice dresses by the way. As tired as I was, I even brushed my hair.

A great shadow passed over us, the drone of engines edged through the air. An airship was passing overhead. It seemed so strangely modern in this setting. Kind of comforting. It was large, ridged framed, with four engines. On its tail was a red shield with a white cross.

"Oh, Caproni," Aleta said, looking up. "A Cz. 3 I think."

"You know airships?" Lucien asked.

"I used to work for Lufthansa."

Lucien nodded, then turned back to staring into the distance, lost in thought.

I stole glances, looking him over more carefully. His uniform today wasn't his best, his boots a little worn and dusty. He had no rings or jewelry. Just a belt with a canteen and a revolver. Despite his apparent energy, he looked a tired.

He seems to collect people, I thought. It must be hard being unrecognized by your family. Maybe that's why he tries so hard with what he has. I couldn't help liking him for that at least, despite our situation and his part in it. He was as much a victim of circumstances as we were, working with what he had just like us.

At Omama's we furled our umbrellas and entered. Lucien followed carrying a big sack.

"Good girls," she said with a smile as she got up to greet us. "You keep using those umbrellas. I will not cover sunburn. Hello Lucien. I got your note about the plan change, and I think you will be pleased."

She turned and called, "Naja, set up the screen. Aba, bring the dresses to show Lucien." Turning back, she said to him, "They will, of course, need adjustments."

Lucien looked just the tiniest bit smug as he explained, "We're going to play on the American angle, which will allow us to break with Paris fashion, and go with the practical. Let's hope we've got this right. Your opinions, Cali, will be helpful."

Omama shooed two very confused young women behind the screen and handed us the dresses. They were, when tried them on, simple frocks. Mine was loose-fitting dark green cotton, with a large open collar folded down. It had a false overskirt, but it had only one or two actual layers of cloth which would help with the heat. The hem was a practical ten inches above the floor. Aleta's was a dark red, which set off the blackness of hair, her round face, and especially the green in her eyes.

"Wear your boots," Omama called to us over the screen, and then to Lucien. "We're using dark colors to make their skin look paler."

When we came out, he nodded his head in approval. "Omama,

as always, you are a genius." Omama was definitely looking happier. Lucien dragged over his bag and pulled out two leather waist belts, and then two gun belts. "Put these on."

The waist belts fit well, but the gun belts were way too big, even over our hips. I held mine up with one hand. Then he pulled out two hats. "I don't know if these will fit. We may have to block and stretch them." They didn't, but we jammed them on anyway. They'd been cut down and stripped of adornment. I could see the outlines where there had been decoration and the felt hadn't faded.

So now I began to get the gist of where he was headed. We looked like a couple of penny-dreadful cowgirls, not that I read those, mind you. That would certainly be against school rules. We were Wild West frontier women, and maybe part-time bank robbers. I started to laugh and then looked up at Lucien, "Cowgirls?"

Lucien grinned. "Armed with pistols and rifles," he said. "You can't compete on fashion and etiquette. The court women he's used to have trained their entire lives in the arts of the court courtesans. I think he will be amused, intrigued by the exoticness, and hopefully held at a distance by the firepower and your potential, as American cowgirls to use it. Bring Crow along to top it off." Then to Omama, "They shouldn't look new. The dresses need to be weathered."

"I think we can handle that."

"You know I'm English, not an American?" Aleta said.

"It's a nation of immigrants," he replied.

"The hats need bands, and feathers, maybe," I said.

"Good!" Lucien said. "Take the hats with you. The belts as well. Decorate them as you will. There are alternatives to the British which he steadfastly refuses to consider. If we can divert him, intrigue him, then pique his greed with thoughts of exotic trade with far away America, he may yet consider a compromise. Besides there's Annie Oakley to consider too." Then he added, thinking to himself. "I wonder if I can interest him in collecting Americana, or better still, hunting buffalo and grizzly bear?"

"Annie Oakley?" I asked.

"Who's she?" Aleta added.

"A cowgirl sharpshooter," I replied.

"He followed her all the way to Milan," Lucien said, with a

smirk. "She was in Brussels with Buffalo Bill's show. Butler took a shot at him."

"He didn't," I said.

"He did."

Annie Oakley. I laughed. I was definitely in good company and I was already excited and brimming with ideas. I wondered if Crow had any Indian jewelry.

The lugger had put out while we were gone. Its loss made the dock look even emptier.

Lucien dropped us off at the gate and hurried off. We were left to explain the plan to the crew. Pa listened with intensity as we explained, running his hands back through his graying hair even more than normal.

"He's out of his mind," Pa mumbled. Then he said, "I guess he's right in one way: it does play to our strengths. We have a day, maybe two, to turn you into frontier women. Crow, I'm counting on you most of all to help us out with ideas."

"Aye aye," Crow said, with a smirk. Crow grew up in Baton Rouge!

So the crew worked with leather punches, drills, thread, and glue, while Pa took us up on deck with the rifle and the revolver.

"This is a Winchester repeater. It's too big for either of you, but considering what you might meet out there, it may be too small. The pistol is a Colt 45 double-action revolver. Again too big for you. I'm going to try to teach you to shoot without injuring yourselves, then you're going to learn to clean them. First, though," he said, his eyes casting about, "we're going to need a target."

We looked around but couldn't find one. We couldn't shoot at the dock, at the other boats--especially not at Red--or even at the open water, where there was nothing to say whether we'd hit or missed. We finally walked down the dock to the Dutchman. The militia guards gave us the eye, but let us leave with the guns. Maybe Lucien had warned them. Oh, and she wasn't really called the Dutchman. We just took to calling her that. She was the "*Kleine Heks*". Little something perhaps? Don't ask me. We had no idea what it meant, which, was why we called her the

Dutchman. So the Dutchman--being at the end of the dock--gave us a clear view of the shore past the fence. We stood up on her stern, near her faded flag, staring down the shore toward the jungle.

"We'll use that snag, just offshore." I could see it in the distance. It seemed far away. "Just so you have an idea as to the sound these things make, I'll take the first shot. You'll want to hold your ears, but try to get used to it. You can't when you're shooting, and it will make you look weak."

He lifted the Winchester and showed us how to push in bullets, lever open the bolt, sight, and pull the trigger. "Hold it snug against your shoulder or you'll bruise," he said. "Sight on the target, and squeeze." There was a great righteous boom. The rifle jerked in Pa's arms, and the water went up near the snag. I felt it in my bones.

"Lord!" Aleta exclaimed. She had taken a step back.

I stood there stunned.

He levered open the bolt and out popped the empty shell. I reached down to pick it up off the deck. It was still smoking.

"Careful," he said. "It'll be hot." It was. I tossed it back and forth in my hands as it cooled. The bullet was gone from the end. I passed it to Aleta.

"We're going to have to fire that?" Aleta said.

"It's not as bad as cannon shells," I replied.

That got a snort from Pa.

"Aleta, we'll start with you. Cali will have the hardest time because she's so small. She can watch you first. It's too bad we don't have a shotgun as well. You might be using those for hunting birds."

Aleta kept closing her eyes and grimacing when she shot, the rifle knocking her back, and Pa kept trying make her keep her eyes open and hold the rifle hard against her shoulder. After three shots she said, "My shoulder is killing me."

"You're not holding it close enough. Cali, you up for a try?"

"Sure," I said. This might be fun, I thought. But when I got it, the thing weighed a ton. I was holding it like he said and he was pushing it into my shoulder, but my aim was sagging. "Pa, this is really heavy."

"Just wait till you shoot it," Aleta said.

When I did, it knocked me flat on my back. Aleta let out a little laugh, but then she was helping me up. I think she was just nervous and worried.

Pa was sighing. "You're going to have to brace yourself, keep your feet apart and lean forward into it. It's your size. You don't have the weight behind you."

"Did I close my eyes?" I asked.

That pulled a little half-smile out of his grimness. "I couldn't see. Feel up to trying again?"

"Yes."

The second time I stayed upright, but I still didn't hit anything, not even the water!

Finally, we both managed to land shots in the vague vicinity of the snag. Then we started over with the pistol. Getting the cylinder to come out gracefully was devilishly hard.

We were dragging our bruised and battered bodies back up the gangplank onto Red, thinking how good it would be to lay down, when Pa hauled us down to his cabin where we were introduced to brushes, oil, rods, screwdrivers, and patches.

When Lucien showed up that afternoon for more fittings, we hobbled out to him, a pair of very sore women. I could see him hiding a smile. I'd have punched him if only I could've used my arm!

In the end, we each got two new dresses. They were delivered to the boat that evening. The crew had done wonders. They pounded, drilled, and polished nickels, stitching them around my hat band. On Aleta's, Tinker tooled a swirly leaf pattern. I really do think Tinker had eyes for her. Both hats looked nice, and the brims were curled up at the sides too. They said it was to keep the wind from blowing the fronts up from our faces. The coins glinted in the sun and made my head feel heavy. We had belt pouches for bullets and more for sundries, big knives, and shoulder bags. Aleta's was made from the lion head, only the fur was trimmed. "It's supposed to be buffalo," Crow said. And we got big canvas back sacks with shoulder straps for our day-to-day gear. Ed tooled a weaving interlocked pattern into our belts and animals onto the pouch flaps. I grabbed one with the eagle before Aleta!

When we finally stood on deck turning around for everybody, we looked good, which was good because that night the invitations to the hunt came, delivered by an Imperial officer, feathers on his polished helmet and all. We were to report to the dock the day after tomorrow, in the early morning. Please pardon my English, but it was damn rude such short notice!

We practiced twice more, saving the rest of the cartridges to take with us. The next day, we tried on the first bits of our ball gowns. They were white! I was already in love with mine, but there was no way it would survive onboard ship. Perhaps we could crate them and keep them in the upper hold, somewhere away from the damp, I thought.

That evening Lucien brought us a pistol and two rifles. One he called a Mauser and it had seen a lot of use. It was longer than the Winchester too, but it kicked the same, and the cleaning rod was built in, which was handy. The pistol was definitely different. The hole in the barrel wasn't as big, and instead of the cylinder tipping out the side to reload, the whole thing bent in the middle. He called it a Webley. Since it used smaller bullets, we decided that I should have it. The last was a big rifle for Crow. Actually, it was more like a cannon.

"My pa had one of these," Crow said, admiring the gun. "Only it didn't have the fancy brass. This has a bigger bore too."

"The Spencer is from my private collection. You would not believe what I had to go through to get the other two," Lucien said. "That Mauser is our old model, but one of the best the militia has. They did not part with it willingly. The pistol . . ." then he trailed off. "The pistol is better left a mystery."

He said no more for a moment, then roused himself as if remembering where he was. He looked at me. "You must try to understand, Cali. Commoners are not encouraged to carry or even own weapons. I'm sure he's expecting you to show up unequipped and at his mercy for everything. He'll have gift guns tucked away somewhere, along with his personal instruction. This will be a shock."

Then he added, almost as an afterthought, "He's quite good you know. I mean a good shot, a remarkable marksman. If the situation wasn't so dire, this hunt, I think, could be quite a treat." Lucien continued on with more instruction about caliber, recoil, stopping power, gun types and makers, and lots of stuff I would happily not remember.

Chapter 15

Logs in the River

I would like to be able to say that I didn't sleep before the big day, but I did. They had to wake me. We gnawed our way through our breakfast of boiled roots, leaves, flatbread, and dried sausage. Then, after a hug-filled goodbye from Ma, Pa, and the crew, Aleta, Crow, and I walked down the dock toward the river steamer, our stomachs feeling full, but still hungry.

There was a lot of activity down by the steamboat. At least

two steam trucks and three horse carriages. The dock was full, mostly crates, but some odd objects as well, folded tangles of pipe and metal which I will describe. And many, many people, some of whom I will introduce as well.

One of the steam trucks was pulling away as we approached. It passed us as we walked, leaving a trail of steam-lit bright white in the morning sunlight. My water bottle sloshed and my pistol bounced with each step. It was going to take a while to get all that gear settled so it was comfortable. We three had backpacks, bed rolls, and Aleta and I our instruments. Lucien had been clear about that. Crow carried the rifles. We were paragons of frontier self-sufficiency. Self-sufficiency as long as it didn't involve walking more than a quarter mile. All that gear was heavy!

As we approached our riverboat, the second truck pulled away and puffed by us, revealing two great contraptions that towered over the litter and sundry of boxes, bags, barrels, and canvas rolls. They were great tangled blocks of metal tubes and barrels, made of gleaming polished brass and steel. On their bottoms they had wheels. The dock workers were preparing to roll one of them onto the deck of the steamship, still docked after its arrival the night of my birthday party. They had laid a ramp for them, but I had my doubts that the steamer could load them that way without tipping and dropping them in the river. What they needed was a crane. They had one of the machines at the bottom of the ramp, trying to push it up, and the boat was already listing.

"*Arrêt! Arrêt!*", came a frenzied call from behind us. That's "halt" in French. Aren't you glad I listened in French class? A thin, bald, bearded, dark-tanned man with black hair and dirty deck clothes loped past us and began jabbering at the workers in French far too fast for me to understand. From his deck hand's looks of confusion, I suspected they didn't either.

"What does he want?" Aleta asked.

"He doesn't want to lose his cargo in the river," I replied.

At his emphatic urgings, they pushed the machine back on the dock. Then he ran through the other cargo, sometimes pushing crates an inch or two across the dock, testing their weight.

"He's going to try to counterbalance the boat while he moves those big machines on," I said. "That's going to be tricky, especially with this crew."

"Maybe we should help. Show the flag," Aleta suggested.

A good idea. Especially since there didn't seem to be any help forthcoming from their nearby British allies, who were just lying about on their deck. The spectators, hunters, attendants, and well-wishers were no use either. They were standing back from the dock with their own gear and bags.

Don't worry. I promise I'll introduce them all in a minute.

"Should we ask your pa?" Crow asked.

"I think so," I said.

"I'll go," Aleta said, and she started dropping her gear. "You know more about this kind of thing than I do."

"True," I replied.

Crow and I helped her out of her straps and then she trotted off back toward Red. Crow and I headed for the short-tempered Frenchman. He was picking boxes and telling the workers to move them onboard.

"Hello!" I called.

"*Pas le temps!*" He waved us off, not even looking up. He then pointed at the dock, "*Restez avec les autres!*"

I was going to have a hard time pretending that I didn't know what he was saying. I deliberately stepped in his way and said, "We can help." I pointed at myself and Crow, and then at Red down at the other end of the dock. The moment he got an eyeful of us, he stopped, his face suddenly blank and confused. He was trying to make out what we were, but without much success. So I pointed at myself and said, "American."

"*L'Américain?*"

I nodded my head, "Yes."

And then he was off rattling out French and I was lost. So I raised my hands and shook my head and he trailed off and stopped. I pointed at his boat, then tipped my hand back and forth. Then I pointed at Crow and myself, then a crate, then made like I was pushing. Now he was focused on us and thinking.

"*Attendez ici,*" he said, pointing at us and then down at the dock. You two, wait here. So I nodded.

He turned back to the dock workers and picked boxes for them to haul across. What I hoped he was planning to do was to slide crates from the center, to the side of the boat, and then back again as they loaded the machines to help them keep the boat from tipping everything off into the river. By the time he was ready, Aleta came back with Pa, Ian, and Tinker. With Pa there to speak French, things went smoothly. While we were loading, the steam trucks came back led by a shiny black steam carriage, its polished brass glinting in the sun. In the back seat was the prince!

I could see him casting about through the people on dock, and then finally on deck as they drove up. He saw us pushing crates. The carriage rolled to a stop and I could hear him, *"Nein! Nein! Sie müssen nicht!"* He was pointing at us.

"I don't think he likes us working on deck," Aleta said.

"Was machen Sie? Sie sind Fräuleins!"

So we straightened up, I sighed and grabbed my hat and jammed it on my head, and then we walked back to the dock from the boat deck where we had been working. When we got there, we found he had started berating the French captain, who probably couldn't understand what he was saying, since it was in German, but was showing the proper angst and fear that a confrontation with a prince called for. Once we were facing him, we both curtsied as Lucien instructed. I tried to go as low as I could, but I wobbled and messed it up again. Really, I needed to practice this. I will never be a woman of poise and grace doing it like that. Lucien came up behind him, clearly trying not to laugh. Leopold stopped and stared at us both.

"Was ist dies?" he said, staring at us. The whole dock was quiet, all work stopped.

"We're here at your invitation, my lord," I said and Aleta repeated it in German. "We're here to hunt!" I added with a smile.

Leopold blinked for a moment and then escaped with a "Yes, of course," and retreated back with the spectators. We grabbed our gear and followed. Somehow our presence seemed to disturb him. He kept his distance, but sometimes, I could see him glancing at us. He didn't seem happy.

This worried me. More than anything, I wanted to repel him, but we needed some kind of trade dispensation, or at least a pardon for docking in Boma, so we sat down on a crate with our gear and I thought. Maybe it was time to pay out a little line. I turned around to Aleta and asked, "Feel up to playing some music?"

"Sure. You feel up to it? He's standing right over there."

I didn't answer, but pulled up my case and opened it. The

sweet smell of the wood and varnish rose up. The heat and humidity brought the life in the wood out, but it made it hellish to tune. Then we played for him. Nothing complicated. Just simple little tunes to pass the time, stopping and starting to discuss which way the music ought to go. We didn't look to see who was watching. We just played.

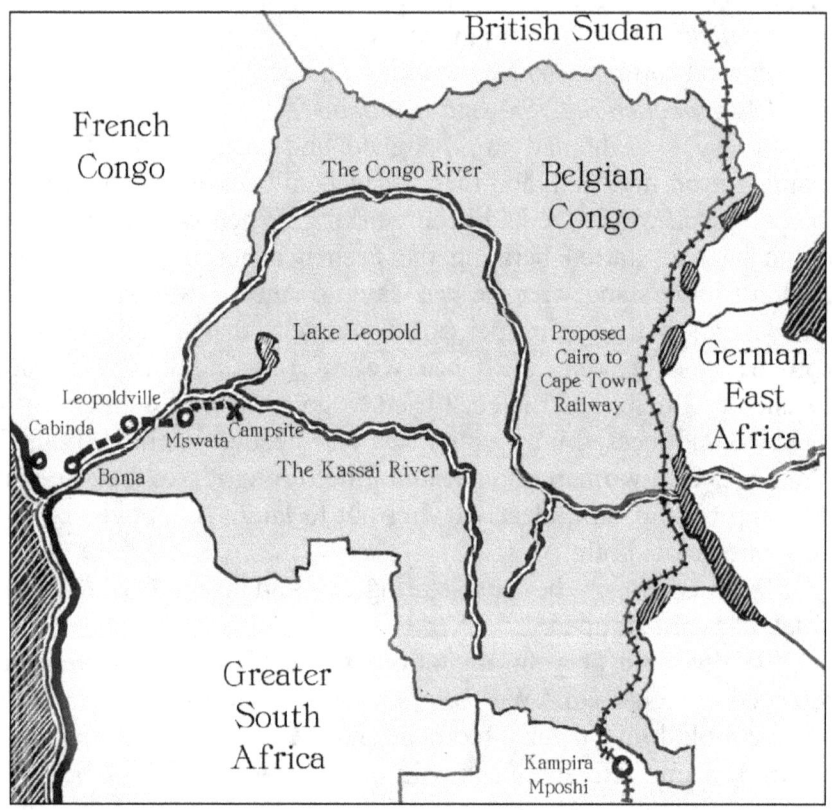

Oh, and I promised you a description of our fellow hunters, didn't I? I didn't know their names then, so I'll save that for later. By far the bulk of the crowd were servants and soldiers, all imperials, none of them helping to load! They were all men wearing various uniforms, numbering about thirty, all armed to various degrees.

There was Lucien, whom you already know, and who was being annoyingly aloof. He wasn't wearing his black uniform, just a wide-brimmed hat, shirt, pants, and boots. Then the guests, five men and one woman, along with a couple of wives waiting to see their husbands off. The men wore various baggy shirts and trousers, belts of bullets, big knives, big hats or helmets, boots and canvas spats. The men got to roll up their sleeves, which is so unfair. I got the feeling, from their asides to each other and their accents, that two of them were English and at least one was German. The woman, Belgian or French, wore a long dress with mildly puffed sleeves, an open bodice, high collar, a wide-brimmed hat, topped off with a parasol. She looked bit overheated with her collar buttoned up her neck, but hid it well. Women's collars are insane. I couldn't see her foot gear under the skirt, nor could I get a good look at her face. She was in her late 20's or maybe even 30.

The prince wore a blousy white shirt with a wide-open collar. No lack of ventilation there! His big handlebar moustache stretched down under his long nose, down past his small mouth, his hair was short and somewhat curled. He was wearing green canvas riding pants tucked into his shining calf-high boots. He chatted merrily in German to the Brits, still glancing our way occasionally. His servant, or perhaps aide, stood quietly next to him holding his helmet, which was high-topped white canvas, with a great silver and gold badge on its front.

We meandered around various tunes until three dockworkers came for our crate. It had been over an hour since we had arrived, and I was beginning to realize that our boat had no cabin and no below decks. Just a closed hull with an engine on top. Where were we going to go to relieve ourselves? I hoped we would find out soon.

We had only just gotten our instruments put away when a servant came by with a tray. On it were tall narrow glasses like tall thin stalks. They were crystal with geometric patterns cut in them that glistened with little rainbows in the sun. They made the wine glasses we saw in France seem very plain. We each took a glass and then heard a pop, and Leopold was standing with a wine bottle spilling out foam, laughing as it ran down the sides of the bottle.

"*Komm!*" he said, motioning us over.

He was pouring out the contents of the bottle into the glasses, while another servant prepared the next. Everyone was laughing and smiling. In the wine went, into my glass, foaming to the top. As he poured our drinks, he gave me an odd searching look. I could see, I think, perhaps, mischief in his eyes. Then he made a toast, looking straight into my eyes. *"Auf der Jagd!"* he said.

"To the hunt," Aleta translated.

First Leopold, followed by the rest, we clinked our glasses together--carefully. I would die if one of these broke. When I faced the Brits to touch glasses, their eyes were cold behind their smiles.

So what did they finally do? They put up a tent on deck. The damn boat, and I'm sorry because she doesn't deserve that, didn't even have a head. Instead they had a railing chair, which is a seat with a hole in it that clamps on to the side of a boat leaving your behind hanging out over the water. An unfortunate lurch of the boat, and in you go to swim with the crocodiles. On the bright side, at least the process did allow a little ventilation under one's skirts.

Ma and Pa came down and waved to us as we left. the prince didn't look happy about that for some reason, but he didn't send them away.

Our boat was called the *Hercule*, which is Hercules in French, and she reminded me of the Nellie Thomson, only much bigger. Hercule's captain was Émile Savoie and she had a crew of six, all black. Unlike the dock workers, Émile seemed to be able to keep his men fed. Émile fed his boilers wood instead of coal, which smelled much nicer and made less dirty soot. Unfortunately, it burns a lot faster than coal so they had several big piles of it onboard in various states of dryness. The deck was full of crates and gear as well, which didn't leave much room for us. Everyone sat about on top of the stacked cargo as we made way up channel.

The deck was divided into definite class divisions which decided where you could sit. the prince and his party, including us, had the bow, which was away from the boiler and smoke, and had an unobstructed view of the river scenery. Everyone else sat behind. What sort of divisions were below us, such as between soldiers, servants, and crew, couldn't be seen as I was never allowed to go back.

We were watching the river go by when Lucien climbed over to Aleta and me and, with an amiable look, said, "His Highness would like to greet the two of you. If you'll follow me." He waited for us to pick up our cases. All our other gear had been spirited away by servants. Lucien didn't even give us a "how are you doing," which made me a little worried and maybe a little angry. I hoped he wasn't going to be like this all trip. He coached us for this meeting, but I still felt a bit of panic. But, I had nowhere to go but forward!

The servants and crew had built the prince a little room out of crates, with a canvas awning roof. In the center, he had a table and four folding chairs. Around the sides crates were places for others to sit on. He was sitting in one of the folding chairs, drinking tea. The other guests were there, including Nigel. Really, I will introduce to them all soon! We both started to curtsy (I was getting better at it) and said "My Lord," but he waved at us to stand up, tut tutting. Lucien translated for us.

"There is no reason for formalities here," he said. "We'd miss all the game if we spent our time like that." He motioned us toward the chairs Lucien was holding out for us. "Please sit down. It's too hot to stand about out of the shade."

We both said, "Thank you, My Lord," and took our seats, stowing our hats on our laps for lack of any place better. Lucien took the last chair.

"Tea?" the prince said, and began to pour without waiting for our reply. It was strong and black. "I'm afraid there's no cream or sugar. We must make sacrifices here in the colonies. It will be weeks before the next shipment comes in."

"We might be able to help you there, My Lord," I said. "We could send you a couple of pounds of sugar to tide you over."

He looked at us for a moment, and then blinked. "Really?"

Nigel cleared his throat and added, "We could send you some, My Lord. I'm sure Janus has some." That must be the remaining ship.

"And why didn't you offer before?" Leopold replied. "We've shared tea often enough."

Nigel looked uncomfortable, "We didn't realize there was a need."

Leopold looked at us for the first time with an honest smile. "I would be grateful for some sugar." After a sip from his cup he asked, "Our Congo must be very different from America."

"We spend our summers in the Caribbean, My Lord. Mostly around Jamaica. This reminds me a lot of the Black River. Swamps, mangroves. We have jungle, but alligators instead, and herons too. Well, in the South actually, which isn't part of our country at the moment." I had started to babble, to which I apologized, but he held up his hand to stop me.

"Your war must be difficult."

"Yes, My Lord."

And he shook his head again. "Please, we can drop the honorifics as well." He continued, "I can understand about your war. We have suffered through enough wars ourselves. Our poor Belgium is everyone's doormat. Is food getting tight yet?"

"No, but we are running out of men."

For a moment that seemed to surprise him and then concern him. "Lucien, how can that be?"

"This one is different . . ." Lucien began to try to answer in both English and German, but the prince, realizing this was being rude to his guests, shushed him and said "Later."

"You are so very quiet. You are the English girl?" he said to Aleta.

"Yes, Sire," she replied in a very nervous voice.

"Have you been with the ship long?"

"Three years." We had worked this out ahead of time.

"You were out practicing with rifles, I hear."

"Yes. I'd never shot one before," Aleta said. "They thought I ought to know a bit about them before we went out."

Then he turned back to me. "So you've shot before. I have heard that the frontier is always very close in America."

"Yes, it is. The woods and mountains are never very far away." Then I continued, "I can understand how Belgium must feel. We always seem to be at war with somebody. We only just finished a war with the western Indians and the Mexicans. And now this one." That last bit came out a little bleak. But I took a breath and continued, "In the last one, the Indian Nations overran some of our cities before we pushed them back. That was only a few days away by train from Boston, our home port."

"You have an Indian with you," he said.

"Crow?" I asked.

"Yes."

"Crow has been crew since before I was born. He stayed onboard during the war. And we have Ian now, who has to hide during this one. He's a Southerner."

"So you prefer to be neutral and not pick sides?"

"Yes, Sire, we're shipping merchants. War is bad for business."

"See, Nigel, they're not spies," he said to Nigel.

Nigel turned red and stammered, "No, of course not." I could see laughter in Lucien's eyes.

That was Nigel Prendergast, by the way. Sir Nigel Prendergast. He has a moustache, but it isn't as big as His Highness', which is probably on purpose. He had a long narrow nose, like the prince too. He and his aide, Howard Milford--notable for his spectacles and lack of facial hair--were, as I have already stated, the administrators for the front company that represents the interests of the British Crown in the Congo.

Our tea progressed peacefully. Lucien was right. If it weren't for the chains holding Red captive, this trip would have been pleasant. Leopold was doing his best to be nice, which made it hard to believe he could allow people's hands to be cut off. And he served good tea.

We were making our way east, upriver, at an amazing ten knots. Sometimes steam engines are the best. The shores were closing in, the river here being only about 200 yards wide. The swamp and grass had given way to barren hilltops and jungle-lined river valleys. We passed clearings on the shore with beaches and small villages as well as, of course, crocodiles. They looked like logs floating in the water--at least that was until you shot one.

This was demonstrated by another of our guests, Alard Daems, the Growers Association port administrator. His job was to make sure supplies headed east and rubber headed west. We finished tea and were left to wander while his highness went to inspect the railing chair. Standing by the railing, watching the river go by, we spied M. Daems, who was expounding on his hunting experience to Mme. Emmaline Verbeeck. Mme. Verbeeck was very rich, and was in the Congo to review her investments. She also spoke English! Mme. Verbeeck had expressed doubt that the logs M. Daems had pointed out were truly crocodiles, so M. Daems had gone off to get his gun. She was translating for us, although I had a pretty good idea what they were saying.

"And so you live in Antwerp?" I said. "We've been there, but not since I was little. I was born offshore, heading in to port."

"Then that makes you Belgian! At least in spirit. Have you been to Belgium, Aleta?"

"Yes, several times. The last time I was in Antwerp was two years ago, when I was working for Lufthansa. It's a beautiful city. It was winter and we had snow."

"Were you there for Christmas?"

"No, and I was working. There was no time to sightsee."

"Then you have my sympathies. I doubt there's ever been snow here!" she said.

"Mme. Verbeeck, I have my rifle," called M. Daems.

"*Oui, bien sûr,*" Mme. Verbeeck replied.

Up over the box pile puffed M. Daems, lugging a huge monster of a gun. Really, more of a cannon, all brass and iron.

"Whoa! You're going to fire that?" I said.

Mme. Verbeeck's head turned back to me. "Whoa?" she said. "Is that English?"

"Yes, it's for horses," Aleta said.

"It means slow down," I added.

Mme. Verbeeck stifled a laugh.

M. Daems was not about to let himself be ignored. "It's a .5 BPE. It will stop anything."

Mme. Verbeeck was, if nothing else, polite and so she turned back to M. Daems with a friendly smile. "Yes, of course it is. And you were about to demonstrate its properties for us."

"Yes. Its operation is very simple," and off he went, telling us about caliber, slug size, and powder weight. I looked around at the river, trying to guess which crocodile would be the one to meet its maker. Mme. Verbeeck was doing a wonderful job of pretending to listen. And then finally he seemed ready to shoot. I noticed that he was bracing himself much like I had to. It must have had a huge kick. I could see the crocodile he picked, soaking in a group of fellow "logs." Harder to miss that way, I guessed.

I thought I was ready, really! But when it went off, I was still knocked back. There was a great deal of smoke, which obscured our target for a moment. When it cleared we could see that the log was thrashing in the water, and that its fellow logs were beginning to take an interest in it.

Naturally, the sound of a shot drew every man on the boat. They climbed over boxes, came around the rail, stood on top of things to see. "What did you hit?" was the general reaction. The crocodiles were coiling around each other in the bloody water, a good reminder not to go swimming, and Mme. Verbeeck was watching the empty shoreline while the men all congratulated M. Daems and compared impressions. I thought I might like Mme. Verbeeck.

Whom did I miss? M. Massart, Giliam Massart, the gun merchant. He works for Krupp, the arms maker, and was one of the few who didn't look to see who took a shot or what was hit; at least I should say that I didn't see him looking. He was a very quiet man, always writing in his notebooks. I only found out about his business by asking Mme. Verbeeck later on. She said that the real question was, who was he here to sell guns to? Mystery, something we really needed here.

Lastly was Herr Metzger, Dieter Metzger. He was following the prince around, like us, trying to buy rubber, only in his case it was on behalf of the German government. A hopeless errand. He wore spectacles and oiled his hair back, even though we were in the tropics, which must have been terribly uncomfortable as he sweated. Some people are just crazy. Unlike the French speakers, he had no problem speaking directly to the prince.

Lucien said that it takes a lifetime to train to be a proper royal courtier. This is entirely true. I was, on this trip, a babe in the woods at the mercy of wolves. For an example, I give you Mme. Verbeeck after M. Daems had left to stow his rifle.

"You understand French," Mme. Verbeeck said, in French!

"*Merde!*" I said. Did I say that? I didn't say it out loud, but she knew I said it anyway!

"You must be careful when you're listening," she said in English. "You're moving your eyes to follow the conversation and reacting to what people are saying. Look at something else, like you're waiting."

I could do nothing but nod my head slightly.

"Don't worry," she said. "We all have our secrets," and she

gave me a little smile. "You'd hardly be worthy of being here if you didn't." Then she laughed. "What possible reason could there be for someone so young to be here amongst all these crocodiles?"

Did she mean in the water or on the boat?

"He's interred our ship," I said.

Then something fell away and for a moment I could see the gears turn in her head. She sat back and gave me a hard look. "Oh," was all she said. After a moment she looked down at my case. "You play the violin. Can you play something for me?"

"I would rather not," I replied.

Then the sun rose in her face and she laughed. "Ah, so you declined."

Aleta and I look at each other in shared confusion.

"It's nothing," she said, trying to reassure. "I know your secret. It's only fair I tell one of mine. Did you know that I am a commoner? When I was young like you, I was an actress! The toast of Paris. I think I'm here to help you," she said. "This explains why I was invited. Oh, Lucien, you are brilliant."

And so, going by what I could follow from that, I felt that perhaps we had an ally.

The crocodiles were still winding about, trying to get a lock on the kill, as we left them behind. I sat on a crate watching the shore. Aleta was off trying her luck with the railing chair. She was not feeling well, which wasn't surprising considering the food we've been getting from shore, when who should crawl over to my perch but Nigel. He sat down next to me.

"Good afternoon, Miss Carmichael. Please allow me to express my sympathies as to the impoundment of your family's ship."

"Yes, thank you." I was, by that point, wary of everyone, especially those pretending sympathy.

"I think we could be of some help in obtaining its release," he said.

"Oh, really?"

"If your father is willing to sign with our company, I don't think that trade with the Congo would be any problem, no matter what the political situation here might become."

A cartel offer. "That's really very generous, but we already have permission papers from the government," I said.

"Aside from general policy and strategic decisions, the British government has little say here in colonies, especially ones they don't own. Besides, we're an independent company, run by the Belgian government. My offer is real though. We're always on the lookout for good captains and we definitely need hulls."

Red is not a "hull," and there was no way I was signing her over to a cartel. He was looking for an implicit contract. In this case, a promise from the daughter on behalf of the father. A pretext to force Red into the cartel. The next step would probably be to replace our "crew" with his own men, leaving us only nominally in charge. What an idiot he must have thought I was! Why do you think we brave Florida instead of working China? To avoid such deals. So I fell back on an old negotiating defense. Claim a need to defer to an absent higher authority to delay decision.

"I'll tell my Pa about your offer. I'm sure he'll be interested in a steady route, especially during war." Then I decided to pull him along. "It's nice to hear English. The only person I can talk to is the Duke of Tervuren and he only translates."

"I can sympathize. Europe is a land of so many cultures. My work carries me to so many places. The only place I can relax is at home."

"I wish I could speak German," I said.

"We would help," he replied. "Language, if you signed with us, would not be a barrier. We could supply you with appropriate translators for any route. But you have your friend, Aleta don't you? It can't be too much of a problem."

It wasn't, but I wasn't about to let him know that. "She's new, and I can't always trust what she says. It's not like she's regular crew yet. And I think she likes Lucien."

Nigel snorted, "Not surprising. He has quite the reputation."

Does he? "And I'm worried by the people I see in the streets, back in Boma. This isn't a friendly port," I said.

"What, the hands?"

"It's not only that," I said.

"So you know what that's about?" he asked.

"Maybe."

"Perhaps I'm not the best one to tell you about it." He thought for a moment, then decided to forge ahead. "Well, really it's about conserving ammunition. The colonial administration doesn't like passing it out. If we gave the militia too many bullets they might start shooting at us instead of their fellows." I nodded for him to continue. "The militia are required to turn in a right hand for every bullet fired, to make sure they aren't wasting it. One bullet, one life. It's all because of that rebellion we had." He could see that I was gaping. He frowned a bit and continued, looking off into the distance, "Well, they miss sometimes, don't they? They have to find hands somewhere."

That rocked me back. I didn't know how to respond.

He looked at me again. "You really didn't know?" I think I saw genuine sympathy and surprise in his eyes. The game had slipped for a moment.

"No."

"Oh." He turned his head back and stared at the river. "Well then."

We sat quiet on the crates for a bit until Aleta came back, "The Captain said we're coming to rough water and that we should climb higher and hold on."

"Yes, of course. It's that part," Nigel said. "We'll have rough water until Leopoldville."

So we climbed up a bit. The sun was bright. The water was clear now, a rocky bed. The waterwheel was sloshing. And the shore was no longer covered in forest, but with huge round rocks of black stone, ten, twelve feet in diameter, tumbled smooth by the river. God, I thought, what the river must become to turn boulders like that.

The water was picking up speed. We began to lose headway as the current held us back. Swirls and chop broke the water around us, wavelets breaking over the bow sending water running across the deck. But we plowed on. I wasn't worried. This boat obviously did this regularly. This is why she had a closed hull.

Nigel was right, we had unsettled water all the way in to port. We reached Leopoldville that evening, with the slanting sun lighting the town and riverbank. The docks were even more primitive than Boma. They were sitting back in a little calm bay among the rapids. It was summer and the river was low, which made for a climb to the dock top. Looking around, I noticed they had no crane. How were they going to unload?

The answer was brute force labor. The stick-thin black dockworkers formed human chains, standing on each other, clinging to the pilings like ants, passing the crates up hand over hand. Dozens of hands hoisting each crate upwards while clinging to the sides of the docks. And there on the dock were the militia with their guns ready, their clips filled with bullets, each one a human hand.

"Oh good," M. Daems said. "We're in time for dinner."

The jungle had been cleared back from the harbor and filled with neat rows of plantation trees. Leopoldville spread out in narrow patches, here and there, between the groves. Our destination was up on a hill, along a long dirt road. I was actually looking forward to the walk after our confinement on the boat, but they had been expecting us. Twenty imperials on horseback rode down to meet us, bringing us horses. Our gear would come later, loaded on the backs of black men.

I had never ridden a horse in my life, but I was certainly not about to look like an idiot. They were huge. Just getting my left leg up to the stirrup was a stretch, and yes, I admit it – I do read those penny dreadfuls. Once I was up, though, I was clueless. The horse moved around waiting for instructions, the ground miles below. I had reins. I knew what they were, but I didn't know what to do with them and I was determined not to rely on Lucien, since he seemed to be distancing himself from us. Aleta was still on the ground trying to figure out which leg to use to climb on.

"Mme. Verbeeck!" I called, and she came trotting over to us.

"Yes my dear?"

"We don't know how to ride horses."

"An American who doesn't know how to ride?" And she was hiding a laugh again.

"Yes, I'm embarrassed to say, I don't go on shore as much as I should. We mostly rent carriages. As far as I know," I said, again from the penny dreadfuls. "He should respond to rein. But it isn't working."

"He's a warhorse. You use your back, heel, and knee. Do nothing, just relax or he may jump. Pass me the reins and I'll lead."

Then Leopold came riding up. "*Was ist los?*" he asked.

She replied in French. "They use rein in America and she is

confused." She was covering for us!

"*Auch*," he sighed. Auch was right! Then in French he replied, "Pass me the reins." We had heard his French!

She said to us in English, "Give His Highness your reins," which we did, with thanks.

"Was the river ride comfortable?" he asked, with Mme. Verbeeck translating.

"Yes it was. The rapids were exciting," I replied. Aleta was just sitting there as we were led along. It wasn't like her to just sit.

"Not the same as the ocean," I said.

"No. Certainly not. I have a ship of my own. It's bigger than yours though. A dreadnought."

Dreadnoughts were about the biggest things in the ocean. Certainly the most dangerous.

"I wish it had been there when we were crossing the Atlantic."

"There was trouble?"

"Yes. A Confederate fleet and a Union fleet were fighting over us. We were very lucky the shells all missed."

"You were there on the boat when this happened?"

"Yes." Then I smiled. "I was soaked to the bone from the spray."

Aleta gave herself a shake and added, "Tell him about your cabin."

"I wasn't there for that one."

"Your cabin?" Mme. Verbeeck gave me a searching look.

I sighed. "A shell went through my cabin. But that was a different trip."

"War can make travelling dangerous," she said.

"It's very bad for business," I replied.

We arrived at a row of whitewashed buildings with smoke coming out of two chimneys on the largest. Our dinner I hoped.

Leopold was off his horse and helped all three of us down, even though it was clear that Mme. Verbeeck needed no help.

Aleta and I were given a room in our own little house. It had rough mud brick walls and two straw beds draped over with netting. Our maid was a black woman, thin as bones. She didn't speak English, French, or German. She pointed at us and then herself and then the door. Completely confusing! Then she grabbed the top of her blouse and yanked it up and then pointed at herself again.

"I think she wants our dresses," Aleta said.

"That makes sense. They need washing," I replied.

"Oh!" exclaimed Aleta.

"What?"

"We're probably supposed to dress for dinner! We have no clothes."

"You're right. What are we going to do?"

She plunked down on her bed and began to rub her temples. "We'll just have to wear our clean day dresses," she said.

"Are you okay?" I asked.

"I have a headache." Stomach problems and now a headache.

So we were undressing and Aleta said, "You know, life with you has been about the strangest thing I've ever experienced."

I laughed. "Mine has certainly been more fun since you came along," I replied.

We donned our change of clothes without a bath, and awaited the call to dinner. We didn't have to wait long. It came as a gentle knock on the door. "Please bring your instruments," the imperial said in French.

Dinner was in the large building, in a room with a long table with seating only for us, the principal guests, and Lucien. When we entered I heard Herr Metzger say to M. Massart, "*Ah, unsere schönen Ablenkungen sind angekommen.*" M. Massart turned on him rather too quickly and started to speak, changed his mind, then chided, "*Höflichkeit bitte.*" Aleta whispered in my ear as I was sitting, "He called us beautiful distractions." I thought that was odd as well as rude, but the prince seemed amused.

"M. Massart knows German," I whispered back.

"It makes sense if he works for Krupp," Aleta replied.

Crow wasn't there. I hadn't seen him all afternoon. He was probably eating with the servants. I hoped he was getting food. We were going to have to find a way to ask about him.

The conversation was complicated because of the language issues, Mr. Milford, M. Daems, and yours truly not knowing German. It got to be so bad that we might as well be writing each other letters. If only we would all admit that we could speak French--most of us at least--if not all, then we wouldn't have any problems, I thought. The translations went on and on and about the time the salad was served, I couldn't take it anymore and I did something stupid.

I looked at Leopold and said, "*Je sais que vous parlez français!*" I know you speak French.

"Yes. I do," he replied in French.

Then I worked my way around the table repeating it, or, for the people I wasn't sure about, I just said, "*Je ne suis pas sûr de vous.*" I'm not sure about you. I saw averted eyes and, I thought, some begrudging nods. "Now we can have a proper dinner," I said. "Proper" was in English because I don't know the word for proper.

Herr Metzger said in French with indignation, "But my French is very poor!"

Nigel cut him off. "The word is '*correct*'," he said.

"Correct?" I replied. "Really?"

"Yes."

"*Maintenant nous pouvons avoir un dîner correct?*" I asked.
"*Oui.*"

At least this amounted to conversation. Giliam was still silent and aloof. Sadly, this solution left Aleta out, but she had hardly said or eaten a thing all evening. She looked kind of gray.

Desert was some sort of pudding. Frankly, it was nasty. The cook had no clue. Leopold just snorted in disgust, then looked up at me. "Could you play something for us, Miss Carmichael? Save us please from this . . ?" he asked, pushing away his pudding.

How could I refuse a plea for pudding salvation? I looked at Aleta, "Can you play?" She shook her head. I could see shadows under her eyes. "May I play?" I asked, and she nodded. Something was wrong with her. Oh please don't get ill here, I thought. Tropical diseases are just about the worst kind.

So I stood, feeling somewhat alone. I rosined my bow and tried to find some sort of tuning amid the humidity. Aleta was looking ill and I had never been or felt so very far from home. It was like we were on the edge of the cliff at the end of the world, and I wasn't playing this game well at all. I decided on *Vitali's Chaconne.* Honestly, it just popped into my head when I thought of pudding salvation. Everyone was watching me, so I turned aside a little so I wouldn't have to look at them.

Once I launched into the music, the sound cut through everything, my doubts and fears, and the room disappeared and I rolled from note to note twisting them to my whims. It's an awful work, but it can be a very romantic piece with effort. You can fill it with melodrama. The key is to shift from sweet to sad, a little sharp, a little flat, back and forth with sobbing vibrato. I drew the notes out each heavy, the vibrato ringing, then pulling back, rolling them in confectioner's sugar only to slice them back down, building slowly and falling back, like surf over and over again, worrying about Aleta the whole time. Was she all right? Would it pass? Over and over, I shifted between the music and worry, until I was at a loss and altogether too tired. So much so that I almost stopped. It was the heat and the day.

But this wasn't practice. I wasn't alone. I had to finish. I pulled last notes out in anger, close to tears. I would not succumb to this! I rose up again, bringing it finally to a close, slicing through the silence of the room with the last note.

My chin rest was wet with sweat. It had become annoying. It was the humidity. I must find some kind of cloth, I thought. The doors had filled with servants watching. Mme. Verbeeck had an odd smile on her face. She slowly began to clap, breaking the silence, with the rest of the room soon following. They had been staring. Confused, I bowed.

I was tired, and worried about Aleta. I looked at her with concern. Then I said to the room in French, "We cannot continue. I apologize, but we must retire."

I practically had to carry her in, she couldn't stay upright. I felt her forehead. She was feverish! I gave her water from our pitcher to sip.

the prince's doctor came soon after dinner finished, with a gentle knock on the door, and after examination said she had dengue fever. He gave us pills for the fever, to help her sleep. And they did help. She said her headache was less, but they weren't enough to stop it and she just got worse.

It was hours after dinner and she had fallen asleep and I tried to wake her to drink some water. She had stopped sweating and I was worried, but she wouldn't wake. She was so pale and so hot. I knew then that I had to get her back to the ship, to Red, where we could take care of her. I was running down the walkways in the dark knocking on doors, when Lucien came with a lantern. People looked out their doors and windows, candlelight from their rooms spilling out past their night clothes across the darkness. I heard muffled discussion, but I was trying not to cry. I couldn't stop pacing. Then Lucien was there.

"The doctor is with her," he said. He made some hand signal to someone amongst the others.

"Lucien, I can't go on," I cried. "These people have no idea what they're doing."

"You have to. We have to leave her here."

"They're so desperate, they'll steal her medicine to feed their families."

"There's a hospital here, run by Baptist missionaries," he said, holding my shoulders, trying to calm me. "They have a German doctor and trained nurses. We'll leave someone to watch over her."

"What kind of hospital can they have here?" I asked skeptically. "May I see it?"

"Yes, of course," he said. I think he wanted to say more, but we weren't alone. "But we must hurry. We have to leave early if we're to make our next stop before dark." Imperials appeared behind him.

"Let's go and pack her clothes," he said. He let go, walking past me to lead, expecting me to follow. "Do not pack her knives, guns, and ammunition," he said. "They'll only be stolen and someone might get hurt. Keep her flute too."

I took a step, then two, then I was following. At our door we were met by Crow and another man. They had a stretcher.

"Oh, Crow! I've missed you!" I ran the last few steps and gave him a hug. I was crying all over again.

"Hello, Missy. I've been here." He hugged me close for a moment, then rubbed my shoulders. "Don't worry."

Inside our room, Crow knelt down by Aleta and felt her head and then pressed his finger under her jaw, then shook his head. "She's sick all right. Hot enough to fry eggs. Getting a rash too. If the doctor didn't say different, I'd say she has measles."

"Come," Lucien said. "She has to go to the hospital."

Crow and the soldier lifted her on the stretcher while I gathered her things. Mme. Verbeeck met us in our house's hallway. There was a moment of worry on her face lit by the light from our candles as she looked at Aleta, but quickly hidden.

Outside, we were met by a man with a torch. We walked into the dark, the moon behind the trees, pitch black in the shadows, silver gray in between. In the distance I could see a light or two, a gray shape. We were following a trail that took us further up the hill.

"How is she?" Mme. Verbeeck asked.

"She's very hot and I can't get her to wake up," I said. I felt numb dread.

"I hear this doctor is quite good," Mme. Verbeeck said. I didn't believe it. Nothing was good in the Congo.

"I will see for myself," I said flatly.

"As any friend should," she replied.

"I spoke French to His Highness," I said to Lucien. I think I was going crazy and babbling. At that he looked back with a little smile.

"You did," he said. "And I think it may have been for the best."

Ahead we saw light from windows, windows with real glass.

"We're here," Lucien said. It was the hospital. We had to walk around the building to get to the entrance. The hospital itself consisted of two long whitewashed buildings with mud walls and thatched roofs. Between was a mud brick paved courtyard. In the center were two open fires and many people. Family members of patients, I thought; all black and desperately thin. Both buildings had large double doors facing the court. We went in through the doors on the left, lugging the stretcher. Lucien seemed to know the way.

Inside it looked like a barn, with just the thatched roof above and dirt ground below. Sitting on the dirt floor were more people, the room lit by a single lantern. I was about to say that this won't do when a white woman in a loose skirt, much like mine, came out a side door. "*Was ist los?*" The men sat the stretcher down. She knelt beside it and felt Aleta's head. "*Fieber. Sehr heiß.*" She stood and motioned for us to follow her back through the door. "*Komm,*" she said. Through the door, inside, was a proper room that stretched away before us filled with rows of real beds, each with clean sheets and bedstands. She picked a bed and pointed, "*Stellen Sie sie hier. Ich werde den Arzt erhalten.*"

187

"She's getting the doctor," Mme. Verbeeck said. Two other women, both black, were going from bed to bed helping patients. On each wall hung large wooden crosses.

The doctor, when he arrived, was older, but not yet graying. He washed his hands in a sink by the door. *"Was haben wir heir?"* he said as he approached her. *"Fieber, ausschlag,"* he lifted her lips and eyelids. *"Kein Blud."* He looked up at us and said, *"Dengue."*

"Fever, rash, no blood. It's dengue," Mme. Verbeeck said.

" Zwei Tage und wir werden wissen, wenn sie leben wird."

"Two days and we will know for sure if she will live."

"Does he know her chances?" I asked.

"They are good. The next two days are the hardest, and someone will always be here with her."

"I will stay," I said.

"You must go on," Lucien said. "You'll both need a ship after this and there's your family to think about. You aren't finished."

"But I can't leave her alone!" I was almost ready to cry again.

"I suggest you write a letter to leave for her," Mme. Verbeeck said. "There is nothing you can do here that won't be taken care of. She will not be alone." And then she smiled, "Besides, they speak German here, and her German is better than any of ours except for Lucien and His Highness himself."

I did finally write her a letter, scribbling away at the scrap of paper they gave me. I kept having to wipe away tears. Lucien came for me, to bring me back to our room, and found me holding her up, trying to dribble water into her mouth, the only aid I knew.

Chapter 16

Mswata Trading Post

We were under way the next morning with me curled up between two crates sobbing as the dock shrank in the distance. The staff had come early that morning to take away my things to the boat. I didn't come out for breakfast, but was eventually led onboard by Lucien, in a daze. I sat on the deck, leaning against the dusty wood of the crates, my heart broken. I could hear His Highness and the rest talking sometimes, when they raised their voices.

"It was that fool! They were in that warehouse all night and the next day!"

"But will she be all right?"

"We're damn lucky it wasn't malaria!"

Eventually, Crow came by with some food. "Feel like eating? You ought to or you'll get sick," he said. "It'd be a shame if you were dead when the boat gets back to pick her up."

I had to think about that. "Give me the food," I said, a little angry at his being right. "I'll eat what I can," which turned out to be a fair bit.

The food did help. But it was a wicked need to use the rail chair that finally drove me out of my hole. Walking around brought back some sense of the world around me. On the way back, Lucien caught up with me.

"Feeling any better?"

"Yes," I said. To be frank, it sounded weak.

"Would you like some tea? We're having some over at His Highness' table."

Tea would be nice. Jousting with Leopold, not. "I'll try," I said.

The table was set nicely. The prince was sitting with Mme. Verbeeck and Nigel.

"Oh, there is our young musician. It's good to see you moving about," Leopold said in French.

"We have been a bit worried," Mme. Verbeeck added with a friendly smile.

They seemed cheerful. Even Nigel looked at me with interest. I suspected that I looked like a bit of a mess, but they seemed to be willing to ignore it.

"Try some tea," Leopold said and he poured. It was steaming and very black.

How did they heat it? "Oh!" I said, "I bet they sit it on the boat's boiler."

"Hmmm?" Leopold said. He looked at the pot a for second and then said, "I suppose they must." Mme. Verbeeck was amused and Nigel was just alert.

"This is very good," I said. It was too. "Thank you."

"Thank you for joining us," he replied. "We are sorry for your friend, but we are glad it was only dengue and not worse, and we could not have been in a better place for it to take hold."

My French not being that good and his accent thick with German, I found I was missing words, but I got the gist of it and nodded my head to thank him.

"We've been thinking about the future of your ship," he continued. "And we believe we have a solution that will satisfy everyone." Not if Nigel is involved, I thought. "Nigel has kindly offered to extend their company contract to cover your ship."

"Under what . . ," I stopped and look at Mme. Verbeeck and said in English, "Conditions?"

"It's *conditions*, just pronounce it in French," she said in English.

"Oh. Under what conditions? Would we fly our flag? Could we choose our own cargo and ports? Under what conditions would the contract be . . ." and then I look at Mme. Verbeeck. "Voidable?"

"Ooo, I don't know that one either," she replied with a frown.

"*Résiliable*," Nigel said. He frowned.

"*Was ist das?*" his highness said.

"*Aufhebbar, vielleicht?*" Nigel said.

"Ah, good thinking! What about these questions?"

"These would naturally be up for negotiation," Nigel said.

"All of our crew are owners. What control would your cartel have over our personnel?" I asked.

"All of your crew are owners?" Nigel asked.

"Yes. I own one-sixteenth myself. Would we have to use your bank?"

"You are an owner? Where do you bank now?"

"In Boston, naturally."

Nigel clearly didn't expect me to have a clue about business matters. His highness' smile was growing.

"Sir, if you expect some sort of . . ." I said, momentarily lost. And then to Mme. Verbeeck, "Implied?"

"*Implicite*," she said, covering her smile with a sip of tea.

"Of course. If you expect some sort of implicit contract from this discussion then I'm afraid that you will be disappointed. Any contract we enter into must be voted on by the owners." There, I thought. Invoke the need for higher authority. I leaned back and stared at him, taking a sip of tea.

Leopold burst out laughing. "A merchant's daughter! Nigel, you have met your match."

Nigel was holding his tea, but had stopped halfway to his mouth. He remembered it suddenly, blinking at it like its presence was unexpected, then continued on to take a sip. "You do surprise, Miss Carmichael."

Should I attack? I was definitely in the mood. "Sire, Mr.

Prendergast's cartel does not service the Americas. Looking at the ships in port, I wonder if they currently have the resources to do so. With our contacts, we could easily organize such trade. American ships trading with the Americas, British ships trading with Europe. There is room for both."

"That!" Nigel snapped, slammed down his hand. "Is not possible!" He had sloshed his tea into his saucer. When he realized where he was and put it down carefully, looking a little surprised. "I apologize, Your Highness. What she proposes would violate our exclusivity agreement."

"Are we discussing what is good for Britain or what is good for Belgium?" I replied.

"Yes Nigel. We are building up unshipped surpluses and are in wont for supplies. More ships would help everyone," His Highness said.

"And more varied goods," I added.

"If the Congo is to continue to receive our protection, then you must honor the contract," Nigel replied. He was losing his temper again, I thought.

"Does that contract include the land necessary for your railroad?" I asked.

Now everyone was looking at me.

"Which railroad would that be?" Nigel asked.

"You know about the Portuguese African colonies, of course?" I said to the prince. Now Nigel definitely scowled.

"Nigel?" Leopold asked. He had to already know about it.

"Portugal ceded them to England," Nigel replied. "They were losing a great deal of money, with no end in sight. We felt that we might be able to make a go of it."

"Their government toppled because of it. There was armed rebellion in the streets," I said.

"I think, Miss Carmichael, that you have been hearing stories," Nigel said.

"I was patching bullet holes in our hull all the way from Lisbon to Cadiz. We were commandeered to move soldiers."

"Shells, now bullets!" Leopold said. "You live an adventuresome life, Miss Carmichael, but I'm afraid that I must retire for a bit." I think he was trying not to laugh. "Please, finish your tea. It is too dear here to waste." He rose and headed in the direction of the rail chair. I definitely heard a chuckle.

Nigel wasn't finished though. He switched to English. "Miss Carmichael, if you continue to carry on like this, we may be forced to withdraw our offer."

"As I said, I cannot agree to anything without consulting the crew." There would be no implicit contract.

All of this time Mme. Verbeeck had said next to nothing. She poured herself another cup of tea and then finally added, "Why would it be so difficult to create some sort of American sub company, some sort of division of assets? I have heard you complain in the past about your difficulties with finding ships to cover your territories. Wouldn't American ships under contract to your concern fill that gap? Merely pay by the shipment rather than control the ship?"

"There is the difficulty of the American war. We trade with both sides. We would have to hire from both, they would have to work together under this system if we are not to take sides." Then his face got darker still. "And then there are the needs of the Empire herself. We need the flexibility to shift shipping at will, especially in times of war. Contracts, like you propose, would flee conflict."

"Red can't fight Mr. Prendergast, especially not for England," I said.

He tossed down his napkin, "That's where you're wrong Miss Carmichael. There's far more to fighting than guns," he said bitterly. Then he stood, "I too must retire, excuse me," and he walked away.

Once he was gone, Mme. Verbeeck gave me a mischievous smile. Motioning across the table she said, "It appears that the battlefield is yours!"

━━━━≈✳≈━━━━

I sat again amongst the crates, watching the jungle, the water, and the "logs" go by. The afternoon sun was hot, but I had shade from the crates behind me. I heard a noise above me and looked up. Who should be climbing down, but Crow!

"Hello, Missy."

"Hi, Crow," I said listlessly.

"Oh don't feel down," he replied.

"It's this heat."

He chuckled, "You should go over near the boiler."

"I should. Their rig might be interesting."

"They distill their own water," he said.

"Really?" I said, brightening up.

"The Captain built it himself. The boiler heats the coils."

"We should have something like that on Red. We could use Ma's oven." Now I really had to go see the boiler.

"Sure would be nice," he said, looking pleased. "Hot fresh water baths would be great."

"That is if we ever see her again."

"Oh, don't talk like that," he said. "The odds on us are going up."

"Odds?" I asked, suddenly interested again.

"Well, yes. The servants do just about anything to pass the time. Especially gambling."

"They gamble on their employers?" Could the day get any stranger?

"Hell yes," he said with chuckle. "Nothing better."

"So what are our odds?" I asked, a little afraid to hear them.

"'Bout one in five we keep the ship, three in five we survive."

"Better than even," I said. "That's hopeful."

"It is when you know that our survival was one in twenty yesterday. You're doing great."

"I should have put some money down before we left."

"Don't worry," he said, his gold tooth shining. "I did. Figured we had nothing to lose."

For the first time in a week I let out an honest laugh.

"They treating you okay?" I asked.

"Better than you I think. Most of those servants are pretty good people. They have to stick together to survive."

"I can't budge the Brits," I said, sighing.

"That's 'cause they want the territory. It's going to be war, sooner than later. They can't compromise. Most people are trying to figure out where to hide until it's over."

"Are there odds on his highness?" I asked.

"Yup. If he's here when the war starts, it's one in six. He isn't the king, just an heir."

"That might be useful," I said.

"I suppose it might," he said with a little smile. "Your pa was smart the way he brought you up, training you in the business, and now it's paying off."

"I hope so."

"Keep fighting, Missy," then he was back on his feet. "I've got to get back."

"Don't go far, Crow."

"I'll be right here." He smiled, and then he was up and over the pile of crates.

I sat back down and watched the river roll by for a bit, back to feeling melancholy again. I missed Aleta, which made me think of my violin. So I pulled down my case from the crate above me. The bow seemed fine so I started to try to make sense of the tuning. The sun had been on the case; she was hot, but cooling down. Dry in the case, now damp in the air. Impossible. But I would not be foiled and kept working at it when who should show up but Lucien. I was so popular!

"Hello," he said. "I hear you did well against Nigel." Then he saw that I had put down the violin. "Oh, don't let me stop you. Your work is quite amazing. I hadn't realized just how much with only the one other time I heard you play."

"That was my first time on a public stage."

"Then I am blessed," he said with a little bow of his head.

"Odds are not good that this violin will make it home."

"Oh no, not at all. Your family's future is in doubt, but everyone has finally managed to agree that somehow we'll find a way to get you out."

I had no response for that, so I stared at the river for a bit, and then set about trying to find some tuning again. It had settled to an even temperature and I finally found sense in it.

I started to play a Negro work song, plodding and sad. It was, as I remember it, a plea for mercy. The weight of work matched by the weight of the sun and the beating heart, although I doubted that Lucien knew that. It had come drifting up from the furnace vent at school. I thought of Aleta and began to hum along, my piping soprano filling in her flute. Lucien sat on the crate above me and stared at the water as it went by.

We stopped for the night at *Mswata*, a trading post about 20 miles south of the Kwa river, beaching our boat on the gravel shore, the current trying to pull her stern about as her bow dug in. But ropes were tossed and tied off, new stakes driven next to those already there, and the boat fixed in place so that when the ramps were set and we walked down, there was no shift, the stern firmly fixed.

Mswata was little more than a large log blockhouse, a huge pile of cut wood, and a mud-brick cookhouse, all enclosed within a wood palisade. Imperials were waiting for us at the beach even though the post had, as I had been told by M. Daems, its own militia contingent. Apparently supplies and men had been shipped ahead for us all along our route.

Trading posts in the Congo were built to serve the steamer network that plied the Congo's rivers. They supplied fuel, secured places to rest overnight, and provided embarkation-debarkation points for cargo. Some of them were also militia posts representing the local law.

Our arrival had been well planned. Equipment, people, and tents with cots were already set up, waiting for us outside the palisade. They had built a fire too, with folding chairs and tables. We were served a very welcome, very good dinner almost immediately after we had walked off the boat. We ate sitting in our seats by the fire, which kept away the worst of the insects. We had noodles in broth, bread, cheese, glorious oranges, and wine – which I declined. I think, perhaps, His Highness seemed disappointed by that. He offered it to me several times over the course of the evening, extolling its virtues. My share, however, was not wasted. It left more for the men, and they got very "jovial."

After dinner, M. Daems was cleaning his gun as we sat by the fire.

"Did you see how the thing turned? Fifty caliber clean through, end to end, and still not dead!" M. Daems said.

"It was remarkable. I would hate to meet one of those brutes in the water," Herr Metzger replied.

"Shame we had to leave the hide," added Leopold. "Remember though, Daems. No shooting on the hunt unless it's an emergency. I'll tell you when we reach the killing ground."

"Yes, yes, scare the game and all," M. Daems replied. "It was a good shot though."

"Yes. A fine shot," the prince said. "If you had waited until it had its mouth open, it would have gone clean down the center and left the hide unscarred!" Which got a general laugh. "That would be a story to tell."

"Assuming you could have kept it out of its friend's teeth," added Nigel, which incited more laughter.

Not the brightest of conversation. M. Massart, again, contributed nothing. He had his notebook with him, but chose to sit with his glass of wine and stare into the fire instead. Mme. Verbeeck had retired early, which was beginning to sound like a good idea. Lucien was nowhere to be seen.

"Massart," the prince said. "You're too damned quiet."

"Yes, my Lord, I have been told that before. It's just that I can think of nothing to add, except perhaps to note that M. Daems' shot was doubly remarkable for having been made from a pitching deck." He gave Daems a sidelong glance, his eyebrows raised, as if saying, "is that sufficient?"

Daems broke into a broad smile. "Yes, it was wasn't it?"

Casting about, longing for escape, I noticed how everything was lit a beautiful deep blue under the trees, in the summer twilight. "Your pardon, my Lord, but I'm going to take a walk."

"Don't cross the perimeter," he warned.

"I won't," I called back.

Away from the fire, the insects began to buzz around me. I batted at them but it was no use. Smoke was rising from the trading post cookhouse inside the palisade. The forest stood like a dark wall beyond. The cleared perimeter was silhouetted beneath the dimming orange sky. Strangely, although they had set up tents in the servants' area as they had in ours, they had no fire. They were camped on the other side of the post and as I walked toward them, I crossed downwind of the post itself. That's when I noticed the smell. It smelled like the latrine trench and burning meat. I was about to go to the gate to look when I was intercepted by a guard.

"I'm sorry, miss, but this is as far as you can go," he said.

"I would like to see Crow," I replied.

"Is there a problem?" he asked.

"No. I just wanted to make sure that he's comfortable."

The guard looked relieved. "Don't worry, Miss. Everyone is well taken care of. But you have to stay within the party area."

"Yes, of course," I replied, a little bewildered. This, unfortunately, drove me back to our fire and the conversation of my hunting companions. I should have followed Mme. Verbeeck's example and retired early.

I noticed that the jungle had lit up with sound. All around us were creeks and chirps. What could be brave enough to be awake at night in a jungle like this making such racket? Whatever they were, there were a lot of them, in amazing variety.

Leopold, who always seemed to have one eye on me, saw me looking at the woods, listening. I had wandered back to the fire.

"They're frogs and cicada mostly," he said.

Frogs I'd seen, but I had no idea what a cicada was. "What's a cicada?"

"They're insects, an inch or two long. They live in the trees. The natives eat them."

"Are they like crickets?" I asked.

"No. More like a moth with a hard shell," he replied.

"They eat them?"

"They fry them mostly, but when they're hungry enough, they'll pop them straight in their mouths."

"How awful!" I replied, which got snorts from Mr. Milford and Herr Metzger.

Leopold, and perhaps some of the others, were, I think, taking pleasure in my discomfort. Smiling, he continued. "Oh, my dear, there are worse . . ."

He was cut off by a roar in the distance, out in the dark. Every head turned toward it.

"Leopard, I think," Nigel said.

"Something just died," the prince said.

"Quite," Nigel added.

That was enough for me. I excused myself and went to my tent. Inside, of course, the soldiers had set up two cots, one for Aleta and one for me, both draped in mosquito netting. The candle lamp was sitting lit on the little folding table. They hadn't heard about Aleta. The news couldn't travel quicker than our boat. Looking at the cot brought all my weariness and loneliness crashing down on me in a great wave. It was all I could do to change to my sleeping dress. I didn't even brush my teeth. I stared at her bed as I cried myself to sleep.

Chapter 17

The Hunt!

I woke with the first light of dawn. Everyone was still asleep, which was nice as there was no one around at the privy. Back at my tent, I thankfully brushed my teeth and felt much better for it. Down at the fire, a servant brought a most-blessed cup of tea. I almost cried with gratitude. The men still had yet to rise, but I could hear servants knocking on their tent poles. I was blissfully alone, free from talk of guns and death, enjoying what would probably be the only comfortable breeze of the day, when Mme. Verbeeck sat down next to me.

"Good morning, my dear," she said in English. "I hope the men weren't too boring last night."

"I couldn't offer an opinion." I might have rolled my eyes.

"Circumspection," she said, clearly amused. "You're learning.

I hoped you would follow my lead and retire early. I could hear some of it and you have my deepest sympathies." A servant brought her a cup of tea. She sighed with pleasure. "A cup of tea will brighten any day."

I asked the servant, "May I have another?"

"Yes, miss," he replied.

"They wouldn't let me visit Crow last night," I said.

"They wouldn't. It's not proper," she sighed.

"They didn't have a fire!"

"Yes, His Highness, I think, likes to feel he's isolated in the jungle. A second fire might also split the party's attention."

"A possibility," I replied.

Mme. Verbeeck just smiled.

"And while I was walking," I continued. "I noticed an awful smell coming from the trading post."

"Is there?" She frowned for a moment, then said, "Well, we don't need awful smells, so I think we should avoid it."

"Do you know what it might be?" I replied.

"I've investigated things like it before."

"And?" I asked.

"It's best to avoid them," she said, and took another sip.

That morning, when we embarked, I noticed that we passed the trading post on the upwind side.

The Congo River widened again and we made good time. Really, steam power is amazing. Imagine being able to cross the Atlantic diagonally, across the doldrums! We could go straight from the Canaries to Boston and never go near Florida, and work inland ports without worry as well.

As we worked our way north, we saw the Kwa River's silt trail miles before we saw the river itself. The water of the Congo and the Kwa seemed strangely reluctant to mix, instead, choosing to flow side by side.

An hour out of camp, Crow climbed over the boxes for a visit!

"I heard you tried to see me," he said.

"Yes, but they wouldn't let me."

"It's that class thing." Crow shook his head. "If there's something to not like about Europe, it's class."

"They didn't let you have a fire!" I said.

"Yup. Kept us away from the trading post too," he said,

shaking his head. "That Lucien made sure nobody got near."

"I wonder why?"

"Word is, they keep prisoners in there," he replied.

"How awful!"

"Probably, or that Lucien wouldn't be worried," he said, with a frown.

"At least he didn't ask me to play a song last night."

"Some folks were hoping he would," he said.

"Really?" I asked.

"Yup. It would've brightened more than a few people's day."

"He was too drunk to ask."

Crow smiled. "And none too happy about waking up this morning either, I hear."

That finally worked a smile out of me. I do love Crow.

We camped for the hunt at the fork of the Kassai and Kwa rivers, our boat beaching on a sandy stretch on the north shore. A camp for us, again, had already been built, its golden lanterns shining across the river water in the blue twilight as we approached.

Logs had been placed around the fire for seating, and tea had been prepared, the smoke from the fire providing blessed relief from the insects. A table had been set for us for dinner, but I wouldn't leave the fire and its protection. Others joined me in the circle and soon we were all lounging around the fire's light, holding our plates in our hands as we ate.

"This is the way a hunt should be," said M. Daems. "Roughing it."

I didn't think M. Daems had ever roughed it in his life. He ought to try standing watch in heavy seas and freezing rain, I thought, but I said nothing. Down at the beach, the soldiers were still working by torchlight on unloading, Captain Savoie's voice rising over the racket of the frogs.

M. Daems saw me looking at the boat. "Dammit, Lucien, where are the blacks? You didn't bring any. Your men can't be doing all the work."

"The nearest village is 75 miles away. We picked this spot for its security and isolation."

"Still, a boatload or two of them would make things easier," Daems muttered.

"No. It would make things harder," he replied crisply. "We would be watching them instead of the perimeter. We're going to travel light, in short one day excursions."

"One day's march?" Daems looked aghast. "That's not far enough in."

"This is virgin forest. We're the first whites, perhaps the first people ever to see this patch of forest. I think we'll see things," Lucien replied.

They talked more, but I couldn't listen. I found M. Daems to be very disagreeable so I stared at the fire instead. When we retired, I again had a whole tent to myself, with two cots. This time, her flute and guns lay on the bed.

The next morning brought rain that came down in waves, battering the top of the tent. I went out to look for the ditch and ran into Mmn. Verbeeck, doing the same. We laughed when saw each other, soaked to the bone, our dresses ruined beyond any point in caring. I took a big leap and jumped in a puddle hitting her with water, only a little bit by accident. Then she retaliated by kicking more water at me, laughing. When an imperial found us splashing and asked us if we needed help, we couldn't stop laughing to answer. He sent us in the right direction. The privy trench was flooded, but we used it anyway. I made it back to my tent, but had no clue what to do after that. I had one dry dress. To put it on now would be to ruin it, so I shucked off my bodice, put my nightgown back on, and crawled back into bed.

I think I must have slept, because the rain had stopped and the sun was shining. Even with all the humidity, steam was rising from everything. It was late morning, the green forest towered over us, the river drifted by below, mud squished and stuck to my boots. Then somehow, somehow, we had, of all things--a luncheon with a white tablecloth. They had set a buffet. We had canned peaches, which I love, and butter! How could they have accomplished this? I doubted there could be a single cow within a thousand miles. And of course, Leopold's lovely and most welcome tea. A glance down toward the river revealed that Captain Savoie had pulled out, probably back down river. The stakes they had driven last night to moor him were still there, so I expected that they were planning on his return, but for the moment, we were stranded.

Oh, and those contraptions that worked so hard to load back at the docks in Boma? They were down near the beach, men climbing all over them with wrenches, unfolding them piece by piece. Even as they took shape, they still made no sense to me.

I was trying to keep the insects away from my food as they served me, when who should bump into me but the elusive M. Massart.

"Pardon me," he said. His accent was definitely French.

"Oh, no problem," I said. I was waving the bugs away from my plate. They had net basket covers for the dishes, but you had to clear the air above the plate before you could use them.

"Miss Carmichael, isn't it? We really haven't had a chance to be introduced yet," which was nonsense. It's just he never talked to anyone!

"M. Massart." I said.

"Yes, Giliam Massart," he replied, seeming a little at a loss.

"Cali Carmichael." I looked at him squarely, daring him to go on.

"Cali?" he asked.

"Calista, really, but please don't. It's Cali."

"Ah, the sea goddess." He let loose a tentative smile.

"Yes. I've heard you deal in munitions."

That seemed to draw a thoughtful frown. His eyes seemed kind. "Yes, I'm a colonial representative for Krupp."

"But you're French."

"These are cosmopolitan times," he said. "Are you going to sit next to the fire?"

"It's the only way I'm going to be able to eat this food in peace."

"May I join you?" he asked.

I almost laughed. We had been sitting together for last two days.

"It would be a pleasure." I was raised, as you already know, to be a gracious hostess.

We were walking down to the fire. Several of the others had already had the same idea.

"It's interesting that I didn't hear about any munitions in your manifest," he said.

"People have been talking about our manifest?"

"Oh, yes."

"Really?" I asked.

He nodded back.

"Well, I've been kicking myself for that," I continued. "Shells would have been difficult since we didn't know what weaponry you all use here, but percussion caps, powder, and lead would have been smart purchases."

"I'm sure His Highness would have welcomed them." I think he sounded a little surer. I suppose it felt more natural for him since we were talking about munitions.

"But it's odd you should kick yourself," he said.

"This whole trip was my idea."

That seemed to baffle him. "But I heard that you are all shareholders. There must have been a vote."

"There was, but our manifest was based on my library work."

"I see." He thought for a second. "I think," he paused. "I think that you did very well for your first trip here. That pyrethrum has been a godsend."

"That was a lucky find. We got that from a Confederate ship berthed next door to us in Le Havre."

"Confederate?" he asked, a little surprised.

"Oh yes. We merchants don't fight. Especially if there's money to be made."

"Still, Confederate. There must be some disincentives for trading with the enemy."

"Well, yes, sometimes, but that particular ship owed us," I said. "We helped them defend their ship from rioting soldiers."

"Rioting soldiers?"

"Union soldiers!" I spat. "Our own soldiers, rioting, attacking Confederate ships in a neutral port!"

"Appalling," he said, although he didn't seem appalled. "However, I find the implications to be interesting." His voice had changed. The meekness had evaporated.

"It could be Confederates attacking us next time." I gave him the eye.

"Very true." He seemed to be sizing me up. "So, you were fighting on the docks?"

"No, Ma and I were defending the gangway." He nodded his

head, as if he had guessed.

He glanced toward the fire and the rest of the party. Then gave me a little smile and asked innocently, "Did you get any of them?"

I nodded and, in a whisper, said, "I got two. With a crowbar."

He chewed on that for a second and then rolled back and laughed out loud.

The elusive Mr. Massart was far less elusive after that. He gave me a cheery hello that afternoon when we were gathered to discuss tomorrow's hunt.

The metal contraptions had unfolded into mechanical men made out of sticks. They were squat and heavy, with armored torsos like barrels. Where there should have been hands, the things had what I could only guess were weapons. Round arrangements of tubes, like tubes made out of tubes, fed by belts of bullets that travelled along tracks. There was always someone near them, polishing and adjusting them. They looked very formidable.

"What are those things?" I whispered to Mr. Massart. He's an arms dealer. He should know.

"The knights?" he asked.

"Is that what they're called?"

"They're heavy-weapon platforms, used primarily to support infantry. They're here to help protect His Highness."

"Will they be on the hunt with us?"

"I doubt it. They make a lot of noise."

"They look scary," I said, looking back at them.

"That's certainly on purpose." We stopped walking and he looked back at them. "They also pack a hell of a lot of firepower."

"They seem like a lot of trouble. Could we be in such danger?"

"Africa is a risky place." He dismissed it, as if it were a given.

"Still, I doubt even lions would bother with us," I said.

"No, these are for the people kind of predators," he said.

"Rebels, or perhaps assassins?"

"Possibly. Who knows?"

"The British?"

His head snapped around, his gaze sharp. He frowned at me and looked like he wanted to say something, but then we heard the call for our pre-hunt meeting.

"We must talk," he said. "There is business we need to discuss." He got up with a sigh, and added, "Later." Then we walked over to the prince and the rest of the gathering guests.

The meeting went like a council of war, with intelligence reports and timetables. Apparently the scouts had seen signs of leopards, an elusive, much-sought-after prize. We were going to concentrate on the wooded regions to the south in the hopes of "bagging" one; as Nigel put it. Everyone was keen to start the hunt. I suspected they were looking forward to tomorrow as if it were Christmas.

When I got back to my tent, I looked at Aleta's flute and guns still sitting on her cot. It would have been better, I thought, if they had taken her bed away. It only depressed me.

After dinner, they were playing cards and passing around a flask. Even Mme. Verbeeck! Apparently, judging from the sums being bid, a great deal of money was changing hands. It was interesting at first, but I quickly grew bored. I didn't understand the game and couldn't appreciate the intricacies of it. We very rarely played cards on the ship as we were rarely had enough of us together at the same time. And, of course, I had no money to play with. I retired early.

There came a knock on my tent pole just before dawn. I answered and was out of bed before I could think. It was shipside habits. As I geared up, I looked at the Colt pistol on Aleta's cot. It had twice the hitting power of my Webley, at least according to Lucien, and it was American to boot. So I switched belts, then I picked up my ten hellish pounds of Winchester and hung it over my shoulder, just as Pa had said. It was certain as church bells on Sunday that it was going to weigh even more by the end of the day.

Sandwiches and tea were waiting for us as we gathered at the fire. His Highness had changed clothes. All finery and shine were gone. "Good morning, Miss Carmichael. I feared rain again, but we have a fine day. It's a good omen."

"I hope you get your leopard, my Lord," I said.

"One for each of us!" he replied with a wild grin.

Then I saw Mme. Verbeeck. She was wearing a sensible dress, still buttoned to the neck, with boots peeking out beneath, a wide-brimmed hat, and a beautiful rifle covered with engravings and gleaming brass. Despite all of its gilt and flash, the thing seemed to be of impressive caliber.

"*Guten morgen, Frau Verbeeck,*" the prince said.

"*Guten morgen, Milord,*" she replied.

Then she looked at me with a smile, "It's not fair you know, that you Americans can wear such easy clothes."

"I'm afraid this is only for the countryside," I replied. "In the cities, we are as crazy as Parisians."

"Oh good, that is a relief. One does not want to suffer alone," she said with a melodramatic roll of her eyes.

"May I say that that is a most impressive gun you are carrying," I said, which got a snort from his highness.

"It was my husband's."

"Was?" I asked, a little worried.

"You didn't know? I'm a widow."

"Oh dear, I'm sorry," I apologized.

"You couldn't have known." She waved it away. "It's been over a year now."

I was aching now to find out more, but this was hardly the place, lady of manners and grace first after all. And we had no more time. We were called to our horses. I grabbed another sandwich and held it in my mouth as I mounted.

Another river boat had arrived in the night and had unloaded horses, fodder, and more troops. We were going to ride for a while, I was told, in order to get some distance away from camp. As we moved into the forest we made a column of guests, servants, gear, and soldiers. I could see Crow back behind us in the turns. He saw me looking and nodded and smiled.

The path we were taking was very narrow and animals fled in front of us; colorful birds and little apes in the trees all running for the hills even though our horses and tack made very little sound. In the stagnant humid air every noise seemed loud. My horse was being led by the imperial riding in front of me. Each time his horse jumped and climbed over an obstacle, I knew I was next, and sure enough, a lurch and a jolt, and I had to hold on for dear life. I was grateful we didn't have side saddles, or I would have been down in the brush in the first five minutes. We rode for an hour to a clearing--really more of a break in the trees, but still filled with dense brush. It was there that we left our horses.

Crow made his way over to me. "Morning, Missy," he said, shooing away a fly.

"Morning, Crow," I replied.

"They say we're going to hunt from here today," he said. "They have it all scouted out."

"That's good, because I don't think I could find my way back." I couldn't see the sky or the sun.

"Sure you could," he smirked. "You know where the river is."

"That's true," I said, brightening up.

"We're only a few miles from camp too." He was looking around at the forest. "I doubt we're going to find any leopards, though. Not with all this noise."

"Think so?" I asked.

"Maybe. Kind of reminds you of Jamaica, doesn't it?"

"Jamaica had better birds," I answered smiling. Unlike the Congo, Jamaica is full of good memories.

"That sure is true. Seen some parrots though."

"I heard them," I said. "I was trying too hard to not fall off the horse to look."

That got a chuckle, but then a big, vivid-blue hummingbird came buzzing around us like some angry insect. It was hard not to duck and dodge. In the next instant it was off buzzing around the horses, who shifted nervously. "Now that's something," Crow said.

"Sure is," I agreed.

Lucien walked through the crowd tapping guests on the shoulder, motioning toward His Highness, and then moving on to get the others. He didn't even say "hi." I had, at that point begun to doubt him. Had it all been an act to pull me into this?

We gathered around the prince, like at the start of some team sport. He was in the middle, crouched down, giving instructions.

"Each of you may bring one and only one servant. We will have two men in front to clear the trail, then us, then the servants and soldiers."

"Not too many, I hope," said M. Daems. "We've been too noisy already."

"Ten, I think, to cover us and help carry, and the doctor of course. They will follow at a distance. No unnecessary talking. We will advance in two parties, about 200 yards apart."

Naturally, I was in the prince's party. We were advancing with

Lucien, and Mme. Verbeeck. Each group had two experienced hunters and two regular guests. The last thing they did was check their watches. We had to return by 3:00, which gave us seven hours.

The hunt began with a lot of shoulder patting, handshaking, and wishes of good luck, then we were off into the brush. Just like that, with no real trail. We were climbing right through and over it, knocking down the brush as we went, at least until we were back in the darkness of the trees, where the undergrowth began to thin. It made a thick green ceiling over our heads.

His Highness, naturally, led the group, followed by M. Massart, Mme. Verbeeck, me, and then Lucien. We followed the trail that had been opened for us by the forward scouts, trying to be as quiet as possible, but every noise seemed to be cacophonous, even our breathing, in that humid stillness.

What did you see, what did you see on your hunt Cali, I hear you ask! Amazing animals? No. I saw leaves in my face, mud, ant trails, and things to climb over. At least for the first few hours. We stopped occasionally while Leopold looked around, and then we continued on, and on. That was, until we got to the elephant road.

The first sign I saw of its existence was an uprooted tree. It had been literally ripped from the ground! The trunk had to have been a foot thick, pushed right over! We broke through the brush and roots into a wide gap of trampled greenery and uprooted trees. It ran like a road across our path. I could even see bits of blue sky above. I had seen drawings of elephants in books at the library. They were immense, but this – such strength!

In the center of their road was a stack of stones, left by the scouts, pointing the way across. We were soon back under the trees. After another 10 minutes of walking, his highness waved us to a halt and stood staring at the trees, looking for leopards I figured, when we heard a boom off to our right, followed by two more. Birds I never knew were there went flying up from the trees around us. Something crashed through the brush ahead of us, but was moving away fast. The other party had found something before us!

Chapter 18

An Unfortunate Incident

We heard a little piping trill from the brush ahead. the prince had a small silver whistle on a chain around his neck and he used it to answer. Out of the brush came our scouts. They were, of course, imperials, but out of uniform. Only their helmets identified them. They conferred in whispered German with Leopold, then moved back into the forest. Behind us we again heard movement, and Leopold again used his whistle. It was our support column. They had another whispered conference, and then it was our turn to move forward.

The day wore on. We had to have covered miles, creeping along through the brush. Gradually, the ground started taking on a definite downward slope. Following it, we saw light and a thinning of brush ahead. We had come to a cliff, but I couldn't see down further than six feet. It could have been ten or a hundred feet down. At the cliff edge two branches had been laid neatly on the ground, clearly marking our trail. We were to turn right, down a game trail. Big things had been moving that way and we had a clear path. Something scampered across the branch above me and then up the trunk, startling me. It was gray and I thought "big rat," but after a moment I realized that it was a gray bird. A bird that climbed trees!

On down we went, slowly crawling over damp rocks until I could hear water below. the prince pointed to the rocks at our side as we veered to skirt them. Oozing away from us between the rocks was a snake, very long and bland gray like old porridge, at least seven feet long.

I was thinking that there might be a break in the trees ahead when His Highness practically stumbled over the scouts. They had been waiting for us.

We were down in a river gulley. Word was passed back. "Watch for crocodiles." Crocodiles? They could be sitting right next to me, I thought, panicking. The brush thinned to beaten mud banks. Many trees sported debris piles pushed up against them from very deep river floods. In the distance, I thought I could hear splashing and digging. Maybe a grunt, or two? I decided then and there that I didn't like this place, but his highness was still watching the trees for leopards, happy as a boy out of school for the summer.

Word was passed back again, "We're downwind." I realized there was a breeze, which was nice. Downwind from what? We proceed forward slowly, the scouts flanking the prince. The trees shifted to palms, with breaks and blue sky between them. The brush turned to reeds. Muddy ruts led into breaks between them. A bird above called and suddenly everything was silent. It took off with an angry squawking, its beautiful long tail trailing along a moment after it took flight. We stood still, waiting for the forest to recover. It smelled like a stockyard.

His highness had shouldered his rifle and drawn his pistol. But I, Cali of the Sea, not Cali of the Jungle, was too frightened to let go of my rifle, even to chamber a round. We broke cover onto a wide mud flat that didn't so much bank the river as merge with it. Wading in the shallows were tall, long-legged, birds with sprays of black and white feathers. Beyond stretched brown water, the sun-sparkled surface broken by stray debris. Debris that twitched off flies. They were ears and eyes, just above the water. They were not crocodiles. There was a sudden stirring as we passed, as whatever it was that was submerged moved about. Whatever they were, they were huge, leaving great wakes and waves up the shoreline. They couldn't be elephants, unless they all had their trunks underwater, I thought. Two of them suddenly rose like whales, coming toward us, revealing gaping maws of brown teeth like broken tree branches. Someone yanked me back. The river water had broken over my boots. I had been standing there transfixed!

We showed haste, moving inland. the prince didn't seem interested in the water elephants, for which I was truly thankful. They stood there, behind us in the shallows watching us. We were making for a rocky outcrop that reached down toward the river. The scouts moved ahead. Apparently that was the place where we were supposed to meet the river, where we were to watch the water for our prey coming to drink. We had come out too far west of the outcropping. It's so easy to get lost in the jungle.

The ridge top had few trees, mostly just brush, and on the far side a steep slope that ended in a short mud flat. We crawled over the top and peered down into a herd of striped antelope splashing across the water from the far side to our bank, about thirty in all. the prince motioned for us to stay down, then pointed at his gun and shook his head no. No shooting the antelope.

I sat lying low on the ground, very uncomfortable. Like everyplace in this country, this ridge had ants. A thick trail of them passed a by a foot in front of me, but they seemed to take no interest in me. They were carrying pieces of leaves, each cut out in a circle, which was most curious. I pointed them out to Mme. Verbeeck. She smiled and nodded.

The antelope drank on the run and were gone like ghosts into the forest in a manner of minutes. Both the prince and Lucien had binoculars out, nice ones too, and were scanning the forest. The sun was on my back and it didn't feel good so time went by very slowly. The support column had come up behind us, but they were staying behind the ridge where they had trees and a breeze. Then Lucien tapped the ground to get Leopold's attention, and pointed at the far bank. Coming out of the trees were lions. One male and several females. Leopold shook his head. We were too far away. He motioned that we needed to move down the ridge, closer to the water, and of course closer to all the things in the water. Which was, I suppose, why we came here.

Getting down quietly was not easy. The slope was steep and we mostly slid. There would be no retreating back up. Whatever it was that came, we would have to stand our ground against it. At the bottom we sat in a much cooler spot. I was daydreaming when suddenly it began to rain birds, black and white with long orange legs. They settled like a cloud along the edges of the river amongst the terns and herons. One and then another was grabbed by things that slid out of the water and dragged them in struggling, their neighbors taking little notice other than to dodge. The birds were followed by big brown pigs, who come trotting out of the woods on our side, oblivious to our presence. The pigs seemed to be more interested in the mud than the water, spending their time on the bank. Following them were several crocodiles, who slid quietly from the reeds down those ruts I had seen before, and into the water. I suspected the crocodiles were probably interested in the pigs. Then, as the black and white birds began to leave, down came green parrots who lit at the water's edge. When the black and white birds took off, it sounded like heavy rain on a tin roof.

Still, we saw no game appropriate to his highness' needs, and it was time to head back. Getting out, however, would not be easy. We headed down river through the brush, but were forced to stop by the presence of crocodiles in the grass. The men conferred and it was decided that we would move down to the river's edge, toward the water, to walk in the open on its red clay slope. Ahead was a break in the trees, where the ridge was climbable. When we got there, I realized with dread that it was the elephant road. the prince pointed up it and whispered, *"Dépêchez-vous!"* which is "hurry" in French. There really wasn't much choice. It was this path or make our own.

You would think that being trampled flat by elephants would make it an easy path, but it wasn't. It was a tangle of broken branches and shrubbery, about thirty feet wide. We were half way up, in the worst possible place, and you must surely have guessed it. Along came the elephants! They were crashing along the path and down the slope, quite unstoppable. We were clinging to the slope, trying to aim our guns. They were monsters with great flapping ears and trunks that reached to the ground. The noise as they descended was indescribable. Like the wrenching of great rusting machinery and the rumble of an earthquake. The ground was vibrating beneath my knees.

I heard Mme. Verbeeck let loose a "*Jésus doux!*"

Lucien yelled, "Find cover!"

Find cover where? If I let go I'd go tumbling down the slope, I thought. Everyone was scrambling for the sides of the trail but me. I stood there like an idiot gawking at that huge wave of gray. Then I raised my rifle and fired. Next I knew I was tumbling down the hillside. When I slid to a stop I found I'd lost my rifle. I rolled back upright and drew my pistol. I could hear firing all around and a great river of elephants came rumbling down the hillside, some dying, others charging, some in my direction! I fired and fired. Clouds of smoke were drifting around me. Someone was lifted and thrown, their body twisting crazily in the air. I had to reload, but I couldn't make my hands work. Ahead of me, lying on the ground, was my rifle. I dropped the pistol and ran to it. One of them, wounded, was rising in front of me, a great black silhouette in the smoke. It was stumbling forward, gathering speed. I picked up the rifle, raised it, and cocked and fired. Blood blossomed from its head, but it was still somehow moving. I cocked the lever again, the spent casing spun past my eye glinting in the sun, and fired once more. Its legs gave way underneath as it slowly stumbled forward to plow into the ground at my feet.

My knees buckled. I dropped my gun, my hands shaking, to sink to my knees sobbing. The shooting gradually quieted, then somebody was there with their hands on my shoulders. They yelled, "She's over here!" and there was Crow. He lifted me up and I put my head on his shoulder and cried in great heaving sobs. We were in a sulfurous fog that drifted slowly downstream. It revealed a battlefield in front of us. I let go of Crow and stared at the great gray mounds of ear, tusk, leg, and trunk. Many were still moving, being dispatched by soldiers. Where are my guns? I started to frantically look for them. My rifle was on the ground, tears falling on its gray metal as I grabbed it and chambered a round.

"Slow down, Missy," Crow said. "It's over."

"It's not over," I sobbed. "Not until we're out of here." My pistol was behind me on the ground. I hopped back and pick it up, Crow following. It was empty of course.

"I think you ought to sit down for a bit," Crow said.

He had me by the shoulders trying to get me to look at him, but I was trying to open the cylinder to remove the shells with my shaking hands, still holding my rifle. Then, there was someone's pack and I was sitting on it and Lucien was offering me one of their flasks. "You need to drink some of this," he said. It tasted like kerosene and dirt, and I was immediately sorry that I swallowed for I started coughing. I was so thirsty! I pulled out my water bottle and drank, the first normal moment in my day. Then I finally pushed out the shells and reloaded the pistol. A soldier came for his pack, the one I was sitting on, followed by Crow.

"It's time to go," Crow said. The sun had shifted, time had somehow passed. "We've got to get back to camp. Think you can walk?"

"Yes," I said. "Let's go." I was more than happy to go.

This time, the climb up was successful. The other party had joined us. They had removed two of the elephant's heads and were carrying them lashed between long fresh cut poles. We had wounded as well, Mme. Verbeeck among them. She was unconscious, lying in a hammock of bloody elephant hide, strung between two poles. M. Massart was dead. His muddy body was bent, his head rolled too easily from side to side on his purple neck. I wondered if he had a chance to shoot. Who had he been here to sell guns to? I would never know.

Crow was walking with me now. There was no need for quiet. I realized that he had been talking.

"We saw what was coming, but we couldn't get there. We had to shoot from the ridge. Everyone ran but you Missy. I am some kind of proud of you. You just stood your ground. You'd have been dead, but you just stood your ground," and then his voice trailed off. He was quiet and we walked. I could only see his back, but I thought Crow was crying.

We arrived back at camp at dusk. The horses offered little help with our burdens, so we proceeded at a walk. The mood was subdued. About half way back, Mme. Verbeeck awoke with a groan, and then a grinding moan that almost led to a scream of pain. The doctor offered chloral hydrate to help her sleep through the trip back to camp. She refused for many hours before finally relenting. Then we watched her with great care lest she choke and to keep the flies off. Leopold and I were the only unwounded. Lucien had deep lacerations, which we bound. Walking gave him great pain and blood leaked from his bandages. Altogether, in my opinion, the day's hunt had been a great disaster, but the prince was pleased with his trophies and seemed ready to shrug off the loss of life. He insisted one of the elephant heads was mine. Maybe, I thought cynically, we could use it for a masthead.

"It's not the animal," he explained. "But the story behind it that makes a good trophy," he told me as we walked. "This was one I'll enjoy telling to visitors." He patted the bloody head. What trophy will he take from me and what stories will he tell, I wondered?

"I have no place to keep trophies," I said. "I live on a ship."

"I doubt you will forever," he said.

"I want to."

"And I want to sit in the jungle and hunt, but someday I'll be king and this will come to an end."

"Kings can do what they want," I replied.

"Sadly, no. There are many reasons why they are the weakest piece on the chessboard. I can barely control what I have now."

"I doubt that."

"But it's true. I've changed my mind about your ship for instance. But if I let you go, the British would certainly retaliate."

"They can't have any more troops than you do," I replied.

"True, but we get our bullets from them and our militia could easily be incited to revolt. It would not be difficult to surround and, with their control of shipping, strangle us. Besides, they don't need to do that. All they need do is neglect to ship us quinine or citrus fruit."

"Then trade with us."

"When would you be back? Six months, a year? You'd not only be dodging Confederates, but British too."

"What about your neighbors?"

"The French and the Germans? I will not trade with the

217

Republic and the Germans are on the other side of the continent."

"According to our charts, the river goes all the way through to Lake Tanganyika and then on into German East Africa."

"I will not deal with the Germans," he said flatly.

"There must be a solution."

"Please let me know when you find it," he said, and then walked ahead.

That night in camp there were fewer of us at the fire. Mme. Verbeeck was still asleep. Being the only other woman in camp, I helped the doctor to change her clothes, straighten and set her limbs. Ma would have been a big help here. Frankly, I thought her stitching was better than that doctor's.

We were stitching Lucien when the doctor said, "You'd make a good nurse, my dear."

"I hope not. We see too much of this these days," I said.

"I guess injuries will always follow seafarers." He had started up Lucien's leg.

"Yes," I said. Lucien's grip on my arm tightened. "Especially during war."

Lucien was gritting his teeth, despite being a bit drunk. Then I heard him speak.

"We almost lost you today," he said, between breaths.

"We came closer to losing you," I replied. "I can't lose you, Lucien. I'm running out of friends."

That got a chuckle between winces. It was a rare moment when I could talk to Lucien. I deserved information.

"Why won't his highness trade with the French and Germans?" I asked.

"The Republic booted out their monarchs, many of which were his relatives. They're also somewhat disrespectful," he said cryptically, between breaths. "I don't know why he won't deal with the Germans, but he's quite hard-headed on the subject. He will get angry if you pursue it."

"Do you think we'll go hunting tomorrow?" I asked.

"Yes," he said, his voice was hoarse. "And you have to go."

"No." I will not! I screamed inside my head. I was holding his shoulders and perhaps I pushed him too hard against the table. It started bleeding again. He ignored it.

"If you don't," he said. "It will only be his highness and Nigel. If he dies, by accident or on purpose, Nigel will take your boat."

"There's M. Daems."

Lucien rolled his eyes. It was clear what he thought of M. Daems. "There can't be any accidents tomorrow."

The doctor looked at Lucien. "If you think there will be trouble, then we should assign more men."

"You know he won't let them go in the hunting party itself," Lucien winced. "Only the guests."

"But she's just a girl."

Lucien gave a grim nod, but continued, "She's the only guest left and she has as much a stake in this as any of us. Maybe more."

I could tell the doctor wasn't pleased. By the time I made it to bed I could barely walk. What I really wanted was a bath, but I was grateful for the bed, which I fell into. Somehow they had given me clean sheets. What a waste with me still in my dirty clothes, I might have thought, had I not already been asleep.

When morning came, I woke, still in my clothes, lying face down in my bed. There had been a knock, hadn't there? Movement brought pain and, as I peeled my things off, I could see why. I was a mess of welts and scrapes. I was down to my skivvies when I changed my mind. I didn't care if it meant missing breakfast. I was taking a bath. I pulled back on a minimum of clothes and looked outside for the first servant or imperial.

"Excuse me," I called to a servant. "I really need a bath. Is it possible?"

"Madam, there isn't time to heat the water."

"Cold would feel great," I said with a smile, and I wasn't kidding. You can get very tired of hot and humid very quickly. "Just some kind of tub and some soap, if possible."

"Yes ma'am," he replied and ran off. Me, "ma'am"! I laughed. He was more than twice my age. I'm going to call him "sir" when he gets back, I thought. I hobbled back into my tent to wait for the bath to arrive. When it arrived, and it did quite quickly, it was a low tub carried by two men. They were painfully careful not to slosh water when they put it down. Like I wasn't going to slosh it all over when I used it. They left me soap, a washcloth, a brush, and a towel and I thanked them profusely. It was as cold as I hoped and it felt great. I even washed my hair, princes be damned. If I was going to die today, then it was going to be with clean hair. I scrubbed out my scrapes and cuts. There didn't seem to be any infection, at least not yet. So on went clean clothes onto a clean me and for a few minutes at least, I felt good. I finished it all off by pulling on my mud-caked boots.

Breakfast was sandwiches again. I ate as many as I could, then grabbed two more to carry with me down to the fire. I was late, but Leopold was later. He'd taken a bath too!

Both Nigel and M. Daems nodded to me. M. Daems actually said, "Good morning." Nigel looked a bit surprised. Maybe I was tougher than he thought.

"Miss Carmichael," the prince said when he arrived. "I was wondering if you were going to attend after yesterday's setbacks."

"How could I miss it?" I replied, ambiguously.

"That's the spirit!" he replied with a jovial smile that ended with just a hint of confusion.

We shared greetings all around and then it was down to business.

"We will proceed today as a single group," he said. "We will bear to the east of our course yesterday. We are crossing the river to work the other side. The scouts have found a shallow ford we can use, with a knoll just to the east on the far side. We're hoping that the far side of the river will be less disturbed."

I thought that going in that water, even in the shallows, was foolish, but I held my tongue. We were planning on using the horses most of the way, for which I was truly grateful. The less walking the better. Under my clean clothes, I was a mass of hurt.

We formed up, I again to be led on horseback through the brush, this time by his highness himself. We moved single file through a world of green. While we rode, I pushed three more rounds into my rifle to replace those I fired yesterday. I looked at the thing closely for the first time. The brass had been buffed to a creamy smoothness by years of care. I had never seen my father working on it. He must have done it sitting in his cabin alone.

Our column made a fair bit of noise. Despite our best efforts, any wildlife not deaf kept clear of us. I was very grateful for an uneventful ride. I would have been happy to ride along all day and see nothing.

We crossed another elephant path, and then another. Thankfully, they were empty. I learned later that we were skirting open grassy areas that the elephants had cleared. I think we had all had our fill of elephants. Then something hit my head. "Ow!" I said, and looked up. Up in the trees were dozens of little black and brown apes, looking very put out by our presence in their forest. I couldn't say that I blamed them. They ran back and forth across the branches above us, chattering and screeching. Fortunately the horses paid little mind to their missiles.

After hours of humid green, we were again going downhill through the familiar progression of flora, trees to palms, rock and black dirt to packed clay, and then the river. Really, Omama should be happy. Except for the boat ride, I'd hardly seen the sun on this trip. But here it shone blinking bright. The river was wide and fast, flecked with white, its rocky bottom clear, in view and close to the surface. The column proceeded straight across, splashing through the water, raising a swath of brown silt from under the shifting stones, which flowed away in the current. The mud on either bank was pitted with animal tracks, not a square inch unmarked. I thought this would be a great place to set up our ambush, but apparently the prince did not, and we were back into the forest again, heading east. I learned later that he felt that our scent would disturb the area and that the wind was wrong for our approach. He wanted to hunt in a place untouched.

Back up we went, the far side of the river being much the same as the near. If we were surprising animals, then they were gone by the time I arrived. I couldn't even see the ants from horseback. The clearing in which they chose to picket the horses was a spongy meadow with a treacherous-looking bog in the center. Its edges, though, were firm enough and if you stayed back from the center, the insects weren't too bad. We were a lot further away from camp than yesterday. It would be a long way to carry any wounded back.

We got more sandwiches, this time wrapped in waxed paper to make them easier to carry. Today, because of the distance, we only had four hours in the area before we had to return. Our vantage point, though, was very near. The scouts darted into the brush and we waited the prescribed time before we followed. For me, today was different. This fear was different. I knew what could happen. I thought, perhaps, that this must be what it felt like to knowingly go into battle.

We were advancing along the scout's path on rising ground. I saw a shadow in the brush, then another. I tapped Mr. Milford on his uninjured shoulder and pointed. He nodded. He had seen them too. The shadows broke and were gone, crashing through the brush. Then more on the other side and more movement through the brush. How could the scouts have missed this? I finally got a good look and saw they were monstrous black apes.

Then one came into clear view, standing directly in our path, staring at us with its twisted human face, big as a man. It howled at us with an inhuman voice and we stepped back without thinking. Ripping plants from the ground, it flung them about as if mad, slapping its chest! The creature was clearly insane. His Highness raised his rifle and shot. The rest vanished like ghosts. The shot had raised the birds from the trees and the noise had, for a moment, deafened us.

The ape, when we examined it, was easily taller than me, thick limbed, packed with muscle. I found its resemblance to human to be very disturbing. Those similarities aside, it was easily 400 pounds with long arms like clubs and, most amazingly, hands instead of feet! It was an abomination. I stood aside while the men picked at it. The scouts checked in and then the support column. The men had some discussion as to what part constituted a trophy with these beasts. His Highness was for the whole animal, but his servants argued bravely for practicality. It was too large, so they settled on its head and pelt.

We again proceeded. The support column would take care of the butchery. I'd been watching Nigel, and so far I hadn't noticed any indication that he intended to harm the prince. He seemed perfectly amiable. I was inclined to think that Lucien's fears were unfounded, at least here. They argued over the ape like old friends. Why was Lucien worried?

Our pace this time was slower. Leopold was waiting for the jungle to calm down after the shot. When we made the ridge, it was noon. My sandwiches were waiting. I was opening my second one when I heard a deep, droning hum, and something large was buzzing around me. It landed on my sandwich, a great huge black and yellow hornet, big as my thumb, and then another, dodging back and forth. I could hear everyone's exclamations. I dropped my sandwich, paper and all and they were on it. Two, then three, four. One took a moment to shoo me back, darting at me and weaving about, but it soon joined its friends. So much for lunch. At least I had managed to eat one. Others were not so lucky and had to go hungry. No one, thankfully, was stung.

Our excellent position, before the wasps, had a good view of a wide crossing point. The expanse of trampled mud between the river and the forest was centered perfectly. The river was full of animals, and more came from the trees. But the wasps had changed that. We saw them now, not just on our sandwiches, but in puddles, on fruit, and dead animals. They sounded like zeppelins flying overhead. The men argued, but I knew that we couldn't stay there. Inevitably we moved down the ridge.

Our new position was oblique to the shore. Our shots, if we found any, would be low and further than His Highness wanted. We would not be able to take our pick of the herds. Worse still, we'd made noise. The wind was still with us, but this place was no longer pure and undisturbed. I could tell it bothered him. I could plainly see lions down by the water. They trotted down from the forest while we were relocating, but the prince was distracted and unwilling to commit. Maybe they were too easy? He was unreadable.

It was then that I realized that he needed a story to tell. Just shooting a lion wouldn't do. He needed to face it. He wanted drama and danger. He could go to hell, I thought. How many of us had to die for his stories? I rolled over and looked up at the sky. It was nice to see blue, even if the sun stung. I couldn't care anymore. Nigel could do whatever he wanted. To hell with this prince!

The day ended with just the ape "in the bag."

That evening, M. Daems was my friend.

"The trick is, Miss Carmichael, to always face them in the charge, never back down, go for the headshot. The hunter must dominate! You did very well at that."

"Thank you, M. Daems," I replied, rolling some kind of noodle around in my mouth. It was filled with something, like a pillow. Simply amazing. Royalty eats well, even in the jungle.

"Please call me Alard," he said, glancing around at the trees. "The African jungle is no place for formalities."

"As his highness has said," I replied.

"Especially if our interests may possibly run together?" he said.

"How could that possibly be?" What was he up to?

"We both need goods moving, which they are not at present doing," he said.

"Open trade would be good for everyone. I think ultimately even for the British, if they could see their way to it," I replied.

"Oh, I agree. Shortages limit production. Shipping problems limit profit. I think we are both interested in making money," he said.

"We are merchants." Let him take that as he will.

"The industrial nations of the world are all yelling for rubber," he replied.

"Our country certainly is," I said.

"Maybe the solution to the problem is to find another protector for the Congo instead of Britain," he suggested.

"Communication is the problem there. Contacting potential allies and, of course, the stubbornness of the British with their existing contract."

"Yes." He looked at me with a slight smile. "We are very isolated here."

"Certainly here, we are," I replied. Where was he going with this?

"But the ball is coming soon. The possibilities for business there are endless. The Congo has many neighbors. Perhaps you could propose some to his highness. Just to the north are the French for instance," he said. But then he sighed. "His highness is renowned for the steadfastness of his thinking, but if he were to enter the event with a more open mind, the possibilities might be endless. A woman, might move him. Might open his mind."

This was the last thing I need! I wanted to yell. I had no patience for it. "Sir, I could not possibly have any idea as to what you are talking about!"

He sputtered for a moment, then muttered, "You misunderstand me. I was only speaking of theory." Then he picked up talking again about the ape, a subject which I was not even remotely interested in. I was, at that point, thoroughly tired of M. Daems. I excused myself and decided to visit Mme. Verbeeck.

She was alone in her tent, in her bed, pale and feverish. Someone should be watching her, I thought. At first she seemed asleep, but as I looked down at her, her eyes opened. They looked yellow in the lamplight.

"Could I have some water, please," she whispered. She had a pitcher and cup on her stand. I lifted her head to help her drink.

"You look like a chewed bone," I said.

"Thank you for being honest," she replied. "I feel like one too." Her voice was weak.

"I think that if you can avoid infection, you will recover," I said.

"That's a big *if* in the tropics," she replied.

"I'm watching my injuries."

"Did they stitch you as well?"

"No," I replied.

"I'm afraid I shall look frightful, if I should find another husband," she said with a smile.

"If he's a good man, it won't matter." I smiled back.

"There are so few of those," she replied.

"I've heard that."

"Did you know that I was an actress?" she asked.

"Yes, you told me on the boat."

"Yes, I did. I was the toast of Europe. But then I met a good man." She seemed to doze for a moment, but opened her eyes again, "Do you believe in magic?" she said.

"Back in Jamaica, I know people who can lay curses and make charms. They claim they can raise the dead."

"You are so full of stories," she smiled. "Well, I've made magic. I met a good man. I wanted him so much that I wove spells around him until he could look at no other than me. They were very deep spells. I poured my whole soul into them." Then she was at a loss for words. She looked at the cup and I gave her some more water. I could see she was crying. "Finally, though," she said. "In the end I found out that he had really woven a spell around me."

"I'm sorry. I don't understand."

"You are so young." Her eyes were full of pain. "He was killed by the British." She looked to see that I was listening. "At least I think he was. He led the opposition in the privy council. He wanted to build a navy."

"How sad."

"Hopeless and melodramatic," she mumbled. She seemed to be drifting. A tear escaped and rolled down toward her ear.

"Sit still," I said and felt her forehead. She had a fever in the worst way.

"Someday you will meet your man," she continued, ignoring me. "Maybe you already have. I think you will end up having to fight for him too."

Then she opened her eyes again. She look alarmed. "Go find Lucien. Send him here," she said.

"Yes, ma'am."

I squeezed her hand and as I left the tent I heard her mumble, "American."

Lucien was by the fire, listening to the others work out the story of the ape. They all looked up as I approached.

"Lucien. Madam Verbeeck is asking for you. She has a fever. I'm afraid for her. She needs to see the doctor."

"Do you know where his tent is?" he asked.

I shook my head no.

He looked back from the fire, into the darkness, "Hilaire!"

"Sir?" came the response.

"Bring the doctor to Mme. Verbeeck."

"Sir!"

Then Lucien was off to her tent, and I was back again at the fire with M. Daems.

She died that night, although I didn't learn of it until the next morning. It seemed the path I had chosen to follow was to be littered with the bodies of my friends.

The next morning it was raining with an intensity that could best be described as racket. The pounding drops visibly dented the roof of my tent when they hit. Today was the last day of the hunt. I did not see Mme. Verbeeck this time on the way to the trench.

We had to get back for the ball. It was the day after tomorrow. The invitations had already gone out. But he was determined to hunt to the very last minute, deaths or not. So we waited for the rain to stop. And it did, damn it, midmorning.

I had heard of her death through casual conversation and was lying in my bed too tired to cry. Somehow I knew, even before I'd heard. Her ghost had been lying in the empty bed next to me when I woke. She was looking at the other ghost, standing by the tent pole, M. Massart. He was trying to tell me something. He so wanted to, but I couldn't understand. I honestly tried.

They vanished into wisps when the knock came on my tent pole. It was time to start.

The ground was wet and the mud stuck to my boots. It didn't feel real. They were someone else's boots. I had to go back into that green wall. I almost broke at the thought of it, water dripping and trickling around me as I stepped around stones. I gripped my rifle. There was no need for me to reload since I hadn't fired a shot yesterday.

We were to move out directly from camp. There was little time left to hunt before we had to leave, so we had no need for horses today. Instead we would walk straight into the jungle bearing northeast, straight into the heart of it.

The scouts broke a path into the dripping brush. I didn't care this time about the apes in the trees, looking like little deformed humans, may the Lord have mercy on their twisted souls. They jeered us from above, as they should. We were walking single file over fallen trees, across streams, looking for rocks to step on, pushing through endless green. We had no destination today. This was simply trusting luck.

Two hours into the woods, a great big antelope, half again as tall as me. It went leaping through our party. I dropped down and watched it arc right over my head. It was red-brown with white stripes, clean and beautiful. I can still laugh at the joy of the sight. It would have been truly beautiful, but for all the guns. the prince went after it, of course. They were all giving chase, bounding through the woods, looking for a shot. For a moment I was alone.

I could hear their footfalls and voices away through the brush. Then I felt a magnetic force behind me, it pulled my head around and up. It was Mme. Verbeeck and I could feel her hands on my head. She turned me and there, above, draped over the branch, was the boneless form of a cat. A leopard. Its yellow eyes looked at me calmly.

We stared at each other.

There was a boom in the brush that somehow echoed. The cat looked casually toward the noise, an unsolvable injustice, then put its head down and became, again, part of the branch.

"Miss Carmichael!" I heard. "Come this way." It was one of the scouts, calling for me to follow. I turned and bounded after them. They had brought it down. It was now graceless meat. Another head for His Highness. A successful hunt. He was happy and we rejoiced as good subjects should.

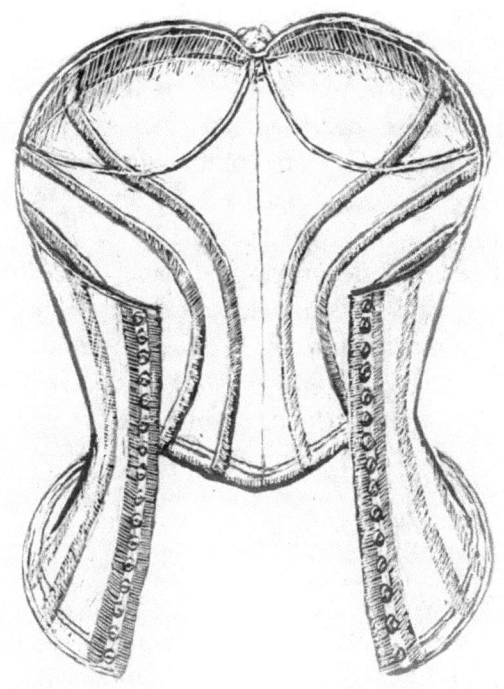

Chapter 19

Dengue Fever

The next morning before dawn we were back in a boat, splashing down river, the camp far behind. It wasn't the Hurcule. This one was smaller. It carried only us and our things so we sat light in the water and made very good time. Strangely, I had no desire to look her over. I felt listless and drained.

The dock in Leopoldville was as high as before, but there on the dock was a familiar face! She was sitting on a box, propped up by two black women. My cheeks were wet. They'd been dripping on my dress.

The boat was going too slow and the captain was a navigational idiot! His inept docking took twice as long as it should. I was heading up the side of the dock before the boat was three feet from it, the ladder practically in my way. She was crying. I ran over to her and sat down on my knees so I could see her. She was covered in red spots, but I hugged her anyway. We sat for a minute and sobbed together. Lucien and Crow walked up behind us, and I felt Crow's hand on my shoulder.

"She is over the worst," one of the women said, a nurse. "Just don't let her scratch or she will scar."

I couldn't seem to stop crying. "I have your flute," I said, but she said nothing. She smiled. The world broke into jumbled piles of fragmented memories for me. We had some kind of lunch. I'm told I played well.

After lunch, the boat headed again down river over rapids and deck wash. I didn't care. I didn't care. I sat with Aleta until we hit Boma.

Red was still where we'd left her, chains and all, the setting sun striking her side. Crow and I had two imperials carry Aleta in a stretcher even though she insisted she could walk. Her fever was gone, her spots were getting better, but she was still very weak and I really doubted that she could. She could barely talk. When we got to Red, there was no one on watch except the militia men! What the hell was wrong?

I leapt up the gangway yelling, "Who's on watch?"

At first we heard no response, then Ma came barreling up the stern companionway, followed by Tinker.

"Oh, my love, you're back," she said, tears welling in her eyes. She lifted me off the deck with a hug like a hurricane.

Tinker was a bit more reserved, "Hello, Cali," but he had tears in his eyes too.

"Where is everyone?" I said.

"We've had fever," Ma said.

"Oh, no," I said. A thread of cold ran down my back. They'd been sick, like Aleta! I was ready to run for the deckhouse, when the lead imperial called from behind me.

"Ma'am! What are we do to with your friend?"

I had to stop. "Follow me. I'll show you where to put her," I called.

But it's hard to get a stretcher down a companionway. They're quite steep. We were discussing how best to accomplish this, me being impatient, wanting to get down there see how bad things were, when Aleta got fed up with us, stood up behind our backs, and walked down on her own – then promptly fainted at the bottom.

Please, oh please, don't let her fever come back, I thought as we helped her up. I may have said that out loud.

Everyone was sick except Ma, Tinker, and Ian, who was asleep when we got there.

Mackie was dead. Mackie was dead! Another friend gone.

He died on the second day of the fever. I guess he was just too old. He never really got to enjoy his new cabin. Pa was sick in bed. He had spots too, but he could talk, and he was happy to see me.

"Cali," he said weakly, his head rolling toward me. "We were worried." That's all he could manage. He fell back to sleep.

"Where is Mackie?" I asked Ma.

"They have a graveyard here. We had to bury him there. I'm sorry we couldn't wait. It was too hot and there were too many flies."

"Is everyone else going to recover?" I asked carefully.

"Yes," and she crossed herself, which was something I'd never seen her do. I looked at her closely. I could see the shadows under her eyes. It had been a hard time.

"How's our food holding out?" I asked.

"We're eating. They're still sending us supplies from shore," she replied.

"Well, that at least is a mercy."

I was too numb then to think about Mackie. We had too much to do. It was time now to cook. We sent Tinker and Crow to bed. We'd wake Ian soon so Ma could get some rest too. Ma showed me some of what she had learned about cooking our new African food. Ed was sleeping in Mackie's cabin. When I opened the door to bring him his food, it hit me. Mackie was gone. There was Ed, looking very pale, sleeping in Mackie's bed. My body grew heavier and heavier as I fed him. As I was helping him back to the cabin from the head, I started to cry. He didn't notice. He was near fainting as he rolled into bed and I covered him. I closed the cabin door quietly, and leaned against the wall next to Mackie's door and started to sob. I found it difficult to move after that, but we had so much that needed attending to.

That evening, after getting food and water into everyone, I went down with a lantern and checked the ship. We had a big pile of laundry, dishes to clean, the cistern was low, and the bilges needed pumping. Since it was dark, I decided to start with the pumping, the bilges first and then the cistern. Then we'd have the tap water from the cistern to boil for the laundry and to do the dishes. I rigged the deck pump and set to it. But it really takes two to pump and it was hard with only me. Eventually Ian heard my plight and hopped up on deck and grabbed the other side. "You should have called me, Cali."

"Now there's nobody on watch down below. What if someone has a problem?"

"Then they'll have to wait."

"We can't stay this shorthanded. We're going to need an extra hand, even if we manage to get out of here."

"You sure have that right."

"I wonder where all those Dutch sailors went?"

"With British around? They surely were pressed or worked for free just to get passage out of here."

"Probably so. Won't hurt to ask around though."

Next morning I was asleep, dead to the world. So dead, even to ship habits, that Lucien actually knocked on my cabin door. I had no warning from deck watch. Ship discipline was completely gone. We had been laid that low.

"Cali?" a voice called.

"Huh?" said a very confused, very blurry Cali.

"Wake up, Cali!" Tinker called, and gave my door a good bang. "Honestly, sir, she's not usually like this."

"Lucien?" I was awake.

"Time to rise," he called. I think they were laughing.

"Give me a minute!" and I started pulling on my one halfway clean dress. Somehow we were going to have to do laundry today.

"Any chance of getting Aleta up?" Lucien asked.

"She was fair weak, yesterday," Tinker said.

"I doubt it," I said, through my door, "but we can check." I was out and down on deck in two minutes, running a brush through my hair.

"Very impressive," he said, like he meant it. "Most women would take at least a half an hour to face a visitor."

"Thank you," I replied curtly. "Tinker, what's the status on breakfast?"

"I'm working on the coals," Tinker replied. "And I better get back to it." He headed forward to the galley.

"Lucien, we have to feed everyone. There's practically nobody left standing."

"The fever was that bad?" he asked.

"Mackie's dead. Half the crew is down," I replied.

"I'm sorry."

"We need help. Do you know any sailors looking for berths?"

"How many do you need?"

"At least one, two would be better."

"I'll see what I can do," he replied. I could see the gears turning in his head.

Lucien helped us with breakfast. He even helped us carry the weak to the heads. Pa looked better than yesterday, in fact everybody did, but they were still weak as babies. Pa could sit at the table! Unfortunately, that meant he could make me talk about the hunt.

He said nothing when I told him I killed an elephant, then less when Lucien said it was at least three. His tired eyes looked at Lucien. I knew he was angry. Lucien was supposed to protect me from these things, and Lucien looked embarrassed. So I told Pa about the elephant head, how His Highness was going to have it stuffed for me.

"What are we going to do with that?" Pa asked.

"That's what I said too," I said. "But he insisted. I was thinking we could use it for a masthead. Nobody has one of those." That, thankfully, got a smile out of him. Then I told him about taking on extra hands, and he agreed, reluctantly, that it was a good idea, at least temporarily. It would be difficult though. We're not used to strangers.

Aleta made it to the head on her own, but she surely wasn't going in any carriage today. I caught her leaning against the bulkhead too tired to climb up to her cabin by herself. So it was only Lucien and I, riding to Omama's, me with my umbrella. I hadn't opened it once on the trip, but I didn't want Omama to know that.

I noticed even more airships moored above the aerodrome than before, at least thirty, so I pointed them out to Lucien.

"They're here for the ball," he said. He looked tired. "They're coming from all over Africa."

"His Highness is so popular?" I asked.

"No. But he throws a nice party and he's as interested as everyone else in making connections at this point."

"Doesn't he know everybody already?"

"Change is coming. Everyone knows it. They want to know which way to jump. The ball is a chance to glean information and make alliances."

I wondered how much I could really trust Lucien. It wasn't just that I wanted to, it was that I needed to. So I decided, after a moment of indecision, in for a penny, in for a pound.

"Lucien, M. Daems is working for the French government." How would he react, what would he do? Would he tell the prince?

Lucien looked surprised.

"He can't be," he replied, and then he frowned. "Can he?" he said. "I would know. How do you know this?"

"He wanted me to seduce his highness, to encourage him to make a trade alliance with France."

"Have you thought that Daems might be working for his highness?"

It was my turn to look surprised. "He wouldn't!"

"He would."

That is court life. Give me the open sea any day.

We were clopping through the dusty brown streets, talking, when I realized that I'd hardly noticed them. I guess it hadn't taken long to get used to the poverty and people running away from us, which was disturbing.

Omama's shop looked exactly the same, even though I felt like I had been away for a year. She tisked and shook her head when she heard about Aleta.

Oh, but now we have the dress!

First bear in mind that I'd never worn any of this gear before. It was completely new to me. It started with thin tall tight stretchy hose and garters (which itched by the way), then new bloomers that stopped just below the knee. "We better get the shoes next. You won't be able to bend after the next part," Omama said, which sounded ominous. They were not shoes. They were cream-colored torture devices that squeezed my feet until I could barely feel them. They had narrow high heels on which I would certainly wobble as I walked. Then a loose chemise, my light bodice gone. And here it came--the corset. I was warned to make sure everything was where it's going to be, because there would be no adjusting after it was laced, and lace it they did. It took both women. They pulled it tight and I could barely breathe, then the demon women waited for me to breathe out and then pulled it tighter still! One of the demon women told me, with a smirk, that it was ribbed with steel!

Underskirts and then finally the dress! White silk with bows on the shoulder tops and back. It had a train of folds of glistening cloth that followed me like a waterfall. I was all neck, and open in front practically down to my breasts. The ballooning sleeves were cinched above my elbows with white ribbons. Omama was right. I couldn't bend to save my life.

Omama was tisking at me and shaking her head. "It's a good thing, girl, that you don't wear the same style of clothes all the time. You've got no tan lines, but you've still seen too much sun. We'll need makeup."

"Let me see," Lucien said on the other side of the curtain.

"Go on," Omama said, fluffing my hair so it was even.

So it was time to launch her. I took the rig out for its maiden voyage, and the sparkle in Lucien's eyes was worth the pain, and that I was about to faint.

"No hat?" Lucien asked.

"That was last year, Lucien, but we're going to add a hair piece. Oh! And there's a fan." She picked up a long narrow stack of lacy cloth from the table and brought it over. "Have you ever used one of these?" she asked.

I shook my head no.

She showed me how the bottom was hinged, then she opened it slowly revealing the lacework backed by thin slats of wood. Then she closed it and then with a flick of her wrist, snapped it back open.

"Think of it as a shield," she said. "I think you'll need it where you're going."

Omama rolled everything, including Aleta's dress, loosely in with a roll of plain cloth, except the fan. She pressed that into my hand and told me to practice with it, which I did all the way back while trying to balance my umbrella. I could see the shoes on the seat beside me. Mine were creme silk with a bow on the toe. I decided the only good thing in the whole outfit was the fan, which was fun.

She also sent along the two demon women who had laced me in as well. They were carrying satchels. They did not smile

More airships had arrived, at least forty over the airfield now. I couldn't count how many below, loading and unloading.

"There's one other thing we must go over," Lucien said as we were going through the nicer shady streets near Omama's. "There will be dancing. A lot of it. You must at least waltz."

"Dancing? I don't dance," I said, which brought a stifled snort from one of the demon women. The other only smirked. I spared them a glance of venom and then turned to Lucien, "but I'll try my best."

I was planning on working on laundry when I got back, but Lucien and the demon women had other plans. Luckily, Lucien had planned ahead. Two men had been dispatched to help out on the boat. They weren't sailors, but their help freed the standing crew to do the boat work. And they left me free to fall into the clutches of the demon women.

After my bath, apparently, it had been decided that my fingernails were a mess and my calluses unsightly. I tried to explain that I needed some of them to play my violin and only after Lucien's vouching for my need, did we enter into negotiations as to what I would keep. They aimed to soak and grind them off with pumice stone, like we use on the deck! I was going to need my buffalo hide gloves to do my work again.

We ate lunch on the move, the devil women taking turns working on me. The paint was drying on my nails when--and please believe me when I say that my nails looked so funny when I was back in my deck clothes--Lucien took me up on deck to waltz.

Waltzing is not bad, once you got the rhythm of it. Fun even. One, two, three, one, two, three, his hand around my waist as we swirled about. The hardest part in waltzing is not bumping into things as you fly about. Oh, and Lucien and I flew! It was glorious.

I didn't want to stop, but I had done so well that he decided to try a grand march, which we would do at the start of the ball. Grand marches are a way of introducing everyone to everyone else at the start of the dance. They involve linking arms and walking about in pairs. It was very confusing! I could see the order in it, but remembering what to do when was difficult. I'd much rather waltz, especially with Lucien. Finally, he had to leave to get ready himself, and I was back in the clutches of the demon women. They were eyeing my hair.

We were working on it up on deck until the afternoon breeze picked up and we were forced to go below decks. Ian brought extra lanterns and the locker doors on the west side of the ship were opened to let in the setting sun through the portholes. Pa dropped by for a moment, and Aleta come out and sat for a bit to watch. "I'm dying to see your corset," she said. One of the demon women snorted. They really were evil.

They used a touch of some powder to lighten my sun-darkened face, and the slightest touch of rouge on my lips to make them red, and then it was time to gear up. On it went. Aleta wanted to help pull on the corset laces, but had to sit down for dizziness. They were all, all, very evil! One layer after another until lastly, they gave me long white silk gloves. They went up above my elbows.

When I finally stepped out on the deck in the light of the setting sun, the crew were all there waiting. I had my violin, as per Lucien's request, and my fan, which I flicked open. Other than Ma's tears, there were no woo-hoo's. Everyone was staring, so I tried to curtsey--and promptly fell over.

Everyone was offering a hand, helping me back up. Luckily the deck was clean. "Sorry about that," I said. "I'm going to have to try that again. Can I have a shoulder to hold on to?" Tinker and Ian were both up. Wally tried to stand but fell back down. I got in nine or ten tries before I saw Lucien's carriage approaching.

He was in his all-black dress uniform with a red and gold sash. He had medals on his chest and a big one on a ribbon around his neck. His hat was under his arm as he walked, his sword shining by his leg, his boots gleaming.

"Permission to come aboard," he called.

"Lucien, you don't need to ask," Ma called back.

"Tonight is a night for formality," he said, and clicked his heels and bowed to Ma. She giggled! I had never heard my Ma giggle before.

He had a package in his hand, and when he looked up at me he had a sly look in his eyes and a hidden smile.

"Almost perfect," he said. Then he walked over to the deck house and started to open the package. "I must apologize for its lateness. These are family heirlooms. They haven't see the light of day in a very long time and I can think of no better occasion to bring them out, nor a more fitting place for them to rest. I had them shipped in with the mail courier."

Everyone gathered around him as he opened the box. Inside the box were pearls and a gold bracelet, but all I heard was an "Oh," out of Aleta and lot of indrawn breath. I couldn't see them! I couldn't get close. The crew were all ooh'ing and ah'ing. I couldn't move for all the tack I was wearing and the crowd around them.

"May I see them?" I asked, in a quiet voice.

Lucien looked up at me with a mischievous smile and said, "of course." He picked them up carefully and carried them over. Nestled in a red velvet lined box was a necklace, ear rings, and a bracelet.

He started with the necklace. His fingers on my neck felt like heaven. I could feel the pearl's weight and warmth. They seemed to caress my skin. How can something so inanimate be so warm? The demon women had to help Lucien with my gold rings. I could almost cry that we didn't have a mirror on board.

Then I had a thought. "Crow, could you get the signal mirror, please."

"Can do," he said, and ran below decks. It was only a small plate of polished steel, but it was the best we had.

The bracelet had pearls too and in the middle was a little watch, so small. It had been wound and set. "They're so lovely," I said.

"No," he said. "They merely mirror the wearer. Happy birthday." Then he lifted my hand and bowed and kissed it. "Now, you are perfect."

That got an "aw" from Ma. She was a sucker for these things. That night, though, I was lovely. It was a feeling that was completely new to me.

Crow came back with the mirror. Someone else stared back at me in the rippled reflection. She was smiling.

Lucien then took my arm and escorted me down the gangway, and believe me, I needed escorting. We waved as the carriage pulled away, me practicing my fan flick. At the gate we were met by a troop of imperials on horseback, black uniforms and gleaming metal, and together we rode into the deepening gloom of the city.

Chapter 20

My Introduction

We were riding further into Boma than I had yet been, past Omama's part of town, into the tree-lined streets and mansions near the aerodrome. The road was choked with carriages, all full of people. I knew we were getting closer because we came across a militia checkpoint. A formality only, and we were waved on, only to be stopped again a little ways further on by another checkpoint. This one was manned by imperials. The carriages were being scrutinized, but Lucien was a pass to anywhere, and we were waved through with just a glance.

Leopold's colonial estate was ringed by a wooden palisade. Imperials walked the top, lit by torchlight. We passed through yet another checkpoint at the gate. Inside were more soldiers, tents, and glistening metal knights, just like those on the hunting trip. Their metal tube and stick bodies were unfolded and ready. Close-cut lawns, hedges, and stark white statues stretched before us.

Our escort left us at the gate, apparently their mission complete. So we were alone as we rolled down the gravel lamp lit driveway.

The prince's mansion was brightly lit. He had gas light shining in his gardens and lighting the facade of his house. Where was he getting it, I wondered? There's no coal in the Congo.

In front of the house, passing under a covered section of driveway, carriages were waiting in line to unload. Most were filled to or even beyond capacity, which I thought strange until I realized that those flying in wouldn't have their own carriages and had to share.

I notice Lucien looking at me and smoothed my dress. His smile was sweet.

"Any last-minute instructions?" I asked.

"I'm afraid to make any suggestions," he said. "You've bested every plan I've made so far. I think this time I'll sit back and watch. If I think of anything, I'll tell you." Then he looked down at my hands. "You have your invitation?"

"It's in my case," I replied.

"Good. You'll need it when we enter. A silly formality really, but it's part of the ritual, and it spares the doorman the chore of remembering people's names."

"Will there be any representatives of the German or French governments here tonight?" I asked.

Lucien's eyebrows went up. "Several Germans, the governor of East Africa for one, Baron Friedrich Grumman. No French. His Highness can't avoid the Germans, even if he won't deal with them directly. So much of our equipment is manufactured there. But he will not invite the French.

"I've also heard that Krupp sent another representative," Lucien continued. "A Maximilian Schuster. Which is strange," he added, almost to himself. "That happened very quickly. It's too bad the last one didn't live long enough for me to find out what he was up to."

"Surely you saw his notebook," I said.

"Just botanical notes. Apparently he was an amateur scientist," Lucien replied.

"He was very quiet."

"An understatement. What are you thinking, Cali? The Germans can no more help us than the Dutch government could help those poor souls down the dock from you."

"I don't know." It was annoying because something was nagging at me. It was more than M. Massart's ghost. "At least I think I don't know. There are a lot of important people here tonight."

"Hence the security," Lucien replied.

"It's odd that he doesn't like the French but he likes Americans."

"Europe is home to him," Lucien said. "America is far away and exotic. Remember that all the monarchs of Europe are related. Many grew up together. His Highness spent his school years in Germany with Wilhelm the Second, their current king. The royalty killed or displaced by the Republic were members of his family and the Republic's representatives are all commoners who often have a dislike for the respectful protocols that his highness is used to." Then he gave me a little smile and said, "You do too, but in your case it's out of naiveté rather than rudeness, and it can be, on occasion, charming."

I could see the aerodrome clearly from where we were, the tethered airships loomed over us, great orange and gray shapes, silhouetted in the last light of sunset. And then we were at the front of the line and men in livery were there to help us from our carriage. But Lucien waved them away and came around to help me down himself. I actually shivered. His hands felt so sweet, especially the one on my waist. It made me want to waltz again!

The openness of the grounds let in a bit of breeze, so rare in Africa. The orange of sunset cast dark blue shadows. Like all great buildings, the prince's mansion started with stone steps and tall wide doors. We walked up the steps.

He had a cloak room just inside the entrance, like the count's mansion in Le Havre. I was surprised it wasn't empty. Coats are a burden in the African heat, but men wore them anyway and women wrapped themselves in their furs. I checked my violin in and was given a small square of ivory with a number on it.

"Lucien, what am I supposed to do with this?" I asked.

He snorted. I think he was as nervous as me. "We forgot to make you a purse," he sighed. "Here, give it to me. I'll keep it safe," and I handed it over.

We were passing down a wood-paneled hallway lined with sculptures and paintings which, to be blunt, were not to my taste. They dripped with syrupy colors, showing people in wigs playing in gardens or little fat naked angels. The statues were all nearly or wholly naked women.

What did I ever think we could gain by coming to the Congo?

I was positive it would be hot inside, considering how hot it was outside, but amazingly it wasn't. The hallway was lined with gas lamps and I could see fires in the rooms as we walked past, but the air was cool. I even felt, for a moment, a cool breeze. Looking down I saw that the builders had added holes in the baseboard, covered in wire mesh. The cool air was coming from them. Did he have in-house refrigeration, like a giant ice house? The idea of it, the extravagance, was staggering.

Halfway down the hall we joined another line of guests which formed up before another set of double doors. One by one, couples were led in, their names called aloud within. Most were normal Misters and Misses, but a few were royalty.

At the door, Lucien stepped aside with real regret in his face. "You must make your entrance alone," he said, and bowed. I reached for him, but he pulled away.

"No," I said.

"You must," he replied. I could see pain in his eyes as he backed away.

I panicked and began to follow him, but the doorman was in front of me, his eyes locked on mine, distracting me while Lucien backed away.

"May I see your invitation, please?" he said.

I realized I had been clutching it in my hand and reluctantly handed it over.

"Thank you," he said.

He firmly took my arm and led me toward the doors. We stood there facing them together for a moment, side by side, while I tried to breathe. Glancing back to look for Lucien, I could see the couple next in line looking at me. The woman seemed concerned. Then the doorman nodded to the two men in their white wigs and livery standing at each side of the doorway. They nodded back and swung the doors open.

They bowed as I passed.

The doorman, having entered first, stood in front and banged his staff on a much marked square of polished wood.

"Miss Calista Carmichael!" he called.

Too many heads snapped in my direction too many different expressions to read. Why should so many care? It was a large room filled with guests in their finest. Moving amongst them were black servants with trays of drinks and couches or perhaps lounges on which many of the women sat, most of them attended by men. Then I realized that I had been standing too long in the doorway, staring at the room and its guests. I tried to breathe and then moved forward down the two steps to the room's floor.

Almost immediately I was intercepted by one of the servants. His tray was full of the same tall thin wine glasses we had at the start of our hunt. I took one and thanked him. A sip told me it held that same slightly sweet, bubbly wine. I needed to avoid this, and anything else alcoholic if possible.

I heard music and a quick glance around the room revealed that it was coming from behind a folding partition on the far side.

According to Miss Brunche's etiquette class, the purpose here was to mingle, but all I saw around me were strangers, men in black and women a rainbow of colors. Then a face I recognized. It was Nigel. Had I no friends left alive? I needed someone to make introductions for me. If not a friend, then perhaps an enemy, so I walked over to him.

"Sir Prendergast," I said, and curtsied. I was learning, practice makes perfect.

"Miss Carmichael," he smiled. "You look lovely tonight. No longer the frontier woman, I see," he said with a smug smile under his long droopy mustache.

"No sir, most of us spend most of our time in cities, now," I replied.

"Miss Carmichael, may I introduce Mr. Linfield Spencer. Linfield, she's the one who brought down an elephant with a pistol."

"Is she?" He smiled. His teeth under his mustache were coffee brown. He was fat. How can anyone be fat in the Congo? "I heard about that. Amazing. You don't look capable of hurting a fly." He leaned toward me as he said that, like he was talking down to me.

"I'm not sir, except when cornered," I replied.

That got a throaty laugh. Nigel just smirked. I was thinking that I was going to dislike Mr. Spencer.

"Mr. Spencer manages river traffic," Nigel said. "He owns half the boats on the river." That's how he stays fat, I thought. He has his pick of incoming cargo.

"It's a very long river . . ." and was about to ask about navigational hazards, especially between Boma and Lake Tanganyika, when he interrupted me.

"About 3000 miles long, and we have to cover it all," he waved his hand through the air to encompass all of Africa. "We link all the villages and towns together. Without us, there would be no transport, no trade," and he began to carry on about his importance to the colony and I realized I had made a mistake in my approach to the subject. I was rescued by an older woman with gray hair and a significantly less tight corset, who came up behind me and joined our conversation.

"My dear, you should sit down. It's going to be a long evening," she said. She gave apologies and led me away by the elbow. "I'm sorry I couldn't get to you sooner, but I'm not as quick as I used to be."

She did seem to have trouble making headway.

"You had to run into Linfield first, you poor thing. You'll think us all boring blowhards." But then she laughed, short and quick. "But then, maybe we are!" she added with a light in her eyes. "Here I know your name, but you don't know mine. I'm Emma Baudouin. Please call me Emma."

She led me to a couch that seemed to have been left just for us. "You've done so much to lighten the burden of this dreary jungle. In only a week you've turned everything upside down. Our little rabbit with teeth!"

"Rabbit with teeth?" I asked as we sat, arranging our dresses.

"His Highness is notorious for bringing one or even two women home regularly. In the bag, so to speak." I was aghast at her frankness. But she just glanced sideways at me to check on my reaction and continued. "Oh the scandal and trouble it causes, but that will all change soon. He'll have to marry or renounce his claim on the throne." I realized that she was feeding me information.

"Did you bet on me?" I asked, with sudden realization.

And she burst out laughing, which turned heads in our direction. "Yes, of course I did. I love a longshot. You're every bit as clever as I've heard," she said. "I think I would help you even if I hadn't."

She paused for a moment and eyed me over. "So let's look at this dress. Stand up." She squinted at me. "So this what the new flowers are wearing in Paris."

"No, ma'am," I replied. "They're wearing wide hats and bustles."

"That would be the dames, my dear. Not the new flowers. Omama is never wrong." She looked up from my dress. "But you were in Paris?"

"No, ma'am, Le Havre, getting close to two months ago."

"That would explain it then. You must see Paris someday." She smiled.

"We have a ship," I said. "We tend to stay near the coasts."

"Of course, your ship." She mumbled, looking uncomfortable. Then she changed the subject. "I hear you were in Portugal."

"I'm sorry to intrude," said a thin dapper man, his black coat unbuttoned, his chin white from a recently removed beard under a sun burnt nose and cheeks. "May I join you? Did I hear you say Portugal?"

"Here they come," Emma said, and then to me, "You'll have your own flock soon." She looked up with a bright smile, "you were listening, Henri."

He smiled back, "One must, if one is to find the best conversation."

She gave me a stern look. "Be careful of him." A servant came by with a tray. It was covered with little crackers, each with something on top. I was hungry, despite the corset, and took one. Emma saw me and frowned.

"Careful," she said, just as I took a bite. It was spicy and had an awful texture. "It's made with a local snail," she said.

Henri was smiling at me and then, to tease, popped the entirety of his into his mouth.

"Don't be cruel, Henri," Emma chided.

I didn't know what to do with the thing. I wasn't going to eat it! I had to take a sip of wine to cool my mouth.

"You need a plate, dear," Emma said, as she saw my distress and she waved to a servant.

So I got my plate and we were all settled and I began to tell about our adventures in Lisbon. By the time I was going into the currency collapse we had at least ten men standing about us with more listening in the wings. It was a wall of black suits! News of current events seemed to be in short supply here. At the point where I was recounting the slaughter of civilians in the street I met dissent.

"Impossible," said one.

"You saw this yourself?" asked another. I had forgotten all their names by now, there had been so many introductions.

"We were filling bullet holes all the way to Cadiz."

"It was in the papers," said a voice with a German accent.

Then, when I was at the part about having to ferry troops, we heard a great pounding on the floor and the doorman cried, "His highness, Prince Leopold Ferdinand Elie Victor Albert Marie, Duke of Brabant!" Everyone stood and bowed, with me just a beat behind.

"Fashionably late as always," I heard Emma mumble.

The trouble with being short is that you can't see anything in a crowd. I could hear people greeting him as he moved about, but I couldn't quite pin down where. Maybe I could dodge him, I thought. But then the wall of black coats parted and there he was, dressed in white gleaming trim and glistening black boots.

"There you are, my dear, as elusive as ever." He was speaking French, as was everyone that night. I suppose he had given up on his pretense of speaking only German. It was for me I suppose.

Smiling, he bent down to kiss my hand. My smile was a little stiff as I successfully curtsied.

"I don't see your Indian bodyguard," he said.

"Surely I'm in no danger here?" I replied.

"No, of course not." My question seemed to set him back for a moment.

"My Lord," came a voice from behind him. "I would like a word with you."

A frown crossed his face. "We have the whole evening." Then he added in German, "*Ich werde sicherlich Zeit für alle haben.*"

"There are some matters of importance we must discuss, about Portugal."

He heaved an irritable sigh. "Yes, of course, Victor. Pardon me, my dear," and he was off surrounded by a buzzing hive of men.

I was back on my couch, but Emma was nowhere to be seen. Then I heard a quiet voice beside me.

"Masterfully played." It was that German accent I'd heard. I looked up at a small, wide-faced man with watery eyes. He had a wide, lipless smile. "He'll be busy for a half an hour at least," he said, looking toward the prince.

"I've been reviewing my predecessor's notes," he continued. "And his entries on you were quite startling, but I see now that he may have been right."

"His notes were all scientific observations," I replied.

He shrugged his shoulders, "There are notes and then there are notes."

"Are you Mr. Schuster?" I asked, and I saw a slight twitch in his smile.

"I'm so very sorry, my manners," he replied. "Yes I am. Maximilian Schuster, I work for Krupp Industries. You may call me Max. I'm the new area representative for southern Africa."

"Calista Carmichael." I tipped my head toward him.

"A pleasure," he replied, with a slight bow.

"I'm so sorry about M. Massart," I said. "He was a very pleasant man."

"Trouble unfortunately comes with the territory."

"Yes," I replied, with sadness. "But there's been too much of it."

"The Congo is a difficult region to work," he said as he took a sip of his drink. "Definitely too much death. But still death, at least for us, can be good for business." He seemed to ponder for a moment, and then smiled. He was, I think, quoting something. "The Congo is a trap that ensnares all." Then he took a drink of wine.

"It's certainly ensnared us," I said.

"So, your ship is still at the docks?" he asked, suddenly alert.

"They have her chained."

"Do you know who has the keys?" He looked concerned.

"No," and then I realized that I may have made a mistake. Where were the keys? "Perhaps the harbormaster?"

"I would suggest you find out. Quickly." His look was grave.

"Tonight." I said, and he frowned for a moment, then gave me the slightest nod. Something was going to happen tonight. Something that meant running for the ship.

"Giliam wanted you to know," he said.

"I know," I replied. Again, that seemed to startle him.

"He also felt that we might have business to conduct," he said. And then he added with a little sadness, "But I think it will have to wait for another time."

"Miss. Carmichael I presume," said a new voice behind me. We were approached by yet another black clad man, followed by two more, which brought my conversation with the very interesting Herr Schuster to an end.

Chapter 21

The Final Dance

Another thump of staff on floor, doors were thrown open, and a liveried man called, "Dinner is served!" We all rose and moved en masse to the next room. It was much like the first, only it had a long table covered in dishes and silver.

As I passed through the hallway I saw Lucien with the guards, watching from a hallway. I veered in his direction. A guard attempted to direct me back to the hall, but Lucien waved him away.

"What's wrong?" he asked.

"I need to know who has the keys to the boat chains," I asked as quietly as I could, looking at the guards around us. We were not alone.

"The harbormaster." Then he frowned, annoyed. "I think."

"It's important. I must know now."

"Something is going to happen?" he asked.

"Yes," I whispered. "Soon. Something big."

He motioned to a guard and said quietly, "Go tell the ground crew to prepare his highness' airship." He turned back to me and took my hand; leaning forward he whispered in my ear, his breath warm, "I'll find out."

"Thank you," I replied.

Then I had to let go. I had to go back! He'd been holding my hand, but he just used it to turn me toward the line of people moving on to the next room, the dinner hall.

Inside was a buffet, with guests picking up little dishes and forks. I finally had a proper view of the other women guests. They were mostly older, but I saw some young women, one that I thought might be my age. She saw me looking but turned away.

All of their dresses were fantastic, like inverted flowers or great fluted bells. Many had jewels around their necks and flowers in their hair. Their dresses flowed around them as they walked, which made wonder about mine. I tried to look, but that damn corset wouldn't let me!

Across the room, the table stretched before me, lit by hundreds of candles, the silver and porcelain glinting in the flickering light. We were to pick and choose between the finely cut meats and breads.

I did not drink wine, at least generally, so I wasn't a good judge. They are complicated, with many subtleties even within the same variety. But I think that his highness must have had them all. There was a table just for them. I was relieved of my nearly full glass, only to be offered a more traditional wine glass filled with white wine. It smelled pleasant, nearly tasteless. Then Emma was at my side again.

"I'm sorry to have left you my dear, but I was called away," she said. Then she frowned at the buffet like it was a patch of bad water. "The trick, my dear," she said, after a pause, "is to eat just a little from here and there. Eat too much and you will be ill."

"I can barely breathe. I don't see how I can eat."

"You must eat something or you'll faint during the dance. It's a delicate balance."

We steered toward the table. The china was lovely and looked familiar. I turned a plate over. English.

"Is something wrong with it?" Emma asked.

"No. I think we may have shipped its like before," I replied.

"I'm afraid we get all of this from England. We're quite dependent on them."

the prince's staff had laid out an obscene variety and quantity of different foods, especially considering the starvation outside.

But the food was in here, not out there, and so was I. I tried to choose from the ones I had never seen before. I thought to avoid the fish, we got enough of that on board, but the smell hit me like ambrosia, so I took a little bit. It was amazing. All the food was amazing. I could see the wisdom of Emma's warning.

There were a dozen different shapes of fork. Emma tried to explain.

"That's a meat fork, but so is this, but only for cold meat. This a cheese fork, an oyster fork, a pastry fork, and . . . oh, I can't remember what that one's for."

Then I noticed that girl was beside me filling her plate.

"Oh hello Marguerite," Emma said, rather flatly I might add.

"Emma," Marguerite replied crisply. "Is this her?"

Emma sighed, then continued distractedly. "My dear, this is our new Marquess de Maintenon, Marguerite," then she mumbled past some names, brushing them aside with a few waves of her hand, "du Pont." She had not looked up from the table.

Marguerite frowned at her in momentary fury. She was about to reply when Emma added distractedly, "Just married," while picking up a piece of meat.

Marguerite let out a tiny growl then looked at me and said, "You must be Miss Carmichael."

"I am," I replied, wary.

"I see you've been to Omama's," she said, eyeing my dress.

"I have," I replied, trying to smile.

"It's nicer than what he buys most."

I almost dropped my plate.

"Really Marguerite," Emma said. "The evening is difficult enough for her."

"Oh yes, of course, pardon me," she said, but I don't think she meant it. "I saw you talking to the Duke of Tervuren," she said.

"Yes. He helps with translation."

Emma looked up and eyed Marguerite with suspicion.

"It looked like you two have become friends," she said. Her eyes were averted, staring at something more important in the crowd. "A prince, a duke, and all this nobility must be very heady stuff for a commoner."

"Marguerite was just married," Emma said. "What were you before?"

"Marguerite!" an older woman called. She was walking through the crowd toward us. "There you are. You are needed over here."

"A daughter. A rich one," she said, and then curtsied before turning to the woman.

"Do you think she bet against me?" I asked, as they walked away.

That got a chuckle from Emma. We began to walk back to our couch.

"Who was that who called her away?"

"Her mother-in-law. Not a bad woman, but I think a bit strict for Marguerite's taste." Then she sighed. "And not strict enough for mine."

I sat on a couch with Emma, holding my plate, my wine glass on a low table beside me. Servants were walking around passing out fan-shaped cards to the women and pencils with tassels to the men. When I got mine, I found that the first line was already filled in. It said "Leopold."

"It's a dance card," Emma said. She seemed surprised that I didn't know. She looked at mine and winced. "That sly devil," she said, as we sat and nibbled.

The men went from couch to couch, like bees to flowers. We had, around us, a considerable cloud of men. Their talk consisted of empty flattery, that was until they realized I was far more interested in talking about economics and trade, popular subjects in the Congo. As such, our couch was always surrounded and my card quickly filled up. Emma was quite knowledgeable herself. No one stays in the Congo for anything other than business.

His Highness hovered in the distance, his white uniform almost glowing amongst the black, in his own pool of followers. I suspected that he chose white instead of his usual black on purpose, just to stand out.

A servant came with a tray and more wine. They were always taking my glass away and bringing a different one, even though I had barely tasted any of them. Each one was subtly different. Emma watched this process for a while and then leaned over and whispered in my ear, "he's trying to get you drunk." And it was true. I had no way of knowing how much I'd had.

Then a soldier came over and said quietly to Emma, "Dutchess, could you please come with me. There is a problem."

Dutchess?

"What is it?" she replied, annoyed by the interruption.

"It's a matter of discretion," the soldier replied.

I turned to her. "Please, I think it may be important."

"Then yes, of course," she replied quickly. She huffed to her feet and closed her eyes. "I'm sorry, my dear, I must leave for a moment, but you're doing very well on your own." Then she said to the servant, "Take me were you will."

I was sure that she would not be back. I hoped she would be safe, no matter what it was that Mr. Schuster was alluding to. If it involved the need to run for our ship, then it had to be something on the order of insurrection, a coup d'etat, or perhaps assassination. The British must be about to make their move.

But I had been drifting and missing the flow of the conversation. How impolite! Miss Brunche would scold. M. Marchal was espousing the need for tariffs on the new German wines flooding France from the east.

"German wines are of little concern to us since we do not trade with North Sea ports. The North Sea and Baltic are far too cold to my taste anyway. But as merchants, we oppose tariffs in general, as they are impediments to trade," I replied. There, how was that?

Dinner progressed, luckily without Marguerite. I'm not sure

how I would have fended her off without Emma. I saw her occasionally on the other side of the room. She had far fewer men at her couch.

So far it had been a standoff between the prince and me. My wall, sadly Linfield among them, against his. I smiled. It was his pride this time that worked in my favor. He had to be the center of attention. He needed me to come to him. But then again, maybe he was waiting for the alcohol to do its work.

Through the heads, I could see another servant heading my way. He was carrying my case. "Ma'am, his highness has requested a song." It had been fun in Spain, but I was getting tired of playing for my dinner. What hadn't I played yet, I thought? I'd played practically everything in my school folder appropriate to a formal occasion, but . . . but that most hated Bach piece. Perhaps, I thought, this was its place.

So I stood and excused myself, and walked over to the buffet table and put my case down. When I lifted the lid, that smell, oh I loved that sweet smell of that wood and rosin! It drifted up around me.

Those standing around me grew quiet, watching, my back straight. The music from behind the partition stopped. The sound of my tuning spread quiet across the room. I stood and came out from behind the table, alone to the center of the room.

"Bach's Second Partita," I called. My voice sounded so small, echoing in the emptiness of the room.

I raised my violin in the empty silence. Perhaps I can care about this piece, I thought. Maybe just a little. I took a moment to collect my thoughts, and then dove in. It came pouring out with each stroke, without bidding. My hurt, my anger, flooding the room with wandering melancholy.

They stood around me as I played, their suits black against the shadows, the women pale as ghosts. To hell with them! I pushed them away, they were trees, they were the jungle. the world narrowed to a small circle around me.

I cut and rolled notes, double, triple, sometimes even quadruple stopping them. Four bars, four bars, vary it, slow it, pulling the notes this way and that, turning their ends to weave them together, each clawing at the last, then four bars more again.

The sweat drops gleamed on the wood under my hands despite the cool dry air.

It's supposed to be a dance. I turned it into a durge, filled with my hatred and anger. A string of wolves to claw at their senses. The Giga was supposed to be happy, but I chopped down on each note, stabbing the earth, trying to kill the ground beneath me, every elephant, every ape, every log in the river, then ending, back again to that dissonant theme. I tinged it with insanity. I turned it into a murder ground, just for that prince. But it cut into me too. This magic does.

I was in the middle, I had to stop, to breathe. Why was I crying? Around me came the crash of applause, but I hadn't lowered my violin. They knew nothing. It wasn't over. Nothing in the Congo is over without death.

So I ignored them! I launched into the Chaconne, making it a conversation, no an argument! The audience drew back. I could see them stir. I bled out pleas met only with dismissal, then complaint. I lead them to futility, fear, and flight, followed lastly with resignation to the inevitable. I used my music to damn them, and they accepted it.

In the end, I drew out that last note across the room, twisting it. Death, death and darkness.

When I lowered my violin, I heard distant applause, sound, people congratulating me, all shadows. I felt nothing but welling tears. So many good people had died, all because of this idiot prince and his wretched colony in hell.

I stood there numb, until, again, there came the pounding. They all turned from me and looked. It was the doorman. I used the moment to dry my eyes on a napkin and put away my violin. He called, "prepare for the grand march!" My blood ran cold. Now came the part where I, your Cali, would fall flat on her face.

We lined up two by two, ladies on the left, men on the right, holding hands. I was paired with someone new. I didn't like his smile, which made me thankful for my gloves as I held his hand.

Whoever they were, the musicians hiding behind the partition had made their escape to the next room unseen, to a new partition, behind which they struck up a tune. The double doors were swung open and in we walked. Thus began the march.

The hall was high-ceilinged, filling both stories of the house. To the sides were stairs that led to balconies and the walls lined with chairs. Above, in the center, were four large chandeliers, their gas light sparkling in shrouds of cut glass. The walls' sconces too were draped in glittering cut glass. The effect was nice, but I couldn't help but compare it to that dead count's mansion in Le Havre. The Count made Leopold's efforts seem simple and garish.

We marched in, a long line that coiled around the room. Then somehow, with all the shifts in partners, I ended up with Henri, who gave me a big smile. I couldn't feel relieved. He shouldn't, I thought. Bad things happen to my friends here.

The lines broke apart, sending us around the room in different patterns, me trying to follow along. Most made it look so effortless despite their various states of inebriation. We walked around and around holding each other's arms until everyone had managed to walk together at least once. I locked arms with Leopold several times, which was when it happened by the way. My dress caught on something, notably Marguerite's shoe. I heard it tear. She had stepped on it!

I let go of High Highness' arm to look, which made him stop as well, which broke the pattern of the dance.

"What's wrong?" he asked.

"My dress," I replied. "It's torn." I was so angry. This was so unfair!

"Sorry," Marguerite called over her shoulder with a smile as she was whisked away in the lines of dancers.

"It's just a dress," he hissed impatiently. "It can be fixed!"

Maybe to him, but it was my first and only. The ruff on the bottom had come loose.

But! I am a lady of social grace and poise. I breathed, and calmed, then stood and actually smiled at him.

"It's nothing," I said. Then we resumed. He took my hand and we moved on. I didn't cry.

The dance finally ended and there, around the edge of the room, were padded armless chairs. I'd barely managed to plant myself in one, inspecting my dress with dismay, when the music started again. A waltz I thought, at least by the beat. I sang hosanna, a dance that I knew, but who was there in front of me but His Highness sporting a mischievous smile. He was first on my card of course. I suppose I shouldn't have smiled at him.

"May I have this dance?" he asked.

"How can I refuse," I replied.

There was no doubt about what was in his eyes this time as he took my hand and led me out into the dance floor. Then his arm was around my waist and around and around we went. He was staring at me, I was trying to look at the walls, ignoring the smell of cigars and whiskey, until finally he opened with, "You can't elude me forever."

"Was I trying to elude you?" I replied

"The chase only makes the end sweeter."

"My end?" I actually looked at him.

"Of course not!" He looked alarmed. "You will be well taken care of."

"I'm not a whore," I replied tiredly, turning away from him again. I was trying to look down to see if the torn ruff was dragging.

"No, you are not." He frowned.

"You have nothing I want," I said.

"I know that. It's another thing that makes you prize worthy. I have nothing except your family. I can help them leave in comfort. By airship. And I can see that you are compensated for your ship."

"It's our home," I replied. "It's where I was born."

He frowned again. "Even still, it's not mine to give."

"Then we are we both prisoners."

He looked annoyed, he was missing steps. "Everyone is a prisoner to a certain extent," he said. I think he had wanted to wince at that, but was too proud. He had envisioned a different conversation. Things weren't going to his plan.

"You say your people are your jailors, but I think it's really the British," I replied.

"The British are under contract to me." That made him angry.

"They will destroy you eventually, just like they did Portugal," I continued.

"In time, I will be rid of them," he said. "We have plans."

"Be rid of them now," I said. He almost stepping on my foot.

We just missed the couple passing behind me. "Make a deal

with the Germans. Offer them a trade partnership. Tell the British they must share or get out. The Germans are here tonight."

"*Die Handelsflotte* is small," he snapped back, clearly angry. "It lacks the foreign contacts, and I will not deal with that cripple Willy! He always wants to be first!" We had completely lost track of our waltz.

Wants to be first?

"It's not spread thin like the British and you only need the contacts you need," I continued. "You don't care about tea or spices. Your market is Europe and America."

"And!" His voice was raised, people were looking. "How do I prevent a revolution? Our own troops will revolt." We had stopped dancing, but his hand was still around my waist.

"How many troops are in East Africa?" I asked. I backed away from him.

"They're too far away!" he said, stepping forward.

I stood there. I looked at him squarely, standing my ground, the other dancers swirling around us. He didn't know, I thought.

Lucien hadn't told him. In a quiet voice I said, "How strange."

"Strange? Strange how?" he asked, but the music was ending. For some reason I couldn't understand, I felt the need to reassure this viper who was probably about to lose everything, all because of some slight during his childhood.

"It's nothing," I said instead, feeling annoyed. I waved him away. As I turned away, he tried to follow, but the situation was awkward and my next dance was coming. It was Henri, of course. His one chance to upstage a prince.

"By your leave my lord?" Henri said.

"We are not done," he said, looking at me aghast.

"No, not yet. But soon," I said. Then I turned to Henri.

the prince stared at me in disbelief. What was he thinking? I thought. Was I arrogant? Ungrateful? I looked back at him with pity. I only needed to delay until the Germans hatched their plot.

The music was starting and I took Henri's hand. I gave Leopold a little curtsy and said, "Pardon me, your highness." Then Henri was whisking me about. He was a very silly dancer and a relief after the prince. I could finally relax and enjoy myself a little. He liked to swoop, which I must admit was fun, although a bit dangerous in my heels. I laughed despite my mood. In the end I curtsied and he bowed, and I looked at him with a little sadness. I wished that I could tell him to run. I have always hoped he made out alive, but I never met him again. Was the rest of the evening going to be as melancholy as this?

We got a break from dancing after that. Across the hall, I saw them escorting Marguerite out. She spared me a dark glance as she turned. It was a relief she was going.

The orchestra had picked up a light little tune. It was an odd one I'd never heard and I begin to trace out the notes in my mind. I saw Leopold through the door of the smoking room, pacing back and forth, smoking like a chimney.

But I was thirsty! There had been nothing to drink but alcohol all evening and even with the low cut of my dress and the mansion's cool air vents I was hot. So I eyed the punch bowls.

They looked harmless.

I looked at the servant manning the ladle and asked, "Is this alcoholic?"

He replied in nearly unintelligible French, "I don't speak French," then repeated in Dutch and German. So I took the cup he offered.

It smelled alcoholic but not strongly so. I sipped it. It was fruity. I went over to Evrard, another new friend, and asked him,

"Is this very alcoholic?"

"No, it's lovely." He was drunk. Great. Where could I get some water? I could see no sign of Lucien so I walked over to the partition where the musicians were hiding and glanced around its edge. Inside were seven musicians, all in normal street clothes. I darted inside, past the partition.

"I'm sorry, ma'am, but this area is not part of the party," the cellist said, not missing a beat by the way. He was brilliant. His long gray hair was pulled back in a ponytail.

"I'm just looking for some water," I replied.

"Hey, it's the violinist," the clarinetist said, as he paused at a break to turn a page. They all nodded hello.

"Love your work," their violinist said.

"Yours too, thank you." I nodded to him with a smile and a little bow. I meant it too. They were good.

"If you don't mind sharing the cup, we have some." They had a pitcher and a mug on a little table.

"Oh, bless you," and I poured a cup and drank greedily. "What is this song?" I asked, gratefully holding the cup.

"Mozart, ma'am," the cellist said. "The Church Sonata, the third."

"It's lovely. I want to play it too."

They came to the end and were changing music. "Get your violin," the horn player said. "We're a bit sparse on these."

"I can't. It would be rude, and I doubt they'd let me." Then I felt a breeze behind me. Luckily, I had just put down the cup.

"Ah, there you are, my dear," the prince said. He had regained his composure.

"My Lord," the cellist said. "We were just explaining to the lady that this area is not part of the party."

"I'm sorry," I said. "I don't see other musicians that often. I couldn't resist."

"Understandable," he said, and firmly took my arm to lead. "Please rejoin the party. You have been missed."

"Have a good evening," they called as I was led away.

"Thank you," I called back.

"Your next dance partner is waiting for you," Leopold said.

He seemed very happy about it.

"Yes, of course," I replied, suspicious.

Men and women were lining up in formation on the dance floor. I had no idea what to do or where to go. My partner was an elderly gentleman. When he took my arm, I said "Please, I'm going to need help with this. I have no idea how this dance goes."

"Not a problem love," he said, but he was drunker than Evrard. He planted me in the correct spot and said, "Just follow me." But when the music started, his group went left and my group went right and I had to dodge to keep up. I caught on fairly quickly though. The dance had three basic moves, the bow-curtsy, the hold hands and walk about, and the cross over. The problem was anticipating the next move. It wasn't so bad when he was there to lead, but very often I was left out to fend for myself. Then I had to hop to catch up. When it was over, I glanced over at Leopold. He was hiding a smug smile. It was clear that my performance had been quite comical.

After that, the evening began to deteriorate as the alcohol took its toll on the guests. The crowd was thinning as people went home. As I danced by the drinks table, I could hear requests for tea and coffee, all met by the familiar "I don't speak French."

Leopold didn't seem to notice. His eyes followed me like Knockers on a stalk. Finally, the worst happened. A loud argument had ended with fists. Guards had to be called and the men helped away. It was then that I noticed, when all movement had stopped, that the Brits were still here. I could see M. Daems and there was Nigel, but the Germans were gone. All of them, and I had been introduced to several. I moved through the crowd looking at the faces on top of the black coats. They were gone and no one seemed to have noticed. Those that should were too drunk.

Leopold had become furious. The dance was in a shambles. He waved over two imperials to follow him, and they walked straight up to me. "Follow me, Miss Carmichael," he said. And I was led away from the ballroom through side doors.

"Your Highness, there's something you . . ."

"Shhh!" He angrily cut me off.

I followed him through a side room with couches and ash trays flanked by the soldiers. We went down a corridor, upstairs, down another hallway, then to a large door, which he opened and ushered me in. The guards, he stopped at the door. The room was high-ceilinged with a large window facing forest trees silhouetted by the glow of the city. Glow of the city? Since when did Boma have lights? He had a large ornate desk in front of the window and bookshelves lining the walls. I was standing in the middle of the room as the door clicked shut behind me.

He turned from the door and faced me. His face was flushed and angry. "Cali, you have ruined my party. You have ruined everything."

I could see no way to reason with that. "Your Highness," I said. "Is it to be rape along with blackmail?" He snarled something I don't want to repeat and charged toward me. He aimed high to slap me or grab me by the hair, but I stepped aside and pushed him over. It wasn't that hard. He was a bit drunk and that hell-spawned corset actually gave me a little spring.

So he was sitting on the floor bewildered, wondering how he had gotten there, I was standing over him, wondering if I should help him up, when the study door swung open with a bang and in strode Lucien, out of breath. He was about to make some announcement, perhaps intervene on my behalf, but instead stopped, confused by the scene before him. Tonight, clearly, nothing was working out like anyone expected.

We had a moment of frozen time, which was finally punctuated by the sound of breaking glass. the prince frowned, trying to make sense of it. Lucien's eyes darted around the room. But I found it first. It was a window pane!

"The window," I said. Then, a knock on the outside wall. I knew that sound. "Lucien, I think someone is shooting at us!" And like that, the spell was broken. We again had purpose and the past moment was gone.

"Your Highness," Lucien said. "We must get you to your airship at once."

the prince, a bit unsteady, started to rise from the floor. I reached down and gave him a hand up. "And why would should that be?" he asked. "Thank you, my dear," he added. We were apparently back on speaking terms.

"There is a riot, backed by militia," Lucien said. "Apparently, someone's given them bullets."

"The British?" the prince asked.

"The Germans," I replied, and both men looked at me. So I stared back. "I tried to tell you!"

"How can that be Lucien?" Leopold asked.

"Look at a map," I said. "You share a border. And I still don't understand why you can't trade with them." Two more glass panes shattered. "Pardon me, but I think I'm going to move to the hallway," and I started to make my way to the door.

"Out," Lucien said. He grabbed the Leopold by the arm and pulled him along after me. In the hallway were a dozen imperials, still in their dress uniforms, but now with rifles and bullet belts.

Lucien turned Leopold over to the guards. "Get him to his airship."

"What about my guests?"

Oh, now he cares, I thought.

"We're planning on moving them to the aerodrome and evacuate all we can by air. If things go badly, the rest will go by water," Lucien replied.

"Lucien," I said. "Red is the only ship at dock. We don't have enough supplies to feed ourselves. The next free port is in the

Canaries."

"Let's not argue. It's not come to that," Lucien said.

"Lucien, I think the Germans are invading. We can get to Loango."

"That's French," he said.

"Unlike this colony, they might have food."

The soldiers and Leopold were just standing there, watching us argue. "There's no time for this," Lucien said, shaking his head.

"We have francs," I replied.

"Oh, now I understand," the prince said, half to himself. "She loves *you*."

Lucien rolled his eyes and let out a sigh of exasperation and said to the guards, "Get him to his ship." At an order from their sergeant, half the guards detached themselves and practically dragged Leopold down the hallway, the prince watching me all the way.

Then I turned back on Lucien. "Lucien, really, we have francs," I repeated.

"Dahomey," he replied, with a little smile. We started walking quickly the other direction, half the guards following us.

"The Slave Coast?" I cried.

"It's British. They're still our allies."

"It's full of pirates!"

"The French will seize the ship," he said back.

"The British will certainly. We're American. The French have always been our allies."

"St. Helena then," Lucien said.

"The wind's the wrong way." I shook my head.

He stopped and looked at me with a smile. "I can see how you got into trouble."

I looked up into his eyes and felt a little frightened. It's always been his eyes. The way he looks at me. I knew then that what Leopold had said was true.

"We have to keep moving," he said. "People are dying."

In the ballroom the guests were slowly being sorted. Those with airships shouted their destinations, collecting passengers. Most though, were arguing with the imperials that were blocking the doorway out. A clerk was sitting at the refreshments table taking names of those in the city that needed evacuation. I heard a couple tell him the names and location of their children as we passed by.

Lucien was, as always, a passkey to anywhere. The guards at the door helped us past the crowd. Soon we were at the front entrance.

The horizon toward town glowed even brighter. The orange firelight and smoke blotted out the stars, the smell of wood smoke was heavy in the air. Gunfire crackled and popped in the distance.

"What now?" I asked. I saw a soldier fire two rounds from the palisade wall down into the city.

"Good question. I need information. We need to find out what's going on," he replied.

He glanced around at the confusion of soldiers and civilians as they rushed back and forth across the lawn. Then he set off at a brisk walk, which I was having a hard time keeping up with, my high heels sinking into the turf. He realized the problem and slowed down.

Looking at my dress, he shook his head. "What a shame," he said. "Now which problem do we solve first?"

"Are you going to dress me as a soldier now?" I asked.

"It's a thought." He smiled. "But I think you're a bit too small for the uniform. We have to find you better shoes, at least." A volley of gunshots rang out from down the street, just outside the walls. "There isn't much time," he added.

We headed for a large tent on the far side of the front lawn. Soldiers and crates littered the ground around it and I could see horses behind in rows. Lucien walked right through the lot, past the guards who saluted, and into the tent. The guards who accompanied us waited outside. I could hear a horse ride up behind us as we entered. Looking back I saw soldiers jump up to meet it and help the rider down. Inside, lit by lantern light was a table with maps and two portable desks. Officers and clerks, some still in their dress uniforms, were busy at work. The air was thick with cigarette smoke.

"My Lord," someone said, and they all snapped to attention.

"Status," Lucien replied. "And see if someone can find better shoes for her. Clothes would help too. Something easier to move in. Something that doesn't stand out." Then he was at the table with the officers. The courier, down from his horse, entered behind us and delivered several sheets of paper rolled inside a metal tube.

While Lucien and the officers talked, I looked out the tent flap. The fires had spread with flames visible just over the wall. Someone's house was burning. The courier came up behind me, looking over my shoulder at the city as well.

I asked him, "Do you know where I can get water?"

He smiled. "Yes, ma'am." He unhitched his canteen and passed it over. As I drank I couldn't help a little moan of relief. That prince and his stupid parties.

I passed it back. "Thank you so much."

"No problem, ma'am," he said, as he snapped it back on his belt.

I realized that Lucien and the others were talking about me. I heard Lucien say, "and she'll need weapons too, at least a pistol."

"Unlike the civilians, at least we know she can handle them," replied the officer, which kind of made me feel a little proud.

Men entered and left. The clerks wrote notes and passed them to couriers. The officers argued over the map table. Then Lucien walked over to me and said quietly, "We still hold the aerodrome, but the road to the harbor has been cut. There's too much gunfire close to the harbor to risk flying in." Then he cursed. "I wish we had air cavalry or at least tanks. Knights are good for quick strikes and defense but damn useless for sustained attack." He ran his hand through his hair just like Pa. "I told him, but he had to have his toys." Then he continued, "We hold several positions in the direction of the harbor as well as the harbor itself, but they need relief. They can't hold for long without supply. If we can link up with them, then together we might be able to break through to the harbor. We can make a stand there." I understood very little of that. But I think that was more for himself than me. And, I think that perhaps, it was almost an apology as well.

"We're going to evacuate the mansion. That means you're going to have to accompany the attack toward the harbor. In the back of course. It's the only way to get you back to your boat." Then he sighed in exasperation. "I almost forgot. You'll need these. Keep them safe." He handed me three large keys.

"Where am I supposed to keep them?" I said, looking down at my dress.

"More appropriate clothing is coming. Be patient. All of this is going to take a little time to organize."

More couriers came and went. We heard occasional explosions nearby. House boilers, someone said. Then a soldier came in out of breath, with an armload of clothing. "Here, ma'am," he said. "They belonged to one of the gardener's sons."

"I hope they got out," I replied.

"There's no getting out of this, ma'am. We gave them guns and put them in the line."

Somehow, they had found me pants, a shirt, socks and boots. No bodice and I wasn't going into battle in a corset. It would have to be bare breasted like an Amazon.

"Where do I change?"

"That's a good question," Lucien said.

I finally changed in the corner, they turned their backs. Lucien himself undid my soon to be discarded corset. I so wished it were someplace private, just the two of us. But see? There was a bright side to this! Oh, I itched when it finally let go. Then I pulled my hair piece out, pulling my hair back in a ponytail, tying it with string I got from one of the clerks. I had to save something of that dress, all that work of Omama's laying discarded on the dirt floor in the corner. It was my first ball! So I carefully folded the silk gloves and stuffed them in my pocket.

They gave me a pistol and a rifle. A Mauser, newer than the one we had. This one had a knife attachment, but they took it away from me. Apparently it takes special training to use. They all looked a bit relieved when I pulled open the bolt and pressed a clip into the magazine. The pistol was another Webley. I had ammunition belts over my shoulders, my own canteen, and a well-worn--if slightly too large--pair of boots on my feet. I was, for the first time since I woke up, comfortable.

I was the only one there with nothing to do, so they sent me to the house to pick up supplies. We were all going to have to carry everything we could. The first place I went was the cloak room. It was still full of jackets and furs. There, on the floor, next to a shelf, amongst the fallen finery, was my violin case. I picked it up and held it like an old friend.

The room where we had first gathered and only this evening had been sipping bubbly wine, had been turned into an infirmary. The wounded were laid side by side across the floor, the wood parquet smeared and puddled with blood. A doctor was working on a man who was lying on a beautifully carved table. The orderlies were holding him down as they worked. I could see blood. I was back in the hallway before I realized where I was going, leaning against the wall, trying to catch my breath. He was screaming. It echoed everywhere.

Following the flow of people, I found myself back in the ballroom. It was now a hive of activity. People had pulled all the food from the kitchens, stacking it by the armload on the floor and couches. Everyone ran to and fro, trying to get ready. I could hear bits of conversation. Apparently, the aerodrome had come under fire and airships couldn't land. The harbor was the only route left.

Someone handed me a backpack and told me to fill it as full as I could. There was blood on the shoulder strap. Where had they gotten it from? I stuffed it with bread, which I pressed flat, as the soldier next to me was doing. They had those roots I had tasted back on Red, sausages, cheeses, and some canned goods. One of the cans I picked up was caviar. After the backpack, I began to stuff my pockets, moving the keys and pearls to my case. Then Lucien came up behind me and whispered in my ear.

"The attack toward the harbor will start in thirty minutes. We need to get to the front yard."

I looked up at him. He looked worried.

He grabbed my backpack and we headed toward the front door, passing the infirmary again. They were carrying the wounded out on stretchers, following us out. Looking down at the stretcher beside us as we walked, I saw a boy no older than me. His arm, bandaged from his shoulder to his elbow, was still bleeding. He needed better stitching and tighter wrapping. I wanted to help him, but there was no time to stop.

Chapter 22

The Retreat

We were standing under the inky shadow of the wall, waiting for the start of the attack. The carriages with the wounded and civilians were spread out over the lawn behind us. Around Lucien and I stood hundreds of soldiers and civilians with guns.

Dirt had been piled around the gate to block the enemy from

shooting through. The gates, after all, were only iron bars, and I could see past them to the street beyond. Outside, hundreds of figures were running back and forth, thin as sticks, silhouetted by burning houses.

Then the gunfire outside suddenly picked up, wood splintering from the wall posts. Someone was ringing some kind of bell nearby. A man fell from the wall above us, landing with a dead thump nearby. It was a blessing I couldn't see him clearly. All around us our soldiers were standing up. We heard the officers calling, "Fall back!" Lucien grabbed my arm and pulled me along, running for Leopold's mansion. Everyone was taking cover behind hedges, statues, and wagons. The wounded could not run. Lamps were put out inside the command tent and they were running out through the tent flap, the clerks frantically trying to roll their maps as they ran.

"We must find cover," Lucien said, out of breath. But it was too late.

Figures were pouring over the top of the wall, almost like water, yelling and screaming, some with guns, some with spears and knives. They hit the ground running toward the house and us.

Our men began to fire, the reports popping like rain, but there were so many of the enemy and they came so fast. Those men in front stood and meet them face to face as the dark wave came at us. The men manning the knights had climbed inside and slammed their doors shut.

Then the knights came to life. They started with an explosion of steam jetting down their sides as they fired their boilers. Bullets ricocheted off their armor, ringing like bells, unnoticed. Each stood slowly, picking up speed, their arms swaying back and forth as if stretching.

"Down," Lucien yelled.

We dove into the damp turf, bullets whizzing over us like angry bees. The knights began firing. They poured jets of white fire from their arms, tearing through the attackers, the pipes in their arms spinning. Their metal frames gleamed in the flashing light of their guns, sweeping through the attackers like scythes through wheat, taking one step after another toward the enemy. When they had finished, the normal din of gunfire seemed almost quiet. The attack had ceased to exist. Nothing was left of the enemy but bodies rolling and moaning, and ground plowed loose in great clumps. I could hear the knights on the far side of the house, doing their work there too. At an order, our men rose up and charged those enemy still left. They tried to run, panicking, but they had no place to go. Their backs were literally to the wall. Every one of them was killed. It was then that I learned how the knives on the guns worked. The soldiers were using them on the enemy wounded.

Lucien kept me down for a few minutes more, even though the firing had stopped. Then we were up and running back to the wall, stepping around and over the bloody and torn dead. We were regrouping, but had little time. Men were cutting wounded and dead horses loose from the wagons, leaving them to be pulled by those that remained.

Then the gunfire outside began to pick up again. They were going to attack once more, but we couldn't pause. Plans had been set. Our attack had to start on time.

A red starshell went up, lighting the ground around us in dancing red and black shadows. The knights vented steam and stood up again. After a few last minute adjustments from their mechanics, they walked forward with great thumping steps through the front gates. Literally through them! Nobody bothered to open them. After their passage, the gates hung loose for a moment and then fell from their hinges with a ringing clatter. I could see the white light of the knight's guns outside.

Then our men clutched their rifles and followed them through, like a great dark river. Unlike the enemy, they made no sound.

Bullets were picking splinters off the outside wall. The din didn't stop. It's the stuff of my nightmares.

Lucien had gone. He had gone to lead the attack. He had kissed the back of my head, his hands on my shoulders. I squeezed his hand, and then he vanished. I was in too much shock to be surprised. I realized then, that he was the only noble who had stayed behind to fight. He could have left with the prince. I think he had stayed for me.

We heard a whistle call and it was our turn to move forward with the wagons. We had been pulling the dead from the wagons to make room. There were more in the street, along with so many of the enemy. Soldiers were still stabbing them. I saw two flashes of light in the window across the street followed by reports. Some of our wounded were crying out. We hauled them up as best as we could into the already full wagons, but we had to hurry. The knights were already down the street and we had to move forward. Too many wounded were hopeless. The doctor said no. We had to leave them, even when they cried out to be taken. When I looked back, I saw that one of our officers was killing those we left with his pistol. The enemy would not show them that mercy.

I followed along with the wagons and the children through burning streets. At each stop we sorted through those in the wagons, removing the dead to make room for the living. We left their bodies in the dirt.

I will remember no more.

Sometimes I see bits of it in my nightmares and at their worst, sometimes, when I play. Often, for some reason, I remember reloading, the golden shells bouncing as they hit the dirt in the firelight, still smoking. I've been told that we broke through the enemy several times to rescue refugees and that our column grew as we moved.

We reached the harbor at the first light of dawn, the sky twilight blue behind towers of smoke from the burning city. We had taken the harbor gates. I was still clutching my violin and my pistol, but my rifle was gone. My ammunition belts, too. I must have given them away. Inside the harbor walls, the warehouses were nothing but black ashes, smoke, flame, and rubble. The defenders had fought their way back from the walls to the docks. I stood at the gate, staring across a sea of bodies, wagons, and people moving past.

Red was there, still chained at the docks. Her deckhouses and upper hull were torn by gunfire. Figures began standing up on deck. I could see soldiers and civilians too. They had been preparing to make their final stand from her decks when we arrived. Then I saw Crow and Pa. I was staggering forward, then lurching into a run.

Someone called "Cali!" There was no gangway and I stopped, momentarily confused. Ian and Aleta called to me. They shoved the gangway across but I could no longer move. I was down on my knees crying, clutching my case. Hands lifted me, carrying me aboard. Ma was hugging me and then Pa.

"My violin case!" I cried.

"It's here Cali," they said. "It's here."

"The keys are inside."

I heard Tinker and then Crow, "whoop" and "woo hoo!" And then I heard the sound of the chains sliding into the water.

We had to unload our cargo back onto the docks to make room for refugees. I got to help clear out Mackie's cabin. He had precious few things. In his desk drawer was an envelope with some locks of my hair. They were thin and copper blond. I must have been a child. He had picked them up after a haircut. I couldn't move after that. I sat in the corner and cried. Lucien and Ian sat with me until I calmed down.

It took six runs to move all of the refugees to Cabinda, a trading post with a small dock just north of the Congo River estuary.

First the wounded, mothers and children, then the men and soldiers. Three days and nights. An orderly withdrawal.

After the first night of rage and fervor, the rebels lost steam. You couldn't put your head over the harbor wall, but I think the Congolese were happy to see the back of us. Enough blood had been spilled.

I didn't find out what happened at the aerodrome until ages later. the prince escaped in comfort, as did all the royalty, having been warned by Lucien and then escorted to their airships. Those that were left had to wait for evacuation, which was just as slow for them as it was for us. The British, paid of course by the Belgian government, gradually ferried everyone to some kind of safety.

That didn't help the six thousand troops and ten thousand civilians who were trapped inland. A few were ferried out one way or another, all with harrowing stories, but most just disappeared, swallowed by the jungle.

As I said, I have since heard so many trite sayings about the Congo, the dark land of death, told to me by people who know nothing! The one that comes to mind here is that all the roads through the Congo use skulls as cobbles. The sad fact is, they don't build roads in the Congo. There's only a river. A river filled with logs.

Lucien waited to leave until the last load. The leader's responsibility. We took a chance and reloaded our cargo as well.

It was then that we finally had time. We stared at each other as we headed down river, too tired to speak, the river drifting by, his hazel eyes so sad. Everything had all turned out badly. When the dock at last came in sight, we heaved ourselves back to our feet to help lower the sail and then throw out the bumpers. The docking was a bit hard. Everyone was exhausted.

Food was short at first, but a British airship came by on the second day and unloaded ten tons of canned goods.

We would not be going back shorthanded. We were going back loaded with passengers, most of them paying, some of them working, all those who wanted to get to the Las Palmas Aerodrome. Pa found a way for even the poorest.

We were getting the passengers settled, their gear stowed in our few remaining nooks and crannies, when we found Lucien waiting for us on the dock. We all wanted to shake his hand, to thank him for all his help, but he kept looking at me.

Then finally he turned to Pa. "Excuse me, sir, but may we have a moment alone?"

Pa stopped and looked at him for a moment, then nodded his head.

"Let's go," Pa said. He and the crew all turned and begin to walk away without a word.

Lucien looked down at me. "I'll miss you" he said.

"I'll miss you too, you know I will," I said, starting to cry. I knew this was goodbye.

Then he reached over and carefully kissed me. It happened so fast but it lasted forever and my arms were around him and he felt wonderful, my tears cold on my cheeks.

"I'll find a way to send for you," he said.

I wanted to sing.

"Don't wait too long."

"You need to finish school," he said quietly, brushing his lips across mine.

"There isn't much left."

"Perhaps more than you think," he said, pulling back and looking at me with a smile. Was that mischief in his eyes?

"What does that mean?" I said, running the tips of my fingers along his hair. I wasn't sure what to do.

"There are things in the works," he said.

"When?" I asked.

"Soon."

Cali's Songs

All of Cali's music and any other songs mentioned in these pages are available on YouTube. Below is a list of suggested examples, although many more exist.

Squid Jiggin Ground
"The Squid Jiggin' Ground", The Squid Jiggers

Jack Hinks
"Jack Hinks Sept 11 Vancouver Great Big Sea", Great Big Sea

I Be So Glad When the Sun Goes Down
Sounds of the South

I Don't Do Nobody Nothin

No More, my Lord
Alan Lomax Collection

Pat Murphy's Meadow
Con O'Brien

She's Like a Swallow
Lucia Micarelli

Fantasia
Sabicas

Flamenco duet for guitar & violin.

Los Amores de un Torero
Carmen Amaya
(She will teach you what you need to know about flamenco)

Sonata for Piano and Violin in G Major
Joseph Haydn

Chaconne from Partita N° 2
Johann Sebastian Bach – Hilary Hahn

Chaconne for Violin and Orchestra
Tomaso Antonio Vitali - Sarah Chang

Church Sonata No. 3 in D major
Wolfgang Amadé Mozart

Bibliography

The Internet is a great source for information, but if you want real detail about a particular subject then you're going to have to turn to books.

Basil Greenhill
The Merchant Schooners
Naval Institute Press
1951

This is simply, to be blunt, the best book you'll find on merchant schooners. It describes in detail the schooner down to the last rope and plank. It categorizes types and where they were used, the lives of their crews, and the economics of their operation. I'm truly grateful to have found this obscure work.

Patrick M. Royce
Royce's Sailing Illustrated
Sinclair Printing and Litho, Inc.
6th Edition, 1974

A practical handbook on the ins and outs of sailing, told in a manner that even I can understand, as described by a fellow writer/artist. It's a general book on sailing, not specific to schooners, however it contains much that pertains to all.

Captain Alan Villiers
Men, Ships, and the Sea
National Geographic Society
1962

An excellent collection of National Geographic magazine

stories about the sea. I found it helpful in description of storms, the nature of waves, and in general the sorts of things that go on day to day on a ship.

John A. Butler
Sailing on Friday
The perilous Voyage of America's Merchant Marine
Brassey's
1997

Although a history of the U.S. merchant marine, it gives great descriptions of the less romantic side of merchants. The economics that drive the ships and the day to day concerns that threaten them.

Lastly, I suggest you look up the *Congo Free Republic* for an mind boggling piece of history that has largely been swept under the rug.

A Note on Pronunciation

This is the second edition and I've had a lot of encounters with English speaking readers, and I'm sad to say – every one of them has mispronounce Lucien's name. Some of the renderings have been worse than chalk on a chalkboard (not that there are many alive who remember that singular sound)! To think I would name an important character, a romantic one, "Luchin"! This is French. I blame it on the Internet and inexcusable laziness. Take an interest in the languages of your neighbors.

The place I like to go for pronunciation is Google Translate. Set it to English/French, type Lucien into the English side, then press the speaker button on the right. "Loosia-", shorten the "oo" and add just the slightest hint that an "n" may follow. Toss a little nose and upper pallet in as well. Listen to the weight of its parts.

Do you think that Cali speaks with a Boston accent? She hardly knows the place. She's closer to a mix of dockyard pirate and a whiff of Irish trill, sans the chain smoking growl. It's a bit as if Popeye were a sixteen year old girl, if you can imagine that, and as the stories progress that will drain away. Events, her constant exposure to French and Aleta, and the efforts of her maid, Sara, will change her. And don't you ever dare say "Pippi Longstocking" to me, nor will you compare her Paris house to Villa Villekulla!

So let's get started. Most of foreign words are pretty obvious, at least to me, but some bear attention:

Alard Daems (Gr.) A-lar Dames

Aleta (Sp.) A-leta

Bondurant (Fr.) Bon-durrant (twirl the r)

Cadiz (Sp.) Ka-di

Claveloux (Fr.) Clev-lou

Coup d'état (Fr.) Cou-de-ta

Cuerdas (Sp.) Qware-ddas (roll the d)

Émile Savoie (Fr.) A-mille Sav-owa

Emmaline Verbeeck (Du.) Emma-line Fer-bake

Giliam Massart (Fr.) Jul-i-am Ma-sar

Hercule (Fr.) Air-culle

Le Havre (Fr.) Le-ure-hav-a

Lucien Antoine (Fr.) Loo-sia(n) Ann-twan

Metzger (Gr.) Metz-ga

Mswata (Swazi) Msz-wata

Marseille (Fr.) Maar-say

Poiret (Fr.) Pwa-ray

Réis (Port.) pl. ray-ees, sing. ray-el.

Iilittate Akdisshé (Crow) – I don't yet know how to pronounce this. Crow is second generation, born and bred in Baton Rouge and although he is technically Crow, his mother was a local Choctaw. He's considered Confederate even though the Choctaw Nation did not join the Confederacy, instead remaining neutral, and the Crow Nation itself sided nominally with the North. He stays onboard when docked in Boston to avoid the whole mess.

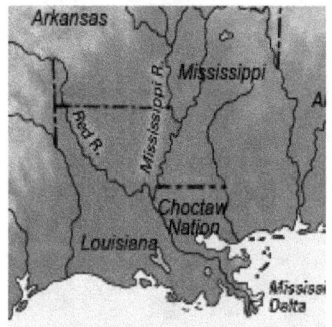

Tervuren (Du.) Terr-vu-ren. Tervuren is just east of Brussels, close to the king.

Villa Villekulla (Swed.) Villa-Villekoola

Turn the page for a preview
of Mark Bondurant's next
Calista Antoine adventure . . .

A Bad Crossing

Available October 2016 from
Bongo Books

Chapter 1 – Bad Memories

The wave rose from the starboard dense and gray, thick with debris, filled with black stick figures. It passed over us, a wall of water. With all our sheets out we had no time to come about and over we went, the deck listing, then tipping, everything falling. I'm dragged under the dark gray water, screaming. The water screamed, screamed like rusted metal, filling with long white teeth, and then. And then they were on me. The stick figures. Black faces and hands pulling at me. and pulling, until I drew my pistol and fired, their heads exploding one by one. The blood and fire. Wagons turned. The dead and dying littering the ground. And I'm trying to scream, but I can't breathe, and there's a great pounding, and hands grabbing me.

"Cali!"

I'm kicking and fighting, my pistol melting in my hand as I try to grip it.

"Cali, wake up damn it!"

I think they were trying to shake me without getting kicked. Then I realized where I was, in my cabin. It's dark except for the dim rectangle of my cabin door and the lamp light from the stair. I can see Pa and Ma. They're standing in my door trying to hold my legs. I'm lying on my back sobbing, tangled in my covers.

"Cali, you awake now?" Pa asked. But I couldn't answer. Not yet. Just great heaving sobs.

"Cali, please answer," says Ma.

"It's the night terrors," says Willie. I couldn't see him, he was behind Ma and Pa. I must have woken the whole ship. He sleeps in the bow. Willie lost his wife and kids in a flood. He must know.

"I'm awake," I croaked. How long had I been crying? "Oh Ma," I said. "Pa." I twisted about to the bottom of my bed so they could reach me, their arms warm and sweet.

It was fall of 1892 and we were two days out of Las Palmas in the Canaries, all the passengers we ferried out of the Congo were gone, off to the aerodrome or looking for other passage to Europe, and we were just Red again and there was no reason I should feel this way. We escaped from the Congo, we got away. Better than got away. We had our cargo, and money. We won, even though they lost. They all lost everything, even their lives. What will they call it now, the German Congo?

I could feel the water moving past the hull, the surge of the waves, and the blessed creaking of the mast in her step, and I knew that I was home, and my Ma and Pa were there. And Knockers. She's meowed below my door. I could see the whole crew. How loud was I?

"Pass her up," I said, hanging out the door, reaching down toward her. Crow picked her up carefully and put her down on my mattress. "Oh Knockers," I said, turning to hold her close. She purred. "I'm OK. Please go to bed." Sleep is precious on a ship.

And then I realized something. "Who's on watch?" It starts as a whisper and ends in a growl. Nobody's on deck! Léon, he's new crew, let's out a cough and turns and runs. Tristan and Léon stayed on after Las Palmas in the Canaries. They had no money and nowhere to go, and we needed the hands.

"Sorry Cali," says Tinker, and he turns and heads for the wheel too, which gets a general chuckle from the rest. I love Tinker, but the watch is more important than me. If something happened to the ship, we'd all be dead. Ma and Pa gave me a last hug and go to their cabin. They all leave, saying goodnight, until there's just Knockers and me. She seemed to want to curl up at my feet, which was just damn brave of her. The lamp light shining in from my cabin door was comforting. I left it open. It helped.

My watch came up at 6:00 a.m., which as third mate is my right. I was out of bed at 5:45. We had gray skies that promised rain, the air was warm and wet, storm for sure, way late in the season. So I dragged my wet weather gear with me up on deck, all of it stiff dark green waxed cotton. Tinker was at the wheel. I passed Léon and didn't recognize him. The new faces were confusing and I found that for a moment I was shaking. I had to stop to breathe. But it passed, and I told him to get Tristan out of his hammock. I saw Tinker give me a worried glance as I took the wheel.

But the deck was surging under me and the wind was at my back. I stood in the worn spots, staring forward at the binnacle, checking her heading. She tossed, stretched out before me. 154 feet, riding low, the rising sea breaking over her bow, all blue in the morning light. I could feel the pull of the wind whistling in her rigging, her sails taught. I inspected them with a critical eye. We'd have to pull in the gaffs before she hits, I thought, but it could wait for breakfast. I loved that wet and cold wind, washing away the world. Mme. Verbeeck was standing watch with me, the deckhouse visible through her gray form. She stood in the blue light in the ball gown she never got to wear, staring into the waves. I knew she was there to watch over me.

And there, coming up the companion way, was Ma. She's brought coffee! "Thanks Ma," I said, as I carefully took the hot mug, the wind making little wavelets in its top. Heaven. Tristan was late on deck, but I left that to Pa.

We were heading straight toward Florida, and the Confederate States of America. We really had no choice. It's the way the wind and currents flow. We were aiming to do what we always do, run past as fast as we could and hope they didn't notice, which made the coming storm a boon. We'd ride it all the way north hidden in its wind and waves.

It was the fall of 1892, the fourth and nastiest year so far in the war between the north and south. We in the north and I expect the south as well, had been bled white by the carnage. The land and sea crawled with great machines that reaped lives like crops, blighting everything around them. This stupid, and I mean that in the most literal sense, war was looking to be the death of everyone.

It had certainly tried, time and again, to kill us. So far we were still here sailing the sea, but so many of our fellows had sunk into the depths, the bottom of the Atlantic a garden of ships and bodies of seamen and their families.

A rogue gust blew my hair in my eyes. It's coming soon, I thought. I didn't think Tristan had ever seen a storm, at least a real one. I yelled to him.

"Tristan!"

He'd been on the bow. He knew he was late. He had to make his way back.

"Get your wet weather gear," I yelled over the wind and surf. "Then stay close."

"Aye Cali," he yelled back. He could feel it too, though he didn't know it. It's a nervous thing.

"Oh, and take this mug back to Ma."

Last spring Red took a shell passing Florida just like we were aiming to do now. We can all thank everything thankable, and I mean everything, that her hull was too soft to set it off. It took out a mast and went right through the porthole in my cabin. And now, thanks to the nature of the trade winds we were heading back there again, past the Bahamas and then Florida, on our way north home to Boston.

I figured we'd had to have been making phenomenal 12, maybe 13 knots, running all out with the wind this blessed storm brought. Maybe, I thought, I'd ask Ian to toss out the chip to get a reading just to know. We wanted to turn north before we made sight of the coast even though the islands were all neutral, hoping not to be spotted and pursued. The storm would make that harder. It could blow us almost anywhere, even onto a shoreline.

It'll be a shame when we take in the gaffs, I thought, wishing one of the regular crew had been on deck so I could ride the bow, but we were listing enough. The peaks were practically breaking over the port gunnels on main deck. I bet we had pumping to do. We'd certainly have it that night.

We were loaded with rubber, African hides, ivory, and sundries, worth more than its weight in gold. The best cargo we'd ever brought home. What's more, our purses were full coming in. Considering what we'd been through, this was only fair. We were chained to the docks in Boma, Congo, for five weeks, living on weeds and bush meat while some prince tried to use my family as blackmail to get under my skirts. Crazy, huh? I even had to play Bach like I cared. And it all ended in a war. We had to fight our way through the streets . . . Then there was the coup d'état in Portugal, and the riot in Le Havre. I was thinking then that I would be floored, absolutely floored if we lived through the war.

Ed came up to take the helm so I could get breakfast. The rain had started and I didn't have my rain gear on yet, me still in my sloppes, so I was a little wet. No reason to track water through the hold, so I crossed the deck to the forward deckhouse. Down in the galley it was warm, like I'd forgotten what warm was. My fingers tingled.

Red's galley is beautiful. Tinker had been carving the beams for years, seaweed, mermaids, whales, gradually covering everything. Ma punked down a plate on the table in front of me and another mug of coffee. We had fresh bread, olive oil, eggs, and romesco, bought at my insistence after Aleta introduced it to me. I bought two big jars of it from a restaurant. There are good things in this world, and romesco is definitely one of them.

"Hello," Aleta said, literally climbing in through the hold. We had no walkways below decks this trip. We were loaded to the gunnels. The best kind of thing for a merchantman.

"Morning," I replied. "Storm coming. You feel up to it?"

"I should ask you," she said, trying to smile. "Are you OK."

I had to think about it. "No. I'm not."

"You sure made a ruckus last night."

"I guess I did," I replied quietly.

"Want to talk about it?"

"I don't know what good it would do. It was just things that happened being mean all over again." Then I looked at her. "Maybe you could tell them to stop."

"Stop," she said.

I laughed. "I don't think they'll listen to that."

"I don't know about that," she said, smiling for real. "If they're listening, then they've got to be using your ears."

"That makes sense," I said. Then I laughed. "So leave me alone!" I said and Aleta laughed too.

I was trying to eat my breakfast fast, but still enjoy it. Oh, I do love romesco.

"We're going to need all awake soon to bring in the gaffs," I said. I was kind of trying to warn her to look for her weather gear.

"It's a storm isn't it," she said, looking grave.

"Don't worry, it's the best kind."

She frowned. "How long do you think it will last?"

"Days. A week?"

"That might be too long. I need your help."

"What?" I asked, a touch worried.

"I want to try on my dress."

That threw a big smile.

They made ball dresses for us in Boma. I had to throw mine away. Really, it would have been ruined in the battle and would have made me a big target. But Aleta couldn't go to the ball because she was still recovering from dengue fever. She'd stuffed her's into her cabin unworn, which was too bad because they were something incredible. All I had left of mine were my silk gloves that went all the way up my arms past my elbows! And my pearls too, of course.

"That would be so fun!" I said. "You can wear my pearls too."

"I don't think that would be a good idea," she replied. "I'd be worried they'd end up over the side."

"What good are they if they don't get worn?"

"True."

She didn't put up much resistance.

"I hope it's aiming to hit Florida," I said, referring to the storm.

"It would serve them right, shooting at us."

"Or maybe the Carolinas. Those banks don't get enough water."

So we were winching them down, thinking about the jibs as well. Well not me. I was at the wheel, when a great gray shape loomed out of the rain off the port. She was big and I could see the outlines of her turrets through the mist. We lurched over her wake, coming up on her astern, the churn of her propellers white against her dark gray.

"Hard a starboard ho!" I yelled over the wind, spinning the wheel. We drove back toward the gray mist, trying to put distance in between us. I had no time to give warning, no time to identify them. On deck, everyone was scrambling to reset the sails.

"All hands on deck!" I called.

Wally was reaching for the bell, but I yelled, "Belay that." We needed to wake the crew, but not the enemy. He nodded that he understood and ran for the hatch.

Then another shape loomed up in the rain to our starboard. We were in the middle of a fleet! It was coming right at us. The gaping barrels of her guns loomed over us. We cut across her bow with only a hundred feet to spare. From somewhere the damp air carried the sound of a bell ringing on her deck, loud and sharp, but no shots fired. They were running like ants up there, her blue sailor boys running for their combat stations. They were ours, but that wouldn't stop them from sinking us first and looking second in this weather. At least they were as surprised as we were.

This is why you never leave the wheel unattended.

As the mist closed in around us, I watched them fade. We crossed the wake of another, but couldn't see her. Then I turned thirty degrees to the port. We stayed on that heading, north northwest for an hour, just to put distance between us. No more ships. We were clear. Then it was across the wind and back east again. I figured maybe ten miles between us, gradually widening if they held course. But then we had that storm coming and once that hit, who could tell?

It was after lunch that Willie came and sat on the pile of rubber sacks across from me. I was below mending rope by lamp light. It's always chafing and we're always mending it. He picks up a piece of tarred yarn and starts worrying its frets, which comes apart in his hand.

"Where's the twine," he asks.

"Down on your left," I replied.

He grunts and steps down to reach it and almost loses his pipe. Don't worry, it wasn't lit. Not near all that rubber. Once he gets the ball, he cuts off a couple of feet with his knife and sets to winding.

"That dream you had," he says.

"Been having. Wasn't the first."

"That's the way they go."

"Do you still have them?"

"Sometimes," he sighed.

"It's been what, twenty years?"

"Something like that."

"Do they get easier?"

"Mostly."

"Sometimes worse?"

He frowns a bit and starts working his way back down the line, looking for wear. "Best if you don't hide from it."

"I'm not hiding."

"Maybe," he said. Then he looked up from the rope. "There are things you'd have to be loopy not to hide from."

"I'm not hiding."

"Don't shy away from thinking about it. Thinking about it on your own helps. When you choose to. Not it."

"That makes sense. I suppose I have to."

"You will, one way or the other. Think about it that is."

"So, it's a wound that needs air."

"That's about it."

Willie was right, and I've tried. And, over the years, I've laid it all open. I've sat with some of the best and talked about it. I can remember everything. But the wound is still there, still demanding more air.

That evening I was at loose ends below deck wondering when we were going to start pumping. It's a crazy feeling to be below decks in a storm. All that water, all that rain is coming down around you, shaking and grinding everything, and yet there you are. Dry in clean lamp light. I rocked with the decks for a moment, reveling in it. I was a little worried. Aleta was up on deck, standing her watch. This was her first real storm. She was the only new crew up there and I wanted to follow her up, but she had to see it on her own. My Ma and Pa sent me up during storms when I was much younger, although it must have given them sleepless nights. I could be brave too.

That crazy storm, and it was a righteous big beautiful one, begged for music so I climbed up to my cabin for my violin, sliding open my cabin door. My cabin was right above the rope locker. It was about two and half feet high and about six feet long, although some of that was taken up by my sea chest. A palace on a ship. I had my own porthole and a door that slid closed. Inside I had all my things, like a little nest.

My violin, my new violin that I got in Cadiz, was in its case next to the bulkhead. My old violin of twelve years was kept on top of it, but it wasn't there. I mean the case was, but the lid was open and the violin gone. Alarmed, I felt around and found it

tangled in my covers. It got caught in my thrashing about. When I
lifted it, I realized her neck was broken, hanging by its strings. It's
crazy but this brought tears. I had been crying a lot lately. Her
worn wood looked dull next to the new exposed bright broken
ends. I sat there on the deck under my cabin door holding her. I
grew up with this violin. I didn't have many things, but the things I
kept were very dear to me. I was alone. Everyone else was on deck
or forward. Then somehow I was up through the hatch.

The wind wailed around me, sheets of rain stung my skin and
tore at my night dress. I was drenched in an instant.

"Cali!" someone called, but I ignored them.

I was walking barefoot, the best on unsure decks, if you can
stand it. The surf washed around my legs as waves broke over the
deck. The din of the storm reminded me of something else for a
moment, but there were no fires, no bullets. I almost stopped, my
legs weakened. But this wasn't it and I was off again, up the
ladder, onto the stern, near the bulwark holding on to the lines.
Waves crashed and churned around us.

"Cali, what are you doing?" It was Pa in his big japara coat,
meaning to pull me back from the railing. Even he was soaked
despite the waxing. But I shook him off and reached up and flung
her out into the gale. She was gone from my hands the instant I let
go, vanished. Snatched by the storm. I was left there alone,
gripping the ropes.

Did I do that?

"Cali, get below," he was yelling at me.

"Aye Pa," I replied. I turned and made my way back below,
gripping the handholds on the aft deck cabin. Back down in the
lamp light, the hatch closed, the steps wet, me drenched making
puddles that raced back and forth on that rare piece of dry deck as
it tipped. She was gone, buried with no ceremony, twelve of my
seventeen years, given as an offering to a storm. I couldn't
remember not having her.

My new violin greeted me, the incense of wood and rosin rose
as I opened the case. She was beautiful and I loved her too. I didn't
care about rosin or tuning. I just played, rolling with the waves, I
didn't care what, Mme. Verbeeck a dim outline in a dark corner.
After a few minutes Crow stepped into the lamp light and sat on
the ladder. I suppose Pa had sent him back to watch me. He didn't

say a word. He sat and listened as I played.

The storm decided it liked the Carolinas and hit somewhere below Cape Fear. Bad luck for them and good luck for us. We were free and clear all the way north. No coastal patrol boats for us! Just sweet sailing in blue water and cloud marked sky. I swapped watches with Ian so I could have the afternoon free with Aleta. We told everyone what we were doing and to stay out of the bow.

When we pulled out the dress, I could see that it was wrinkled and had lost some of its starch. But really, who cares? This wasn't a ball. This was fun!

Our biggest problem was her hair. We had plenty of fresh water. We'd just had a storm and the cistern was full. Ma heated some up so she could have a proper bath that morning, but after it was washed, what did we do with it then? All we had was some combs and the hair piece. The pins they used on mine were lost in the dirt. They were only bent wire, but we didn't have any. What we had was string. The trick would be to tie it so it wouldn't show.

Ma and I sat Aleta in the kitchen on a stool and fretted over it, trying this and that. Trying to get her hair to stay up. The thing is, her hair is so long and straight. It's nearly black too, so cornstarch wasn't going to do it. We tried. It turned to a crusty white that came off in flakes. We finally hoisted it up with braids and string under a bun held in place with my and Ma's combs. We cut the ends off the string at the knot and tucked them inside. We couldn't find a place for the hair piece, which was sad because it had pretty little silver silk flowers.

First, before the corset, we had bloomers, garter and socks, and a chemise. Our corsets were something of a frontier compromise. They didn't have proper boning available so they ribbed them with what they had, which was steel. It made them somewhat less forgiving than a normal corset. Frankly, I wasn't sorry at all to dump mine, but you needed it to fit in the dress. She made noise when Ma and I pulled on it, which was kind of funny. Eventually even she had to laugh. I had my foot on her rump to get leverage. I waited until she breathed out to pull too. Fair is fair.

It was then that we realized that it was a mistake to have done her hair before putting on the dress, which had to go over her head. We managed it, but it was a near thing. Underskirts first, a loose stiff weave that fluffed out like foam. Then a thin bustle. Then over her head it went, one arm in, then the other. You can't bend in a corset and we had to work to get her second arm in. Last it was all the buttons up the back.

We couldn't paint her nails. We had only two colors of ship paint, white and black. I don't know why they painted mine anyway. I had gloves and shoes. Like anyone was going to see my bare toes. The shoes were crème colored with "low" heels that laced up your calves. They were narrow and I think hurt her as much they had hurt me. Then the gloves. They are very tight and slow going to get on and off.

Lastly, and with great ceremony, my pearls! She didn't need rouge. She was blushing enough as we put them on. Last, the pearl watch bracelet. I had wound and set it first.

She was simply beautiful. The dress swirled around her as she moved. I bet mine had done that too. I thought of the flamenco dancer in Las Palmas and liked the idea that I might have looked even a little bit like her.

The crew were all waiting up top. She emerged, rising from the deeps into the sun, carefully stepping up the ladder as we held her dress for her. The white of her dress made everything around her seem dull. There was no sound except the sea, the rigging, and their indrawn breath. Tinker was the first to leap up and bow, followed by the others. She looked absolutely royal.

We were sailing around Cape Cod, heading past Monomoy, watching the whales. For the new crew, this was crazy new. Even the old hands were out on deck. I was leaning on the railing with Ma. We had a beautiful day, perfect sailing weather, a rare event around Cape. Whales and calves out there frolicking, showing fins and dorsals, big as ships. I was glad there weren't any whalers about, but then worried why they weren't. Had they been lost to the war or perhaps moved to safer waters?

After the encounter in the rain we'd seen no war vessels, just sails, damn few of them too, all the way down the coast. We were in the home stretch, Boston just ahead. We made the lighthouse on Brewster Island that night, then the channel, and Lovell Island, and finally President Roads.

I couldn't sit still. I was still having problems sleeping. I was up at four in the morning and then again at seven, playing my violin. Aleta kept watching me, worried all the time. Maybe Ma and Pa too. We all have to sleep, but sometimes it's a hard thing to do.

The cutter with the inspectors pulled alongside at 11:00 a.m., which was pretty quick. With war losses and risk, traffic was as thin in harbor as it was along the coast. They shook their heads as they crawled over our cargo. We made way for them as best we could, but the hold was very full. There was talk of putting off inspection until we docked and could unload. But mostly I think it was what we brought. Everyone was dumbfounded. We were the first American ship to haul in a load of rubber to the east coast in four years. Most trickled in by train from California, the final leavings after having passed through half a dozen middlemen and nationalities.

And then there were the pelts. There were no tariffs or rules on African pelts in America in 1892. No one knew what to do with them other than their being entirely a sensation. During the war, people looked to anything for relief and zebra and elephant were nothing but myths from another world. Once we docked, we had newspaper men trying to get our story. They walked up the gangway with no leave. One took an actual photograph of the pelts, still on their pallets as they sat on the dock. I had deck watch then and they ignored me and tried to walk on board. Who would stop for a 17 year old girl, and a small one at that? I had to push one off the gangway before they would listen which, to my shame, was funny. Luckily he could float. It was ebb tide though and the water was filthy.

Once we were unloaded and the warehousers and auction houses took over, I'm told bidding for our pelts was very vigorous, as it was with our rubber too. That tree bark was picked up by the government. Apparently it's used in medicine. And our ivory, as expected, was accepted with a shrug. The war hadn't done prices for non-war related luxuries like ivory any good. People either couldn't afford it or had no time to use it.

But I wasn't there for any of that. I was back in school uniform. Back at the Carrigan School for Young Women in Boston, which is where I stay most of the year. What? Did you think I was raised at sea? I've had a thorough and responsible education. Mind you they had to search around a bit for a uniform that fit me which I could wear until my new ones arrived from the seamstress.

I was now one of three 17 year olds. Not many girls make it to 17 and still stay in school. Most are working on marriage by then. My school had only one 18 year old and she wasn't happy about it.

Chapter 2 – Goodbye

Mrs. Pettett was still there even though it felt like I'd been away for years and years. Really, it had only been an extended summer. She was there in the echoing front hall to look me over, the cool stone a relief from the fall heat. I stood there with my violin case and my sea chest. I was wearing my boater and best dress by the way, but not my comb. My hat still had its blue ribbon which, considering all the places we'd been, was amazing. I had left most of my things back in my cabin. My wool watchcoat, my sweater, my knit hat, all would not go well with my school uniform. Neither would my duck pants, gray knit socks, and cotton shirts from the sloppes – all hard worn – do either.

When I was little, someone would come to help me with my chest, but I was a big girl now so I had to lug it up the steps from the carriage myself. Honestly, it doesn't weigh that much. I really don't have much in the way of possessions. Just underthings, sundries, and a couple of night dresses. Most of my things, like my precious *Standards of Training, Certification, and Watchkeeping,* and my shells had been destroyed with my cabin. The only book I still had was my copy of Dracula, which I figured was going to make me very popular at school.

Ma and Pa had learned long ago to say goodbye outside. Parents were considered an uncomfortable distraction and were not encouraged to wander the halls. We hugged and cried. They were going back to Caribbean to do another sugar run and it might be the last time I saw them. And there was no Mackie to drive the carriage. We had Ian this time, which was something more to cry over. So saying goodbye took a while.

Inside, Mrs. Pettett looked me over with a critical eye as always and tisked.

"Just your violin and that old chest again. I suppose you're wearing your only dress too. We were wondering if you'd make it back."

You might think that was meant to be mean, reading it here, but she said it with a little smile. The smile was something I hadn't noticed before and to me it felt a bit odd. I wasn't sure what to make of it.

I bobbed my head and said, "Yes, ma'am." I was then, as always, at least outside the bounds of the Congo, a lady of etiquette and grace.

She led me at a brisk pace down the hall to the dorms, to a bed not far from my previous one. Next to it was a dresser I would hardly use, and a shelf and a desk. The room held five other girls, all of whom were off at class. I knew from experience that that bed would be pitching that night. It can take weeks to get over being at sea, to get your land legs back.

There were workmen there in the room as well, pulling holes in the walls and running pipes. The wood floor was a mess of broken plaster. The school was getting electricity and I had to step over rolls of wire and broken plaster as we made our way in. No more doing work by lamplight this winter. I wondered what it would be like. I eyed the wire with interest, bright copper wound in black cloth.

"We'll send for you when the seamstress arrives," she said. "Here is your schedule."

We used to have a tailor, but they're too useful in wartime. All of them had gone to war. Now we had a war widow, a Mrs. Bennett. Mrs. Pettett had written my schedule on a sheet of notepaper, leaving it on my desk.

"Don't be late," she said as she left.

Picking up the paper, I saw that I would be just in time for French. I pushed my chest under my bed and headed for class.

I said bonjour to Mrs. Claveloux.

I completely stood out, not only being the only girl not in uniform but now being substantially taller. I was the eighth girl in the class, taking the next to the last seat. It wasn't the worst, but it was almost the worst. It was off to the side in the dark, away from the windows. Someone had let the ink dry in the well too. I would have to clean it, but since I had yet to be given my school box, I had no pen anyway.

"Bonjour Calista," she said.

"Bonjour Mme. Claveloux," I replied.

" Avez-vous passé un bel été?"

Did I have a nice summer?

"Il a été mouvementé," I replied. It was eventful.

This seemed to set her back. I'd spent the last three months speaking practically nothing but French. My ten years of study had stood me well. But she seemed surprised.

"We went to France, Portugal, Spain, and the Congo," I added, in French of course.

"Did you use your French?"

"Yes, quite a bit."

She nodded and moved on to the next student. Really, the day's lesson seemed silly. I said as little as I could and spent most of the hour daydreaming about Lucien. Would I ever see him again?

I swear, when I think about him I get scared and what's weird is that I enjoy it! But then I start to worry that thinking about him will somehow use him up, that he'll disappear, which is crazy. But then again, maybe he was gone already. It was just a kiss. My one and only. I went around and around, jumping from fear to joy to worry to fear again. He was a world away on the other side of an ocean. I thought maybe I would try to write him a letter. I'd need to find some money first.

Next was music and I swear that Mrs. Hartnoll actually gave me a momentary smile when I walked in. My teachers were all doing it that year. All the girls in the class seemed so young and all their lessons so basic. It was hard to sit and listen. When she finally got to me I was sitting waiting for the class to end. Everyone was making a racket except me. Her hand reached around from behind and placed some music on my stand. It was a violin piece by somebody named Saint-Saëns. The paper looked new. She must have just bought it.

"I didn't think you were coming back," she said.

"For just a bit," I replied. "I didn't think I would either."

"You have a new violin." She was standing there in her prim dark blue dress, looking down at my case. "May I see it?"

I said nothing, but leaned down to pick up the case. She lifted her carefully, running her hand across her wood. I could tell she could sense it too. There is something more than just the scent of wood and varnish. She gave me a strange look.

"This will do." Then she continued levelly. "I heard you went to France." She had pulled up a chair next to me.

I nodded my head.

"Did you get to hear any performances?" she asked.

I shook my head slightly no. "But I got to play in Spain, in the street, in a club and a restaurant."

I don't think she liked that. She seemed troubled, but said nothing. She opened the music. "Work from here. Let's see how far you can get tonight." She handed me back my violin and walked on.

I'd never noticed it before, but she seemed smaller, grayer. She looked tired. Had she always looked like that?

Thumbing through the piece, I realized it was full of thirty second notes! There was nothing for it but to roll my eyes and sigh.

After class, out in the yard, Dae, my apparently now ex-friend, didn't believe a single word of my story. She stopped me at the elephant stampede and said, "Enough." She wouldn't let me continue. Apparently I've become a teller of tall tales. Perhaps I should join the circus. Certainly no Dracula for her.

My first night went well. The first nightmare didn't come until the second. I suppose I had to settle in. I was twisting and thrashing in my bed and the girls in my room were in a panic.

Apparently I had made some noise. Poor Lorraine was back in the corner scared. I was loud enough to have woken girls from near rooms. They were looking in the door.

"Calista!"

My hands were out trying to protect my face.

"Calista, wake up!"

I could see a face looking down at me, and a candle I thought, but I couldn't figure it out. It's hard for me sometimes to remember where I am when I wake up from a bad dream.

"Calista?"

I was blinking at her, still not recognizing her. But she was Mrs. Miller of course, our dormitory mother. I was still crying and in no state to talk.

"Calista?" she asked again, still trying to hold me down even though I had finally settled.

I nodded yes.

"You poor dear. Just like my Bill. You'd think you'd been in the war." Then she turned to the others. "It's over. Go to bed."

They left one by one. Poor Lorraine climbed over the foot of her bed be rather than come closer. She's only seven and I was truly sorry I put such a fright in her.

"I'm sorry," I said weakly.

"Don't you worry dear," cooed Mrs. Miller. "You couldn't help it. There's no helping these things."

"May I have some water?" I asked.

"Yes, of course." She got up and went to my dresser. My cup and pitcher were there, next to my basin. We even have chamber pots under our beds, just in case you're too scared of the dark to make it to the head. "You drink this and when you're ready, we'll try to sleep again."

It takes me forever to go back to sleep after a bad dream. I couldn't keep her up with me.

"I'm okay now," I said.

"Are you sure?" she asked. I don't think she believed me.

"Really. I'll be fine."

"Well, we'll see." She was tugging my covers back in to place. "I'll keep an ear open for you."

She got up and shooed everyone back to bed with me laying there awake in the dark for I don't know how long. I must have gone back to sleep eventually because morning came. Mrs. Miller had knocked on our doorway, going from room to room. They do that every morning. For once, I didn't want to open my eyes. To be honest, I was embarrassed.

Nobody said anything though I know they wanted to. Nothing at all! We had porridge, eggs, and toast. Meat was in short supply because of the war. Eggs were more common. They couldn't be easily stored or shipped to the front. Since we docked in Las Palmas, we'd been eating pretty well so the loss didn't mean much to me. I've been told that the poor were lucky to even get eggs. I dreamed of the glorious oranges and melon we had in Spain while I ate.

There was whispering of course. Soon the whole school would know about my noisy dreams, then everyone from here to the docks. What was I going to do? What was I going to do tonight? Would they come again?

Naturally, they did. That very night. Twice. Why should being at school make any difference? Dracula or not, spooky screaming tall tales Cali was never going to have any friends again. I was called in to the office at lunch. It wasn't Mrs. Pettett the schoolmaster, it was Mrs. Keckland, the head of the school!

She was old and gray and her office was all wood and carpet. It was going to be hard getting electricity in without breaking something. I'd only ever seen her in the halls and then only once or twice a year. I have been told on good authority that she was the Daughter of the founder, Mr. E. J. Carrigan.

"Is this she, Janet?"

"Yes, ma'am," Mrs. Pettett said, giving her head a little bow.

"Come in, take a seat." She waved at the one in front of her.

I wanted the one near the window, but sat where I was told.

"Your family was in the newspaper?"

"Yes. I think so," I replied.

"You were in the Congo wasn't it?"

"Yes, ma'am."

"There was a war there."

"Yes, ma'am."

"Louise was right," she said to Mrs. Pettett. Then she looked at me. "It seems you brought something back with you."

I couldn't think of anything to say. I wasn't quite sure what she meant.

"I believe it to be the soldier's terror. Traumatic hysteria." She looked down and tapped an open book on her desk. "I've been trying to read about it, but these books are out of date. Mostly sheer nonsense." She pushed it back to make her point.

"Fear not," she continued, with a little smile. "We aren't going to send you away, although we might try to find you some help. More common than a cold these days. We'll have to find you someplace to sleep. Can't have you keeping everyone awake."

This was a lot to swallow at once. It hadn't even occurred to me that they might send me away and now I was staying.

"I am right in assuming that your time in the Congo was unpleasant?"

"Yes, ma'am," I replied. Really, it was almost a squeak. I wanted to try again, just to correct her impression of me, but I thought it might make it sound even worse.

"You haven't been having any hallucinations? Think you're in places you aren't? Seeing things that aren't really there?"

I paused for a moment, thinking of M. Allard and Mme. Verbeeck, but they're real. "No ma'am."

"Frightened confused in situations that remind you of the Congo?"

I blushed, which was enough of an answer for her.

"Yes, well," she paused, looking again at her book. "Apparently, in most cases, eventually, this can go away on its own. It can take years though. Mrs. Pettett has told me about a therapy, the talking cure, which can be helpful. Perhaps we can see about that. It might help that you're so young." Then she turned to Mrs. Pettett. "Janet, any ideas where we can put her?"

"I was thinking the caretaker's room."

"In the basement?"

In the basement.

"It would be quiet."

"Yes. It would. It would have to be cleaned." Then she looked at me. "It's a frightful mess down there right now."

In the basement. I knew it.

"Yes, ma'am."

They weren't kidding. It was a mess down there. That's where the furnaces and coal for our heating were and the narrow stairway and floor were sooty. It was dark too. No gaslight down there. The only outside light down there came from little windows up near the ceiling and there were none in my room. It would be candles and lanterns, even in the daytime.

We hadn't had a building caretaker in years, not since our old one died. He died in the bed I was supposed to sleep in! At least I got a new mattress. Since his death, his room had been used for storage.

I didn't do it all on my own. Mrs. Milliken and our coal man Leroy helped. Some of it went upstairs and some was plunked down in a pile in the hallway with an old blanket thrown over it.

My room was big, perhaps eight by ten feet. Plenty of room for a bed and desk. My sea chest went right under my bed. They gave me matches, candles, and a lantern, so I could work, and a big round steel alarm clock that ticked loudly as it worked. It was a palace!

I would have to go upstairs through the kitchen to get to the head which would certainly require a candle and matches. I took a bucket from downstairs and cleaned it so I could use it to carry water. A bucket is so much easier to carry than a pitcher when you're holding a candle and trying to open a door.

I went to sleep in fear that the caretaker's ghost would show up, but he didn't. I suppose Mme. Verbeeck kept him away or maybe he was nice enough to be a gentleman. Perhaps it was the new place, but I didn't have any bad dreams that night.

Every morning the alarm would ring so loud in the quiet that I would leap out of bed before I could think, grabbing the ringer to stop it. Then I would practically faint, standing on the cold concrete with my bare feet. I dressed alone, hearing the echoing voice of Leroy singing to himself as he worked. He started early shoveling coal to heat the building. Then I climbed the narrow creaky stairs in the dim light from Leroy's lamp, saying hello as I climbed. Up in the kitchen it was warm and full of smells of breakfast. Sadly, they didn't let us have coffee, just tea, but I could get my cup in the kitchen! Unlike the dining room, everyone in the kitchen said hello and smiled.

"There she is," they would say. "Would you like your tea dear?"

The kitchen women were nice. But it lasted only four nights. It was Wednesday, and the other girls had finally started talking to me. It was my ears. Lydia wanted to see my pierced ears. I still had my gold loops. Then Carol and Rachel were next.

Then it was my room! They wanted to see my room. I wasn't sure they were allowed down there so we creeped past the kitchen. It was after dinner and the kitchen ladies were doing dishes, so it was noisy. Leroy was gone too, the furnace and boiler winding down for the day.

It's pitch black down there in the evenings after Leroy's gone with only the dim orange glow around the furnace door for light. He won't leave a lamp on with all the coal about, but I had a box of candles by the door. I lit one and then others for everybody and then down the narrow wooden stairs we creaked. I swear they acted like we were investigating a tomb! They wanted to see everything, but you can't go far down there because the coal dust gets on everything. We went as far as we could though. Then we huddled into my room. It's just a bed, my sea chest, and a table and chair, but everyone was impressed despite the endless clanking tick of my clock. I think it was that the caretaker had died in it. Maybe being Creepy Cali was going to be okay.

The end came when the lawyer found me sitting, let's be honest, asleep in English. "Calista?" they called from the classroom door, as if calling gently would interrupt the classroom less.

"Yes, ma'am," I replied.

"Please come to the office."

They lead me down the hall. I was pretty sure I wasn't in trouble. I'd only been back a week, but that didn't mean this wasn't trouble. And there it was, waiting for me in the school office, a short rotund man sweating in the autumn heat in an ill-fitting wool suit. Behind him workmen were banging on the wall, knocking holes in the plaster for the new pipes.

"Miss Carmichael?" he asked, as if they would bring him an imposter.

"Yes," I said. Get on with it.

"You have not been easy to find." He looked at me over his spectacles. I stared back at him. "I represent the estate of one Countess Emmaline Sophie Verbeeck of Belgium."

Now I was giving him the eye, "Yes?"

"There is a matter of a bequest and some paperwork associated with it."

"Bequest?" I asked, now completely confused.

"Yes. She apparently set up an endowment to the Royal Academy for Music in Brussels. It's contingent on you and another young women, Aleta? You wouldn't happen to know where I can find her and perhaps her full name?" I nodded yes and then no. "It's contingent on your attending the institution. You are to be sponsored by," he paused and looked at a paper. "A Duke of Tervuren."

"Oh, Lucien," I said. Mind you the women in the office were gaping.

"It covers your room and board, certain expenses, and a monthly stipend."

"Oh," it was almost a whisper.

All I could think was that I'm going to get to see Lucien again! By the way, he wasn't wrong about the paperwork and they wanted me there at "my earliest possible convenience." The last thing I got from him was a zeppelin ticket! I was leaving in ten days on the SML Bremen. SML stands for *Seiner Majestät Luftschiff*, his majesty's airship!

So this was goodbye, probably forever, to the Carrigan School for Young Women. Perhaps to Boston itself, a city I had lived in half my life but had never really seen.

I hauled my sea chest and violin alone down the hallway to the entrance hall wearing the dress I had arrived in. We're civilized. We had washed it! I left my loaner dress on the bed. I had only met the seamstress the day before and my regular school clothes wouldn't start arriving for a week.

Mrs. Pettit was, as always, waiting to see me off. Then Mrs. Hartnoll came walking in, out of breath, there were tears in her eyes and she was having trouble speaking. I was stunned. She gave me a hug and thrust another piece of music into my hands. It was a symphony by someone named Beriox.

"I knew you would do it," she said.

"Go to music school?" I grunted as she hugged me.

"Make something of yourself," she said, looking at me. "You can be so much more than just someone's wife. Please, promise me that you won't stop playing. Not for anyone."

"I won't," I said, very confused.

Then she mumbled something I couldn't understand and turned

quickly away, walking quickly up the corridor, dabbing her eyes.

I stood there stunned. I had no idea what to do. My teachers had always been something other, distant taskmasters, something to be listened to or avoided. The thought of a teacher crying was almost frightening.

"She said you were always her greatest student," Mrs. Pettit said.

"I am?" I asked.

"Well," she said, with a little smile. "You're not a bad one at least."

"Oh."

She didn't pinch my cheeks as usual, settling instead on straightening my hair and resettling the blousing on my sleeves.

Outside Ma, Pa, and Ian, were waiting with a rented pier office wagon. No steam carriages for us. We're certainly not rich. There were, of course, lots of hugs, even though I'd only been gone a week. Then we clopped-clopped down Hannover Street from Beacon Hill toward the waterfront, dodging steam carriages and trollies chugging by leaving their trails of smoke and puffs of steam, ice and milk wagons, and people who don't seem to care if they got run down. Luckily our Boston streets are much wider than European ones. Many of the streets are dirt as well which isn't so bad as long as it isn't raining. The cobbled ones make everything rattle, although on the plus side they don't rut.

Since steam carriages began to fill the road, people had lost all respect for horses. People walked right in front of us expecting us to stop in time. One man even popped our horse on the nose, dodging its teeth as it tried to bite. He had a mischievous smile and gave me a wink, which made me laugh.

We passed the waterfront warehouses and trade shops, then the harbor itself, a forest of masts and funnels. A steam ship whistled, echoing away in the cool fall breeze. The smell of the harbor, tar, salt, sewage, old fish, and cooking food, all told me I was back home.

Red Jacket

If you liked the story, and want to help the author, then please rate it, or even better - review it - on Amazon.com

Mark Bondurant

MAX AND Mrs Stroud

A STORY OF LOVE AND DESTRUCTION

www.ingramcontent.com/pod-product-compliance
Lightning Source LLC
Chambersburg PA
CBHW070832280626
47161CB00015B/486